T0020022

WE SHALL RISE

EDITED BY
JOHN RINGO
& GARY POOLE

WE SHALL RISE

A Baen Books Original

Baen Publishing Enterprises
P.O. Box 1403
Riverdale, NY 10471
www.baen.com

ISBN: 978-1-9821-9193-1

Cover art by Kurt Miller

First printing, June 2021
First mass market printing, June 2022

Distributed by Simon & Schuster
1230 Avenue of the Americas
New York, NY 10020

Library of Congress Control Number: 2021010458

Pages by Joy Freeman (www.pagesbyjoy.com)
Printed in the United States of America
10 9 8 7 6 5 4 3 2 1

As always
For Captain Tamara Long, USAF
Born: May 12, 1979
Died: March 23, 2003, Afghanistan
You fly with the angels now.

For Delores Hamilton
for starting my long literary journey
and nurturing a never-ending sense of wonder.

CONTENTS

Foreword

GARY POOLE

Just over seven years ago, Ringo and I decided to catch a movie at our local cineplex. It was a popular zombie apocalypse flick that featured a big name actor, had a big budget, and was based on a pretty interesting novel. And in true Hollywood fashion, the film proceeded to ignore almost all the good science of the novel to create a "Hollywood ending" that pretty much threw all semblance of science (and reality) out the nearest window.

To say we were disappointed was a bit of an understatement.

And in true Ringo style, when presented with something that offended his understanding of science and storytelling, he opened up his laptop and began to type.

A lot.

Three months later, he had finished the first four books of the Black Tide series. Because he really *does* write that fast when the muse is cooperative.

But he wasn't just pulling things out of thin air.

ix

Far from it. He spent countless hours in e-mail discussions and phone consultations with a wide variety of scientists who have deep knowledge of the biosciences. John's simple goal was to create a scientifically believable plague that didn't involve what he likes to refer to as "hand-wavium." The input from the various MD's and PhD's and graduate researchers was invaluable, and led to what I feel is one of the most scientifically strong bases for any plague-based post-apocalyptic series out there. And judging from the popularity of the novels and anthologies, I can safely state that I am not alone in this belief.

So what happens when a fictional plague that began in the Far East and quickly spread around the world moves from fiction to reality?

Well, if your name is John Ringo, you get a lot of e-mails and social media posts along the lines of, "You predicted this!" And yes, the parallels between the Black Tide virus and the real-world COVID-19 virus are obvious. But, thankfully, the real-world pandemic did not involve people stripping off their clothes and trying to eat their friends and neighbors.

It has, however, been a very unusual period of time in which to put together a post-apocalyptic anthology. There's something very surreal about watching the news and thinking, "I already read this story." But, while the news focuses only on what is happening now, our goal as storytellers is to write about what happens next. To not get caught up in the minutia of everyday life but to think beyond. Beyond tomorrow, beyond our towns, beyond our countries. I have written in previous forewords about how I feel that for a post-apocalyptic universe with a mind-bogglingly catastrophic death toll, the Black Tide series is all about hope. As John so elegantly put it, "To hell with the darkness. Light a candle."

As strange as it may seem, having been involved with the series since its inception, I was much more hopeful about how we, as a species, would handle a real-world pandemic. Because even though all of the many stories told in the novels and anthologies were fictional, I feel strongly that they were based on deeper truths. And the truth is that we overcome everything. Just look at how fast we were able to develop multiple vaccines (!!) using cutting edge mRNA technology that was in its scientific infancy less than a decade ago, which just shows you how resilient we are as a species. When confronted with a world-changing problem, we came up with world-changing solutions.

It's what we do.

Before COVID-19 even existed, John and I had been approached by our publisher to put together a third anthology after the success of the previous two. We sat down and tossed around ideas of themes and came up with one we thought would work well from both a storytelling standpoint and as an intriguing challenge to the writers we invited to participate. The theme is, simply, resurgence. It's not just a case a "what happens next," it's deeper than that. We wanted to delve into how humanity has always risen above whatever challenge the species has faced.

Back around 75,000 years ago or so, a great super-volcano in Sumatra erupted, sending thousands of cubic kilometers of magma and rock into the air, spreading ash as far away as Africa and China, dropping global temperatures by as much as 18 degrees. Mankind, which was still largely centered in Africa and Southern Asia, was nearly wiped out. Experts believe that *homo sapiens*, which had grown to a population of nearly a hundred thousand, fell to less than 10,000 individuals, with some putting the number at close to just 2,000.

So how did we not only survive, but overcome the devastation of our environment? Cooperation.

The few surviving members of humanity relied on their social skills to work together to overcome a global catastrophe. And that is the key to our survival as a species. By working together for a common goal, which in this case was nothing less than avoiding extinction, early humans were able to adapt and overcome to the point where 75,000 years later we have orbiting space stations and are in the development stages of human colonies on the Moon and Mars.

Not bad, eh?

And along the way, the race has been faced with countless challenges. Wars, pestilence, plagues, famine, natural disasters, and so forth. And we're still here and stronger than ever as a species.

The other key trait that separates humanity is persistence. We're arguably the most stubborn lifeform on the planet. From our days of hunting in the vast African savannas where we simply wore down our prey to our current civilization, we just don't quit. Whatever the challenge is, we figure out a way to overcome whatever challenge is placed in front of us and learn to overcome and adapt.

So let's extrapolate our real-world history into the fictional universe of the Black Tide series. The "zombie plague" has killed or turned somewhere along the lines of 90% (or more) of the human population around the world. Think for a second how you would react if nine out of every ten people you know suddenly were dead or reduced to being an unthinking (and often extremely violent) animal. How would *you* survive?

In Ringo's world, the uninfected have survived by cooperating and refusing to give up. Not just family units, like the Smiths, but in larger groups. And not just survived, but thrived (for various values of thriving). Sure, civilization as we know it has collapsed, but we as a species are not the type to simply say, "Oh well, might as well give up and die." No, we are inherently stubborn. We have a will and a spirit that drives us to go beyond mere survival. We look at the cards that we are dealt and bet the pot that we will not only survive but thrive.

Social Distance

KEVIN J. ANDERSON & REBECCA MOESTA

I
Dale

"This is going to be the most grueling, most difficult survival challenge any of you has ever faced," I said, looking at their faces, a few of them already sunburned and sweaty. I watched the expressions of the nine high school students change as the grim reality washed over them.

We stood together in the Utah desert surrounded by endless blue skies and jaw-dropping stretches of red rock pinnacles, canyon labyrinths, scrub brush, pinon pines, yucca plants. And no people.

"We're on our own here." I shifted the heavy backpack on my shoulders and tightened the strap to carry the weight low on my hips. "We'll give you the skills, but you have to put in the work." I glanced at the other two adult guides for this CanyonTrek adventure. I wanted my introduction to sound like a pep talk. "You're going to love it."

Preston—thin, bookish and thirty-eight, five years younger than me—wore the most expensive hiking

1

clothes and had the most earnest expression on his face, taking his job as a CT counselor so seriously that even his fellow guides couldn't have fun.

Judy, whose age I put somewhere between sixty-five and infinity, was a leather whip of a woman who had spent twenty years in the army, the rest of her life in the desert, and could probably tie a boot lace with her teeth. She had seen it all, and was probably the most competent person in this part of southern Utah.

The nine teenagers looked up to me, though, as the ostensible leader of the expedition.

"Dale's right," Preston said, nodding to me. "These three weeks are going to all be about your personal growth, meeting new challenges, and becoming a better person inside." He pressed his palm to the center of his chest and spread his fingers as if he expected angels to spring out of his heart.

Ophelia, a spunky fifteen-year-old with a dark braid draped over one shoulder, snickered. "Three weeks without cell phones, computers, air conditioning, toilets. Oh, joy." The other kids seemed cautious, still getting a feel for the situation.

"We're good to go," Judy said. "It's time to walk the earth." She strutted out with a trekking pole in one gnarled hand. Her hiking boots looked as old as the Dead Sea Scrolls and yet sturdier than my own.

Our group set off together along the desert path, on our way to the horizon and back. Fortunately, we had topo maps.

Exploring new landscapes and building stronger people was what the CanyonTrek brochure said, and the parents of troubled teens gobbled it up.

As we walked, Bridger and Logan took the lead.

Bridger looked like a squeaky-clean Boy Scout, though I knew he had been suspended for bullying his lab partner in chemistry, while Logan had been caught selling alcohol to classmates. Marco, a broad-shouldered Hispanic student who had lost his spot on the varsity soccer team when his grades took a nose dive, hurried to join the other two.

"Ten miles the first day," I said, "while we still have energy."

"Who has energy?" Shaylee asked with a dramatic groan.

I pressed my lips together. I'd hoped to make at least half a mile before the complaints started. "Could be the most beautiful miles you've ever seen," I said. "When we get to the Needles Overlook, it'll take your breath away."

"I can hardly breathe now," panted Noah, a scrawny, freckled thirteen-year-old, the youngest member of our group. He was on the high-functioning end of Autism Spectrum Disorder, which made him intensely knowledgeable if you were interested in his particular obsessions, or annoying if you weren't.

"As you walk," Preston said, as if reading from a handbook, "be aware of your reactions and consider what you might write in your journals tonight. It's all part of the experience."

"Homework already," Ophelia said. "Oh, joy."

"Personal growth," Preston corrected. "Not homework."

"Can't call it homework, anyway," Noah added in a flat tone. "We aren't going home for three weeks."

"Right," Judy said. "Think of how strong you'll be when you're done." I couldn't tell if she was being sarcastic or not. Her voice was usually a combination of tough chick and prune juice.

CanyonTrek, headquartered in Moab, drew most of its patrons from the troubled teens of wealthy, frustrated parents along the Wasatch Front, hoping to wear down their unruly kids and teach them discipline by sending them on the "experience of a lifetime." There were plenty of reasons these teens ended up on our expeditions. They might be oppositional, blowing off school, drinking, taking drugs, rebelling against stepparents—the possibilities were endless.

By offering fourteen- or twenty-one-day expeditions in the spectacular canyonlands, CT proposed to empower students by instilling a perspective of honor, self-reliance, and balance. The brochure also asserted that participants would realign priorities and find inner strength through the beauty of nature.

As far as I was concerned, the arduous job of schlepping a heavy backpack for mile after mile, day after day, should be adequate to settle turbulent or distracted minds. Always worked for me. Preston, though, had planned a curriculum filled with personal-centering exercises, conversation starters and, of course, the daily journal of their thoughts.

"I thought this was going to be summer camp," said Ava. "Like riding horses, weaving lanyards, singing around the campfire."

"Way better than summer camp," I said.

I liked to be out here, especially in uncertain times. The world seemed nuttier than usual at the moment. The headlines were mostly about some kind of flu epidemic in New York, Los Angeles, and other major cities. In most cases, violence seemed to follow within weeks of each outbreak. Democrats accused Republicans for not offering enough medical and financial assistance, while Republicans blamed Democrats for creating the environments in which the virus flourished. I couldn't stomach the news, which seemed less informative than argumentative day after day.

One more reason to stay away from the cities, if you asked me. I was glad to be out in Red Rocks country, deep in the desert, even with nine surly, difficult kids. It was still better than any normal day in Salt Lake, or going to board meetings at the tech center.

This was the fourth group I had led for CT since taking a golden-parachute retirement from my tech job in Salt Lake. The severance package was big enough to keep me in pleasant, comfortable freefall for a long time until I figured out what I wanted to do next. And I loved the backpacking experience.

My favorite area of the state was this wild segment of Bureau of Land Management canyon country adjacent to the Needles District of Canyonlands National Park. Arches Park was always crawling with tourists, especially this time of year, mid-June with the kids out of school and the days warm. Before long the desert would show its angry side and temperatures would rise.

I led the group along our planned route, a network of trails and four-wheel-drive roads. Over the three weeks of our character-building expedition, we would go more than 150 miles along with whatever side trips caught my interest. Trekking overland, finding our own campsites, following the maps to little known springs and water sources, and killer views.

Our first main destination was an overlook, a dot on

the BLM map with an informational sign and a gravel half circle for parking at the edge of a mesa drop-off. Ahead, we could see the vista of the Needles District and its incredible, surreal formations. In its wisdom, the BLM had installed a metal pipe barricade at the edge of the overlook to keep people from falling off that particular twenty-foot section of the cliff.

"Sure glad they put safety first," Ophelia said, grasping the pipe fence and shaking it. Her parents were intellectual property attorneys, and she was bright and spoiled and a bit of a wise ass.

"Just enjoy the view for a minute," I said, wanting to drink it in myself. It was indeed enough to keep the rambunctious students together and quiet for a minute. I said, "Reminds me of a story about a Scottish shipbuilder named Ebenezer Bryce who became one of the first settlers in all this Utah desert."

"He was LDS—a Mormon pioneer," Shaylee pointed out.

"Bryce Canyon was named after him," Preston added, as if pleased that he knew the answer.

"Bryce Canyon," I agreed, "is one of the most beautiful and complex canyon systems in the state, a wonderland of multicolored rock forma—"

Noah broke in. "Did you know that Bryce Canyon isn't actually a canyon? It's a series of amphitheaters along the edge of a plateau, and they're full of those lumpy rock spires called hoodoos."

I let out a sigh. "Thank you, Noah. Very informative, but back to Ebenezer Bryce. When he came along and found that amazing area, supposedly the first white man ever to see it, you know what he wrote in his journal?" I looked at the nine young people, holding their attention. "He called it 'one hell of a place to lose a cow.' That's it."

Some of the kids dutifully chuckled, while others held onto gloom or aloofness as a matter of pride.

I felt a sudden urge to get through to them. "Don't be a Bryce. Learn how to look at everything around you, not just in terms of the hard work it might represent, but in terms of the wonder—of what might be," I said. I was getting a bit zealous, but I couldn't help myself. "Learn to enjoy beauty that's not about entertainment, computer-generated scenes, getting people to like what you post online—none of that. Look at everything around you and realize each sight is a mental snapshot, a moment in time."

With a curt nod, Judy spoke up. "Only guarantee in life is that things change."

"Right." I took up the baton again. "Time won't stand still. You'll never see exactly the same thing in the same way ever again. Deserts are different from seashores or rainforests or snowy mountains. They're all amazing, all distinct. Let yourself be enchanted." I scanned the group for any reaction.

Ophelia rolled her eyes and Logan made a scoffing sound. While Ava and Isabel looked attentive, Noah watched a lizard sunning itself nearby. Bridger and Shaylee were whispering to each other, and Marco folded his arms across his chest, while Zane seemed to be playing a drum solo in the air.

I took a deep breath before plunging in again with a stern tone. "This adventure may not be your choice, but there's no opt-out button. You're here. You'll learn survival skills and how to work as a team. You'll get sweaty and sunburned. Your feet'll be sore and you may discover some muscles you never knew you had until they started aching. But you'll be proud of what you accomplish. By the time three weeks in the wilderness are up, you'll be stronger, braver, and more resourceful than ever."

"And more in touch with your inner selves," Preston said.

Judy hooked her thumbs into her belt loops and her eyes narrowed as she stared out at the vista nodding in appreciation.

That was before we ran into the first zombies.

Ophelia Journal

Day 1. Is there any more ridiculous assignment than journaling? My shrink makes me do it. Won't work any better here than it does at home, but here goes.

I'm trapped in the wilderness with 8 other students and 3 counselors who think they own us for the next few weeks.

Dale acts like the chief. Okay-looking for an older guy, but he must be like 45. Pretty sure of himself and definitely on the bossy side. I like it when he jokes.

Preston's on the wimpy side. He actually meditates. So dorky. Says he was an Eagle Scout. No surprise there. His clothes look more stylish than practical, like he's posing for a magazine. Talks in that annoying super-friendly voice that therapists use.

Judy is a tough lady. Not sure she was ever fifteen like me. Looks like a piece of beef jerky with a chunk of dandelion fluff stuck on top. Says what she thinks but keeps it short and snappy. Some people would call it rude, I call it refreshing. If we say "shit" or whatever she always says "language!" meaning not to use bad words, but I'm pretty sure she's got some "language" in her, too, depending on the situation. I'll wait and watch.

This morning's first lesson was "hygiene." Beyond embarrassing. Who wants to talk about digging cat-holes to poop or bury blood? Yich. Plus, the spot has to be just right. Seriously. Six inches deep, at least two hundred feet from any water sources, trails, or camp. Use hand sanitizer. Blah blah blah. Hope my period doesn't arrive while we're still out here. But it will. Insanely awkward. Anyway, we already had that mortifying lesson. Ach. Ick. Ew. Backpacking is hard enough without adding that extra serving of torture for us girls. Whyyyyyyy?

Day 2. This is so not a vacation. Why would anyone choose to camp? I. Would. Not. Everything takes ten times as much work as at home. We have civilization for a reason, so why put ourselves through this by choice?

We can't just go to bed. No. We have to put up tents. We can't just nuke food and eat it. Again, no. We either have to build a fire or use those dumb little gas stoves. Then add water to dry food that all joy has been drained out of. Don't even get me started on doing dishes, either. Everyone has chores every day. That's on top of ten or more miles of hiking! It's impossible to get a minute to ourselves, and then we have to journal.

And Utah in June? June! Whose brilliant idea was that?

Today's main lesson: protecting the environment.

We can't just throw stuff away when we're done with it. No, no, no. Whatever we "pack in" on our trip, we have to "pack out," including trash. WTF?

Next lesson was finding and purifying water with our portable filters.

Day 3. The lowdown on my fellow inmates.

Bridger is LDS, which means Mormon, but he doesn't like to be called that. Says he loves to read, and plays guitar, drums, and piano. Weren't allowed to bring books or instruments, so I bet he's frustrated. I hear him humming a lot.

Noah is only 13—youngest in our whole group. Pretty sure he's high-functioning on the Autism Spectrum and klutzy like my cousin. His aunt's a veterinarian, so he knows a lot about animals. He drones on and on about them. All. The. Time. Plus he blurts stuff out at random times and doesn't notice if we look confused or shocked or whatever. He doesn't pick up on social clues. His mom teaches special ed, which is probably a good thing, considering.

Marco is tanned and decent looking. I approve. Why is he on a CanyonTrek? Got suspended from the varsity soccer team when his grades did a swan dive in the winter. Didn't say why. He's obviously smart. I mean, he speaks three languages fluently, but he mostly talks about movies and TV shows.

Logan generally keeps to himself. He's an Army brat and moves around a lot, so maybe not good at making friends? Tall with lanky shoulder-length hair, so I thought he was a stoner, but I could be wrong. He obviously works out because, well, muscles. Really nice muscles.

Zane is hard to sum up. Straight dark hair that falls across his blue eyes. Dimples that make me stare like an idiot. Kind of like that actor on *Vampire Diaries* that I've been watching for the past few years. He gives me a strange feeling when we talk, like he thinks a lot more than he says. He's kind and helpful but not in obvious ways. He just glides in and does things without being told and then he goes right back to what he was doing. What's that about?

Day 4. It's totally quiet on the trail. No music, no TV, no phone. Can't even text Skye and Maren. So boring here that even writing in a journal seems interesting. Preston and Judy read everything we write (seriously? when??). Preston is going to start helping us "process" our thoughts starting tomorrow. So... there's that humiliation to look forward to.

We did lessons on stuff they called navigation and orienteering, or just "nav." Reading topographical, aka "topo" maps, using a compass, remembering shapes and markers in the land around us, judging directions and time by the sun. Useless stuff like that. I mean, we've all got GPS on our phones, right? (If they would let us have our phones.)

Day 5. The staff focused on more "outdoor living" skills. (For the record, I refuse to ever get into outdoor living.)

Agh! They teach us stuff and then make us practice. Like we're little kids taking piano lessons. When they test us at a skill, Dale always asks, "Can you do that?" in kind of a drill sergeant voice. I learned fast to just answer "I can do that." Because if we don't say it, Dale makes us practice again about 20 bajillion times. So no thanks. From now on, "I can do that." Even if I can't.

There are only four girls in our group including me.

Ava is an airhead, but I like her. Not everyone can be brilliant like me. She's fourteen and nice—maybe too nice. Marco told me her parents sent her on a CT expedition because some jerkfaces at school convinced her to steal test answers for them. She got caught, of course. She has a pretty voice and wants to sing as a pro. Maybe she and Bridger should put together a band.

Isabel is such a Goody Two Shoes I don't know how she got sent here. Saint Isabel does everything the counselors tell her to without complaining. I don't trust people who are too good. They're usually judgy as hell.

Shaylee is LDS like Bridger, but they never met before this trip. She's my age but does acting, dances ballet, plays flute and piccolo, blah blah blah. Oh, and writes poetry. Give me a break. What is it with these LDS kids and "The Arts"? I just added her to the pop band in my mind with Bridger and Ava.

Last: I'm me. My parents are IP attorneys and they're always away. Even though a TV practically raised me, I've made straight A's since middle school. No tutors. Just me. But that didn't seem to warrant my parents' attention, so I developed an unhealthy interest in murder scenes and decided to be a forensic scientist. CSI stuff. Instead of worrying, my parents arranged for me to watch some autopsies in person. Huh. Turns out I can handle seeing real dead people, so that works out. Yay, me. The parents didn't even notice I was rebelling, so I cranked it up a notch. Started raiding the liquor cabinet regularly, then bought Adderall from school friends to keep my grades up. Brilliant, right? Eventually (better late than never) my parents caught on, and here I am.

Day 6. Almost every day Dale finds a time to say, "That's what adventuring is all about: solving problems." (Or you can insert traveling or navigating or cooking or getting along in place of "adventuring.") So apparently everything is all about solving problems.

Dale: Can you solve problems?

Me: I can do that.

Hah. We'll see.

Day 7. Hike. Sweat. Learn to act as a team. Sing. Hey, I'm not half-bad at this singing stuff. Maybe I'll learn to play bass and join the rock band. In my head, I've named it Cat-hole Daze.

Days 8–14. Blah blah blah. You get the idea.

‖
Dale

When I trained to become a CanyonTrek counselor, they supposedly prepared me for any emergency situation—which meant I'd taken a first-aid course and sat through PowerPoint presentations on various scenarios.

Fifteen days into our three-week adventure, Judy, Preston, and I had made some progress filing the rough edges off our teen adventurers. The most drama I expected was minor personality clashes, blisters and scrapes, inadvertent dehydration, wishing for the comforts of technology, or missing their families. Most of them had begun to appreciate what they had in their homelife.

I never expected Preston to get bitten by a rattlesnake.

In late June, Utah's canyon country was getting hot, and our by-the-book counselor decided to wear shorts, low-cut socks, and trail-runners for comfort, leaving his legs exposed from knee to ankle. Preston took the lead, enjoying the morning vistas, while the rest of us followed by twos and threes, with Judy at the middle of the group and me bringing up the rear with Noah.

Preoccupied by the view, Preston didn't see the rattlesnake sunning itself on the red rocks. The snake did see Preston, though, and was so startled that it bit him on the calf. His yelp was high-pitched, like a girl getting free tickets to a Taylor Swift concert.

Zane bounded forward as the rattlesnake slithered into a wide crack between the rocks. "Shit, that's a big one!"

"Language," Judy shouted automatically, running toward our colleague faster than I thought she could move.

Noah assured me he was fine, so I ran to the front of the group.

Preston collapsed to the ground, sagging onto his overlarge backpack. "It attacked me! See where I'm bleeding? Oh, it hurts."

Judy instantly dropped next to Preston.

As I arrived, I glanced at Zane. "Did you see what it was?"

Before he could answer, Ava, the most delicate of our girls, answered helpfully. "It was a snake!"

"It bit me!" Preston said, although we had already established that.

"I'm pretty sure it was a rattler," Zane said. "I saw the diamond patterns on its back. But it could have been a gopher snake."

"It wasn't a fucking gopher snake!" Preston cried.

"Language!" Judy snapped. She had shucked her backpack and was frantically opening the zippered compartment to get the first-aid pack and snakebite kit.

I slung my pack off as well.

Not at all squeamish, Ophelia knelt beside Preston, wiped away a trickle of blood, and turned his leg to expose the bite marks. Two neat little punctures, with the skin around them already starting to swell.

Zane investigated the crack in the rock where the snake had disappeared.

Bridger joined him and poked at it with his trekking pole. "Want me to get the snake out, just to make sure?"

"No!" both Judy and I said.

"Can't risk two snake bites," I added. "Treat Preston on the assumption that it was a rattlesnake."

Noah ran up to stand near Bridger and Zane, breathing hard.

Ophelia frowned. "But aren't rattlesnakes rare out here?"

"Somewhat," Noah agreed, trying to get a look at the snake in the crack. "Statistically, injuries by bee sting are way more common. And only about five people have died from snakebite in Utah in the whole past century."

"So this is a once-in-a-lifetime thing?" Ava asked.

"Sure," Noah answered. "I'd say this definitely qualifies as a special event."

"I'm not feeling exactly special," Preston said. "This is really starting to burn and it feels like needles are stabbing me!"

"I think I see the snake!" Bridger said.

Marco came up behind Zane and Bridger. "Hey, I'm pretty sure rattlesnakes are protected under Utah law."

I opened my pack and dug down to the bottom to get out the emergency sat phone we affectionately called "the bat signal." Out here in the Canyonlands wilderness, not even within the boundaries of the national park, a mobile phone wouldn't get a signal at all, but CanyonTrek—"safety is our number one priority for the protection, comfort, and education of our young adventurers"—assigned one expensive satellite phone per group, and I carried it.

We were just over two-thirds of the way into our trip, so I knew our exact location: as far from help as we could possibly be. Fortunately, out of caution and common sense, we had filed our route map in the Moab offices. With one call I should be able to summon a search-and-rescue helicopter team. CanyonTrek was a card-carrying member of Utah Search and Rescue Assistance, so the rescue team would come in like the cavalry. I knew the admins carried pricey insurance and made regular donations to USARA in case some troubled teen went off the trail and broke an ankle.

I switched on the sat phone and waited while it searched the sky for a signal. The bars danced and blipped. Apparently, the satellites were shy today.

Meanwhile, Judy deployed our snakebite kit. Her

brows were drawn together, her gaze intense as used a plastic disposable razor to scrape the fine hair off Preston's leg around the bite marks. "Next we clean."

"I can do that," Ophelia said, opening the sterile alcohol wipes, and lightly swabbed away the blood and dirt from the area.

"Now for the handy extractor pump," Judy said. She pulled out a plastic tube like a large syringe, fitted a suction cap on the end, and positioned it near Preston's leg.

"Snakes," Marco quoted. "Why did it have to be snakes?"

Preston glowered at him. "This is not a stupid movie. I can feel the venom working."

"When you panic, your pulse races," Judy said. "And that just spreads the poison around—so calm down. Somebody sing *Kumbaya*, okay?"

I thought she was being sarcastic, but Ava took Judy's words to heart. Sitting behind Preston, Ava put a hand on his arm and sang softly. Shaylee stood close by and hummed along.

Noah approached and looked over Judy's shoulder, as if this were one of their lessons. She pressed the extractor against the lower of the punctures, but Noah grabbed the syringe away from the wound. "That's the old way. It's not how they treat snake bites anymore."

Judy gave him a shrewd look. "This has been SOP—standard operating procedure—for as long as I can remember."

Noah shook his head. "No tourniquets. No cutting. No sucking."

"Really?" Ava sounded disappointed.

"Why listen to him? He's just a kid," Preston objected. "Read the instructions in the kit!"

"How'd you hear about the changes?" Judy asked Noah.

Ophelia spoke up. "His aunt's a veterinarian, remember? He knows endless mind-numbing details about animals and medicine."

While they went back and forth, Isabel, the quiet girl, got out Preston's water bottle and gave him a few careful sips.

Just then, my sat phone locked onto a signal, and I punched the preprogrammed number for CanyonTrek HQ. It rang eleven times without being answered. "So much for emergency preparedness." I was starting to sweat myself.

Several of the teens looked at me with concern. I hit redial, and the bat signal rang seven more times before someone finally picked up.

"Thank god!" I said. "This is Dale from Group One. We've got an emergency situation. Preston got bitten by a rattlesnake. Please send the rescue chopper immediately." They would acquire our location from the bat signal's built-in GPS so I didn't waste time giving directions. "I'll get our group to an open area and set out some signal flags."

Over the phone, I could hear shouts and havoc. Maybe they were having a rowdy party at CT headquarters.

The answer I got was not at all what I expected. A strained, feminine voice shouted in my ear, "Who is this? Where are you? Can you send help?"

I was pretty sure it was Desiree, the office manager, but I'd never heard her sound so ragged.

"This is Dale—and you're mixed up. I called you for help. I need an urgent medical evac for a snake-bite victim."

"Snake bite?" Desiree's voice rose with hysteria. "A snake bite! Are you crazy? That's the least of our problems." Something was definitely wrong. Desiree was usually so poised and cheerful.

"Can you put Bob on?" I said. "This is an emergency."

"Stay where you are," she said. "You're better off." It sounded like total chaos around her.

Her voice came through so loud over the sat phone that our whole group could hear her. "Moab is overrun! The epidemic spread. People from the big cities, trying to escape that virus a couple weeks ago? They swarmed out here and brought it with them! They're going crazy!" In the background I heard shouts, furniture being knocked over, a great crash, and the distinct crack of gunfire.

"Oh god, they smashed right through the door!"

"What is going on over there?" I said, pressing the bat signal to my ear.

"Bob!" Desiree screamed. I heard more gunshots, splintering wood, shattering glass, simultaneous yells. When I heard Desiree's voice again, it was a hopeless wail that abruptly changed to shrieks of agony. The phone fell to the floor with a clunk, and then I couldn't tell what the sounds were: Some kind of scuffling. Panting. Wet noises...

My throat went dry. What could I do? The students around me were staring, puzzled, and not nearly as terrified as I thought they should be. I switched off the bat signal.

Judy looked up from the snake bite wound. "Are they coming? What did they say?"

I tucked the bat signal back inside my pack. "I think we're on our own."

While Judy reread the instructions with the snakebite kit, Noah rattled off a list at break-neck speed. "Step one, move a safe distance away from the snake. Step two, have the victim rest on the ground. To slow the spread of venom, keep the bite at or below heart-level and keep the victim still and calm. Step three, get medical help as soon as possible. Antivenom is the primary treatment."

"Which we don't have." Judy said, looking at me. "I guess we can't count on anyone coming to help, huh?"

I shook my head. "Sounds like folks in Moab are worse off than we are. So what comes next?"

Noah continued with his list, as if it were a first-aid spelling bee. We covered the snakebite wound with a clean, dry dressing, even used a Sharpie to outline the discolored area and write the time, so we could track the spread of the damage. Preston groaned.

Noah finished, "Step eight, if medical help can't reach the victim, do not wait: take the victim to medical assistance. Left untreated, damage may be permanent or fatal."

"That sucks," Logan said.

"Sucking is obsolete," Noah said.

"No undoing a snake bite," Marco observed. "You need antivenom. It's a race against time."

"That's it then," said Zane. "We take Preston somewhere that has real medical help."

"It's always something." Judy set her jaw. "We'll handle it."

"That's what CanyonTrek is about: learning to solve problems," I repeated.

Sweat stood out on Preston's forehead and he didn't seem to be following the conversation. "You're just going to leave the venom in me?"

"Whatever's necessary to get you help, buddy, that's what we'll do," I said, starting to choke up. How often had I been annoyed with Preston, taking him for granted instead of treating him like my friend? I gave myself a mental kick. No time to agonize about my feelings. We had to get going.

Ophelia got out a roll of stretchy white bandage.

I pulled out the topo map and unfolded it on the rocks. Logan, who had proven excellent at map-reading came up beside me and Bridger joined us a moment later. I showed them the area we had been exploring and the trail of faint dots, which indicated a mere "suggested route" marked by occasional rock cairns. We were in the deepest desert wilds with the darkest night skies and the greatest solitude. Also the farthest from help.

"Now I know where we are," muttered Bridger. "We're screwed. That's where."

Logan gave a soft laugh, but did not let himself be distracted. "Judging by the terrain, we must be here." He pointed to the map and traced the faint dots.

"Good. I agree," I said. "That means it's about five miles total from here to these four-wheel-drive roads." I ran a finger from our position to our first goal. "We have to move Preston. With some help, he should be able to walk on his injured leg. Camping's free-range on BLM lands, so let's hope we find somebody with a vehicle."

"No helicopter?" Preston moaned leaning against a rock while Ophelia and Judy finished securing the bandage around his calf. "Shouldn't I just lie here and rest?"

"Pfft," Shaylee said. "You told us we couldn't stop and rest just because we were tired."

"You weren't bit by a rattlesnake!" Preston said. "Damn kids are so spoiled!"

I frowned at him, because this certainly wasn't Preston's usual philosophy of how to deal with reluctant young people. "You could stay here," I agreed, "but since there's no helicopter coming, it'll take forever to bring help. We may arrive too late. If we get you to those Jeep roads, you'll be better off." It wasn't exactly ideal, but we were SOL regarding the speedy rescue we'd expected in an emergency.

I was haunted by what I had heard on the sat phone. None of it made sense. I put away the map in my heavy backpack and zipped up the saddlebags. "Okay everyone. We've got to move out. Empty Preston's pack and distribute the items amongst yourselves. No telling what we might need."

While several of the kids darted off for hygiene breaks, very careful to watch for snakes, Zane and Ophelia emptied Preston's backpack and distributed the weight evenly among the hikers. Judy helped Preston lace his hiking boot. "We want to support your foot, but not too tight. That thing's going to swell like a sonofabitch," she said, then caught herself. "Language, sorry."

Ava and Judy helped Preston to his feet. He looked wan but determined to hobble. Judy offered him the option of using her sturdy trekking pole in addition to his own, like crutches.

"We can make a human crutch," Logan said. "You put one arm around my neck and my arm goes around your back. We'll need someone to help from the other side."

"I can do that," Marco said.

Preston agreed, so the young men put on their packs and supported him, one on either side. "Okay, let's blow this joint," he said.

Feeling the urgency, I set off, raising an arm to get everyone's attention. "This'll be tough, but necessary. Today we keep up a fast, steady pace, eat some miles. I believe you can do it. We need medical help for Preston, so let's get out to where we can be found."

The whole group murmured their agreement. No complaints. They understood the seriousness.

Before long, the hike turned arduous, although the map rated it as "easy." Up to that point, the days had been pleasant enough, with highs around eighty degrees. Today, Mother Nature chose to throw ninety degrees at us.

We wound our way through the slickrock, yucca, and saltbush, disappointed that we couldn't take the time just to enjoy the alien-looking hoodoos, red rock mounds striped with white frosting. This area had always held a primeval wonder for me, but now it felt like a nightmare landscape.

Finally, when we found the four-wheel-drive road, I realized that the term "road" was gracious and optimistic. The red powdery soil was punctuated by boulders, ruts, and deep washouts. On the bright side, I could see tire tracks, so someone had driven here since the previous rain...whenever that was. We were forty miles from a paved highway, but we knew the way out.

By late afternoon, Preston was getting more and

more miserable, his face gray and sweaty, his lips drawn back in pain. He finally insisted that we rest. Leaning on a rust-colored boulder and propping up his foot, he fumbled with the bandage.

Judy clucked her tongue. "Better leave it alone. That sucker is swelling up."

"I want to see," Preston said and unwound the fabric to expose his leg—angry red and swollen, with scarlet lines tracing up past his knee. "Oh, this is bad. I'm going to die of a snake bite! This is ridiculous."

"Wrap it up again," I said. "Keep it clean, and let's get going. We'll find somebody."

Marco patted Preston's shoulder. "Bro, in the words of the philosopher Dory, 'just keep swimming.'"

The sun was low on the western horizon and the temperature was already beginning to cool, mercifully. "We can make a few more miles down the road before nightfall." I tried to sound hopeful. "If someone is camping out here, we'll see the lights or the fire."

Preston groaned. "Great, we can roast marshmallows."

Two students chuckled despite the seriousness of the situation.

Marco tried to stay upbeat. "Come on, champ. Never give up. Never surrender."

We moved down the 4WD road, and within an hour we crossed a low swell, and I could see across the desert ahead. I was overjoyed to see a battered recreational vehicle parked off the road in one of the makeshift distributed campsites. "There, Preston! See, I told you."

"Woohoo!" Ophelia said. "First time I've ever been thrilled to see a Winnebago. We're usually stuck behind one on a slow mountain road."

We moved forward with a target now and with hope, plodding along, each of us taking turns shouting, trying to get the attention of the campers. "Hello!" I shouted. "We need help."

"Help," Shaylee cried.

Isabel and Ava added their voices, and soon we were a chorus. No one stirred in or around the RV, though. Perhaps the people had gone backpacking somewhere and left their campsite for a while.

In a low voice Judy asked me, "What do we do if no one's home?"

"Break in and take what we need." I mentally estimated a 50/50 chance that at least one of these teens knew how to hotwire a vehicle.

"Help!" Zane yelled toward the RV. Then he, Marco, Noah, and Logan bellowed greetings and pleas for help, trying to outdo each other, while Preston cringed at the noise.

As we hiked closer and the late afternoon shadows grew longer, we heard faint noises inside the Winnebago, beyond the curtained windows. The flimsy door swung open.

"Help!" we yelled again.

We were close enough to the campsite that I could make out something on the ground—was it a person? It was. A body, actually. Or what was left of one. A large portion of the skin and muscles had been ripped away in ragged chunks.

The two figures that emerged from the RV no longer appeared fully human. They had pale, blotchy skin, wild hair, blood-smeared faces. And they were naked.

That was when the shit really hit the fan.

III
Dale

The two sickly things that lurched out of the Winnebago came at us fast. Their bodies were discolored, and we could see far too much of their skin, as if they had shambled out of a nudist colony for leprosy patients. They made wild, inhuman, and hungry sounds.

The hope of the RV, the campsite—any sign of life at all in the vast empty desert—juiced Preston with adrenaline. Always annoyingly optimistic, he ignored the warning signs. While the rest of us hesitated, he broke away from Zane and Logan and lurched forward, waving his arms. "Help! I've been bitten by a snake. We need to get to a doctor."

He certainly drew their attention. Both of the things were male, embarrassingly so. Even without clothes or weapons, they had clutching hands and menacing teeth—and they weren't afraid to use them.

The older male charged Preston and drove him to the ground. The counselor fell hard on his back and cried out, "My leg!"

Working his jaws, the scarecrowish creature pinned Preston down and bit into his face, before using skeletal hands to tear at his throat and chest. Each wound drew a wordless shriek from Preston. The sound of it was appalling, almost inhuman.

Backing up toward me, Ava screamed, and several of the others decided that was the appropriate response.

Everything happened so fast. The second creature came at us, wild and moaning. It launched itself toward me, eyes blazing, hands outstretched. Its ragged nails clawed at the space between us, reaching toward me.

I swung my trekking pole so hard it made a whistling sound in the air. I was just trying to batter away the grasping hands, but I brought it down so hard, the fingers snapped like hollow sticks.

Finished killing Preston, the first attacker turned and ran straight into our group.

Zane wielded his walking stick like a tae kwon do master. Logan and Marco waded in, while Noah, Bridger, Ava, and Isabel clustered together, raising their makeshift weapons.

"Och. This is like *Night of the Living Dead*!" Ophelia blurted.

Hearing her, Marco called out, "Original George Romero version, or the remake?"

"Can't go wrong with George Romero," Ophelia answered, dodging the thing that had killed Preston.

I kept fighting away at the ghoulish man who was trying to rip my throat out. I whacked again with my walking stick, this time with more practice, more confidence, and more urgency. I struck my attacker full in the eye, and he didn't even flinch. After all, what was one more wound or gash on his already ravaged body?

Ophelia swung her walking stick, still jabbering in her fangirl fascination. "Now, the *Return of the Living Dead* movies were funny." She whacked at the older creature, Preston's murderer. Blood streamed from the hideous mouth down to his chest. "That's where we got used to the idea that zombies eat brains." To my surprise, Ophelia did not look fazed.

My attacker continued to flail and scrabble, for some reason fixated on me, even though there were plenty of other choice morsels around. At least three of the kids had bolted off into the desert. Good call.

Zane smashed the first creature and yelled for Ophelia to run. She made a break for it, but her diseased attacker sprang forward and clutched her overstuffed backpack, clawing and ripping, as if it were filled with internal organs rather than pack food. She tried to get loose.

I stumbled on something and tripped backward, instinctively rolling to the side, so I wasn't like a turtle turned upside down with my heavy pack. I saw that I had tripped over the gnawed, stripped remains of a third person—the bloody body I had seen from a distance. Wisps of long hair clinging to the skull implied it was an older woman.

I kicked out, knocked the attacker back, and lurched to my feet. As he came at me again, I extended my trekking pole and jabbed as hard as I could with the pointed metal end. I stabbed him right through the neck, like a gladiator with a spear. I shoved again and again, until the point came out the thing's back and blood spouted out. I twisted and wrenched, realizing that my pole was now stuck in the body. The attacker flailed, then collapsed. His snapping jaws slowed as he died.

All the screaming confused the details of what was going on, but the loud gunshot was unmistakable, then a second one. Expecting another attack, I turned, only to see Judy holding a pistol in a cool firing stance, like an Old West gunfighter at high noon.

My jaw dropped.

The older thing attacking Ophelia's backpack gurgled and let go so suddenly that Ophelia lurched forward and landed on her hands and knees. The creature staggered sideways, fell, and rolled face down on the ground with two gunshot wounds in his back.

"Och!" Ophelia brushed gravel from her hands, and Zane helped her to her feet. They scrambled away from the dead corpse, or whatever you call it. Ophelia blinked in surprise. "I guess you don't have to shoot these things in the head to kill them. So, not real zombies."

I wrenched my bloody trekking pole from the neck of my own attacker. "Whatever works," I said.

"What the hell was that all about?" gasped Bridger, then reconsidered. "What the fuck was that?"

Judy didn't correct him for his language, although it shocked me, especially coming from one of our straightlaced Mormon kids. Ava, Noah and Shaylee had rushed over to Preston to give first aid, but he lay unmoving, his face and throat ripped open.

"He's dead," Ava groaned. "They killed him!"

Tilting his head to study Preston, Noah said with odd inappropriateness, "Well, at least he didn't die from the snake bite."

"I may put that in my journal tonight," Ophelia said. She looked over at me and Judy. "Do we still have to do our journals?"

Neither of us answered.

Judy still held her pistol, then slowly lowered the weapon, visibly winding down.

"We aren't supposed to have guns," I said. "CT's pretty strict about that."

She gave me a withering look. "Not supposed to." She sniffed. "I signed a contract to protect these kids. It's a Glock 21, .45 caliber. But CT also says that counselors must be prepared for any circumstances."

"You kidding me? Even from a zombie invasion?"

Judy shrugged.

"Och. Please don't," Ophelia said. "Don't say zombies. It doesn't feel appropriate to me—so trite, so fictional. These were real. Are we sure what they really are? What if we called them living dead—LDs for short?"

I looked over at the murdered counselor. "Preston didn't like to use terms that made people uncomfortable. Something about being politically correct."

Ophelia nodded. Turning abruptly, she went over to Preston's body, sat beside him, and took his bloody hand.

Judy strode toward the Winnebago. "Preston would also have wanted us to understand what's happening and take stock of our resources."

The vehicle's flimsy door had flapped shut. She yanked it open and stepped into the RV, cautiously extending her pistol. "Nobody's home. And nobody's housecleaning, either."

As I followed Judy inside, I could tell that the Winnebago had never been nice, but now it was a disaster, a combination of hoarder and homeless camp under a bridge. Cans of beans, chili, and soup had been pried open somehow, scooped out—with bare fingers, I assumed—and strewn on the floor. Ramen noodle packets had been crunched and devoured, sometimes with half the plastic wrapper.

"Guess they don't just eat brains," I said. "Oh, that's right, they aren't 'zombies.'"

Tucked on a shelf beside the small cupboard, I found two copies of the Salt Lake Tribune. I pulled them out, unfolding the front pages.

"Jackpot," I said, showing Judy.

By now, several of the teens had ventured into the RV with us. Others milled around the campsite. Zane was apparently standing guard in case more of the living dead marched across the open desert.

I read the lead story out loud about a viral epidemic that had surged through the nation's largest cities and soon spread to Salt Lake City. Even smaller areas like Moab suffered unexpected outbreaks, as people fled the cities to isolate themselves from the virus, bringing it with them. I thought of Desiree screaming over the sat phone, and the sound of gunfire at CanyonTrek HQ.

Beside me, Judy shook her head. "This is messed up."

"Hey, look," said Marco. He held up a couple of postcards from the windowsill by the Formica dinette table. "They were going to mail these when they got to the Needles Outpost." He squinted to make out the handwriting. "I think they were an older couple, Linda and Frank, and their son Owen. A couple of weeks ago when people started getting sick, they drove out here to hole up. Frank thought the desert was the best place. They were going to get more supplies from the Needles Outpost before it was too late." Marco shook his head. "The last line says, 'Owen isn't feeling well.'"

I glanced out the open door of the RV. "I guess he got worse."

The mangled body outside must have been Linda. Now we knew who our two attackers were.

Noah came through the door, ignoring everyone, and said, "You probably want these." He handed me a set of keys with a metal fob marked Winnebago and ducked back out the door.

A plan was coming together in my mind. I looked around at the mess inside the RV. In addition to eating most of mom, Frank and Owen had ransacked the

Winnebago's supplies. But our group still had a week's worth of pack food—two weeks if we stretched it, since CT always overplanned. I remembered complaining a few times about the extra weight in emergency supplies. The old me was an idiot. Now I don't mind at all.

The rest of our teen wards clustered around the door looking in.

What could I say after all we had just been through?

I took a deep breath and spread my arms. "Now we have a vehicle."

Ophelia Journal

Day X. I've lost track. Maybe it doesn't matter.

Hi Preston. This one's for you, even though we don't have to journal today. See, I'm still doing my assignments.

I stayed by you for a long time today and said a lot of bad words. A bit inappropriate, but I know you wouldn't have minded.

I can't believe you're gone. Dead. And what an awful way to die. You were really nice, except toward the end and that was really the snakebite's fault. Sorry you went through so much pain.

I don't know what happens now. Wherever you are, I want you to know that I won't forget you, no matter what. I don't think any of us ever will.

IV
Dale

In the aftermath at the campsite, we took care of clearing out and cleaning the Winnebago with plenty of Windex and Pine-Sol and using up a jumbo bottle of hand sanitizer. Everyone read the newspaper stories, so we were up to speed on the end of the world—at least out here. Many of the larger cities were still intact, but hospitals were overwhelmed. The Salt Lake Tribune didn't give us the answers we really needed, though—like what the hell we should do now.

We pitched camp as usual to sleep outside—no one was ready to take advantage of the RV yet. In the morning we took turns digging graves, not much more than uneven divots in the rocky ground. We needed to bury Preston, and it seemed appropriate to do the same for whatever was left of Linda, Frank, and Owen. This part definitely wasn't in the CT manual. In the end, we wrapped the bodies in old blankets we found in the RV, put them in the shallow trenches, and piled rocks on top of them.

As the students picked up the heavy stones for the cairns, Ophelia called, "Watch out for snakes. They can kill you just as dead as the LDs."

Next to her, Zane raised his eyebrows. "LDs?"

The two of them were spending a lot of time together. She smiled. "Yeah, it's short for living deads."

"Why not call them zombies?" asked Noah.

"Because they're not exactly dead and rotting. You saw them—they're diseased. It's a virus, a plague."

"They were naked," Shaylee said.

Ophelia rolled her eyes. "After all we went through, that's what you noticed?"

"Well, they were really naked," she said.

"LDs?" Bridger frowned. "Sounds like LDS."

"Not meant as an insult," I said. "We just need something to call them."

"Exactly," Ophelia said. "Especially if a whole herd of LDs comes shambling across the desert to get us. It'd be stupid to waste time arguing about terminology."

"Why would we? You're the only person who objects to calling them zombies," Logan observed. Before Ophelia could answer, he raised his hands in surrender. "Never mind. I'm not objecting. LDs it is."

"Pfft," Shaylee said.

Several of our group turned nervously, shading their eyes to look across the expanse of hoodoos and red rocks, the rills of canyons, as if scanning for LDs.

"I have to get home," Isabel said.

"We all do." I assured her. I wanted to offer hope, but should I? So far the bat signal hadn't been able to reach anyone who could help us. It was a bad sign for civilization. "We'll find out just what's going on in the world. Meanwhile, it's tight but we can all fit inside the Winnebago. We can go somewhere."

My announcement was greeted with genuine cheers.

I climbed into the driver's seat, took a deep breath, uttered a prayer to any higher power that might be listening, and turned the key.

The engine started right up. It puttered a little, one of the pistons firing erratically, but it seemed to run fine. My joy lasted only a moment, though. I was dismayed to see that the fuel light was on. "Great. They came all the way out here and were about to run out of gas."

Judy leaned in the window, concerned. "Highway 191 is about forty miles, and another fifteen or so to Monticello." Monticello was a small farming community that had a few amenities—gas station, general store, cafes.

Who knew how long the fuel light had been on, or how much remained in the tank? I shook my head. "Not sure we'd make it that far."

Logan came forward holding a map and plopped himself down on the passenger seat beside me. "That Needles Outpost thing isn't very far, though. It's on the park-access road."

I felt a glimmer of hope. I'd been there once, a campground, gas station, cutesy tourist teepees, souvenir shop, and general store on private land just outside the boundary to Canyonlands National Park. "That might do it. We can at least fuel up there, stockpile supplies. No telling how long we might have to stay out here in the desert keeping our distance from people with the virus."

"But I've got to go home," Logan said. "What if my family is in the middle of this? They may need help."

"Mine too," said Ava.

Noah echoed the sentiment.

"It's a safe bet that they're all in the middle of it," Judy said, "and there's nothing you can do to help. Sorry, kids, but they'd want you to stay safe, and the safest place is out here with us."

"Tell that to Preston," Ophelia said.

"Everybody climb in," I said, conscious that the engine was gulping fuel every second I left it running. "We'll get to the Needles Outpost and figure out what to do from there. Maybe they'll have a more recent newspaper."

Leaving the four fresh graves behind, including our lost counselor, everyone piled into the RV. The teens argued over seats. Logan called shotgun, but Judy overruled him, shooed him away, and swung herself into the passenger seat beside me. "You good at maneuvering on four-wheel-drive roads?"

"That's not the question so much as is the Winnebago good on them?" I said. "We know it got this far." As we moved away from the nightmarish campsite, twenty-five miles an hour seemed like reckless speed. We rattled over washboard ridges, hit potholes, swerved around boulders. I was amazed the big recreational vehicle had made it out here, but Frank, Owen, and Linda must have really been determined. I kept glancing at the fuel light.

Right now I could have been in a conference room at my software company headquarters or reading over budget documents, or flying to a trade conference. After my early retirement, I'd stashed my savings and lived on a minimal budget. Spending my days walking around slickrock country had seemed like the perfect idea. I wasn't prepared for anything like this!

And yet if I had been at my normal job, I would surely be in a worse situation now. Our software engineers worked hard, lived in the office, put in ridiculous hours, but were never obsessive about personal hygiene. The epidemic would surely have raged through the offices, and employees-turned-LDs would have torn through the cubicles, smashed computer terminals, and eaten their coworkers in favor of the stale donuts left in the breakroom. I remembered my ex-wife saying that my midlife crisis was going to kill me. But maybe it was the only thing that had kept me alive.

The Winnebago bounced and rattled along the rough road for nearly an hour. I was sweating about the fuel, and my neck and shoulders were stiff with tension, but at least they had been toughened from carrying a heavy backpack. The students tried to play games to distract themselves. Sometimes they bickered, other times they fell into a nervous silence.

We saw smoke, and I slowed down to see another campsite on an offshoot pullout. A small pop-up camper and a tent had been set on fire and actually flipped on its side.

"I don't see any LDs around," Zane said. "Should we have a look?"

"Don't stop," Judy said. "Just get to the outpost."

I agreed.

After what felt like forever, we finally left the jeep road and hit the patched and pitted access road that dead-ended into the national park. The feeling of tires humming on actual asphalt was heaven.

The engine began to putter and cough more, and I recognized the signs of a near-empty gas tank. "We're on fumes," I announced.

I knew we would make it, though, when we saw the turnoff for the Needles Outpost. I pulled down the road surrounded by desert scrub and rock formations, the type of scenery postcards and tourist brochures are made out of. A rustic wooden sign said Needles Outpost, as if it had been carved by some old pioneer.

The campground seemed sparsely populated: a handful of RVs interspersed with white teepees, a few parked vans, a dozen miscellaneous tents.

"Look, there's people!" Shaylee said. "We're saved."

Something set off my alarm bells. Figures moved aimlessly around. Then I noticed that a couple of tents were torn and collapsed, the windows on a van were smashed open, the sliding side door yanked off its tracks. The figures that emerged from some recreational vehicles were pale skinned, blotchy, and naked.

"No!" Ava said in a plaintive voice.

"They're LDs," Ophelia confirmed.

I glanced at the fuel gauge, then ahead to the general store and its line of gas pumps. The Needles Outpost store was a single large building, set away from the main campground. I hoped we'd have enough time.

"No choice. We've got to do this." I accelerated toward the gas pumps. "Soon as I pull up, break into the same teams we used this morning. Can you do that?"

A chorus of voices behind me said, "I can do that."

"Good. We've got several things to do. This is what teamwork is all about: solving problems. Team one, with Judy: work the pumps and fill us up with gas. Team two, stand watch and fight off any LDs that come close. Team three, you're with me. We have to get inside the general store, load up with as much food and supplies as we can possibly grab."

"Don't forget toilet paper," said Logan.

Gasping on its last fumes, the Winnebago pulled into the Outpost.

Judy looked at me and said, "This is going to be fun."

V
Dale

Even though we saw jerky, uncertain figures in the campground, the general store and outpost building looked quiet and abandoned. That could be a good thing or a bad thing.

The outpost building had mirrorlike solar panels on the roof, and three large sausage-shaped propane tanks sat in the rear of the building. I pulled the

Winnebago up to the bank of gas pumps, choosing one in the open on the opposite side of the general store.

Judy looked around with the thousand-mile stare of a battle-hardened veteran. "You could get closer."

"I want some room for movement," I said. "Just in case LDs come boiling out of that trading post, too." The thought of a horde of cannibalistic zombies surging out of the souvenir shop in new T-shirts and chintzy dude-ranch hats almost made me smile. Almost.

"Good thinking," Judy said with a curt nod.

Figures were starting to move in from the group campsites and the cute teepees. "Ready teams?" I said. "Get in and out as fast as we can. Be flexible. This is a fluid situation."

"Mmm, fluids," Shaylee said. "We need to grab some soda, too."

"We'll need to grab some of those camper propane tanks for the Winnebago," Logan said, pointing to a rack of stubby tanks on the side wall of the store. "You know, to heat up our Ramen noodles and Chef Boyardee."

Chef BAD? I hoped the apocalypse wasn't quite that bad yet. "Ophelia, Zane, Shaylee—you're with me in the general store to grab supplies. Judy, you've got Ava, Logan, and Noah to fill the gas and grab propane. Bridger, Marco, Isabel, take your hiking sticks or whatever you need and guard the perimeter. Keep watch."

"Can I keep watch from inside the RV?" asked Isabel in a quavering voice.

"I know it's hard, but I need you with your team," I said. "Remember how we said this experience would teach you survival skills? I expect you all to survive, damn it."

Marco's eyes widened, and he nodded. "I can do that." Several of the others echoed his words.

Zane popped open the Winnebago's door, and we rushed out all at once. The fresh, hot air struck me, making me realize how close and stinky the inside of the RV had been.

"Ooh look. They have showers," Ava said, pointing toward a side building.

A sigh of longing rippled through the group, and I felt it, too. We had more than two weeks of sweat and trail dirt on us.

"No time," I replied. "Better grungy than dead."

"Yeah, it's a tough choice, but..." Zane turned his cocky grin toward Ophelia. I'd seen the two flirting with each other.

Judy headed to the gas pump with Ava and Noah, while Logan ran to the rack of small propane tanks. The three guards fanned out, looking nervous—the most skittish sentry ring I'd ever seen, but I couldn't blame them.

We ran to the trading post. The operating hours were conveniently listed, but the glass doors were locked, the interior dark.

"They're not open," Shaylee said in dismay.

Ophelia pointed to the hours posted on the door. "According to this, they should be."

"That could be a good thing. Maybe it means the store hasn't been ransacked by LDs," I said.

Shaylee rattled the door, as if a few more attempts might magically open the outpost for business. She made a *pfft* of annoyance.

Ophelia pressed her face to the glass and shaded her eyes to peer inside. "Nothing moving in there," she said. "But I see potato chips...and they have a special on Cherry Coke."

"We've got to get inside," Zane said. Before any of us noticed what he was doing, he picked up a decorative rock and smashed it into one of the thick glass doors, producing a hole surrounded by pointed shards and spiderweb cracks. "Now it's ready for customers."

Ophelia scowled at Zane. "Och. Couldn't you have found a side window? LDs probably aren't good at getting through windows. But with the front door broken—what if we need to barricade ourselves inside against an army of living dead?"

"Oh." Zane looked crestfallen, not just because of what he'd done, but because of Ophelia's disappointment.

"You probably don't watch enough movies," Ophelia grumbled.

I pushed a loose fragment of glass away to clear the hole and reached inside to click open the deadbolt. "Let's go."

"Isn't this stealing?" Shaylee said sounding uneasy.

It wasn't anywhere in the CT playbook, but I wasn't going to argue. "Desperate times," I said. "We'll pay for any damages later, when things go back to normal. But we need supplies now."

At the gas pumps, Judy had yanked up one of the nozzles and tried all the buttons. Ava removed the gas cap from the RV. Logan had a camper propane tank in each hand and was lugging them from the rack to the Winnebago.

I entered the dark general store. "Hello?" I called out. "Anybody here? We need help."

My words echoed among the well-stocked metal

shelves and displays. I was relieved to see that other scavengers hadn't already taken everything.

"Okay, quick, grab what you can," I said. "This might need to last us for a long time." Saying this gave me a chill. Since Preston's snake bite, we had been reacting from gut instinct, not thinking more than an hour or two ahead. Now I was planning for a crisis that might last for weeks or even months. I was acknowledging that we would not simply be met at the pickup point by Bob in a CT van that would take these kids back to clean clothes and showers, then into the appreciative arms of their families. That wasn't going to happen.

"Cherry Coke or regular?" Ophelia called out. "They're both on sale."

"Cherry," said Zane.

"Decaf," said Shaylee, then made a *pfft* sound. "No—make mine regular after all."

I glanced outside, where gaunt, hungry-looking figures were moving closer. I counted maybe twenty LDs coming in from the campground, all naked. Strange. Had they come here to "get back to nature," or was nudity a thing that all LDs did?

Bridger, Noah, and Isabel had spread out beyond the RV, holding their hiking sticks. Bridger had picked up some egg-sized rocks and crouched, ready to throw them.

With jerky awkward movements the LDs came closer. Yup. Might turn out very much like a scene from *Night of the Living Dead*, and my mind made no distinction between the original, the remake, or even the spinoffs.

In frustration, Judy slammed her hand against the

metal side of the gas pump. She sent Ava on an urgent dash back to the general store. I met her at the door, suddenly struck by the possibility that the gas pumps might not be working at all. "What's wrong?"

Ava was out of breath and panted for a few seconds before saying, "Judy needs your credit card. Hers was declined."

I fished out my wallet, pulled my Visa from its slot, and handed it over. As Ava ran back to Judy with my card, I yelled toward the gas pumps, "Helluva time not to pay your monthly minimum!"

Judy spread her hands in apology.

I ducked back into the shadowy store. The lack of lighting must have been intentional, because the outpost was solar powered and off the grid.

Zane and Ophelia had shopping carts, while Shaylee carried a basket, running up and down the rows. Ophelia started with candy and chips.

"Get the cool ranch ones," Zane said. "Way better than chile verde."

"Roger. Also getting all kinds of cookies," Ophelia said.

"Remember, this is survival," I called to them, "not snack time. Think nutrition. We need protein."

"I found the Spam and Vienna sausages!" Shaylee said. "Ooh, and Slim Jims."

I shrugged "That's definitely closer." I checked outside again.

Judy was pumping gas now, filling the Winnebago's tank. Ava had gathered several large red gas cans and was filling them at another pump.

"Better hurry," Noah yelled. "They're getting closer."

"Gas doesn't pump itself," Judy said. "It takes as

long as it takes." She looked around warily, and I saw that her Glock was now holstered at her side. Good.

Dozens of LDs were swarming from the campground, as if someone had rung the dinner bell. The Needles Outpost campground must have been pretty full, and I imagined plenty of people had come here to avoid the viral apocalypse. Of course, it only took one bad zombie to infect the whole barrel.

Inside the store, I grabbed a shopping cart and threw in protein bars, electrolyte drinks, and bottled water. I made the mistake of thinking this was all going smoothly.

That's when I heard the distinctive click and ratchet of a shotgun slide being racked, followed by the clink of something small hitting the floor. We all froze. I turned toward the noise and saw a gray-bearded man in a plaid shirt and bib overalls. He pointed a shotgun at me, then swung it around to aim at the kids. "Who the hell are you, and what are you doing in my store?"

With a clank, Ophelia dropped a can of chili on the floor. "Uh, shopping?"

I raised my hands. "We just needed supplies."

"Can't you see we're closed?" His face was drawn and his eyes wary as he stepped closer. "And you smashed my damn door!"

He must have locked himself inside the outpost for days, hiding in the dark so the LDs wouldn't notice him.

"My name is Dale," I said, consciously using a calm, friendly voice. A Preston voice. "I'm here with a group of CanyonTrek students. We were out in the BLM lands at the edge of the Needles, and came back to...all this."

"How do I know you're not infected?" the old man demanded.

Shaylee made a *pfft* sound. "How? We've been out in the middle of nowhere."

I slowly reached for my pants pocket. "Look, we're not stealing. I can pay for everything. We just need to load up our RV and get back into the desert to wait this thing out." I slid out my wallet, opened it, and saw the empty slot where my credit card usually was. I opened the cash section and pulled out a couple of twenties. Normally I carried more... but who needs cash on a Needles backpacking trip?

Judy shouted from outside. "Dale, speed it up! We've got company." Through the open doors I saw her hand the gas pump to Logan. "Finish this," she said and stalked off, pulling her pistol.

Ava filled up another red gas can, returned the hose to the pump, and frantically screwed on the caps.

"Well, now you caught the attention of the campers," the old man snorted. "Nothing worse than dissatisfied campers."

The LDs were rushing toward the Winnebago now. Marco and Isabel swung their trekking poles back and forth, driving a few of the diseased victims back. Bridger hurled stones, smacking one LD in the center of her forehead.

Judy strode up beside him, raised her Glock, and fired with a loud crack. She shot the nearest pale and bloody figure in the center of his naked chest.

"Dale, I did not bring enough bullets for the Alamo here!"

I pleaded with the old man. "Look, we have to get out of here. If you think you're safe, stay." I reached a decision and blurted out. "Or you're welcome to come with us and get far away...but you've got to run now."

"Name's Wendell," he said, lowering the shotgun. "And I'll give us some elbow room." He slipped past us and rushed out the door.

I yelled at the three kids in the store. "Come on, all of you. Take what you can and get back to the RV."

Zane and Ophelia ran up and down the aisles with their shopping carts rattling, while Shaylee set her overfull basket by the door and grabbed a new one. I added all the emergency supplies I could grab to my cart. As I passed the cash register, I swept a pile of batteries in with the mix and trundled out to the RV.

Logan hooked the gas nozzle back in place on the pump and whirled to screw the cap back on the tank.

Wendell stepped next to Judy and discharged his shotgun with a loud boom. The buckshot dispersed wide enough to blast two of the oncoming LDs and knock them flat.

"Back into the Winnebago, everybody!" I yelled. They didn't need to be told twice.

Wendell chambered another round, ejecting the spent shell, and shot again.

I leaped into the driver's seat, jammed the keys into the ignition. Judy fired her Glock twice more, and then the rest of our group piled aboard the RV. Wendell followed them into the back, while Judy hopped in through the passenger door.

"Don't worry, I got your credit card, Dale," said Ava with earnest diligence.

"Thank you," I replied and started the engine.

"Did anyone get toilet paper?" Logan asked.

"*Pfft*," Shaylee said, slapping her forehead, at the

same time as Ophelia said, "Aargh!" and Zane said, "Uh-oh!"

"Not going back," Judy said sternly.

The big RV rolled forward not much faster than the living dead could shamble. I stomped on the accelerator. The Winnebago was a workhorse, slow and heavy, but it did pick up speed, eventually. I was glad we'd used one of the outer gas pumps, because the behemoth couldn't maneuver in tight quarters. I swung a wide U-turn.

Wendell was trying to situate himself on one of the seats in back.

"You might just have to hold on," Ophelia told him.

About ten LDs that must have wandered over from the campground blocked the exit road.

"Crap!" Zane said. "Can you dodge them?"

"Is there another road out?" I barked at Wendell.

"Only one road in and one road out," he said. "Never been a problem before."

"Straight through it is," I muttered. No point in trying to dodge any LDs. I accelerated toward the bottleneck that limited our escape. I braced myself, gripping the steering wheel.

Shaylee screamed, "Look out!"

"Don't worry, they'll jump out of the way," I said, not believing it for a moment.

They didn't. The Winnebago struck a few LDs, scattered the rest, and kept going even as we felt a sickening bump under our tires.

"Just a pothole," Judy said. "Nothing to worry about."

I raced along the bumpy, patched road.

"Just a pothole," I agreed.

VI
Dale

We were home free. More or less. Our RV had a full gas tank and a couple of spare cans. We had food. We had water. We had propane. And we had no idea where to go.

"I want to get home," Shaylee said.

"Forget Moab, just head straight up to Salt Lake," Bridger piped up from the back. "My family's there." He looked around at the other eight students. "Most of our families are there, right?"

"I miss them." Marco's voice cracked. "I never thought I'd say it..."

Into a rising chorus of excited voices and worried demands, Wendell spoke. "That's the least safe place to be right now! I watched the TV until most of the stations went off. Salt Lake is burning. There's a virus spreading. Hospitals are overflowing with flu patients. On top of that, those infected things are everywhere."

"We call them LDs," Ava said, trying to be helpful. "It stands for 'living dead.'"

"You can't know what's happening everywhere," Zane insisted. "We should see for ourselves."

"What I do know is this: driving toward an infected city is the opposite of wise," the old man said. His shoulders sagged. I could see him in the rearview mirror. "Five days ago my wife took the truck in to Monticello to get our monthly delivery. She called to tell me our delivery didn't come, and there were riots in the streets. How? There's only a couple thousand people in the whole town, and none of them are the rioting type. She said 'Don't come anywhere near town—it's not safe.' That was when the call got cut off, and phone service has been down ever since." His voice wavered on the verge of weeping. "Next day, a young couple with a baby stopped here for gas. They came from Monticello, said there were stark-naked people and fires and murders all over town. They escaped. My wife never came back. And I know damn well what's happening out there."

I turned on the radio and scrolled through the stations, getting mostly static except for, oddly, a station that blared brassy Mexican music and another with a vehement preacher railing about the end times. I switched it off.

"It's probably going to get worse before it gets better," I said.

My heart felt heavy for these teens. They were participants in CT because their parents thought they needed behavior modification, boot-camp counselors to toughen them up and straighten them out. Before our three-week expedition, Judy, Preston, and I had met with all of the parents and learned about the home situations so we could understand the special problems these kids might pose. Some of the parents probably just wanted to breathe a sigh of relief at getting the unruly teens out of their hair. Ava had naively thought she was coming to a summer camp.

I'd been through this before. The parents expected miracles from a few days out in the canyonlands hiking and tent camping. They wanted us counselors to force an epiphany, make their almost-adult sons or daughters appreciate the things they had, learn a new work ethic, develop respect and civility. All in three weeks or less. We did accomplish some of those things. Their nightly journals were a good tool to help us assess their progress, but it wasn't magic.

These kids all wanted to go back home, because most of their problems paled in comparison to a deadly epidemic. But having heard Desiree on the sat phone, I could guess what had happened at CanyonTrek HQ in Moab...and maybe all of Moab. We'd read the papers, and we knew what to expect in Salt Lake. These kids couldn't go home. They couldn't help.

As I maneuvered the Winnebago along the narrow winding road through the red rock desert, I said, "I think we should stay here on the BLM lands for a while. We've got food and supplies. We have our packs and tents. The smartest thing is to wait this out, and I'll keep trying to reach someone who can tell us when it's safe."

"That's what we need to do," said Wendell. "Plenty of places to get lost out here. We could hunker down."

"That's my vote, too," said Judy, "so it's unanimous."

"Hey, we didn't get a vote!" Ophelia and Zane chimed in at the same time.

"This isn't a democracy," I said. "It's an oligarchy." I paused for a second then said, "Look it up."

"There's no dictionary," the kids grumbled, and, "We should have a say."

I took a turnoff and left the pavement for another dirt road. A brown Forest Service sign with white letters said OVERLOOK 15 MILES. It seemed a good place to start, to get a feel for where we were.

The road was rough, and its washboard surface rattled our teeth. If Preston were still alive, he probably would have started a group song, like "ninety-nine bottles of soda on the wall." As it was, most of the young people sat in confusion and sadness, trying to absorb what was happening. The RV gave us countless options of where to camp. There were plenty of firepits and open parking areas, no traffic that we could see.

"I made a promise to keep all of you safe," I said to the group.

Judy nodded. "Me too. I just wish I'd managed to pick up more rounds for my Glock."

After the long rattling drive I finally pulled the Winnebago to a stop at the abandoned, nameless overlook. From a high point on the edge of a mesa, it offered a view out across an endless wonderland of hoodoos, rust red pinnacles, and deep-cut canyons.

We all climbed out.

"I found a picnic table!" Isabel said.

I drank in the desert scenery, using it to find a tiny speck of calm deep inside me. Even in a world with a spreading epidemic, upheavals in society, and living dead roaming the streets, I felt a sense of satisfaction. I was taking care of the people I was responsible for. We were safe. For now.

Looking at the landscape, I said to myself, "One hell of a place to lose a cow."

Standing nearby, Ophelia flashed me an odd smile. "But maybe a good place to lose the LDs."

I drew in a deep breath of the warm, dry desert air and nodded slowly. "I agree."

Ophelia Journal

Day 1. I'm starting over. I'm not who I was a few weeks ago.

So this is for me.

Sounds corny, but this is true: We morphed into a family of sorts, with a mom, dad, grandpa, and nine kids. Well, except for one thing. None of us are kids anymore.

Life is harder than before. Gritty. Back-breaking. We all have jobs every day—guard duty, cooking, foraging, inventing, sanitation. There's no choice. We don't argue about it. Who else would do the work?

We solve problems, pretty much around the clock.

Me? I wait, and hope for a future when I can maybe see my parents again. Meanwhile, I'll live the life that I have, not the one I wish for.

I can do that.

Liberation Day

BRENDAN DUBOIS

On the sole dock leading out of Massabesic Island off the coast of Maine, Fred Paige, chairman of the Board of Selectmen for the village, was waiting, seeing the early morning fog still hanging around this brisk morning. The dock was like the middle tine of a three-tined fork, with the other two tines being the stone breakwaters leading out into the Atlantic, protecting the small harbor.

Next to him the other selectman, Paul Lucian, checked his watch and said, "They're late."

"It's foggy," Fred said. "Maybe they're just being cautious. Or lost. What do you think, Chris?"

Chris Allain was about fifteen years younger than Fred and Paul, skinny, with long stringy hair and a face with a bad complexion. But despite his appearance, he was one of the most important people on this island, for he was the best operator of the still-surviving shortwave radio equipment in the volunteer fire department building.

"They sounded legit," Chris said, also looking out to the fog. It was so thick that it was hard to see the end of the breakwaters, where large plywood signs were posted, painted black and orange, with a skull and crossbones, and large letters stating KEEP AWAY. One old cabin cruiser that was partially sunk still bobbed at the harbor entrance, having been there for a year.

"So did the others," Fred said, hands in his dungaree coat. He and Paul both had thick beards. Most men on the island had beards, when the razors and so many other staples disappeared. He and Fred also had holstered pistols at the side—his a 9mm Beretta, Paul's a 10mm Glock—and Chris had a 20-gauge Remington pump action shotgun over his shoulder.

Fred turned to look behind him, at the piled up lobster traps, the trash barrels, and the various buildings and homes that made up the village and island of Massabesic. There was a faint twinge of sadness at seeing the large barnlike structure that was the village's town hall. Every other Tuesday evening the three-member board of selectmen had a business meeting, but now the town was down to two. The third member, Matilda Grant, was once the oldest resident on the island and a constant smoker. She died two months ago after some bouts of serious coughing that brought up a lot of blood and sputum. Lung cancer was probably the cause of death, but there was no need nor ability to perform an autopsy, so she was laid to rest in a freshly made pine casket, like her ancestors.

And at least, some whispered, she had died naturally.

Not like the Clark or Pemrose families, up on the northern end of the island.

He shivered at the memory.

Late last year, as the winter storms had begun, Fred had urged the town to continue the mobile patrols, to ensure trespassers and even the Zeds didn't make it on the island. But he had been outvoted by the other two selectmen—including Matilda, before her death—who had said, "Shit, Fred, you can't expect people to tromp through the snow, night and day. Who's gonna come try to across during the winter? We'll start the patrols up come spring."

That had been that, until during a particularly bitter cold spell in February, the wide sound between Massabesic Island and the mainland—where the abandoned town of Gilbert was located—had frozen. That allowed a number of Zeds to walk out to the island, where they ended up at the homes of Bob and Tracy Clark, and Hank and Helen Pemrose. It had been a slaughter... made worse when Bob and Tracy's twelve-year-old boy Glen, had turned, and they had to hunt down the poor kid for two days, up in the rocky and forested north end of the island.

The patrols had started up the next day, during a sleet storm.

"Fifteen minutes late," Paul said. "Looks like fourth time ain't gonna be the charm."

Fred nodded.

Being out here, prepared to be disappointed, well, that was the job of being head of the little town government of Massabesic, for the princely sum of one hundred dollars a year and lots of heartache.

Not many townspeople had come out here this morning, after the disappointments of three earlier promised visits. Today there were about a dozen or so townsfolk, huddled around, looking out into the fog. A few months after "it" happened, the first promised visit was announced over the radio, when supposedly the State of Maine had secured one of the ferries that did the Portland/Halifax run to make a rescue, but that turned out to be a hoax. A couple of months after that, a rich computer mogul was going to swing by and pick up survivors aboard his luxurious yacht. Another hoax. The third time...that had been rough.

The radio operator talking to their own Chris Allain that third time claimed to be under contract with the famed Wolf Squadron, and he had arrived one late summer day in a Boston Whaler. He offered to shuttle islanders to a larger boat—just out of view, of course—but only if the islanders would pass over gold jewelry or other valuables.

Fred and Police Chief Aaron Swinton hadn't bought it, and when he and Chief Aaron demanded that a test run be made, the guy in the Boston Whaler had cursed them, said, "You had one chance, and you lost it," and he backed away from the dock, and just before he could make a turn, someone in the crowd with suitcases and knapsacks at their feet took off the top of his head with a .308 hunting rifle.

Like that dark day, everybody here this foggy morning was carrying a weapon, bicycles were propped up against the stacked lobster pots, and three horses were tied up the fuel pumps. About three yards away at the end of the town pier was an M2A1 Browning .50 caliber machinegun, secured by concrete blocks and surrounded by sandbags. Gil Pachter, a quiet yet scary inhabitant of the island, who claimed to have been a cook in the Army, had donated the weapon after "it" had taken place. He was standing behind it, hands loosely draped around the receiver, like he was relaxing with intimacy with an old friend.

Fred said, "Well, looks we got skunked again."

His fellow selectman Paul said, "Shit."

Fred started to turn and the younger Chris said, "Hold on."

"What?" Fred asked.

"I'm hearing something," he said. "Honest. Not making it up."

Fred looked out in the fog.

Heard it now.

Low throbbing of an engine.

Some of the townspeople heard it and joined him and the others on the dock.

Fred stared and stared.

Movement in the fog, becoming visible.

A few hoots and hollers behind him.

A black RHI approached with two inboard/outboard engines in the rear, about thirty feet in length, with two men standing at the pilot's station about two-thirds back. Black hard plastic containers and silver coolers were piled high at the bow. At the stern of the craft, a large American flag snapped in the breeze, along with one from the State of Maine.

More joyous yelling, and handclapping, and shouts, and about a half-dozen volunteers surged forward to help tie off the craft.

Fred couldn't talk. He took a breath, remembered the promise he had made back when it started, that never would he let his emotions grab him in public. Not when food supplies went short, not when the Sherman house burned down with no fire department to save those trapped inside, screaming for help, and not the thought of everyone he knew back on the mainland was either dead or changed, never would he tear up in front of his townsfolk.

But not today.

He was weeping, and in looking around, saw he wasn't the only one.

An hour later—after MREs and other canned goods had been offloaded from the boat and brought up to the town hall for later distribution—Fred chaired a quick meeting to introduce their visitors. Both were young, strong-looking men, clean shaven and with clean uniforms. One had short red hair and the other had well-groomed brown hair.

Clean, strong, and confident.

The residents of Massabesic—with more trickling into the town hall every minute as the word spread—seemed to stare at the pair with wonderment, like they were time travelers from the past, where full supermarket shelves, laundromats, and hot showers were everyday occurrences.

The two uniformed men were on stage with Fred and Paul Lucian, the other selectman, and Fred didn't need to use the gavel to quiet down the residents.

They looked shocked, in awe, and Fred couldn't blame them.

"Well," he said, "it looks like the fourth time was the charm after all. Folks, we have visitors here from the outside, and I'll let them introduce themselves to us. Sirs?"

The first one stepped forward, wearing the light khaki trousers and shirt belonging to the State of Maine Marine Patrol, took off his baseball cap and nodded. "Folks, I'm Ward Turner, a Marine Patrol Officer . . . and I'm part of the effort doing survey and relief along the Maine coast, attached to the so-called

Wolf Squadron that's taking the lead in reestablishing the government of the United States, and ensuring the safety of the uninfected. This here is Tim Porter, Lieutenant, U.S. Navy. We've been working together for about two months. Tim, you want to say a few words?"

The Navy lieutenant looked to be about the same age as the Marine Patrol Officer, maybe early thirties, but his face was worn, lined, and looked tired. He was wearing clean blue Navy camo fatigues. He gave everyone a good look and said, "Folks, congratulations. I mean . . . well, this survey and recovery has been going on for a few months, and Massabesic Island has one of the largest populations of survivors. Good job."

Silence, and Fred thought he should be happy or impressed, but instead, he was horrified.

This small island, less than a hundred people, was the biggest survivor population along the hundreds of islands along the coast of Maine?

Lieutenant Porter seemed to sense he had said something wrong, and he said, "Okay, moving forward, I just wanted to admire you folks for sticking together, and surviving, and now I want to let you know that the United States of America—battered—is not beaten, and not bowed. Welcome back."

A couple of people started applauding.

A few more.

Then the entire population of Massabesic Island were on their feet, whooping and cheering and clapping, and Fred joined right in.

When the applause faded away somebody yelled, "Hey, who's the President? I heard over the radio it was that wingbat, Sovrain, the secretary of education!"

Lieutenant Porter shook his head. "Briefly she claimed to be Acting President but thanks to the bravery and dedication of a unit of Marines attached to the Wolf Squadron, Vice President Rebecca Staba and her family were found in a secure bunker at FEMA headquarters in Washington, D.C. She is now the President, and work is underway to reestablish Congress."

Another voice: "You think having Congress back is a good idea?"

Lots of laughter, and the questions came fast and quick after that.

"Any idea where that damn virus came from?"

Lieutenant Porter said, "Above my paygrade, I'm afraid. Lots of theories, nothing rock solid."

"Is it worldwide?"

"Yep," he said, "and President Staba said that while we're recovering, we'll be doing our best to help the rest of the world."

"Fuck the rest of the world!"

More laughter, and as the laughter eased, Grace Moulton stood up, voice quavering, and she said, "I'm just wondering...I mean, there's been so much misinformation and fake news over what radio we can hear...is there some way to find any survivors on the mainland?"

Marine Patrol Officer Turner stepped forward and said, "Parts of the Maine Red Cross are up and running in Rockland, where the relief efforts are centered. They're trying to get a census lined up as to the survivors who are still out there. But it's a slow process...a lot of the infected are still in the cities and countryside."

Grace said, "I was just wondering, you know, because my sisters and brother, and their families, they live in

Portland. And if they were infected...I mean, well, is there a cure? Can they get better? Is there a chance?"

Turner looked to the Navy lieutenant, almost pleading, and Porter said, "No. There is no cure if you're infected. We do have a vaccine—which we brought ashore with the MREs and medical supplies—but there's no cure."

Grace choked up. "But...suppose people are infected. It's not their fault. What happens to them?"

Lieutenant Porter said, "I'm sorry, ma'am. They can only be killed."

Later that day Fred and his wife Lori, along with their daughter Penny and son Ken, ate a feast of MREs at their kitchen table, where an old calendar from last year was still hung by a magnet on the refrigerator door, along with reminder cards for dentist visits and OB-GYN appointments long missed. The refrigerator hadn't run for months, and some days Fred thought its presence was mocking them, reminding them of a better and earlier world.

He and Lori each had macaroni and chili—"My God," his wife said, "have you ever eaten anything so fine?"—and he could only nod with his mouth full.

The kids laughed, with Penny dining on chicken and egg noodles, and Ken slurping up a beef taco with beans.

Fred said finally said, "No, not in a while," glad there were no fish items in the military rations they had received. Cod, clams, lobster, sea bass, halibut, Gulf shrimp...God, the diet had gotten so monotonous, with just an occasional egg here or there.

Twice brave souls—the Monahan brothers—had

taken their fishing boat across the strait to the small town of Gilbert, and had quickly raided the Hannaford's Supermarket over there, coming back with cans of beef stew, Spam, and B&M baked beans. And while Fred and the other two selectmen had publicly criticized them for doing something so reckless, privately he was pleased, and happy that instead of trying to trade their goods for gold or ammo, they had donated it to the town.

The last time...the boat was overdue for a few days, until it drifted up against one of the breakwaters, and young Timmy Monahan was the only one in the boat, and he had turned into a Zed, frothing and bloody.

After he had been shot down, nobody wanted to go on the boat to see if there were any supplies on board, and later it drifted away.

Ken said, "Dad?"

"Yes?"

"What's next?"

He took a moment to relish the feeling of a full stomach, and the sight of a plate with plenty of food left on it. "This afternoon, we get the vaccine. That means we'll be safe from the virus, forever."

"No," Ken said, wiping his chin with an old frayed towel. "I mean, is it safe now? With the Zeds all going to be killed?"

"I don't know," he said, and his wife looked at him and he sensed she knew that he had answered both questions with one answer.

Later that afternoon there was a happy mood amongst the townspeople of the island, as they stood in line inside the town hall to get the vaccine, and the shots were administered by both Marine Patrol Officer Turner and Lieutenant Porter of the U.S. Navy. Moms with kids were first up, and the lines moved along well, and Fred didn't even wince as the needle slid into his upper right arm.

But as the line dwindled away, a loud voice erupted from the end of the line, a male voice that said, "Nope, no way! I'm not gonna get a government vaccine."

Fred walked back to the entrance, were Bud Collum stood at the open doorway, shaking his head. He had on a tattered gray sweatshirt hoodie and patched jeans, with a thick black beard down to his mid-chest.

His wife Tina was at his side, a foot shorter, tugging at his thick arm. "Bud, c'mon, please..."

He shook his head. "Nope. You go ahead and take that poison if you'd like... but I'm not doing it. Who knows what's in it. Could be tracking stuff, shit like that. Nope."

Tina looked to Fred. "Isn't there anything you can do?"

"Tina..."

"Please," she said. "I can't stand thinking of him turning..."

By then Mark Twombly was there, standing behind Bud, and Gil Pachter, the one who had supplied the .50 caliber Browning machinegun, stood next to him.

Next to Fred was the other selectman, Paul Lucian, and Fred said, "Paul, I think we're gonna have to declare another public health emergency. You agree?"

"Yep," Paul said.

Twombly kicked Bud's legs out from underneath him, and Gus twisted an arm, and the Marine Patrol Officer cut away his hoodie, and Lieutenant Porter gave him the vaccine.

In seconds Bud was on his feet, face red with anger, and to his wife, he said, "Tina, you bitch. That's your fault. Damn it woman, I'm gonna divorce your skinny ass."

She was crying but defiant. "Then you should thank me for making sure you live long enough to do that, you moron."

Later in the day, after more MREs and other canned goods were distributed, Lieutenant Porter stood up on the stage and said, "Folks, we need to leave tomorrow, head back to Rockland. But we'll return later in the week, with other watercraft, and get things organized."

The meeting room fell silent.

Fred and Paul were sitting in the front row seats, and Paul looked to him, and Fred stood up. "I'm sorry, organized for what?"

Lieutenant Porter said, "Oh, I'm sorry. I thought it was understood."

"What was understood?" Fred asked.

"We're going to evacuate all of you off the island, for your safety."

Murmurs and some voices perked right up, and still standing, Fred said, "Evacuate where?"

"To Rockland," the Navy officer said. "Like I said earlier, that's where the main recovery effort has been established for the state of Maine. There, you can get fresh food, clothing, and reside in a well-defended community. There's electricity, laundry facilities, and hot showers."

Fred couldn't remember the last time he had taken a long, steady, hot shower, and he said, "But...that sounds nice and all, but will that be a temporary evacuation?"

"Doubtful," Porter said. "Once the effort was made to safely evacuate you, then I'd have to say that you'd be staying there permanently."

Fred said, "But . . . most of us have grown up here. Our families were the first settlers. You can't ask us all to leave now, can you?"

George Dayton stood up and said, "Hell, if it means hot showers and clean clothes, I'm ready to leave now! So what if my great-great-granddad had a farm here. I think he'd be happy to know a descendant had enough good sense to get out!"

Laughter, cheers, and applause, followed by shouts and boos and Fred held up a hand, and no one paid attention, and then Marine Patrol Officer Turner raised both of his arms up, and the crowd grew silent.

Turner said, "We're going to do a survey of the island, and a census, and at eight tomorrow morning, we'll be heading back to Rockland. Before we shove off, we'll meet with anyone at the dock who wants to register so we can bring back a ferry craft to take you off. You'll be allowed one suitcase per person, and no weapons allowed."

The room was now silent.

"Think about it," the Marine Patrol Officer said. "It'll be for the best, to start a new life on the mainland."

He and Lori and the kids talked and debated and argued, and talked some more, with a last minute goal "to sleep on it," but Fred found it hard to sleep. He tossed and turned, keeping Lori awake, and then he went downstairs and tried to sleep on the couch, and that didn't work. Eventually he got up, armed himself, unlocked and unbolted the heavy front door, and stepped outside, 9mm Beretta strapped to his waist, a .223 Mini-Ruger 14 over his shoulder, carrying a quilt from the couch.

As it was just a while before dawn, so the light was faint enough that he could find his way, although even in the dark, he could find his route, which led to a clump of land and rock on his property that offered a good view of the island, sound, and the mainland. He sat down and wrapped the quilt around his shoulders, and thought.

To the north were the buildings of Massabesic village, and he only saw one home with a flickering light inside, a lantern or candle. To the south was the harbor and moored there, along with other vessels of the local fishing fleet, was the dark shape of the Wolf Squadron RHI, where the Navy lieutenant and Marine Patrol officer were spending their night. Many of the townspeople had offered to put them up for the night, but they sheepishly said no, orders were that they would remain with their vessel overnight.

Made sense, Fred thought. It was only through blatant self-interest that most of the small fishing fleet here stuck close to home, because of the dwindling supplies of fuel. And going off to the mainland...who would want to take that chance? But with the good news that progress was being made in rebuilding the nation, it sure would be tempting to a few guys on the island to steal that big powerful boat and head off.

Across the dark strait it was easy to see the mainland and the town of Gilbert, for centuries the closet neighbor to Massabesic. He couldn't help himself, he felt nauseated at remembering those frantic weeks last year when the plague spread. There were the news reports out of New York and Boston, about people going crazy, frenzied, biting and attacking people...and then those people being infected, so forth and so on. At first, the people here and in Gilbert thought it was funny that the big cities were having health problems.

Then...

It got here.

Panic.

Police and National Guardsmen overwhelmed.

Then...the town across the strait started burning.

He and the other two selectmen had an emergency meeting, closing off the island to anyone fleeing the mainland, and the desperate measures here to keep this island isolated.

Firing on speedboats, fishing boats, and even canoes making their way across.

Almost being overwhelmed until Gil Pachter arrived with his M2A1 Browning .50 caliber machinegun, and then the heavy fire sank the approaching watercraft, and that had been that.

Until seeing Gilbert burning down.

Using binoculars and telescopes to monitor the coastline.

A group of people on the end of one of the main docks on Gilbert, who had barricaded themselves, holding up a white bedsheet with the words HELP US! spelled out in orange spray paint.

They had lasted only two days.

The light was now strong enough he could see seagulls floating overhead. The buildings of Massabesic were coming into focus, and he noted the town hall, which had been the meeting place for the GAR chapter, until all of the Union veterans had died off, and then became a Grange Hall, and then the Town Hall.

His bones seemed to ache. So much history here. First settled by veterans of the War of 1812—and most families, including his own, were able to trace their ancestry back to those original settlers—a flourishing community for decades, with farming, and fishing, and some lumbering of tall pines at the north end of the island. Men from Massabesic had sailed from here to serve in every conflict from the Civil War to Iraq and Afghanistan. Writers and poets had summered here. President Franklin D. Roosevelt had docked here for a fishing trip in the Gulf of Maine. . . .

So much history.

And now?

Evacuation.

Leave all weapons behind.

One suitcase per person.

Evacuate Massabesic Island, never to return.

He checked his watch. Just a bit after 5 AM, full sunrise.

Time to get to work.

It was a short and well-remembered walk to the house of Paul Lucian, a weathered light gray Cape Cod house with shuttered windows, and an overgrown lawn. At the stone walkway leading up to the front door, there was a metal post and small bell dangling below. A sign was fastened on the pole:

RING BELL, STAND STILL, ARMS OUT.
OR BE SHOT.

Fred followed the orders, ringing the bell three times, and then stood still, arms stretched out.

Eventually the front door opened up, and Paul came out, wearing worn L.L. Bean boots and a blue robe, carrying a sawed-off double-barrel shotgun in his hands.

He yawned. "Pretty damn early. What's going on?"

Fred said, "Time to declare another public emergency."

"Sure, why not," Paul said. "I can't keep track of how many we've issued over the year. Then what?"

"Then we start going around the town, knocking on doors. Talking to folks."

"Without getting our heads blown off," Paul said. "What's going on?"

Fred said, "I think we need to remind folks about something."

"About what?"

"About what it's like to live here."

Fred checked his watch, looked behind him. It was just before eight in the morning, and it looked like nearly the entire population of Massabesic was behind him, standing on the land rising up from the dock, and the dock itself. There were soft murmurs and talking, and he felt a dark stab of fear, that it wasn't going to work out, that the seductive words of the Marine Patrol officer and the Navy lieutenant would work their charm.

Electricity.

Hot showers.

Three meals a day.

Near the RHI the two men from away came up the dock, smiling, Marine Patrol Officer Turner on the left, holding a clipboard, and Lieutenant Porter on the right, not smiling, just looking like a serious Naval officer who wanted to get back to work.

They both stopped and Turner said, "Boy, what a turnout. Glad to see it. You folks should be proud of yourselves."

He held up the clipboard, took a pen out of his shirt pocket and said, "Okay, let's step up, and don't rush. There's plenty of time, and there's plenty of room at Rockland. One at a time, give us your name, and if you're a parent or a legal guardian, give us the name of minors that will be accompanying you."

His words seemed to hang in the cool Atlantic air.

No one moved.

Fred struggled to keep the expression on his face calm and bland.

"Really?" Turner asked. "Come along, now. Who'll be first?"

Fred didn't dare move, to look behind, to break the mood.

Lieutenant Porter said, "What's going on here? What's wrong with you? Don't you want to leave, be safe? There'll be good food, no shortages, electricity. You'll be safe."

Now Fred looked behind at his townspeople, his friends, all of whom who had done so much to stay alive and together this past year.

He turned back to the two well-dressed and well-fed men.

Fred said, "You said yesterday, 'welcome back.' Am I right?"

The two men exchanged glances. "Yes," the Navy lieutenant said. "Was that a problem?"

Fred said, "'Fraid so. Most of us took that as an insult, Lieutenant, 'cause we never left America. We were right here. America sort of left us, if you think about it. Nobody here on Massabesic had anything to do with that damn virus. But we did what we could. We were isolated. And to tell you the truth, if the whole mainland was infected and everybody was killed off, and we were the sole survivors, then we'd be America, right here, on this island."

It felt like the townspeople—all of whom he and Paul had talked with, face-to-face, before this meeting—were filling him with words and energy. Even his wife Lori came up to him and put a hand on her shoulder.

"And Americans aren't refugees, aren't evacuees, and we don't run," he went on. "This is our home, and this is where we mean to stay."

Lieutenant Porter said, "You made it through one winter, isolated. Do you think you can do that again?"

Fred said "If we have to. We did it once, and our great-grandparents and beyond did so. But we don't plan to do that."

Marine Patrol Officer Turner said, "I don't understand. What do you mean?"

Fred looked back at the townspeople, who were silent.

He finally said, "Before, you said we were isolated. But we aren't isolated now, are we? The country's got a President, there's progress in controlling the infected, there's a vaccine, and you're just down the coast at Rockland. That's not isolation, and we mean to take advantage of it."

"How?" the Navy lieutenant said.

"Trade," Fred said. "Just like was done years back, when this island was first settled. You say you got a safe zone at Rockland. How are you feeding 'em? With MREs and old canned food?"

"Mostly," Lieutenant Porter said. "That's all that's readily available now."

Fred said, "Okay, then, that'll make it easy. We got a small fleet here that hasn't gone out too far because we wanted to ration our fuel, and heck, one or two boats could feed the island regularly. But we make a deal with the government at Rockland, the folks there will get fresh fish, lobster, shrimp ... a lot tastier than your MREs."

Porter said, "And in return for what?"

Fred said, "Some batteries. Regular medical supplies. Heck, even the MREs. They do lighten up one's diet. Oh, and one more thing."

He pointed across the sound. "About twenty miles up from Gilbert, on the Piscassic River, there's a hydropower plant, run by Central Maine Power. Get that up and running, and you power our island, we'll work twice as hard. Our fleet can help out the Wolf Squadron, running supplies out to the other islands, help build back Maine."

He paused.

"That's the deal," he said.

Lieutenant Porter said, "We can't agree to that."

Fred said, "Well, you're gonna have to figure that out. You bring our proposal to whoever your captain or admiral or whatever is; you tell him or her that's the deal from the people of Massabesic."

He thought for a second.

"No, you tell them that's the deal from the Americans of Massabesic."

∽ ⊖ ∾

Ten minutes later and after the RHI left with Marine Patrol Officer Turner and Navy Lieutenant Porter, the townspeople of Massabesic drifted away, and Fred felt exhausted. Was this a victory? Then why did he feel so tired and blue? His wife Lori came to him and kissed him.

"So proud of you," she said.

Fred said, "Just doing my job."

Appalachia Rex

JASON CORDOVA

Long before I removed her head with a twelve-gauge, Sister Margaret gave me solid advice: try your best and rise above the rest. It wasn't until we were in the middle of the zombie apocalypse I truly understood what she meant.

If you're reading this, you know what happened. The world pretty much ended. The lights went off. The party was over. Lots of metaphors were used by those of us who survived. *Survived*. That was the important word because in the beginning, it was all we had. Lock down the school. Avoid the zombies if you could, eliminate and dispose of the ones you couldn't, and keep one another safe. For the juniors and seniors, this meant watching over the middle school girls. For them, it was helping care for the elementary kids who made it. Surviving meant listening on the shortwave radio for only two hours every night to conserve batteries. Later, though, surviving became less important. The next part was harder. We had to rebuild. Like Sister Margaret said, we needed to rise.

This is not a record of the Fall, but the slow rebuilding process those of us at St. Dominic's Preparatory School for Girls had to endure later. I started this because Sister Ann suggested it. Her suggestions are usually carefully worded instructions, and I know her well enough to understand precisely what she meant. Since the first few months of the Fall were only about surviving, I don't really have much to say about that time. It was hard. Lots of my friends died. My best friend, Wren, turned into a zombie and managed to turn three other girls before we stopped it. Well, I stopped it. I had to shoot them all. None of the other girls would do the deed so it fell on me to kill my best friend and the others. I didn't sleep for a few days after that.

"If you don't want to write about the time of the Fall, then don't," Sister Ann said while she handed me one of the notepads from the storage room beneath the Admin Building. They'd been part of donations the school had been receiving for years and, thanks to a lot of donors, we had enough school supplies to last us multiple lifetimes. She lifted my chin and looked me in the eye. "Someone needs to write about how we're going to rebuild. Who better than our class valedictorian?"

She had a point. Granted, I was valedictorian only because the five other girls who had been ahead of me had all turned zombie and then died, but still... if someone had told me two years ago I would be my high school's valedictorian, I would have laughed in their face. Before St. Dominic's, school could best be described as "nonessential." For me, anyway. I had better things to do. I don't remember what they were, exactly, but I know I thought they were better.

Ironically, I'm not the first person in history to have shot their high school's valedictorian just to take their place. Life was odd even before the zombie apocalypse.

Rebuilding wasn't easy. After Sister Margaret turned into a zombie, the only adult who worked for the school and was still alive was Sister Ann. I think having Sister Ann survive actually helped us more than any other person, because *nobody* disobeyed her. I'm not just saying this because she might read this one day, really. Sister Ann had been in the Marine Corps during the Global War on Terror and deployed all over the place. She took her vows to be a nun only a few years back and ended up at our school for some reason. We were lucky to have her then, and eternally grateful now. It also reaffirmed the whole "God works in mysterious ways" saying.

I'm in charge of security. Yeah, weird, I know. How many teenage girls do you know of who run security for a 1200-acre site? It wasn't my idea actually, but Sister Ann's. The girls all backed her decision, though. Especially since I was the only one not terrified of the zombies and had little issue with shooting them.

One of the now-dead staff members who lived on campus in one of the housing units had a gun safe. He was one of those guys who went to gun shows and people made fun of him, but he'd drop like ten grand on a bunch of new guns and stuff. I thought he was a little weird but mostly harmless. Just don't mess with his four-wheeler and you were fine. Once we saw him running around all zombified it was decided we needed to raid his stash of weapons. It was where I picked up Baby.

Look, I don't know guns very well. All I can do

is repeat what Sister Ann told me after I made my selection—in between her fits of giggling after I told her I was calling the gun "Baby." The AR-15 has a pistol grip, tactical sling, an MVG vertical grip, and a green dot sight. Mr. Stitmer had it done up in desert digital camo and it even had a penguin engraved on the side with a rocket jetpack on its back. Sister Ann said it was the most ridiculous thing she'd ever seen but I loved it. I got to keep it, as well as all the ammo that came with it. The only time I don't carry Baby around now is when I shower. Even then, it's in the bathroom with me.

He also had a bunch of rifles in his safe but they were all chambered for .270 rounds. Sister Ann was a little irritated by this but since he had over fifty thousand rounds of ammunition for them, she forgave him a little. Getting these from his house up to the top of the hill without making a lot of noise was a hassle. It meant we had to drive his four-wheeler.

Oh, how horrible. Right?

To be fair, I drove the crap out of that thing. Having the four-wheeler would have made things a lot easier when we first heard about a guy calling himself the King of Appalachia. We knew his real name, of course. Everyone knew who he'd been before the Fall.

Alleghany County is small when it comes to population. I mean, it relied largely on the railroads a long time ago. But since railroads don't make nearly as much money as they used to, and shipping things was easier by truck than train, the area quickly became one of those low-income areas supported by only one business. For Covington and the surrounding area, it was the WestRock paper mill.

In this type of town, everybody was either related to everybody, or they knew others through relatives. I used to joke around with Sister Margaret that you couldn't throw a cat in the area without nailing a Persinger or a Nicely. Unfortunately, some girls in town heard about the jokes (there may have been other jokes involving cousins and third base) and a couple of fights broke out when we were allowed into town on weekends. I started being much more cautious about who I talked smack about. After all, they were probably related.

Sorry, I wandered off topic. The King of Appalachia called himself King Dale. It has a horrible ring to it. The first time we spotted some of the men working for him was during our usual recon mission to the river. They were looking for supplies. We were checking to see if Covington was still underwater. Sister Ann always sent us in groups of three when we hiked down and around to the Jackson River. One to spot, one for site security, and a backup in case someone got hurt and needed help being carried. I always handled security during these missions, though sometimes I snuck out at night to find better spots to shoot from in case the zombies came up to the school again. Don't blame Sister Ann for not keeping a better eye on me. She was one woman in charge of twenty-five girls.

They saw us at the same time we spotted them. It was stupid, and my fault. We hadn't seen an actual human for so long we stopped worrying about what clothes we were wearing. So when a couple of young guys spotted three teenage girls wearing plaid skirts, hiking boots, blouses, and knee-high socks, all armed with either rifles or one seriously tricked-out AR-15, they must have thought they were hallucinating. I would have thought that. A redheaded Catholic schoolgirl with an AR-15?

Only in America...

We scampered off, not going directly back to campus but instead making it look like we were heading towards the old social security office. In hindsight it was stupid, but at the time we were in full flight or fight mode. It never occurred to me they would instantly recognize our school uniforms from St. Dominic's. Yeah, dumb on my part.

The next time we went down there, a note had been left on one of the trees. It had been written on a dry erase board and hung on a large branch. It was a simple message, but one which set Sister Ann on edge. It simply told us to surrender, gave us a meeting time, and to bring everyone still alive from the school with us.

"I'll go and meet with them," Sister Ann told me once the other girls had all gone to bed. News had spread quickly and a few of the elementary school girls were excited. They thought we were being rescued. None of the high school girls wanted to break the news to them, so we didn't say anything. The middle schoolers were the ones who came up with nasty ideas about *why* a bunch of old men wanting to "save" them was a bad idea. That shut the rescue talk down really quickly.

"That's a bad idea," I warned Sister Ann. "What if they just start shooting?"

"Then I die, and the council is in charge of the school," Sister Ann replied calmly. I had to hand it to her. A lot of people could talk the talk, but Sister Ann walked the walk. "Next time you're out on patrol, don't wear the school girl outfit. See if you can go through the clothing closet and find some donations with old hunter's pants or something."

"I should have been doing that from the start," I berated myself. "Stupid."

"No, just shortsighted," Sister Ann corrected me. "We didn't count on survivors coming around. I should have, not you. I'll meet with him, and you'll be my visible second. Let them get an eyeful of Baby. We have three other girls nearby with rifles hiding in the bushes in case they start shooting at us... which I doubt they'll do."

"Why?"

"I don't think they want us dead, Maddie," Sister Ann said as she shot me a look.

"Oh."

"But what I want you to do is get there eight hours before the meet time," she continued after a moment. "Only you. Set up in that old hunter's blind we put up last year and see if King Dale has anybody setting up the way we are. They'll probably get there a few hours before we do. Once I arrive, you come out and stand with me. Let them know we're always watching, always ready."

"That's why you want me getting there so far in advance," I murmured. "That's smart."

"Be prepared," she reminded me. "I have no idea how our meeting with Appalachia Rex is going to go."

Oh, I would be prepared, all right. I was not making the same mistake again.

King Dale may be an idiot, but he had what looked like a freaking tank. I know it wasn't a tank, but the first time I saw it I thought it was a tank. He didn't send any advance scouts ahead, so I spent eight very dull hours watching the dirty waters of the Jackson River swirl about. I could have wiped him and his entire crew out before they'd realize it when they stepped out of the large armored vehicle. Sister Ann gave me explicit instructions to simply observe until she arrived, so that I did.

When Sister Ann walked onto the scene, it created a visible stir across the river. She'd ditched the stole and penguin outfit when Sister Margaret turned in favor of something a little more economical and sensible. Jeans, a hoodie, and comfortable hiking boots made up her normal everyday wear. Now, however, she'd donned her full habit and even wore her veil, which was rare indeed. Only during Mass did any of the school's nuns wear their stiff headpieces that hid their hair. It was psychological warfare; she'd told me the night before. It was meant to send a message.

Sister Ann 1, King Dale 0.

The so-called King of Appalachia stood on the far banks of the Jackson River, surrounded by a large group of people. The river wasn't too wide here but it was definitely deep, courtesy of the Gathright Dam failing six months back. It was also the reason nobody had been able to get up to the school yet. When the dam failed, it also took out the only road bridge and passable route up to the school for miles, as well as the two railroad bridges crossing the river. We'd thought it was a bad thing at first because all the large stores were on the other side of the river, but it turned out to be a blessing in disguise. Not only did the zombies get swept downriver when they tried to cross, it had also managed to stop anyone else from coming to us.

We had a natural boundary to protect us. Other than a small community of houses near the top of the hill by the school and the Moose Lodge, our little valley and mountain top was empty.

This was the first time I'd really gotten to get a good look at the guy Sister Ann had dubbed "Appalachia Rex." St. Dominic's still taught Latin so I understood what it meant. It was the same as what the King of Appalachia called himself, but since we were dealing with hillbillies he probably thought the sister was insulting him. The man wasn't what I would normally call a hick, though. He was tall, well built, and actually wore what appeared to be new clothes. He sported a giant blond beard but since they weren't really making razors anymore I cut him some slack. I mean, I hadn't shaved my legs in months.

We must have been a very weird sight to the men. Armed girls on a river with a nun. I know what men think whenever they see a Catholic school girl, even if she's carrying a heavily modified AR-15 and not in her uniform. Or maybe the fact we were better armed than his group was even more appealing, I don't know for certain. What I did understand, thanks to Sister Ann's "briefing" beforehand (it's what she called it), this was the beginning of a negotiation process. The so-called king believed he was dealing from a position of power.

"Let him," Sister Ann had told us before I started the long hike down. "If he thinks he's in control, he'll underestimate us. He has no idea we've been watching them for days now. Let him believe he is in control, because we all know who really is."

Sister Ann was, and will always remain, a Marine trapped in a nun's habit.

The negotiations did not start smoothly.

"I don't know why y'all calling me Rex!" he shouted at us from across the river. The men around him were armed but he wasn't. Nobody was pointing their weapons at us, either, and all of them seemed to be showing good trigger discipline from what I could see. "My name is King Dale, and I am the ruler of Appalachia!"

"Nice to meet you, Dale," Sister Ann replied back as she raised the megaphone. The young nun was always prepared for everything and, quite frankly, was probably my favorite sister at the school. The megaphone had been in the gym, and it even had working batteries still. "You stay on your side of the river now, you hear?"

"With all due respect, ma'am, y'all are in my domain, and I have right to rule," Dale yelled back. "We're gonna cross that river, and y'all need to respect that!"

"Again, we reserve the right to refuse, since we still live in the United States, my son," Sister Ann replied sweetly. "Since we're not a confederate state in some medieval German principality, you cannot be a king in a republic guided by a legal constitution. Now please disperse and go home."

Dale was flustered. I was just confused. Sister Ann was really smart and sometimes pulled out historical references which even left the former director of our school dazed. Her ability to defuse a situation by simply being the biggest nerd in the room was why her cottage was always on their best behavior. I couldn't even remember when the last real fight broke out in there. She had a way of just keeping the peace with only a look.

"You don't understand what I'm saying here, Sister!" Dale shouted.

"No, I understand you perfectly," Sister Ann replied. The megaphone squealed a little from feedback and she smacked it with her palm before continuing. "You think that because nobody's heard from the government in a year means you get to go and form a new government however you like. This great nation of ours does not work this way, Dale. Have you heard the news? The Navy and Marines have already begun to take back our country along the coast. Parris Island has been retaken. That means more Marines, young man, only eight hours away. You think our government is going to be okay with some tin pot dictator less than four hours from our nation's capital?"

"Bullshit!" He practically screamed. "The government died the day they released this poison onto the world!"

"Language, young man." Sister Ann frowned. I was confused. What did he mean, they released the flu? That wasn't how I remembered it all going down. I specifically remember the words "Pacific Flu" being thrown around, and even rumors than it had been released by some nutjob.

"Sorry!" Dale looked down and kicked a stone into the swollen waters of the Jackson River. "Sister, I have the canned goods, supplies, a tank, weapons, and manpower! What have you got?"

"Apparently I only have the correct side of the river," she called back. "And that is not a tank, but the MedCat SWAT armored vehicle you stole from the Alleghany County Sheriff's Department. It's used for medical evacuations in a live-fire engagement area. Medical counter attack truck. MedCat. Learn your equipment and do better research. Go back to your home. Our school is in the state of Virginia, which is still part of the United States of America and under the guidance of the Constitution. It is not, nor will ever be, part of your so-called Kingdom. Nothing you say will change that, Appalachia Rex."

"God damn it, quit calling me that!"

"Young man!" Sister Ann's voice was stern this time. Even I winced, because you knew you were in deep shit when Sister Ann used *that* tone. I heard one of the girls nearby suck in her breath sharply and hiss, "Ooooooh shit, he done fucked up now" to another. So I wasn't the only one who'd been on the receiving end of a Sister Ann verbal beat down. Sister Ann continued, and boy was she *hot*. "You will *not* take the Lord's name in vain! He did not die for your sins to have you run His name through mud and filth in such a foul and disrespectful manner! This will be the *last* time I warn you. Do you understand me?"

The self-proclaimed King of Appalachia nodded, albeit reluctantly. This did not appease Sister Ann, however. Not by a long shot. We all knew it wouldn't but it was almost funny to see someone else suffer for a change. I would have been laughing my ass off except I knew better. The last thing I wanted now was for her basilisk gaze to turn on me.

"No, I can't hear you," she told him. "What do you say?"

"I promise," he shouted.

"You promise what?"

Oh man; she is not letting him off easy, I thought and watched him struggle for words.

"I promise to not take the Lord's name in vain again!"

"Very good," she smiled, tone sweet and angelic once more. "Have a good afternoon, Appalachia Rex."

"Confound it, woman!"

Well, at least he was watching his language now. St. Dominic's existed for a reason and had a pretty good track record, all things considered. One thing the school was noted for was instilling proper manners while operating as a school. St. Dominic's didn't just teach us how to be independent women, but ladies as well.

She clicked off the megaphone and lowered it from her face. Turning away from the river, Sister Ann motioned for me to come over. Once I was close enough, she started to speak.

"They're going to find a way across that river eventually," Sister Ann said, eyeing the heavily modified AR-15 in my hands. She crossed herself before continuing. "Probably within a week or two. I wouldn't ask you to take a human life, Madison, but if it comes down to it, we can't let those vile creatures on the campus. We have young girls to protect and I can only imagine what he thinks he's going to find if he makes it onto campus. Even if he means well, there might be men in his group who have ulterior motives involving high school girls in uniforms."

"I have no problem with shooting that type of guy, Sister Ann," I told her. "I was the one who shot Sister Margaret when she turned into a zombie, remember?"

"I didn't forget, Maddie," Sister Ann offered me a reassuring smile. "But there is a cost to the soul when taking a life. I'm not sure if there's one for shooting zombies, but humans? Definitely a dark stain."

"No offense, Sister, but I'll let God judge me when

I go to heaven," I told her. "The school's given me the ability to protect others in a way nobody ever protected me. I intend to use it."

Sister Ann rested a hand on my shoulder. Despite the camouflage coat I could still feel the warmth and concern in the gesture. She bowed her head.

"Just...don't come to enjoy it," she told me. "It's addictive and becomes easier if you let it. I saw it many times in the past, in both Iraq and Afghanistan. You start seeing your fellow humans as nothing more than targets, and you lose a large part of yourself when that happens."

"Zombies are one thing, Sister," I admitted, feeling slightly embarrassed. Once again Sister Ann saw through my mask and pointed out what I was truly feeling. I *had* been looking forward to hurting the men across the river. They wanted to do horrible things to the girls who were closer to me than my own family. I'd heard stories from other survivors via the shortwave radio. They alluded to a lot of abuse suffered before they were rescued. I wasn't about to let that happen, not to anyone at the school. Didn't matter if they were my worst enemy. They had a soul, and everything I'd learned while at St. Dominic's told me the soul was most precious indeed. Including my own. "I know it'll be rough, ma'am. I'll be aiming at their legs to start with, it that helps ease the conscience a little."

"God always was a little fuzzy about kneecaps, wasn't He?" she asked, amused.

Sister Ann had been overly generous in her estimates. It actually took them a month to figure out how to construct a bridge and get across the river. In the end, they simply lashed a bunch of logs together and made a floating bridge of sorts. It worked well enough, but before they could test it properly it floated farther downriver. Nobody had tied it off. To be fair, zombies can be very distracting. Especially when they show up in a horde and without much warning.

I hadn't realized the city of Covington was still chock-full of the aggressive types of zombies until Rex and his gang started making all sorts of noise trying to complete their bridge. The idiots thought that just because they didn't see any zombies meant they'd all left. In reality, the zombies probably all went down by Interstate 64 because one of the buildings there was solar powered and featured a tall pole with a lantern and a sign on top. While not the brightest light in the world, it was still the only one around and the zombies were drawn to it. Since Rex and his group had come the most direct route from Lexington, which meant over the hill along I-64 until they exited at State Road 60, they'd unwittingly avoided the zombies—until the chainsaw started, at least.

It was stupid, really. If they'd have gone down I-64 farther they would have found the rear entrance to the school. It wasn't really that big of a secret. Or they could have even just waded across the river. Yeah, it wasn't shallow, but it was easier than trying to rebuild a bridge using logs from the nearby lumber company cut onsite. To be honest, if would have been even easier if they'd just waded across the river and raided the partially collapsed paper mill plant *right there next to the ruined bridge* and did the repair work from the mill's side. Well, what was left of the paper mill, anyway. When the dam went, it had done a number on every building next to the river. Most of downtown Covington remained partially flooded, but still... for a guy who was supposed to be king, he seemed pretty dumb and not the most creative thinker.

He must have really wanted to make his grand entrance to the school with his armored vehicle. Otherwise, he could have just made a simple rope bridge.

I was perched high in a hunter's blind we'd set up on our side of the river when the zombies arrived, drawn in by the noise Rex and his crew were making. These were not the same as the early ones we dealt with up at the school but skinnier. And slower. They weren't the horror movie shamblers though. The zombies were still able to surprise Rex and his crew. It was interesting to watch precisely how they dealt with them from a purely tactical point of view. I took notes because, well, I'd never seen anyone else handle zombies before. Up at St. Dominic's, zombie clearing was always left to me. None of the other girls could do it from up close. Or would, rather.

The first zombie hit the guy who was supposed to be on lookout but seemed far more interested in watching the bridge being built. He didn't even have time to scream before the zombie had latched onto his neck and started chewing away. Between the noise from the river, the loud arguing of Rex's men, and the one chainsaw running there was almost zero chance they heard the poor guy die.

Rex must have sensed something, though, because he half-turned towards the lookout just as the man stopped twitching on the ground. He shouted an alarm as a large mass of zombies appeared from out behind the ruined old Post Office. The group turned as one and the guards were up and ready before the zombies reached their position.

I'll give credit where it's due: they knew what a proper firing line was. They were precise with their shots and didn't seem to waste any rounds. They might not be the brightest bunch but they knew how to defend against an oncoming horde. Zombies dropped in rapid succession as the men fired. Rex's men were clearly good shots, which was something to keep in mind. I didn't want to admire their abilities against the zombies, though. Rex's followers were potentially the enemy, after all.

The group made one huge tactical error right off the bat—they forgot to make sure the scout on the ground was really dead and not just injured. Always double check the body. After killing the zombie who attacked him, they'd just forgotten about him to engage the approaching horde. It didn't take long for him to turn, and even with the gaping neck wound their lookout was up and back on his feet in a matter of minutes. The newly created zombie almost made it to Rex before the so-called King of Appalachia pulled out a monster cannon of a handgun and blew the guy's head off with one shot.

With the new zombie down, Rex began barking orders to his men. I couldn't hear exactly what he was shouting over the gunfire, but eventually they began focusing zombies as they approached. Golden rule of the zombie apocalypse: if you can bring friends to a shootout, bring lots of guns, and even more ammo.

I looked around the area to see if I was still safe. No signs of wildlife or any zombies, but that meant nothing. Sometimes you could almost step on a zombie without waking them up if you were quiet enough. Other than Lucia, I was probably the sneakiest girl on campus. More than once I'd stumbled onto a zombie nest and had to get out of there without waking the creatures up. Fortunately, they stayed away from the railroad tracks and closer to the water. This was helpful because the railroad tracks led straight into the back entrance of campus. Back before the world ended it was also the best route for some of the girls to sneak out at night to meet up with townie boys.

Not that I've ever done anything like that. I've just heard rumors and stuff. I swear.

One of the lookouts suddenly shouted and pointed in another direction, back behind the paper mill. I was still safe but he was pointing up U.S. 220. I turned and followed his arm before blinking, surprised. An ungodly number of zombies were coming down the road, quicker than the original group. These zombies were clearly better fed. There was also a lot more of them. I hadn't seen that many in months.

Where are they coming from? I asked myself as I looked across the river. The area around Covington, including Clifton Forge, had *maybe* ten thousand people in total before everything happened. A lot of them died during the original outbreak of the Pacific Flu. The math didn't add up. Something else to talk to Sister Ann about. Shaking my head, I climbed down from the hunter's blind, jumping the last few feet to save time. Landing on the loose gravel near the tracks, I crouched down and checked to make certain I hadn't damaged Baby any. After a quick inspection I was satisfied. The AR-15 didn't even have a scratch.

I needed to leave. I didn't want to get tagged by

a stray round or a ricochet and since Rex's men were on a shooting rampage the odds were decent of that happening. High-tailing it along the tracks, I headed back towards campus. It was time to report in. Sister Ann was not going to be happy about the amount of zombies still in Covington.

I was right. She wasn't happy at all.

"You saw how many?" Sister Ann asked, clearly bothered by the news. We'd been planning exploratory scouting missions farther out from the school for a few months now, hoping the zombie population had died off over the past year. This sudden arrival of more zombies seemed to have everyone in a down mood.

"A few hundred at least, coming from Warm Springs," I reported. We had all gathered in the dining hall, which had become our de facto headquarters after everyone began turning into zombies. There was a bunker in the basement which had been set up during the Cold War because the Greenbriar, a really fancy resort not too far away, was once a potential target for nuclear bombs since it had been prepped to hold all of Congress in it if a nuclear war broke out. I guess it made sense to want to keep all the girls at St. Dominic's alive should something like that occur, and the bunker was built when they refurbished the dining hall.

Who could have guessed it would be used instead during the zombie apocalypse?

"That's not good," Sister Ann murmured and leaned back in the chair. She glanced at the six other girls sitting with us around the large dining hall table. They were all high school aged, like me, and we all served on the student council by default. "Still, they're on the other side of the river. We're okay for now. Options?" she asked them.

"Stores are good for another four months, maybe five if we stretch it," Lucia Archuleta reported. She was from California originally, like me, and had initially found the quiet Blue Ridge Mountains to be horrible. She'd almost run away a dozen times before settling in. I thought she was just a vapid slut but when the zombie apocalypse began, she was the one who managed to get all the elementary school girls into the dining hall without attracting any attention from those who had turned. I cut her some slack and it turned out she was really good with keeping track of things and a whiz at math. Sister Ann put her in charge of figuring out the food situation, usage, and organization. Everyone had come to rely on her almost as much as they did on myself or Emily. "The problem is protein. We're running low on canned chicken and we're out of Spam."

"And vitamin supplements." Sister Ann sighed. "Those too."

"At least we still have pads and tampons. We need to raid a store though, and soon," Lucia said as she looked at her notepad. "Or we start hitting houses down by the Moose Lodge and take our chances there might be zombies inside them. They had a good stockpile of canned goods the last time we volunteered down there."

"If we get spotted by King Dale and his group, they'll figure out there's a way across the river," Rohena Stephens pointed out. I rolled my eyes but didn't argue. As much as she irritated me, she was right. Appalachia Rex would figure out how we're crossing the river if he spotted us. That would be the end of our excursions, and maybe worse. Rohena continued. "If we head north, then circle back east and check the gas station up on top of the hill along State Road 60, we might get a few things if the zombies haven't destroyed the inside yet and Dale won't spot us. Even if those zombies came from Warm Springs."

"Girl...I'm telling you, that one cute cashier is either a zombie or dead," Kayla Washington remarked with a smirk. "Even if he lived, there's no way he stayed around here."

"Talk all the smack you want, but they had a lot of canned stuff there," Rohena reminded her. "Water's probably gone, but they might have sodas. I know it's not water, but it'll add caloric intake a bit. Maybe some of those vitamin-laced waters? I don't know. Point being, unless zombies figured out how to use complex locks, it should still have some stuff in back. They're only dangerous now if they horde up or get in too close."

"Lucia, draw up a plan for checking out the gas station," Sister Ann said. "It's a low priority, though. At most, Maddie and two others with hiking backpacks."

"People gonna die," Lucia muttered under her breath as she continued taking notes. I almost laughed but managed to turn it into a cough at the last moment.

"Speaking of water," Sister Ann continued, ignoring the girl's comment. "We're still okay with the pump?"

"For now, Sister," Emily Mottesheard responded. She was the only girl at the school who even had a bare understanding of any kind of informal mechanical work. With a little bit of help from one of the middle school girls, Emily fixed all things mechanical for us—as long as the thing that needed fixing had an owner's manual available. "I know some of the girls want to use the solar panel to heat the showers, but without the power from the solar panel we don't have water. They can either have cold showers, or no water at all. They need to quit bit—uh, complaining about it."

"I'll mention it again at Devotionals tonight," Sister Ann promised. "Hand pumps?"

"Yes ma'am, sorry," Emily looked down at her notepad. "I understand the concept behind it but finding water is actually harder than it sounds. Yeah, if we had a lot of pressure we could bring it up from Dunlap Creek. That'd be the easiest way but we would need mechanical pumps for that. Our well pump here is already not doing so well. I was reading about something interesting but we'd have to find a lot of pipes and a natural spring above us somewhere. Basically, water flows downhill, and we just build a gravity well with piping to direct it into the purifiers..."

"Which there isn't any," Sister Ann pointed out.

"I figured you would have mentioned a natural spring flowing down the mountain if there was one," Emily stated. "No manual well pumps for now, sorry."

"How long do you think the mechanical pump will last?" I asked, curious.

"Really hard to say," Emily replied as she looked at me. I could see the worry in her eyes. A seventeen-year-old girl shouldn't be under the stress she was. It was her responsibility to keep everything mechanical running. Then again, nobody should be doing what we had to in order to survive. "They're built to last thirty years and this one was just installed five years ago. If the pipe doesn't freeze or rupture, then we're good for a long time. Last winter was mild. This year? I don't know. Next? Again, no idea. February is always the worst. If it gets too cold and the pipe bursts..."

"We'll worry about that when the time comes, Emily," Sister Ann told us all in a gentle tone. She looked at Kayla. "How are the gardens?"

We'd gotten lucky on that one. The old farm manager who worked for the school had gotten permission years before to convert the old, unused tennis courts into a garden. Because it had been a tennis court, there was a ten-foot high chain link fence surrounding it. It also happened to be between the gymnasium and the dining hall, which was very convenient and close to our little safe haven. She'd also left behind a lot of seed packets so we'd have enough fresh vegetables for years. So far, none of the zombies had taken an interest in it and no wild animals had gotten inside except for the occasional snake...which we quickly learned to leave alone, since they ate the mice and voles who tried to eat our crops.

"Lots of tomatoes and peppers," Kayla said. "Rain's been good enough to keep the potatoes going as well. We should have enough vegetables to can to make it through the winter so we won't have to ration too much. I'm worried about the corn, though. It's got some weird bug on it. One of the farming books mentioned weevils but there wasn't a picture. I don't want to spray them if I don't have to but...if it is weevils, then I'll have to, and we're running low on the stuff. Anybody know a chemist?"

"Okay, keep doing the best you can." Sister Ann smiled. She loved hearing the updates around the council, even if she already knew the details we were all about to share. I think it had something to do with keeping our mental health stable. If everyone was upbeat and talking about what was going right, we didn't need to worry about what was going wrong.

Unfortunately, I was next up, and I was always the bearer of bad news. Yay me.

"Rohena's partially right about one thing, though," I said as everyone else quieted down. "The zombies aren't as much of a threat to us anymore and we should start exploring a bit, though avoid any other people for the time being. I watched Appalachia Rex and his boys do a decent job of handling a mass of zombies. They're good shooters. If they push for us here, we need to be prepared to defend. Before you get all scared, just remember there's only one way up the hill for their tank and—"

"MedCat," Sister Ann corrected me. Even though she took her holy vows years before, Sister Ann never truly forgot her Marine training.

"Yes ma'am, sorry," I automatically replied. "Their MedCat can be stopped at the bridge across Dunlap Creek if we block it with something big."

Dunlap Creek was a good-sized creek which eventually joined the Jackson River. It was a secondary natural boundary for the school, not nearly as wide as the Jackson but almost as deep. It was great for fishing and swimming, and since it was above the river from the paper mill, it was also clean. Even before the Fall it was one of the more popular places the school held public fundraising events.

"Couldn't it just drive across the creek?" Rohena asked nervously. Sister Ann shook her head.

"No, it's too deep on the north side of the bridge," she explained. "Maddie?"

"Their ta—uh, MedCat didn't have a snorkel," I pointed out, recalling all the details I could from the lumbering armored vehicle.

"If the engine goes underwater, it'll die," Emily put in immediately. "Even if it is a diesel, it needs air for the combustion and heat. Unless it's amphibious. Did it look like a badly designed boat? No? Okay, we should be good then. The MedCat probably can't go to the south side of the bridge because the slope down is too steep, and that'll flood the engine as well when they hit the creek, even if the water is down. Which it's not. Supposed to rain more tonight. Yeah, I can see it now. If they push here, we just block the bridge over the creek somehow, only make it wide enough for people to walk through, and Maddie kills them all while staying safely behind cover."

"Or we use it to embarrass them and make them go away once they lose the MedCat," I suggested, remembering what Sister Ann had told me down by the river. Killing them would start us all down a dark path. "Stealing it is a little riskier but..."

"It'll make them rethink everything," Sister Ann finished for me, looking thoughtful, "taking their MedCat from them. It's a brilliant idea. Here's what we're going to do..."

Of course, I was chosen for the dangerous part of the mission Sister Ann jokingly called "Operation Not-A-Tank." I didn't expect anything else. Nobody else was even remotely close to having my skillset. With full hunting gear and my red hair tucked safely away under a black beanie, I blended in better with the environment than normal. The one person who went with me was Lucia, who was dressed similarly. She was the only person I trusted to not wake the zombies *and* Rex's crew. The tiny Latina was not happy about it, though. She let me know about it from the moment we left campus.

"This is stupid," she whispered for the umpteenth time as we made our way down the railroad tracks. We knew already where Appalachia Rex and his crew were holed up at. The gas station that Rohena had been so interested in before was where they had set up for the night. It was pretty easy to see them from one of the perches we'd set up upriver of the paper mill.

Aware that zombies could still be around, I shushed her and made a walking motion with my two fingers. She sighed, held up the letter "B" in sign language to her chin, and jerked it down before giving me two quick waves of her hand. I giggled. We'd barely begun taking sign language before the Fall, but a few of us quickly learned some of the dirty words. No, I'll be honest. We knew all of them since it was the only way we could curse without getting demerits. Back when they were still giving them out it had been a pretty popular way of cussing another girl out without bringing the wrath of Sister Margaret or any of the other nuns down on our heads.

Bitch, please, I mentally translated. Lucia had a point. We didn't need to be silent, merely quiet.

We crossed the makeshift floating bridge Rex had managed to tie up. Surprisingly, he didn't have anybody out there to protect it. Considering they probably didn't have any way to see in the dark, it made sense the longer I thought about it. It wasn't as though the zombies would do anything to the bridge besides cross it, right? He had to be thinking something along these lines. Plus, a school filled with teenage girls protected by a single nun? How dangerous could they be to his plans?

He had no idea what nun he was messing with.

One thing Sister Ann had done before locking the main admin building up was to take all of the hand-held radios. They were good ones, not the cheap sort you'd find at a discount store. They had to be to work in these mountains. Sister Ann had hoarded these radios, keeping them safe from harm and conserving all the batteries we could find. There was a surprising amount, actually, but since most of them were size "D" batteries, we'd only used the radios when I went out scouting. The small, hand-held radios needed "C" batteries, which were in short supply. The "D" batteries we had in abundance were perfect for the shortwave radio, however. It allowed us to keep track of everything going on along the coast, including the exploits of the so-called "Wolf Squadron," even if it was only for two hours an evening. Emily thought we had enough batteries to last the shortwave radio five more years at our current use, so we listened in. Other than chess, which I hated, the shortwave was our only source of entertainment.

I turned my radio on and switched to the prearranged channel. We were risking a lot in using these radios. Anybody who happened to have the same channel we were using could potentially hear us. It was why Sister Ann told us not to talk, merely turn it on and hit the transmit key three times before shutting it back down. The signal was meant to tell her we were safely across the bridge. The next time we were supposed to use the radio was when we completed the second stage and found Rex's stolen MedCat.

The gas station Rex had holed up in for the night was near the river. I was a bit surprised to see it standing complete with glass doors intact and everything. The pumps were gone, but since they were the newer kind with the emergency shutoff valves the gas was probably still in the underground tanks. Contaminated with water, undoubtedly, but still there. Maybe one day we could get to them.

I spotted the MedCat parked directly in front of the door, partially blocking the front entrance. It was a smart idea, actually. It provided them with added reinforcement to the station's main entrance while keeping their vehicle close. The problem with their plan, however, was that Rex had left the keys in the ignition and nobody to guard the MedCat. The doors were unlocked and we didn't see anyone sleeping inside.

Talk about a stroke of luck. It would make what we were about to do next that much simpler.

Locking the doors, Lucia slid into the back area to ensure it was secured as well. We did not want any unexpected passengers during our attempt at grand theft auto. Satisfied it was locked and there was no way, outside of a spare key, of anyone else getting in, I flipped the radio back on and clicked the transmit key three more times. Turning the radio off, I climbed behind the driver's seat and waited. My gaze drifted towards the makeshift floating bridge, which could just barely be seen down the block.

It took a bit longer than expected. I chalked it up to the logs being wet from the rapidly flowing river. Or perhaps the coolness of the evening. But eventually the combined kerosene and Styrofoam packing peanut bags lit the logs on fire. Soon there was a bonfire any southern boy would have been proud to call his own. If anyone had been outside on watch, that is.

I was irritated. Sister Ann and the other girls had worked hard on making their makeshift napalm, and there was nobody from Rex's crew to witness it. I leaned forward and peered inside the gas station. It was absolute darkness inside. This was smart, since zombies were drawn to light. I looked back down at the river. The flames were high in the air now, making short work of the rope lines which Rex and company had used to lash the logs together. The bridge began to break apart, though a few stuck together for some reason. There was a lot of smoke rising into the air. I turned back to let Lucia know what was going on when disaster struck.

I slipped and my elbow slammed down hard on the steering wheel. The loud car horn of the MedCat echoed loudly into the still night. I jerked away from the horn, horrified, and scrambled into the back with Lucia. She was staring at me, eyes wide.

"You think anyone heard?" she asked in a hushed whisper.

As if in response, a keening wail answered. Then another, and another. Hundreds, if not thousands, of angry zombies howled somewhere out in the darkness.

"Shit," I hissed, terrified. "Yeah, someone heard."

Inside the gas station, Rex and his men were awake and running outside. They were well armed but clearly had not been expecting a truck horn to signal for all of the zombies to wake up. Confused, a few tried the doors to the MedCat, only to find it locked. I could hear them arguing outside.

"Who locked the fucking keys in the tank?!" someone screamed. It sounded like Rex, I couldn't be certain.

"Forget the keys!" another voice interjected. "The bridge is on fire!"

"How did the bridge catch on fire?" a third voice asked. "Quick, to the river!"

I risked a peek and saw eight men, all armed with AR-15s similar to mine, running towards the fire. As they drew closer one of them raised his rifle and shot across the river. One of the younger girls was out in the open. I winced but the shot missed. She continued scrambling behind a small pile of rocks but there wasn't enough cover. As the shooter readied a second shot, a screech interrupted him. He turned but the zombie was in too close now, and his screams ended abruptly as the zombie's teeth opened his throat wide. A melee erupted as the zombies poured into Rex and his men. Vengeance was no longer an option. Clearly they were fighting now purely to survive.

"Time to go," I muttered and set Baby safely on a small mounted rack. Lucia climbed into the passenger seat. Checking the dashboard, I was surprised to see the truck was an automatic, just as Sister Ann predicted. I silently cursed. "I owe her three packets of noodles."

"You bet against a nun? Stupid." Lucia grunted as I turned the key. The well-primed diesel engine coughed and roared to life. I flipped the switch for the lights, which drew the attention of all of the zombies—as well as Appalachia Rex and his men.

I revved the engine once and shifted it into gear. The MedCat had a very powerful engine and it kicked up a lot of smoke and dirt as the wheels spun out a little before finding traction. The MedCat slid sideways a little, then quickly straightened out as I barreled over a small group of zombies who were late to the party. I barely registered their impacts as I drove over them in the big armored truck. It was glorious. I preferred this method of killing zombies over any other I'd tried so far. With gore sticking to the windshield and more zombies trying to rush the truck, I decided it was time to get out of there. However, I had one more pass to make.

The image of Rex's face when I shot him the bird as we drove past is one I'll cherish forever.

Sideswiping a zombie and running over two more, I pressed the gas pedal as far as it could go. The big diesel engine roared in response. I'm almost certain another zombie was killed by the exhaust plume alone. A large crowd soon tried to follow us, but the armored MedCat was too fast and soon enough we left them behind. I guided the armored truck up State Road 60, cresting the large hill on the eastern half of the town. From what I could see behind us the zombies were falling behind in their pursuit. I had no idea what happened to Rex and his men but it seemed like pretty good odds they had bolted when the zombies had all charged the MedCat.

"Well, Rohena isn't going to be happy," I commented and slowed down as we passed the gas station she had wanted us to explore a few days before. It had been burned to the ground at some point and now was nothing more than a charred husk of a building. The roof had collapsed in during the fire and the front was completely gone. I counted six bodies near the fuel pumps, all burnt to a crisp. There were signs they'd been gnawed on a little, but with that much fire damage there wasn't much left for a zombie to eat. "I seriously doubt there's any bottled water or supplies in there."

"*Ay chi mama*," Lucia added. "I hope none of them were that cute boy Rohena liked."

"Probably all zombies," I guessed and turned onto I-64. From there we began to head west, the abandoned interstate only partially overgrown with kudzu here. Sticking towards the center of the freeway we passed over the Jackson River, the bridge well above where the mass of water surged when the damn gave way. It was still terrifying, though, since part of the opposite side of the road had fallen off sometime. One of the support beams must have failed on that side.

Once we were across the high bridge, we were home free. I knew the back way into the school was at Mile Marker 10, then we'd have to backtrack a bit to make it to the school. Before I could get off the freeway though, Lucia had me stop.

"Just...wait a sec, okay? Stop the tank," she said. I obliged and parked the MedCat right there in the middle of the freeway. Looking over the fuel gauge, I was surprised to see it at almost full. Rex had gotten gas somehow. I made a quick mental reminder to ask Sister Ann about it.

"What's up?" I asked her as I shut off the engine. No point in wasting fuel. We were completely safe inside the armored vehicle and had time to spare. Sister Ann and the other girls wouldn't be able to return to the school for at least an hour. It wasn't the shortest hike, even following the railroad tracks.

"We could go home," Lucia whispered.

"We are," I said. "We get off at the next mile marker exit and head back to school. This way is safest, just like Sister Ann said."

"No," Lucia shook her head and pointed straight down the freeway ahead. "I mean, *home*."

"Oh." She meant California, where our families were.

It was over three thousand miles away. There was no way we could make it, not on one tank of gas. It was impossible. Yet... the temptation was too real. The idea of driving off, going home. Finding our families and discovering that they all somehow survived. We could use the armored MedCat to go anywhere and not worry about the zombies. Maybe Utah? I'd always wanted to go to Utah and see the mountains there.

I sighed. I knew they were gone. Los Angeles had a massive breakout before the rest of the country had even been infected. It was a mess. The last thing we'd heard over the shortwave before Sister Ann had made us turn it off was that L.A. was half-burned. Fires had torn though Chavez Ravine. The San Gabriel and San Fernando valleys had been devastated by structural fires. Even Orange County, my home, was ruined.

"It's all gone," I reminded her. "Our families. Our old lives. Even if we could go back, what would we find? Nothing will ever return to normal. Not the way it was. I know, deep down, my family's gone. Yours? I don't know. But... why not build something here, for them to come to? Maybe... I mean, if we could get lucky heading west, maybe they'll head east, to us? Luck swings both ways, you know?"

"They wouldn't make it," Lucia said in a despondent voice. "My mama can't drive. *Mi padre* is a horrible driver on a good day, and *Tia* Juanita's car couldn't even get out to Riverside. No, they're stuck there, if they lived... which they probably didn't. I don't know, Maddie. I just want to go home."

"I know. It's a hard decision, but one we need to make. Tonight. So what's it gonna be, *chica*?" I asked Lucia. "Head west, possibly make it all the way there, and find out what happened to our families? Or stay here, be the protectors of the younger girls, and maybe build something better for ourselves here?"

"*Odio cuando tienes razón,*" Lucia muttered in a quiet voice.

"No *habla,*" I told her. "White girl from the O.C., remember?"

"I hate it when you're right," she translated for me and let out a weary sigh. "Let's get this tank back up to the school. I don't think we need to worry about Appalachia Rex tonight. Not as long as we have his tank, and the bridge burned up."

"Pretty sure it did. Plus, that was a lot of zombies drawn to the bonfire. As long as they're not on their way up to the school already, we should be okay," I reminded her as my mind drifted.

In my heart, I'd figured my family was dead months before, but I don't think I'd really accepted it until that moment. The weight of it felt crushing on my chest. It hurt. As annoying as my brothers were, they were still my brothers and I loved them. My parents too, even if they'd shipped me off across the country to a private school to help me figure out who I was. I wiped my eyes as they started to burn from tears and tried to comfort Lucia instead of focusing on my own pain. Home wasn't California anymore, not for either of us. "Besides, you know our families are probably . . . dead, right?"

"I know."

"This is the safest place to be. At the school, I mean."

"*I know!*"

"Hey, it'll get better. The Marines are coming to

rescue us." I tried, but Lucia still appeared upset. It was hard to cheer someone else up while I was on the verge of bawling my eyes out as well. Humor had always been my fallback position. I decided on my one remaining option. "So...you wanna drive the tank back to the school?"

Lucia looked at me, a frown upon her face. She'd stopped crying at least. This was good. "I don't have my driver's license."

"Neither do I. What, you worried about a ticket? Ha!"

Lucia was quiet, clearly intrigued by the idea. Her facial expressions ranged from curious to fearful, with a dash of excitement at the prospect of driving something like the MedCat. I couldn't blame her for any of it. I recognized those facial tics. They were probably the same ones I had on my face when Sister Ann first suggested we steal the armored vehicle. Finally, she nodded once.

"You know what? Yeah, I want to drive the tank up back to the school."

"Atta girl!"

Maligator Country

LYDIA SHERRER

Frank Oberman stood on the front porch of his two-story white farm house and contemplated the sunrise. Like any good Marine at six in the morning, he had his coffee in hand.

And, like any good survivor of the Fall, he had his firearm in the other.

The weapon was a 30-06 Springfield bolt action hunting rifle that his father had acquired after the old man had retired from the Corps in '73. Frank had since added a state-of-the-art scope, but other than that it was in its original condition. He didn't normally carry the rifle around with him while inside the farm's perimeter fence—his trusty S&W Model 66 Combat Magnum revolver was a permanent fixture on his belt for emergencies. But he sometimes spotted deer grazing along the woodline that bordered the front gravel drive, and he never passed up a chance to keep the big walk-in freezer in his dog kennel well stocked. He had eighteen dogs to feed, and those beasts ate a pound and a half of raw meat a day on top of the dry kibble he fed them. It didn't help that the kibble was close to running out.

Raw meat itself wasn't scarce. But since the vast majority of it existed in the form of crazy, diseased, blood-thirsty monsters, it didn't help with the whole keeping-his-dogs-fed thing. He certainly wished he could feed his dogs zombie meat, but butchering and handling the plague-ridden flesh posed too great a risk of infection to their farming community. It wasn't worth it, not while there was still wild game to hunt and they were able to keep their livestock safe from zombies. And they had been able to—thanks to his dogs.

A low canine whine at Frank's feet brought his mind back to his morning tasks. Joe Gallrein, the informal leader of their farming community, had called for a meeting yesterday over their extended walkie-talkie network after everyone had heard that radio announcement from D.C. Apparently the Vice President had been found alive by Wolf Squadron and was officially reforming the government of their glorious US of A.

Oorah, Wolf Squadron.

At times over the hard winter months spent listening to Devil Dog radio, he'd wished he could have been there with them, killing zombies and taking back civilization. But after twenty-one years of service as an MP and then a dog handler, he'd been out of the Corps for going on twelve years now and was pushing fifty-one. Despite his rigorous farm lifestyle and the daily runs he went on with his dogs, he doubted he could have kept up with Shewolf and her men.

Frank gave the woodline one last long, careful look as he finished his coffee, then ducked back into the house to set his rifle on its hooks by the front door. When he walked back out onto the porch, he stopped at the top of the steps and crouched to give each of the three dogs sitting there a thorough rub around the ears.

The Fall was almost a year behind them, and as all farmers knew, there was too much to do to let a little thing like a zombie apocalypse slow you down. Mother Nature waited for no man, and with spring turning into another muggy Kentucky summer, everyone had plenty of work to do to keep themselves and their farms going.

Another whine of suppressed impatience came from the group of dogs, and he shook his head ruefully. "If only humans had half as much energy as you lot. Y'all are just itching to go, aren't you?" This time a chorus of whines answered him, and he chuckled. "All right, all right. I'll get a move on."

Aware of all the chores he had to get done before he left for the community meeting, Frank reached down to the black device on his belt and clicked a button on it three times. The clicks sent electrical pulses to the collars of his night patrol pack whose job it was to watch over the farm while the humans slept. Contrary to popular belief, electric collars were by far the most humane form of dog training and control, not to mention that they worked over long distances and when his dogs were out of line-of-sight. It was a happy irony that they were also perfect for operating in a zombie-infested countryside where shouting and dog whistles attracted the wrong kind of attention. His dogs' collars had an 800-yard range, which covered the one hundred acres of his farm's perimeter fence that the dogs patrolled checking for intruders, predators, and zombies.

Within minutes of his summons, the night pack appeared around the corner of the goat barn. They each jumped the gate to the goat pasture with a powerful bound, then headed across the barnyard toward the house. All Frank's fences were strung with electric wire, so his dogs knew to avoid it.

At a virtual explosion of whines from his feet, Frank blew out an amused huff of air, then gave the command his dogs had been waiting for. "Athos, Porthos, Aramis. Home patrol!"

The two Belgian Malinois—a breed affectionately known as Maligators because of their fierceness and willingness to bite—and the slightly more laid back German Shepherd that made up the day patrol responded immediately to his command. They bounded off the porch, Athos slightly in the lead, and went to greet their counterparts. There was a general sniffing, wagging of tails, and a few playful nips between the groups as they passed each other, and then the "three musketeers" were off to do their preliminary territory check. He'd hardly even needed to train them to check the kennel, chicken coop, goat barn, whelping barn, and the other various outbuildings before they headed out to run the perimeter. This farm was their territory, and they took care of everything in it—man or beast—with boundless energy and ferocious loyalty.

Frank shifted his attention to his night pack as they trotted up the porch steps, considerably less energetic than the day pack. Even so, their eyes were bright and attentive as they gathered around for their morning reward of pettings and gratuitous praise in

Frank's low gravelly voice. The night pack consisted of Aragorn and Legolas, two German Shepherds, and Gimli, another Belgian Malinois. Frank had made the "mistake" years ago of giving his now fifteen-year-old daughter, Maggie, the sole honor of naming all the dogs they trained, and she was a particular fan of the classics. Of course, whether or not Lord of the Rings should be considered a true classic was a frequent point of contention between Maggie and her bibliophile mother.

At least, it *had* been. Before the Fall.

"Get on now, you lot," Frank told his dogs as he stood with a grunt. His three dogs pushed past him and nosed their way through the unlatched door, making a bee-line for the kitchen. Frank heard Maggie greet them with warm affection and many sappy nicknames. All the dogs adored Maggie. Of course, the fact that she prepared their twice-daily meals didn't hurt at all. Frank fed the younger dogs still in training to establish himself as their pack alpha and the source of all things good in their doggie universe. But his day and night packs were old hands and they understood the pack hierarchy without needing that daily reminder. In any case, Maggie was essentially their secondary alpha. She was family, and while they obeyed Frank out of unflagging loyalty and devotion, they obeyed Maggie out of pure puppy love.

Nobody cared about animals the way Maggie did. And animals knew it. Somehow they could sense it, and they responded to her in ways that made Frank shake his head and swear under his breath. He used to swear out loud, but his wife, Sandra, had put a swift end to that after he'd retired and come home from the service. He'd always intended to stay the full thirty years like his father had. But by 2001 Sandra had had enough. It was either come home and be a father to their daughter, or she was getting a divorce.

It had been a rude wake-up call, but a necessary one. He'd brought his family to live near his aging parents and their small Kentucky farm. After a string of ill-fitting jobs, he'd thrown up his hands and taken the leap into small business ownership, building a kennel on the farm and establishing Braveheart Canine Services. It was a logical move, considering his experience and the fact that he preferred dogs to people. In the decade since, Frank had trained over two hundred and fifty police and personal protection dogs. In fact, he'd just gotten in a new shipment of four Maligator pups from the Ukraine last summer when all hell had broken loose.

"Mags?" Frank called, sticking his head in the door. "I'm headed to the kennel. You good?"

"Go on, Dad! As soon as I've got these three goof-balls squared away I'll start on breakfast."

Frank let a corner of his mouth quirk up as he headed down the porch steps. Considering the ten years his daughter had spent caring for and training dogs by his side, it wasn't surprising she'd picked up some of his military lingo. It still made him smile when he heard it, though.

"Morning, Frank."

Frank nodded to Mrs. Rogers as she passed him on the way to the chicken coop. The matron was about his own age, and a close neighbor. Her husband, Mike, had leased land on one of the larger farms just north of them before the zombie plague had got to him. With all their children grown and scattered about the

U.S.—and quite possibly dead by now—Mrs. Rogers had left their small tenant house down the road to move in with Frank and Maggie.

Though he had a lot of respect for Mrs. Rogers and was grateful for her help, he still avoided her. The haunted look in her eyes since her husband's death gave him nightmares. It made him remember Sandra's eyes just before she'd turned. It made him agonize again and again over what sort of humanity might have been left in his wife's mind, heart, and soul right before he'd shot her in the head. Sometimes he felt guilty for how much bitterness burned in his heart, or how much pleasure he took in watching his dogs systematically rip zombies to shreds.

Sometimes. But not often.

Frank pushed the memories away and lengthened his stride so that he soon arrived at the kennel. It was a simple rectangle building of poured concrete. At one end twelve dog runs, six on each side, extended out, with a doggie door for each dog to get inside the building to their own little kennel enclosure. The concrete floor slanted inward so any waste would run down the drain in the middle of the walkway between the kennels. At the other end, the building was separated into two rooms: a combined training, grooming, and vet care room, and a food preparation room which led into the walk-in freezer. A large generator kept the electricity running, though they used it only for bare necessities besides keeping the freezer cold.

Much whining and tail-wagging greeted his appearance, and Frank got to work in the food room portioning out fresh meat, bones, and organs from a deer he'd killed a few days ago. He currently housed six dogs in the kennel, all males, three Belgian Malinois and three German Shepherds. The oldest and most experienced, two German Shepherds named Achilles and Odysseus, were his personal attack dogs that he took out with him when he was on patrol for zombies or doing a scavenging run. The other four, Thor, Loki, Fred, and George, were two more pairs he was almost done training to do similar patrols with a few hand-picked farmers able to manage the high-energy and hyper-intelligent dogs. Last summer he'd also had six more males that he'd trained up and sold, but never delivered due to the zombie apocalypse. They had been rehomed at Joe Gallrein's, the biggest farm in their community with all the livestock and critical infrastructure in need of protection.

The four female dogs he owned lived in the whelping barn. Males he always left unfixed, but females he usually fixed as soon as he could, to keep their semi-annual heats from making the males go crazy. Males were favored for police work because of their bigger size, intimidating look, and aggression, and they were the bulk of what he trained. But females versus males for personal protection was the preference of the client. He could only wonder whether it was fate, or God, or just dumb luck that he'd managed to get four high-quality Belgian Malinois bitches right before the entire world had fallen apart. By now, most quality breeding dogs across the world were either dead or running wild in feral packs. Frank had been able to breed three out of four of his females. The litters weren't large, since he was breeding the dogs a good year younger than was standard practice. But he hadn't felt he could wait. These dogs were the difference between life and death for their entire community, though the first time they'd saved all their lives, they'd done nothing more spectacular than simply show up.

It'd been late last June and he'd just finished loading the four newly arrived dog crates into his camper-covered pickup when he'd witnessed his first "zombification." The Louisville International Airport wasn't huge by any standard, but it still had plenty of work crews to handle luggage—luggage that had been touched by multiple hands of those infected with what everyone now knew had been stage one of the zombie virus. That was what had been so horrible in the beginning. The realization that people could be infected for days without knowing it. That was why it had spread so fast. Well, that and the fact that not enough people had taken it seriously until it was too late.

Him? He'd raised his eyebrows at the avid arguments between Maggie and Sandra about what, exactly, the plague was. Maggie had started using the "z" word as soon as she saw the first video on YouTube of a naked man leaping onto a policeman and violently ripping out the officer's throat. Just because she'd grown up in the country didn't mean she was sheltered. She'd seen enough movies and TV shows to know a zombie when she saw one. Her mother had attempted to be the voice of reason in the house, but Maggie had been adamant. Personally, Frank had experienced enough insanity in his years overseas to know you didn't have to believe in monsters for them to be real.

And preparedness was a Marine's middle name...

At the increased whining from inside the kennel, Frank finished dividing up all the meat and started doling it out to his dogs. Though they trembled and whined in excitement, not a single one barked. It had become known before everything went dark that zombies were attracted to light and sound, but even if they hadn't been, Frank had already been in the habit of training his dogs not to bark except in very specific circumstances when they used it to signal something.

While the dogs ate, Frank scooped poop from the runs, then hosed down the floor. Finally, he got the dogs out one by one and ran them through their morning exercises. Fortunately, they were already almost fully trained, and so the work went quickly. He needed to head out to Joe Gallrein's place soon.

Once he was done with the dogs, he went to the whelping barn to feed the females and check on the pups. The space was actually a storage barn for everything he used to maintain his land and his flock of twenty-odd Boer goats—well, more like fifty now, since most of the does had dropped their usual pairs of kids in the early spring. But he'd converted one end of the barn into several whelping pens for the new mothers, and this morning all was well.

After that it was back to the farm house for breakfast. Mrs. Rogers would take care of the chickens and look in on the goats. The flock didn't need more than twice daily check-ins during the summer since they had two enormous Caucasian Shepherd dogs, Fezzik and Inigo, as their constant companions. Frank hadn't lost a single goat to predators or accident since he'd bought the dogs and trained them up himself. The gigantic breed hailed from Russia where they were prized as fierce herd dogs capable of fighting off wolf packs and bears. Fezzik and Inigo hadn't dismembered any zombies yet, but only because the day and night packs did their job so well.

Maggie fussed at him to slow down as he shoveled cold eggs and fried venison sausage into his mouth at the breakfast table. He gave her a noncommittal grunt that made her roll her eyes and mutter, "Why do I even bother," before returning to clean up duties. Aragorn, Legolas, and Gimli watched his movements from their spot on the floor with hawklike intensity, but were too well trained to beg.

The sun was well up by the time he'd fetched and saddled his mare. Some of the farmers still had working vehicles, but gas was a precious resource and reserved for running the generators and farm equipment that kept them all going. A jaunt down to Gallrein Farms hardly justified starting up his pickup. Those farmers who hadn't had horses in the beginning had quickly acquired them through rescue raids to farms that had either been abandoned, or had their owners fall to the plague. Frank and the others had gathered the livestock left behind before the zombies trickling out of nearby Shelbyville could feast on the helpless animals. Frank had never been particularly fond of horses, but he appreciated their versatility. Plus, his dogs would get fat and lazy riding around in a truck all the time.

It was two miles cross-country from Braveheart Canine Services to Gallrein Farms, but three if you followed the road. Frank followed the road since it gave Achilles and Odysseus room to maneuver away from the thick verdant undergrowth. Nothing had been mowed or trimmed in a year, and nature was taking back her own with a vengeance. Zombies weren't especially stealthy, but that didn't mean you wanted to be bogged down in chest-high weeds when one attacked you. Since the monsters ignored pain and wounds, Frank had trained his dogs to go straight for the neck. They could easily leap up and tear out a zombie's throat, or jump the zombie from behind and savage the spinal cord to break the neck. Either attack quickly incapacitated the zombie so his dogs could disengage and attack other potential targets.

As Frank's mare ambled along under the blue June sky, flanked on either side by his dogs, the man wondered if the Fall could have been prevented if anyone had possessed the sense to use dogs to sniff out the asymptomatic infected in the early stages and get them quarantined. Dogs had incredible noses, and could smell sickness the same way they could smell bomb materials or narcotics. Before the Fall, dogs were being trained to detect early stage cancer in humans. But he supposed things had just moved too quickly. Despite Maggie's animated retellings of gruesome YouTube videos, even Frank himself hadn't been spurred to action until that day at the Louisville Airport when he'd seen the luggage handler rip off his clothes and leap onto his partner with an inhuman howl.

That was when Frank had finally realized that he'd spent enough time speculating.

He'd high-tailed it home, sanitized himself and the four dog crates, then went to Shelbyville wearing a medical facemask to max out every credit card he owned buying supplies. It had been early in the crisis, so stores were still open. Though the down-to-earth country types of Shelby County were certainly spooked, and the hospitals were starting to strain at the edges, no one really understood what was coming yet.

Well, Frank had made an educated guess, and it had paid off.

Long before the lights and cell phones across the country started going dark, Frank had already been hard at work preparing. His neighbors hadn't been too keen on all the extra work he proposed, but after he'd personally bankrolled the purchase of nearly a metric ton of fencing material, they'd finally taken him seriously. After all, they'd all been following the news, same as he had, and they'd spent their whole lives planning ahead to survive the unpredictability of each season.

This was just another season. A really long, heartbreaking, cursed-to-bloody-hell season, but a season nonetheless. Even with all their planning, though, they might not have made it if it weren't for the dogs.

Frank's dogs knew the difference between zombies and healthy humans as easily as they knew the difference between fresh meat and broccoli. That, plus the fact that he always selected pups with a high fight drive—the desire to challenge superior foes—meant that they had adapted to their zombie apocalypse training with ridiculous eagerness. There had been some trial and error at first as he'd experimented with new types of training exercises. But dogs were smarter than most people gave them credit for, and German Shepherds and Belgian Malinois—the preferred breeds for police and protection work—were so smart it was sometimes scary.

What he hadn't had, though, was enough dogs to patrol all their community's dozen or so farms, each several hundred acres in size, with livestock spread out all over the place. Though Frank and several others went on regular patrols to hunt down "leaker" zombies wandering out of nearby towns, it hadn't been enough. After losing nearly thirty percent of their animals to wandering zombies, they'd agreed to consolidate and moved all their livestock to Gallrein Farms where the second set of day and night patrol packs Frank had trained could protect them. That was when they'd renamed their collection of farms "Maligator County," to honor the dogs that fought for them.

Since he was always peripherally aware of his dogs, Frank noticed immediately when Odysseus stiffened and put his nose to the wind, followed closely by Achilles. Pulling his mare to a stop, he sat back and waited for them to signal. Achilles trotted over to join Odysseus by the side of the road, and after a few more moments of scenting the wind, both dogs backed up into guard position in front of him and gave out quiet chuffs. Since he'd trained them not to bark except for very specific situations, this was their way of letting him know they'd found a zombie.

"How far?" he asked in a quiet voice.

Responding together, the two dogs took several steps forward, their attention fixed on a point past the treeline in a field overgrown with ironweed and wild mustard. Their posture meant not close, but not far either. If a zombie was still quite far away, they would lie down. If it was within attack distance, they would crouch in readiness.

Frank frowned and lifted a hand to shade his eyes as he scanned the field. He couldn't leave a zombie to wander freely this close to their farms. On the other hand, they really didn't have time for an extended hunt. Fortunately, zombies weren't the brightest bulbs out there, and rarely needed much encouragement to run head-first toward their own deaths.

After a moment, he grunted and shrugged. "Achilles, ambush. Odysseus, bait. Go!"

The two dogs leapt into action. Odysseus went to the edge of the road and let out a sharp barrage of thunderous barks, while Achilles bounded off into the tall grass where he quickly disappeared. Frank unslung his rifle and readied it as he carefully scanned their surroundings.

Barely five seconds after Odysseus had started his racket, Frank saw a head of matted hair pop up among the ironweed about forty yards away. Fresh, bright red blood was smeared around its mouth as if the zombie had just killed some kind of wildlife and was feasting on it. The face soon disappeared, but then the weeds started to sway in their direction and Frank knew they were in business.

Oorah.

"Odysseus, silent, guard!"

The dog went quiet and crouched, ready.

There was no sound for a long moment except the buzz of insects in the warm summer air. Then came the keening howl. Brush thrashed along the treeline and Frank spotted where the zombie had gotten hung up on the rusted barbed wire fence that separated the road from the field. It was tempting to let his dogs have at the creature, but there was no point risking it.

"Stop whining and get your sorry naked butt over here you stinken' piece of vulture bait," Frank yelled. His voice sounded unnaturally loud in his own ears, probably since he wasn't used to stringing that many words together at once. The insult had its desired effect, though. The creature howled again with renewed blood-lust and redoubled its efforts to claw over the chest-high fence. Deep gouges festooned its naked body, but it ignored them all.

Finally, the rabid thing dropped ungracefully over the fence, picked itself up, and charged through the tall grass toward them. Good. Now, just a little farther—

Completely oblivious, the zombie rushed right past Achilles' hiding place. In a single fluid motion of canine magnificence, the dog leapt out of the grass and onto the zombie's back. Following his training, Achilles turned his head sideways as he landed so that his crushing jaws full of alligatorlike teeth clamped perfectly down on either side of the zombie's neck. The force of a hundred and twenty pounds of pure canine ferocity made the zombie face-plant in the grass. Before it could do so much as howl in anger, Achilles had snapped its neck, almost tearing the head from the body in the process. As soon as the body went limp, the dog released his adversary and bounded back up onto the road to rejoin them, all the while licking zombie blood from his snout.

Odysseus greeted his counterpart with a sniff and a longing whine.

"I know, I know, you old coot," Frank said. "Believe me, sometimes I wish I got more action too. But you had ambush last time. It was Achilles' turn." Frank wasn't replying to his dog for the sake of conversation. While he talked, his eyes scanned the field, waiting to see if any more zombies popped up in reaction to the noise. But nothing stirred, and his dogs resumed their relaxed patrol positions on either side of his mare, telling him loud and clear that they didn't smell any more zombies.

Frank huffed in satisfaction and re-slung his rifle, then clucked to his horse.

Any day that started out with killing zombies was a good day.

Gallrein Farms was an oddity in Maligator County. The dairy farm had been in the Gallrein family for generations, but with the recent industrialization of farming, small dairies across the U.S. had been squeezed dry and hundreds had closed down. But instead of folding, old Joe Gallrein had gotten creative. With an eye toward the rise in tourism and the increased interest in fresh, local, organic produce, Joe had expanded his operation to include a variety of products including vegetables, fruit, and flowers, and had opened up his farm to the public. Before the plague, he'd had a steady stream of visitors attending everything from school education programs, to weekly farmers' markets, to seasonal activities like the summer sweet corn festival and fall pumpkin pickings.

Now, all of that *should* have spelled Gallrein Farms' doom when the plague hit. Tourists meant a stream of potentially infected visitors. But by providence or just crazy good luck, that June Joe Gallrein's son, Ben, had major surgery while his wife, Barbara, gave birth to their fifth child. With all that going on, the old man had decided to close the farm to the public for a few weeks. By the end of the month, Frank had seen the writing on the wall and had convinced Joe to remain closed for the foreseeable future.

And it was a good thing he had.

It wasn't just that Gallrein Farms had milk cows or diverse vegetable gardens. It also had a large number of buildings capable of being converted into everything from refugee housing to a medical clinic, not to mention the greenhouses they already had for growing edibles through the winter, plus multiple generators, and a solar panel array to help keep everything running.

If Frank had been the one to start their little farm collective, Joe Gallrein had been the one to make it thrive. The old man—bless his heart, as Frank's mother had always said before she'd passed away—was the real deal. True country folk: reliable, hard-working, and with a heart of gold. Even though he was nearing his eighties, he still got up before dawn every morning to bring in the cows for milking.

Today, though, Joe wasn't working.

As Frank rode through Gallrein Farms' front gate, nodding to the sentry as he passed, he spotted the old man shaking hands at the entrance to the mess hall. It was really just the concrete-floored picnic area that they'd added walls to, but it served well to feed the farm hands and almost two dozen refugees who lived and worked there. Joe Gallrein's once portly belly no longer strained the seams of his usual blue jean overalls, but that was the only thing that had changed about him since the Fall. Currently, Joe was busy "politicking" as the old man jokingly called it. "Ain't no group'a people as ever stuck together who didn't need a leader," he'd said last summer when the farmers had met together for the first time. Frank was just relieved no one had tried to make *him* get up there and smile and talk to people. Nope. Give him dogs over people any day.

Frank watched the old man out of the corner of his eye as he tied his mare's lead to a nearby tree where she would have shade and a patch of grass to eat while she waited. "Achilles, Odysseus, heel," he said, then headed for the mess hall.

"Frank! Good to see you, boy," Joe said warmly as Frank approached. "You're the last to arrive. A couple of us wondered if you'd make it."

Frank nodded, amused as always at being called "boy" at his age. "Dogs scented a zombie on the way over. Took care of it."

A grave look came over Joe's face as he reached out to shake Frank's hand. "The night patrol took out two at dawn this morning that tried to get into the dairy pasture."

"You burn the bodies and wash the dogs down good?"

"As always, Frank."

Frank nodded, gave the old man's hand a squeeze, then headed for the door. Inside was a group of about twenty, primarily men but also some women. Most of the women in their community, both farm-wives and refugees alike, were either pregnant or nursing infants, so travel was especially dangerous and meetings weren't their top priority.

With a polite nod to anyone who met his eye and a handshake for the farmers he passed, Frank headed to one back corner with his dogs. He preferred to keep to himself, and he used the few minutes of solitude before the meeting started to reconsider a problem that constantly worried him.

Nobody really knew exactly how dangerous zombie fluids were. From what their sole medical professional could tell them—a certified midwife from town who had helped Barbara deliver her baby last June and had then been persuaded to stay—and from what they'd picked up on the radio waves, the airborne flu portion of the manufactured disease had long since broken down. Now the only risk was the blood-borne virus getting into your system. Any little cut or scrape could let it in, in theory. It was why Frank had trained his dogs to love being hosed down, plus he'd taught them a "wash" command. Frank had given it to Achilles and Odysseus on their way over as soon as they'd neared a creek. The dogs had gleefully hopped down into the water, rolled around, and generally gotten themselves completely soaked. It wasn't a perfect solution, but it was the only one they had.

The biggest problem was that nobody really knew who was immune and who wasn't. Between all the surviving members of their farming community and the refugees from nearby towns, about half of them had gotten flu-like symptoms at some point last summer, and survived. Many others hadn't survived, of course. Everyone had lost loved ones, whether to the plague, to zombies post-Fall, or to normal diseases they hadn't had medicine for. But nobody really knew who might have a true immunity to the zombie virus, and who had just survived a normal bout of the flu. They'd heard over the radio that a vaccine had been created, but of course only important people got it. Even if more was created, how would they get it to little ol' Shelbyville, Kentucky?

It was a problem, indeed. All that the farmers had felt capable of doing until now was simply surviving. Survive the zombies. Survive the winter. Survive the planting season. Survive the baby boom. But the radio broadcast yesterday had changed all of that.

"Thank y'all for coming on such short notice." Joe Gallrein's voice rose above the hum of voices in the mess hall and quiet descended. The old man perched atop a table at the head of the room with a grunt and nodded at some of the nearby men. "Duncan, Randy, Bob, glad you could make it. Weren't sure your missus could spare you."

"Spare me?" asked Frank's friend and neighbor Duncan LeCompte. "Today is baking day, and Jane always kicks me out of the house on baking day."

"Course she does," piped up Henry Coffee, one of their wheat farmers who sat in the back. "Otherwise you'd eat every darn thing the moment it came outta the oven."

Duncan looked back at Henry and gave a wide grin, showing off his tobacco-stained teeth. A chuckle rippled through those assembled, but quieted again at Joe's throat-clearing.

"I know we've all got work to do, so let's get started. Pastor, would you do the honors?" Joe asked Mr. Muller, one of the refugees. The man had often protested that he was only a Sunday school teacher. But he was as close as the community had to a pastor, and so he led a short, nondenominational service every Sunday morning in the mess hall for those who felt like attending.

Frank never did.

Everyone wearing a hat followed Joe's lead as he took off his old sweat-stained John Deere cap and bowed his head. Frank was glad he didn't wear a hat. He didn't have any respect left to give to God. Not after what had happened to Sandra.

"Our Father in Heaven," Mr. Muller began in a solemn voice. "Thank you for preserving the life of our Honorable President Rebecca Staba. We pray that you will be with Wolf Squadron and all the military units fighting to take back our country. We humbly ask that you protect us by your mighty hand, and give us wisdom as we seek to make our homes and cities safe once again. Amen."

A chorus of amens echoed him, and then Joe got things moving. "JJ, could you give us a summary of yesterday's broadcast, for them that might not have heard it?"

JJ, or Joe Jr., Barbara Gallrein's second oldest, was only sixteen. But in a zombie apocalypse, you grew up fast. He was mechanically inclined, and maintained Gallrein Farms' radio antenna they'd built with scavenged parts. JJ stood and began to recount the radio message. At his mention of President Staba, there was a general backslapping and quiet celebration among everyone gathered. The thought that their country still survived in any official form was the first bit of news that had given them real hope for the future.

When JJ was finished, Joe took the floor again. "Righty, so here's how I see it. The military may be clearing cities as fast as they can, but they're all the way on the east coast. It could be years before they make it here, and even if we've got food pretty well handled, we need medicine, bad."

There was a murmur of assent, and faces turned as people looked at each other, worry in their eyes. Just in the past few months the community had lost two women and three babies in childbirth, not to mention those they'd lost to seasonal flu and pneumonia over the winter. As if the cursed zombies weren't bad enough.

"That's not even considering our shortage of parts and fuel. The solar panels and stationary bikes help, but they can't meet all our energy needs. We need our electric fences to keep the livestock safe, plus JJ and Teddy might be darn good mechanics, but they can't fix what they ain't got parts for."

They had several working tractors to pull the various tillers and harvesters. Their noise in the fields drew in nearby zombies, but sharpshooters in portable deer stands took care of that. There was no telling when something critical might break, though, and once the machinery was out of commission, things would get a lot harder on everyone.

"Now, we know we can't do a darn thing 'bout Louisville," Joe continued. "They had near a million people last census, and we got barely over a hundred able bodies ourselves."

Sarah Gallrein, Barbara's oldest, raised a hand where she was sitting at the front of the mess. "Don't forget to do the math, Pops. They said over the radio that the survival rate is estimated at about five percent. Plus the death rate from the plague and from the initial chaos was estimated well over thirty percent. So that means there's only about 650,000 zombies in Louisville, not a million."

Old Joe raised his eyebrows and looked about to continue, but Sarah interrupted again.

"Oh! And don't forget that ice storm and week-long freeze in January. With winter weather and general cannibalism, that's bye-bye to a good twenty percent of the remainder. Realistically we're only looking at half a million zombies."

A few chuckles and a murmured "I allus said she was the smart one in the family" answered Sarah's summary.

"Well, I ain't no mathematician like my granddaughter here," Joe replied, a hint of humor in his voice, "but from where I'm sittin' half a mil or a mil don't make no difference to us. We're too few. Now, Shelbyville on the other hand . . ." He trailed off, then gave Sarah a "go on" gesture when she didn't immediately fill the silence.

"Oh, right, um, well I think Shelbyville had maybe fourteen thousand residents, so that leaves about seven thousand zombies."

A grim silence followed her words as each of them contemplated the number. It really wasn't that many people, Frank thought, considering cities like Louisville or, heck, New York. But still it was far, far too many. And after a year of defending themselves and hunting to keep everyone fed, their ammo stores were not up to such a task.

"Why the heck do we need to go pokin' the bear in the first place, huh?" said a voice in the middle of the mess hall. Percy Long had been a seasonal tobacco worker—at least that's what he'd told everyone when he'd showed up begging for food and shelter. He had a generally sour attitude that nobody liked, but he'd survived the quarantine period, and since then had kept out of trouble and done his share of the work, so nobody could complain. "Yeah, we get some leakers drifting out to the countryside. But they're no more'n a nuisance. If we're just talkin' roads to get in supplies, there's plenty'a backroads. Why risk our hides to do the military's job for 'em? Just leave the zombies be, I say. They'll die out sooner or later."

Several upraised voices cut off Joe's attempt to reply, some of them expressing contempt, others voicing similar concerns.

"Now calm down y'all! Didn't you hear what Joe was saying?" said a commanding voice. Ben Gallrein still walked with a limp, but he'd more or less recovered from his surgery last summer. As the general manager of Gallrein Farms, he was known for his level-headedness and common sense. "It ain't just an issue of roads. It could be *years* before any kind of relief reaches us, and we could all be dead by then. Without proper medicine, fuel, and parts, we're dangerously close to the edge, here. Plus, there are two other factors to consider. First, who knows how many other survivors are out there just barely hanging on? The more people we can rescue, the better our chances are. And second, didn't you hear what President Staba said? This isn't just about surviving anymore. It's about living. I don't know about y'all, but I've about had it with zombie this and zombie that. We've been careful for a year, and it's gotten us where we need to be. Now it's time to take back our town, and use the resources in it to rebuild our community."

Cheers greeted Ben's rousing words, but among them a voice was raised in protest.

"But more people means more mouths to feed and more chances of gettin' infected! Fightin' the zombies could wipe us all out if someone brings the plague back here where it's safe."

More arguing erupted, and Frank shook his head. He didn't really blame his neighbors. People were just scared. But fear never won any battles.

"Nobody's suggesting we wade in with clubs." Frank spoke up. His deep, gravelly voice cut through the clamor and people quieted. He didn't often speak at meetings, and many of the refugees were intimidated by him. Well, by his dogs. "Zombies have no survival instincts. It's why my dogs kill 'em so easy. But zombie killing is exhausting work, and the dogs can't take on big groups. We have to use our smarts and the tools we have to figure out some way to kill lots of the bastards at a time. So, who's got ideas?"

Silence greeted his words. There was a shuffle of a boot on concrete and someone coughed as the crowd's eyes roamed, some of them avoiding gazes, some of them staring far away in thought.

"Burn 'em?" Duncan offered around the wad of tobacco tucked into his cheek.

"Can't afford to," Ben said. "Fuel is too precious. Besides, we're trying to save our town and its resources, not burn it all down."

"What if we dug trenches and lured 'em in?" piped up someone else. "They can't climb worth a darn. They'll eat each other eventually."

Several heads nodded contemplatively.

"And who's gonna dig those trenches?" asked Sarah. "We have chores enough as it is keeping the farms going and patrolling. They'd need to be at least ten feet deep, if not more. Plus, how would we lure thousands of zombies into 'em?"

"Radios with big speakers?" JJ suggested.

His older sibling shook her head. "It wouldn't be loud enough. We'd have to dig the holes right in the middle of town for that and it would take days. The zombies would mob us while we worked."

"Pit traps might work in some limited circumstances," Gary Gaines chimed in. "But it isn't scalable enough." Gary was an avid hunter and a crack shot. He was also a big time stock broker—who'd have figured? They'd found him surviving out in the woods after he'd fled Shelbyville. "I know we don't have enough bullets left to kill seven thousand zombies, but we have plenty of saplings. Bows and arrows aren't that hard to make if all we need is crude, short-range killing machines. Teach a dozen men, set them up in strategic high places around Shelbyville with a fog horn or something like that. Rotate when they make noise, so when one is being loud, others can sneak to or from their locations. It'd be a target rich environment. Even if each man only killed ten zombies a day, that's almost a thousand in a week. We could clear out Shelbyville in two or three months."

"Oh, oh, oh! I volunteer to be a shooter!" JJ said, waving his hand in the air.

"Over Mom's dead body," Sarah said.

"Come on, I'm always stuck at home with the radio, it's not fair!"

"Zip it, you two," their father said before Sarah could retort. "It's not a bad idea, Gary. We might consider it if nothing else works. But that'd be pretty dangerous for the shooters, going into town every day for months at a time. Any other suggestions?"

There was a long silence.

"What about combines?"

Everyone in the room turned to look at Mary Smith, the quiet-spoken widow of one of the former tenant farmers they'd all affectionately called "Frog" for his round appearance, bullfroglike jowls, and booming voice.

"My Frog used to run all those gigantic planters and harvesters on Mr. Hornback's land just north. I worried every day he drove 'em that there'd be an accident and he'd get pulled into one or crushed underneath. Their tires alone are almost ten feet tall! And with those big contraptions on the front, they could take out zombies as easy as they take out corn or soybeans, couldn't they?"

This time the silence wasn't dubious or frightened. It was charged with energy.

Frank grinned. He'd always liked Mrs. Smith. She'd come to live in the Gallrein bunkhouse and study under Juliet, their midwife, after her husband was caught unawares by a pack of zombies in his fields late last year. She was a quiet sort, but with a mean streak a mile wide for anyone who threatened those she loved.

Joe called out to one of the seated men. "Teddy, whaddaya think? All that big machinery's been sittin' up in their barns since last summer. Could you get 'em started?"

Teddy Thomas, their only true mechanic, chewed his bottom lip, then shrugged. "Everythin' but the sprayer would'a already been in storage condition by late June since it's all seasonal equipment. And I figure a little tinkerin' outta get the sprayer up and workin'. But if you're thinkin' of using the combines to mow down zombies, they don't really work like that. Insides would get all gummed up with zombie parts and the engine would seize up."

"What if we disconnected the innards?" someone asked.

Teddy scratched his head. "Well... maybe." Then after another pause. "Yeah, I guess it might work. We could try, at any rate."

"Mowers." Frank's voice surprised everyone again, and all heads turned. "Not the little ones. The big, bat-wing ones they use along the interstate. They chew up anything that gets in their way. Did Mr. Hornback have one of those? Take the guards off and any zombie that got close would get cut in half."

"Sweeeeet."

The sound of JJ's awed delight made Frank grin again. A kid after his own heart.

At that point multiple voices chimed in, each bringing up more giant and potentially lethal pieces of equipment that could be weaponized. JJ even suggested they go all Ash Williams from Evil Dead and put a couple of guys in hazmat suits in the back of a pickup truck wielding chainsaws. Unsurprisingly, no one took the teenager's proposal seriously.

By the end of the meeting, though, they had pulled bits and pieces from almost everyone's ideas to make the bare bones of a plan that might just work. It had a lot of moving parts, and there were several months of preparations in front of them. But if it worked, even if it only did half as well as they hoped, it was a start.

They decided on August 27th for Operation Death Parade. They chose August because it was Kentucky's driest and hottest month, and the 27th because it was the anniversary of the by now legendary Last Concert of New York. It was one of the oft-told tales on Devil Dog radio whenever talk turned to the origins of Shewolf. Personally, Frank suspected many of the details were vastly exaggerated, but that was all right. Morale was important, and if they were going to take back the world from the darkness that threatened to swallow them all, then everybody needed something—or someone—to believe in, even him.

He believed in his dogs.

The first order of business was to set up a base of operations in the Hornback's barnyard. The Hornbacks had owned one of the largest farms in the entire state—well over three thousand acres—before the plague had gotten to them. The gigantic, graveled barnyard was where Frank had led one of his first scavenging parties after the phones went down and no one had heard from the Hornbacks in several weeks. Frank hadn't let his dogs take out the poor, zombified family. He'd done it himself with one clean shot each. They'd buried the dead, taken what stores they could carry, and locked everything up tight. But even in death, the Hornbacks did their part to protect the community, as their farm served as a vital source of fuel, parts, and equipment that Joe Gallrein lacked.

Now, though, it was time to open up shop again.

All the big equipment—tractors, planters, combines, even a massive bulldozer—was safely stored in two huge twenty-five-foot-high, concrete-floored barns. Teddy had winterized everything that had needed it before last winter, so they were optimistic he could get it all up and running again. Now, whether or not they had all the tools and materials for their planned "modifications" was another matter entirely.

It took Frank and several refugee volunteers two days to set up the electric fence around the barnyard. The noise of Teddy's work would be bound to draw in any stray zombie for several miles. Frank had even volunteered to shack up in the biggest barn with some of his dogs for the duration, to keep an eye on the place, while Maggie stayed with Mrs. Rogers to look after their farm.

By the beginning of July, they'd confirmed they had enough materials and working machines to enact their plan. So Teddy and his two "in training" assistants got to work in earnest.

In the meantime, as Frank had heard, Gary Gaines had been busy. The hunting fanatic was happy as a bear with a pot of honey to put all his weapons know-how to good use. With a workshop full of welders, grinders, and several kinds of saws at his disposal, he discarded his bow idea in favor of crossbows, as they were easier for beginners to master. With JJ's help, he had a dozen crossbows and hundreds of bolts made within a few weeks. After testing their efficiency on a few zombies that strayed too close to Gallrein Farms, he pronounced the crossbows a success, though only headshots reliably stopped the zombies entirely. For the weeks it took to modify the machinery, Frank had heard all about the exploits of Gary's recruits—which excluded JJ, much to the teenager's disappointment—as they practiced an hour or two every day on straw dummies. They had unlimited ammo, and it wasn't as tiring as training on bows, since each crossbow had a special lever for pulling back the string.

The machinery modifications, while successful as a whole, took all of Teddy's ingenuity and the collective experience of the entire community to complete. Fortunately, most farmers were jacks-of-all-trades, and several of the refugees were blue-collar professionals of one sort or another.

While all the crafting, machining, and target practice was going on, Frank was busy with his scouting team.

Reggie and Russell Dale were brothers, bachelors, and longtime hunting buddies of Frank's. He'd called them last summer as soon as he'd started prepping and had offered them refuge if they brought with them all the guns and ammo they could possibly carry. They'd settled in at Gallrein Farms to train more shooters and help with guard duty. There was no one Frank would rather have at his back. The three of them went on several exploratory missions into town to scavenge supplies for the operation and survey the field of battle. They avoided engaging with the zombies, knowing that even a single creature's hunting howls could quickly draw a mob from every nook and cranny. Frank's dogs were invaluable for helping them avoid groups and lurkers. As long as their team moved silently and stayed out of sight, they could sneak from building to building. Meanwhile, Frank's dogs eliminated any isolated zombies they could catch unaware, attacking like silent angels of death with alligator jaws.

Near the end of August when it hadn't rained for weeks and daily temperatures soared to the nineties, they finally began stage one of their plan.

The first thing that had to happen was road clearance. The Hornbacks had owned a massive bulldozer that they'd used to clear pathways between fields for their industrial harvesters. Joe Gallrein himself volunteered to drive it, using it to shove aside cars and large debris from the route they had chosen. When multiple people insisted it was "too dangerous" and he was "too old," he'd simply asked who else knew how to operate a bulldozer and then grinned cheekily into the deafening silence. Still, they all worried about him, and Teddy had gone crazy adding various protective shields and an indestructible cage of wire hog panels to surround the glass-enclosed cab.

Frank was part of the "backup rescue team" that kept in radio contact with Joe while he worked. Though he reported a sizable crowd was drawn to the sound of his engine as he made his way through town, none of them managed to scale the eleven-foot dozer—as a general rule, zombies weren't smart or coordinated enough to climb anything that mindless scrabbling wouldn't get them over. He left a nice trail of squashed bodies in his wake, which would begin the process of drawing more zombies into the center of town. It was tricky extracting him, as they didn't want to waste their precious supply of diesel driving the crawler all the way back to the farm. So Joe left it on the northern outskirts of town and slipped into one pickup while another drove around and honked to distract the dwindling crowd that had followed the dozer out of Shelbyville.

The second part of stage one required more stealth. Fortunately, the moon was almost full by then, and with the clear skies they had enough illumination to drive without headlights.

Frank had never done much with pesticides before— he used his goats for weed control. So he learned all sorts of new things the night they staged two large metal water troughs at the crossroads of Highway 53 and U.S. 60, just at the eastern end of Shelbyville. It turned out that paraquat dichloride, a weed killer used by industrial farmers, was so poisonous that even a single sip could kill you; and there had been plenty of it at the Hornback's farm. They filled up the troughs with half water, half paraquat, then set up a battery-powered lantern and old CD player nearby, turning both on right before hightailing it out of town. With any luck it would attract a good-sized mob of thirsty zombies, who would drop dead close to the water and draw in even more zombies with their freshly dead meat.

The morning of August 27th dawned bright and sunny, and as Frank stood on his front porch scanning the woodline for deer, he could honestly say he was looking forward to a good ol' country parade. Teddy and his assistant mechanics had spent the last week living in the barns with their pet projects, so he'd been able to go back to sleeping in his own bed.

Maggie joined him on the porch once she'd fed the night pack. For some reason he just stood there, watching the morning sun turn the tops of the verdant green trees a glowing gold.

"Dad..." Maggie began, but then trailed off.

Frank's reverie was broken and he raised the hand not holding his coffee to give his daughter's shoulder a brief squeeze. "We'll be fine, Mags. The dogs have been rarin' for a really good fight. They'll have the time of their lives and we'll be home before you know it."

"I—I know, Dad. I *am* worried about you, and everyone else, of course. But...that's not what I wanted to say." She fell silent, and the silence stretched on until Frank wished he could force his feet to move, taking him off the porch to the uncomplicated solitude of the kennel.

"You know...you know what happened to Mom wasn't your fault, right?"

Frank gritted his teeth as guilt and loss stabbed like daggers into his chest. "I don't want to talk about it."

"I know," Maggie replied, her voice quiet. She slipped her fingers through his, holding him fast and preventing his escape. "But it's not your fault. And no matter how many zombies you kill, it won't bring her back."

"Not why I kill 'em."

"I know that, Dad. I know we have to kill those poor, poor people. I know they have to die for us survivors to live. But at the same time ... I don't want you hating them while you kill them. It isn't right."

"Right or wrong doesn't matter anymore, Maggie. This is the f—the freaking end of the world. If God was ever around, he's not anymore."

"You don't believe that, Dad. Not really. Otherwise you wouldn't have worked so hard to set up our community to survive this horror."

"If I'd known I'd bring back the plague to kill your mother and almost kill you, I wouldn't have done it. Would've left every damn one of them to die on their own." Frank's gravelly voice ached with bitterness, but even as he said the words, he knew what Maggie would say, and that she would be right.

"You don't mean that either, Dad. Semper Fidelis, right?" She squeezed his hand, and he felt his eyes burning. "You took every precaution you could. It's not your fault it somehow skipped you and took hold of Mom so hard. And I have you to thank that I survived it. You and your stubborn, ornery genes that would probably survive anything short of a dirty bomb."

Despite himself, Frank's lip twitched.

"Just ... just promise me you'll try, Dad? Promise me you'll try to have a little pity in your heart, while you kill them? Maybe say a prayer or two? None of this is their fault; none of them deserve to die. Please?"

After a long moment of silence, Frank let out a breath. "I'll try."

"Thanks, Dad," Maggie said, then stood on tiptoe and kissed his cheek. "And you'd better be careful. I need someone to help me train all these goofball pups that you've foisted on me. I can't have my best training assistant getting all eaten up by zombies."

Frank snorted. Assistant? That smart-aleck teenager. He looked down at her and she grinned cheekily up at him. With a shake of his head, he extracted his hand, ruffled her hair, then took the porch steps two at a time as he hurried off to get his dogs ready for battle.

If you grew up in a big city, it was likely you'd go your whole life without witnessing a small town country parade. The kind with tractors pulling tobacco wagons full of candy-throwing 4-H'ers, pickup trucks trailing red, white, and blue streamers, homemade floats driven by riding mowers, and, of course, the ubiquitous fire trucks. Whether it was the Fourth of July, Labor Day, Veterans Day, or the local Pumpkin festival, country towns loved putting on a good parade.

The citizens of Maligator County were no exception, with one small difference: they weren't looking to entertain their audience. They were looking to squash them into zombie paste.

Frank's black pickup was the lead vehicle, with Duncan at the wheel and Frank, his dogs, and Reggie and Russell in the truck bed. It was as hot as hell under the August sun, but the three in the back wore firefighter coveralls, helmets, and goggles anyway, since they hadn't been able to find any unused hazmat suits. The truck itself was outfitted with a sturdy grille guard to protect the front, and like in all the vehicles in their parade, the glass-enclosed cab was protected by welded hog panels. They'd taken the camper off the back to install a seven-foot-tall cage made of more hog panels layered with wire fencing to keep zombies from reaching in. And just in case they got stuck in a swarm, they had two heavy-duty propane torches, ready to melt the face off of any zombie who got close.

Position two would be held by Joe with his now-beloved bulldozer, once the cavalcade neared town and he could get it fired up. His job was to "soften up the crowd" as he put it, and break apart any solid packs of zombies that formed behind the lead truck. For this occasion, the bulldozer's blade would be tilted forward to funnel zombies underneath its crushing bulk.

Third in their grand parade was a 9630 John Deere tractor driven by Randy Davis, a tobacco farmer who'd spent his life behind a tractor wheel, if never one quite so big. The twelve-foot monster he operated was one of the largest on the market and was fitted with a double row of tires nearly eight feet high and two feet wide each. Welded to a frame affixed to the tractor's protruding hood was an honest to God biplane engine and propeller that Teddy had found who knew where. The mechanic had sharpened its blades to a razor edge and it ran at full steam, preceding the tractor like a whirlwind of death. Any zombies smart enough to avoid it would be greeted by the heavy-duty, twenty-foot wide bat-wing mower the tractor pulled behind it. Every guard had been removed and every metal cover had been cut to the bare minimum needed to maintain the mower's structural integrity. What was left was four interlocking vortexes of three-foot blades spinning at over fifty times per second. Any zombie unfortunate enough to come into contact with it would be instantly reduced to mincemeat.

Following about twenty yards behind the tractor to avoid most of the blood and guts splatter was a 9870 STS combine outfitted with a soybean air-reel, also with its guards removed. The massive, twenty-five-foot contraption consisted of rows upon rows of spikes spinning forward and downward, meant to feed soybean stalks into the combine's internal harvesting mechanisms. For Operation Death Parade, however, the harvesting system had been disconnected so that only the air-reel turned, ready to hook any charging zombies and throw them beneath the sixteen-ton behemoth. Unlike the shorter tractor and bulldozer, this fifteen-foot-high piece of machinery had smooth unscalable sides, though they did remove the cab access ladder, just in case. Perched high up in the driver seat was none other than Mary Smith. She had insisted on learning how to operate it, in memory of her husband. Teddy, who had a soft spot for her, hadn't been able to say no.

As an added protection, and to up the parade's swath of destruction, Mary's combine also had a dozen passengers. Gary Gallrein and his posse of crossbow-men, decked out in home-made riot gear, face masks, goggles, and hard hats, crowded around the top edge of the combine. Each was secured to the roof by a harness, and each carried a glut of crossbow bolts.

Bringing up the rear in fine form was a 4830 John Deere sprayer, driven by Billy "Blue" Reardon, one of the Hornback's few surviving tenant farmers who had experience driving industrial agriculture equipment. What the sprayer lacked in terms of protective spinning blades it made up for with an underside that began eight feet in the air, high enough to drive over Frank's pickup truck with ease. It was so tall that they'd worried about it getting tangled up in the street lights, but Frank's scouting had confirmed it would just barely scrape by underneath them. The sprayer was a special touch for all the zombie latecomers to their parade. Not only would it rain down poison into the open mouths of the howling masses running after it like mindless lemmings, but it would also cover every bit of meat and offal the parade left behind with deadly pesticide. Any zombie that fed off the pitiable fallen would soon be embraced by death themselves.

Finally, since no country parade was complete without them, every vehicle was hung with an American flag, most of them hand-made by the pregnant women and new mothers who weren't able to help with the other preparations. Frank had heard about, though thankfully avoided, the dedication service Pastor Muller had held to pray over the flags and dedicate the souls they were about to release to the Lord. Personally, he figured if God had cared at all, he wouldn't have allowed the bastard who'd engineered the virus to have been born in the first place. But he kept his opinion to himself.

At 10 AM sharp, the parade began five miles northeast of Shelbyville, exiting from the Hornback's barnyard onto the cleared expanse of Highway 43. A team had already delivered Joe to his armored bulldozer, and he joined the parade as it turned from 43 West onto 53 South just north of town. By that time they'd already attracted a sizable crowd of naked, emaciated pursuers, drawn from the surrounding countryside by the rumble of engines.

The sight of the stumbling, groaning, empty-eyed people sent the first pang of pity through Frank that he'd felt since he'd been forced to shoot his wife. They were little more than skeletons, and their sunburned skin was covered in cuts, bruises, and sores. He tried not to look too closely, lest he recognize one of them as a long-lost neighbor. The horror—and necessity—of what they were about to do, finally settled over him.

These people deserved better. They deserved peace. And death was the only way Frank could give it to them, so give it he would.

As they neared the horse trough baited crossroads, Frank's truck pulled ahead of the main parade. They took a detour through the local Tractor Supply on the corner so as to avoid the large crowd around the water troughs that feasted on the piles of corpses filling up the intersection. Just before they pulled back out onto the road, they paused to let out Frank's dogs. Then they set off again down Main Street at an easy five miles an hour, headed west to the center of town.

The pickup led the main "Death Parade" by a good hundred yards. Their team's job was to draw the zombies into Main Street from the surrounding buildings and make sure there was as big a crowd as possible for their parade to dispatch—they only had enough fuel to do this once. To that end they had affixed a salvaged police car siren to the roof, and Frank was putting three pairs of dogs to work: Achilles and Odysseus, Thor and Loki, and Fred and George. All his dogs were trained to operate independently once they'd gotten the "seek and destroy" command, and working in pairs meant they could protect each other from surprise attacks, while Frank, Reggie, and Russell provided overwatch protection from the truck bed.

The police siren did its job well—perhaps too well. Zombies flocked to Main Street like children to the Pied Piper's flute, gathering much more swiftly and in greater numbers than Joe had reported on his initial clearing run. Duncan had to occasionally stomp on the gas and ram through the crowds that tried to form around them. The dog teams helped with that too, orbiting the truck in a wide circle, constantly moving, dodging, and snarling as they took down zombies and provided a distraction that kept the monsters from clustering on just one target.

Their combined efforts left a nice scattering of corpses in the street, which attracted even more zombies and redirected many who fell to feeding. Those, in turn, were attacked by their opportunistic companions, leading to a Main Street so crowded by fighting and feasting zombies that Frank worried their parade had taken on more than it could chew. He barely had time to consider it, however, because he was too busy sniping zombies off his dogs. Reggie and Russell had abandoned their guns and were busy using the blow torches to keep their truck from being completely swarmed.

By the time they were in the middle of historic downtown Shelbyville with the city square on their left and the towering court house on their right, Frank could tell they were in deep trouble. All he could see around them was a solid mass of zombies even as more flooded in from every side street. It seemed like the entire city population had migrated inward over the past week, drawn by the fresh meat and water, and had been hiding just out of sight from the hot August sun until their parade arrived. Duncan tried to rev the engine and push clear of the crowd, but the mass of bodies simply absorbed their forward momentum. Soon their tires were spinning uselessly in a quagmire of zombie blood and guts.

Frank stopped shooting and grabbed for his walkie-talkie. "Joe? Joe, come in, we need some clearance help, we're being overrun here." Even though he knew he was shouting, he could barely hear his own voice over the siren, and no matter how hard he pressed the walkie-talkie to his ear, he could detect no reply. He didn't dare remove his ear protection.

As he tried a few more times to raise Joe, zombies began clawing over each other, gaining the truck hood, then the roof. With a string of curses nobody could hear, Frank dropped his hunting rifle and walkie-talkie and snatched up his Mossberg 500 pump-action shotgun. He poured shot after shot into the mob, reloading with practiced ease from the bandolier slung across his chest. His fire shredded faces and chests pressed against the hog panels of their cage, but for every zombie that fell away, another clawed into its place. Duncan belatedly turned off their siren, but it was too little, too late, and he could do nothing to help but hunker down inside the cab and pray.

Frank couldn't see his dogs or hear the shouts of his men through the raging howl of zombies. All three of them stood back to back, desperately burning or blasting away the bodies that were literally burying their truck. Zombie blood splattered them like paint and dripped down onto their helmets from above. Only the layered fencing kept the zombies from reaching through to yank them against the bars and bite or tear them to pieces. Even though the hog panels had been welded and tied down as tight as Fort Knox, the insane, single-minded fury of so many zombies was rocking the entire truck on its wheels and Frank had no idea how long the cage would last.

Seconds crawled by like hours as building panic assaulted Frank's single-minded focus. He held on, until his fingers felt for his next shell and found only the empty loops of his bandolier. He dropped to a crouch and looked for his rifle, but could barely see through his blood-splattered safety goggles. Everything around him was covered in gore. Where was his rifle?

Something hit the truck hard from behind, and Reggie and Russell tumbled down on top of him, sending them all sprawling into the muck at their feet. Frank was suddenly aware of the deep growl of a massive engine close by, a sound he felt through the vibrating truck bed more than heard with his ears.

All three men remained prone as their truck was shoved forward, bumping and sliding over zombie bodies as more of the things tumbled from the truck roof and were jostled from the sides of the cage.

By the time the truck had reached clear pavement, enough of the zombies had disappeared that Frank could see up into the cab of Joe's bulldozer that had just excavated them out of an inescapable scrum of ravenous monsters. The old man gave him a jaunty salute and a wink, then picked up his walkie-talkie.

"Quit goofing around there, you young whippersnapper. We've got work to do!" the muffled squawk of Joe's voice came from somewhere in the truck bed. Frank scrambled to his feet, swiped his messy goggles with the back of a hand, then helped Reggie and Russell up. Duncan took advantage of the brief respite to get the truck going before the zombies had a chance to mob them again, and all three of them held on as the vehicle surged forward.

Looking back, Frank could see the mass of zombies reforming around the bulldozer. But unlike Frank's "puny" truck, the beast of a crawler was barely even fazed by the press. It trundled on, flattening every zombie in front of it. The naked bodies pressed against the sides, trying to go under or over the protective metal sheets. But all that did was get them caught in the treads and crushed or flung toward the rear of the machine.

One zombie had managed to mount the cab, possibly having climbed up from the back, or gotten lucky and flung there from the top of Frank's truck when Joe had rammed it. But even as Frank watched, a crossbow bolt sprouted from between the zombie's eyes and it fell, bounced off the treads, and disappeared into the mass of its fellows.

Once they'd pulled ahead of the parade, Duncan finally turned their siren back on. But instead of slowing to resume their previous pace, he changed tactics. He kept their speed at a steady twenty miles per hour and started doing laps around each block, first to the left, then to the right. Their constant movement kept them from getting bogged down, even if the zombies they attracted to Main Street were a bit more spread out than before.

As soon as they were out of danger, Frank took

stock of his dogs. After a few blocks, he managed to spot Thor, Loki, and Achilles. But Odysseus was missing from his packmate's side, and Fred and George were nowhere to be seen. Frank's eyes burned, and for the first time in his life he hoped to God it was because he was crying. Otherwise, it meant some bodily fluid like zombie blood might have gotten under his goggles and into his eyes. He busied himself shooting zombies instead of thinking about what might happen to him and his gore-splattered men in a day or two. Everyone had known the risk, going in, and they'd done their best to prepare. It didn't matter now that it might not be enough.

As his old platoon leader, Gunnery Sergeant Payne, used to say, "Focus on the moment you have, not the moment you might lose. You'll live longer that way."

As they neared the end of Main Street, Frank informed Duncan of a little change of plans over the walkie-talkie, then used his electric collar remote to call in his dogs. The fight had been much more intense than they'd anticipated, and as few bullets as they had, bullets were easier to replace than trained patrol dogs.

Where Main Street merged into its parallel twin Washington Street, Duncan executed a U-turn and stopped just long enough for the three remaining canines to hop into the pickup bed. Then he took off again, this time down Washington Street heading back the way they'd come. Frank's other dogs were nowhere to be seen, but just in case, Frank sent a "go home" signal to their collars. He hoped against hope they had simply fallen behind and would obey this new command. The kind of dogs he trained were beasts of unsurpassed courage, and if they thought their alpha needed them, they would happily fight until their last breath.

The predetermined route for Operation Death Parade had the entire convoy turning around at the merging of streets and proceeding back east up Washington Street. This would take advantage of the crowd they'd already attracted and give them more area to poison, maximizing the long-term death toll.

Once again, Duncan drove in laps, keeping their speed up while not drawing too far ahead of the parade. They only sniped zombies when they circled back to Washington Street, ensuring the feeding frenzies stayed focused where the big machinery could take care of them. Frank couldn't see all the way down the line behind them, but Mary Smith's combine was tall enough that Gary and his crossbowmen were clearly visible atop it.

He was just glancing back again when he saw Gary rise to shift position at the same moment the combine's engine caught on something and stuttered, jerking the entire machine and sending Gary pitching forward off the corner of the roof. The man's tether held for a moment, and then it parted, sending him slipping and sliding down the side of the combine to the zombie infested ground below.

Frank grabbed his walkie-talkie.

"Duncan! Shut off the siren and turn around, now! Gary just fell off the north side of the combine."

Though his heart hammered in his chest, Frank focused with steely intensity, seeking that unnatural calm of battle once more as he assessed the situation.

Duncan, showing a surprising amount of driving

skill, managed a mid-street U-turn without flipping the big truck, and raced back toward the convoy, knocking aside zombies like bowling pins as he jumped the sidewalk to get around Joe's bulldozer and Randy's tractor. Within seconds, the side of the combine was visible.

But Gary was nowhere to be seen.

As soon as Frank's call had gone out over the open walkie-talkie channel, the entire convoy had slowed. Frank had to make several decisions very fast. He could only hope he made the right ones.

"Everybody, get those machines moving again, now! You need to draw the zombies away from Gary." Thankfully, the drivers obeyed his barked command without question, and he switched his attention to Duncan. "Duncan, I don't see Gary in the street. He probably hit the ground running and is trying to get as far away from this mob as possible. Circle the block and let's see if we can scoop him up."

What he didn't say was that, while he didn't see any Gary-shaped piles of zombies here, that didn't mean the man wasn't already being ripped to pieces somewhere else.

Duncan took the street corner sharply, sending them up 8th Street and away from the main mob. Frank did his best to keep his balance as he knelt by his remaining dogs.

"Achilles, Thor, Loki. Seek human and guard. Got it? Seek human and guard." It was a combination of commands he hadn't used together before, but his dogs were smart. They knew how to seek, they knew what a human was as opposed to a zombie, and they had been well-trained to guard people. As Duncan slowed slightly to take the next corner, Frank unlatched the cage's door and all three of his dogs leapt down and raced off. A few zombies followed after, but the dogs ignored them, loping northwest in a zigzag pattern with their noses raised to the wind.

Frank put the walkie-talkie to his mask once again. "Duncan, I sent the dogs to seek, follow them."

It was fortunate they had the dogs' noses, otherwise they never would have found Gary in time. The man had indeed booked it as soon as he'd hit the ground, because in the barely sixty seconds it had taken them to turn around and make it back to where he'd fallen, he was already two blocks north. With the dogs to guide them, however, they hadn't wasted any precious time circling the block, but followed the canine noses up ninth street toward Northside Elementary School. They found Gary stuck on the fence surrounding the playground. He'd obviously tried to scale it to put a barrier between him and the dozen zombies that had followed him, but one had caught hold of his foot before he could get over, and now his leg was bent at an unnatural angle as half a dozen zombies grabbed for him at once.

Achilles, Thor, and Loki hit the howling group like three furred battering rams. Before the zombies could react, three of them were already dead. Even as half the group turned their attention to this new source of meat, the dogs had jumped on three new targets and were in the process of dispatching them when Duncan screeched up in Frank's truck. Russell and Reggie jumped down first and immediately started taking out the scattered zombies closing in on multiple sides, drawn by the hunting howls of their fellows. Meanwhile, Frank scrambled out and around the truck and went to town with his shotgun, a fresh bandolier of shells slung across his chest. He aimed for knees, dropping the four zombies clawing at Gary to the ground so he could blow their brains out without hitting Gary in the process. Within seconds the group around Gary was dead to a man, and Frank rushed to help his friend off the fence and into the truck.

Frank held the rear as Russell and Reggie scrambled awkwardly back up onto the tailgate. But as they reached down to help him up, a whine and bark of pain met Frank's ears. He turned toward it, shotgun raised, to find three zombies tearing into Loki a dozen yards away even as Achilles and Thor fought with two others nearby.

Murderous rage propelled Frank forward, but his two men caught his shoulders and dragged him back to the truck, struggling and shouting. More zombies were running toward the commotion and Frank knew his dogs would soon be overwhelmed. He yelled at them to heel, but Achilles and Thor fought on, refusing to leave their packmate. Belatedly, Frank dug into his bulky pocket and found his electric collar remote. As he let Russell and Reggie pull him up onto the tailgate, he sent a strong shock to the collars, breaking his dogs' single-minded need to attack even as he yelled himself hoarse for them to retreat.

Finally, just as Duncan stomped on the gas to get them out of there, the two dogs broke off and raced back toward their alpha. They must have been exhausted beyond belief after fighting so hard, but they still managed to catch up to the truck and leap onto the tailgate before Duncan picked up much speed. Frank and the others helped drag them back into the cage where the poor animals flopped down onto their sides and lay there panting desperately. Russell took charge of the walkie-talkie to link up with Joe and the convoy while Frank busied himself checking his dogs for injuries.

He didn't look back at the feasting mob of zombies as they sped away.

Sarah Gallrein estimated afterwards that they'd crushed, chopped up, or otherwise incapacitated a little over three thousand zombies with their deadly parade. Several thousand more would have died soon after from primary poisoning, and another thousand from feasting off those initially poisoned. The first heavy rain would wash most of the pesticide away, but for the moment it was killing every living thing that tried to feast on the mounds of dead, including packs of feral dogs and flocks of vultures.

Frank, perhaps thanks to his famously stubborn genes, survived. Reggie, too, remained healthy in quarantine. Russell, unfortunately, did not. He turned within twenty-four hours, and Reggie was the one to give him lasting peace with a single bullet, honoring his brother the only way he could. All the drivers and crossbowmen had been successfully protected from contamination by airtight glass or simple elevation. Of course, they burned all their clothes and left every bit of gore-splattered machinery in an unused field far away from human contact, just in case.

Gary, miraculously, did not turn. His home-made riot gear had protected him from any scrapes or cuts, and had remained splatter free. Unfortunately, the zombies that had caught him on the fence had dislocated his knee and torn multiple ligaments. Without access to complicated surgeries or physical therapy, he was guaranteed to walk with a limp for the rest of his life. He jokingly said he didn't mind, since he didn't need his leg to pull a trigger.

Frank spent the quarantine week after Operation Death Parade in a silent daze. He'd lost brothers in arms before. He'd had to shoot his own wife. But he had never lost a dog in the line of duty.

Now he'd lost four.

Achilles was taking it just as hard, refusing to leave Frank's side and hardly eating or drinking. Not even news that the community had voted to rename Washington Street, Braveheart Boulevard could penetrate the darkness eating at him.

Once quarantine was over, Frank returned to his farm and his duties, performing each daily chore mechanically. Maggie took over training the dogs. They had stopped responding to him the way they should, and a part of him knew it was because he had withdrawn. He had pulled back from his position as alpha, as if by distancing himself from his dogs, he could distance himself from the pain. Only Achilles stuck by him.

A second week passed, and the farmers began preparations for the September harvest. No one spoke to Frank about the Death Parade, but he overheard Maggie and Mrs. Rogers talking about how Joe was working on bulldozing away the carrion and digging a mass grave, with plans for a memorial service to commemorate the thousands of dead. There was talk, too, of a monument being erected in the center of town. Frank even heard news of more survivors being found by the day, finally freed from their hiding places by the precipitous drop in the zombie population.

He tried to be happy. Tried to care. Mostly he just felt nothing.

A third week began.

Routine was the only thing that kept him going. Every morning was the same. Coffee. Rifle. Porch. It was so dry that he hadn't seen any deer in weeks, but that morning, inexplicably, he saw movement along the treeline. It was a moment before training took over from the surprise, and he set his mug down on the railing to raise his rifle to his shoulder.

What he saw through his scope made him drop his antique firearm to the ground as if it were a worthless piece of firewood. The clatter brought Achilles' head up from where he lay by Frank's feet. Then the dog spotted what Frank had seen and took off like a shot.

Frank bounded down the steps after his dog and ran for all he was worth, feet pounding on the gravel drive. The pair of figures he'd seen come out of the woods did not speed up to greet him. They kept their pace steady, sticking close to a third figure that limped between them.

Achilles reached the group first and leapt about, barking like a two-month-old pup without a lick of training.

When Frank finally reached them, he fell to his knees and gripped Fred and George around their scruffy, muddy, burr-tangled necks, then leaned his head down to touch forehead to forehead with Odysseus. All three dogs held their composure for a moment, sensing their alpha's need. But soon excitement broke through their training and they mobbed him with licks, their entire bodies wagging with the force of their joy.

Frank laughed. He actually laughed. He might have

cried too, but he wasn't really sure. He was too busy attempting to breathe through the assault of tongues and trying to make Odysseus sit still long enough for him to assess the dog's injuries.

Eventually, he gave up and sat back on his rear, content to simply scratch as many necks and ears as he could reach. He heard the front door slam and Maggie's shriek of joy. Then the day and night packs arrived, diving into the fray with yips of excited greeting. By the time Maggie joined them, Frank was flat on his back, covered in dogs, and couldn't think of a single moment when he'd been happier.

Maybe God cared after all.

Fire in the Sky

MICHAEL Z. WILLIAMSON &
STEPHANIE OSBORN

The zombies were dying out.

They weren't really zombies, of course, but the infected people acted pretty much like them. The Kennedy Space Center village hadn't had a sighting in two weeks. The surrounding enclaves reported similar results. The catastrophic collapse seemed to finally have hit a trough.

The workers, including the NASA civil servants and contractors, and the SpaceX people, had survived by being surrounded by water and swamp, judicious use of barricades, and some gunfire. Their stock in trade was technical knowledge. Their neighboring survivors got help with power and equipment, and in turn, they got food to supplement the fish they traded from off the coast and from the Banana and Indian Rivers, and the fresh water they made from a large still in a support building just off the beach.

At heart, though, they were space scientists, and habits persist.

Pete Adams was the newly made mayor. He'd been a senior engineer at KSC on the Flow Team, responsible for spacecraft prep for launch. But the virus pretty much put paid to the upper management. Now he was mayor. The council decision was a mixed election/appointment. He had the technical chops to handle the engineering side, and they decided based on past experience in the field that he could coordinate with the locals.

Today he was meeting with the boatmen who brought in seafood, and transported stuff from the mainland. It was often easier to use water, and had been a lot safer with the infected about. Now they were a bit less necessary, but it wouldn't do to just brush them off.

The boats were everything from pontoons to a small trawler. The crews mostly lived on them these days.

"There are still supplies and transport we'll need," he reassured them. "We're not ending our professional relationship. It's going to be different, though, as more road traffic resumes."

One of them, bald-headed under his bandana and slightly creased from the sun said, "Until the other bridges are repaired. Then what?"

"Then we hope to have other work lined up. We don't want to piss off our neighbors who've done this much for us. Also, we like to have a balance. A couple of the villages want exclusives and to toll the roads. If we all negotiate, we all come out ahead."

"Fair enough. But we're not going to slash rates, either. Diesel costs money, and so do repairs."

"We can keep helping with both."

It was almost colonial-era barter, in the twenty-first century. That's how far they'd fallen.

"Good enough. Thanks for meeting with us, Mr. Mayor."

After that meeting, back in Launch Control, which was as good a place as any to use as headquarters, he got paged.

"Hey, Pete," Assistant Manager Melanie Carter called. "We got a response."

"Huh?" Pete wondered, looking up from the console. When someone had suggested they pick one of the missions in the VAB and actually launch it, he'd ended up on the top of the totem pole, hence his position now. And of the spacecraft in the VAB, the one closest to launch readiness turned out to be the Hina mission. But that didn't mean Adams was on top of things as launch director yet, so he was face-down in the old training documentation. "Stepped in what, now?"

"JPL, dufus," Carter said with a slight snort. "They responded to our ping. They think it's a great idea. They're a little, uh, down in terms of staff right now, but the critical people—at least, for our purposes—seem to have survived."

"Good!" Adams decided. "What can they give us?"

Carter glanced at her clipboard.

"Well, it turns out that their orbital mechanics people have been keeping up with the . . . what the hell do I call it, Pete? Is this thing an asteroid, or a planet, or what?"

"Kinda half baby planet, half super comet," Adams said. "As near as I understood it, like a lot of KBOs, it's a little of both. The astronomy types call it a dwarf planet. It's just an exobody of some kind. Like, interstellar, coming through for a visit. That's the important part."

She nodded. "Okay. So anyway, their orbits guys have been keeping up with it, because they've been cooped up, and bored stiff when they weren't scared to death, I guess. Which means they have the current location of this..." She glanced at her clipboard to get the nomenclature right, "8I/(845982) Hina—I'm not even gonna ask what all that means—as of right now, and they have a better, current trajectory for it."

"Where is it?"

"Right out there," Carter pointed up. "It's just passing Earth's orbit now, and it's as close to Earth as it's gonna get right now."

"Whoa," Adams wondered. "Headed inbound?"

Carter shook her head. "Nope. It's already passed perihelion. It's on the way outbound. Waaaaay the hell outbound, it sounds like."

"Shit. That wasn't what I was hoping for," Adams grumbled. "I was hoping it would still be inbound, and we could fly our probe out to meet it. Instead, we're gonna be playing catch-up."

"Yup. In fact, according to the JPL peeps, we're looking at doing some additional slingshot stuff."

"In addition to the slingshot stuff we were already doing?" he asked.

She said, "Now we're doing different and more slingshot stuff. And we're gonna need to adjust the oomph of the bird."

"Go ahead," he sighed. First they wanted to launch a rocket, now they needed to launch a modified rocket.

"They need to swap out, or otherwise beef up, the third stage," Carter explained. "They think that'll make it a little more likely to actually catch this Planet Hina. What does Hina mean, anyway?"

He squinted in thought and said, "I think it's a Polynesian god—or maybe goddess; I don't remember the briefing two years ago—of travelers, or something like that," Adams said. "The, uh, the International Astronomical Union, thought it would be an appropriate name for an interstellar dwarf planet popping through."

"I guess. Anyhow, we got the stack halfway complete, but now we need to modify the third stage before we install the Hina Probe."

In the Post Apocalypse, they had a mission halfway ready to go, only now they wanted to change it, and he was the chief wrenchbender.

"Lovely. Just great. How the hell do they think we're gonna be able to do that?"

"Well, don't get bent out of shape here, Pete," Carter soothed. "We have options. We got other birds in the Vehicle Assembly Building, in various stages of assembly, and at least one of 'em George says ain't gonna go anywhere because it's been OBE. *And* it's essentially the same launch system—the SHRUGS vehicle—just a little modified for the payload . . . and a bigger third stage."

Adams thought for a moment. The Standardized Hybrid Reusable Utility—Global System was a cross between the ULA's Atlas V rocket and the SpaceX Falcon 9. Both were medium-lift launch vehicles with strap-on reusable boosters, and the third stage could be adapted to need, with the fairings and connectors expressly designed for swap-outs.

"Right, the Pegasus mission?" Adams verified.

"Exactly. It was a comet rendezvous, and that comet's long gone now, back to the nether regions of the solar system. It'll be back around in about another sixty years, by which time that rocket is gonna be a bucket o' rust. So there's that. We can look at what we got there, and maybe we can kitbash from it to ours. Plus, the SpaceX people were always part of this, and you know they got the rapid prototype ability. And we've stayed on good terms with the Air Force flyboys and gals, and Patrick and Canaveral are right down the way from us. You know they got fabbers and machinists out the wazoo."

"Huh. Yeah, good points, all. But do we have time to get that done before the thing is too far gone for us to reach?"

"JPL seems to think so. They've even ginned up the trajectory they want the probe to take. Launch, couple times around Earth, whip around the Moon, slingshot to Venus, then out to this Hina."

"Venus? But if it's going past us right now, don't they want to use Mars?"

"Not in the right place, they said." Carter shook her head and shrugged. "Look, they're gonna pop us a file if we can get the e-mails all cleaned up."

"Okay, that might just work," Adams said. "Let's go down to my office and see if we can't drag in the file, and have a look."

"Done."

He asked, "And the probe is ready?"

"The probe is also put together from its base design modified with whatever sensors we can scavenge."

That actually seemed reasonable under the circumstances.

"Good," he said. "So it's ready?"

"It will be in time for assembly."

"And all I have to do is administrate," he said with a roll of his eyes.

At Adams' next meeting, with a neighboring civic leader, Mayor Binney of Port St. John didn't seem very interested in the update.

Binney asked, "So you're not sending a crew on the irrigation and flood pumps?"

They sat in what had been a diner near the Indian River. It had been cleaned out, but still stank of wet sea and fish rot. The air was clammy. There was beer, though, and some fresh fruit.

Adams said, "We will, but you'll need to provide people we can train up on some of the basics. We're resuming our original mission. This is possibly Earth's only space launch facility. We've got to get back to it." He took a swig of something homebrewed in a Heineken bottle. It wasn't bad.

Binney sounded at least somewhat sincere as he said, "I'd love to see a rocket launch, man. I grew up watching them." His expression was wistful. "But in the meantime, we've got a bunch of pumps that need cleaned and tuned. If you want food to eat, that is."

"Don't you have mechanics we can train?" Adams asked.

Binney shook his head. "Not enough. They're working on vehicles and construction equipment. And your people put these together. We need power, irrigation, and lights. An entire town is depending on you."

"The world is depending on us," Adams said with a shake of his head.

"We have more important concerns first."

"This is the old, 'What about problems here on Earth?' argument that's always been used against space development. We have a chance to do this now. We won't get another on this, and there may never be another before humanity is gone."

"If we die out from lack of resources, that second part is assured."

Adams tried to be politely reassuring. "We're not going to die out. We've got air, fish, sunlight. We got a shit-ton of water if we distill it to get rid of the salt, and that's not hard. Paleolithic people survived with that. We have tremendously more knowledge, materials and support. We're running cryogenics and power already."

"So why can't you do both?"

"Because we're doing the launch with five percent of a normal crew. Everyone is maxed out. We're running long hours, multiple shifts."

"We need the support you promised."

"And you'll get it. Just not on the schedule you want. Be patient, and it'll happen."

Binney shook his head in what had to be practiced, feigned sadness.

"I wish it didn't come to this. But if we're not getting support from you, we'll have to get it elsewhere."

There was only one response to that. "If you can, that's great."

"Good. So we'll open the bridge again, once we're sure we're safe from incursion. We'll talk to Titusville and see what resources they can swap. We'll have to pay them in food, of course. If you change your mind, just let us know."

It was a game of chicken. Binney was betting Kennedy would run out of food and resources before he ran out of tech support. Unless he actually did have help from elsewhere. In which case, why would he care?

In the meantime, Pete realized, it was a good thing he'd warmed up the watermen first. They were going to be the supply line for food and a lot of other things.

Adams woke up in his apartment, basically a cubby in what had been administrative space near the VAB, but it was functional. Lots of singles lived here. The families were in other buildings with better walls, and even in some of the visitor center space.

He had a bike for short trips between buildings, and could call a car for longer ones, fuel being an issue. They were still trying to scavenge electric vehicles, hindered by having to break the security systems in some. The ride gave him fresh air and made him hot and sweaty. In Florida this time of year, though, that was expected.

He had questions for the Monday morning meeting-slash-breakfast; during the outbreak, certain gatherings had become somewhat traditional, and others had merged. He was glad they had coffee, and orange juice. What he really wanted was bacon, but there was some sausage. Good enough.

"How is the fairing coming?" he asked.

"We called in a bodyman," Greg Crooks, head of pad operations, replied.

"A what?"

"An automotive bodyman. He was able to weld, rivet, epoxy, and otherwise make the standard SpaceX fairing fit the SHRUGS second stage."

Redneck engineering. "That sounds...questionable."

Crooks said, "Given the interchangeable stuff, it wasn't really hard, he said. Besides, he's former USAF airframe repair and says he's comfortable through high supersonic, and he's worked on dragsters. We're lucky in that the SpaceX guys say they had the connections pretty well standardized before they built the Pegasus LV. I guess it works or we get a great fireworks display."

Eyebrows raised, he said, "We'll work with what we've got. Engines?"

"They seem sound. We already looked at them from a structural standpoint. The VAB protected 'em pretty well, so there's no rust or corrosion in the wrong places. I got a team going over 'em to make sure they're still up to launch stress requirements."

They were really doing it. They had most of a launch vehicle kitbashed together from three different launch sets. It was taking a bit of work to make everything fit, given there were different models involved as a result of the different original missions, but between the bodywork and the 3D printing and welding of custom parts the SpaceX guys were doing, it was coming together. And a lot faster than Adams had expected, too, given the angle of the fairing had to be adjusted due to the different diameters of the stages. But the CAD designers and their modeling systems had survived the outbreak, and had done wonders in terms of designing custom pieces-parts, then sending them to the 3D printer/fabber people.

Provided everything worked, and didn't blow up during launch, they might actually have a space mission. It wasn't manned, but it was spaceflight. They were a spacefaring species if only an embryonic one. They had to retain that.

"How's the probe?"

Someone from that department, he hadn't caught the guy's name said, "It will be ready for stack assembly."

"We're doing stack assembly now," he noted.

"Yes, we'll be right at the end of our window."

That was a running theme here.

"Okay. I do want to get some sort of technical support out to PSJ to make them happy."

"I've got two pump guys who we don't need for a few days, until we do launch prep testing," Lee Jones suggested. "We can send them and a couple of good mechanics."

He nodded. "Let's do that. Send them down by boat. That should make it clear we're not as dependent on them, but willing to continue our agreement. It's frustrating. They knew the reason we were staying here from the beginning of the outbreak was tech and hopefully relaunching."

"They're scared, Pete."

"Yup. Everyone loves the idea of being independent, until they realize what it means. Then they want someone else to manage things. No wonder there's so many gang lords."

Right then, Carter ran in and said, "Pete, we have a security issue right now!"

He was supposed to engineer, and administrate, and be exec, all at the same time. He stifled a sigh of frustration.

"What is it?"

"Port St. John has a contingent at our end of the causeway and is demanding we furnish mechanical support or they'll come and take it. I gather they mean kidnap people until they get what they want."

Assholes. "Goddammit, we were just about to furnish

some help. All they had to do was ask and send a truck. They assumed a hostile break."

"Yeah, well, it's hostile now."

"Okay, I'll come talk to them."

She shook her head and said, "I really recommend not. You're the primary target for a kidnapping."

He hesitated. Was he really that important? Perhaps he was.

"Okay, then make sure I'm on radio and we'll negotiate that way."

Canaveral had the same security anyone else had—a few veterans with a few guns and limited ammo after shooting zombies. Good luck finding 9mm or 5.56mm anywhere other than a few precious hoarded rounds.

Off in the distance, Pete heard some pistol and hunting rifle fire, and a small amount of rapid fire. He didn't know much detail about guns, but there were definitely at least four different reports. Apparently it really was possible to tell what was being shot by the sound. The rifles were supersonic and cracked even at this distance.

He got close enough to watch through some serious big-ass binoculars—setting up an observation post on top of the Visitor Center along the NASA Parkway—figuring if that wasn't safe, it was all over anyway; it was a good three and a half miles away from the near end of the causeway. Everyone had been cooperative, all this time, through the worst of the outbreak. Now, as soon as the locals thought they might lose support, they got hostile, probably figuring to annex and dictate.

We're supposed to be civilized, he thought. *So much for that. And in only a few months.*

It was a miniature historical battle. Each side had

a dozen men at a distance on the causeway, and each had a handful of boats with shooters bobbing in the water. It quickly turned into a standstill and tapered off. Neither side wanted casualties or to waste ammo. It devolved into a show of force, and eventually the townies retreated.

The next day, Adams asked, "So the important question...who the hell is our new security detail? Because they're...efficient, but crazy."

His own security boss, James Lachlan, said, "Yeah, that's from the guy claiming to be King of Florida."

"That nutjob who was blaring on the radio from Miami?"

Lachlan nodded his bald head. "Yup. He runs most of the peninsula south of Palm Beach, and all the way over to Tampa."

"And we're trusting him why?"

"He heard we wanted to launch. He offered security services in exchange for getting to watch the launch from the old observation stands. And he ran off the rabble from Port St. John."

"What's this costing us?"

"Nothing. At least, as far as I can tell. He's brilliant when he's not stoned, and then he gets rather weirdly metaphysical, but he said something about, 'Light that earth joint aboard the Mothership and share the smoke with the void.' I gather he considers the ability to watch as payment or something. Anyway, you've seen the patrols. They showed up with six tricked out SUVs with machineguns, and they have entry control covered and a couple of overwatch locations. They've been very polite to all our people, and very effective at stopping visitors and referring them to our visitor center. He also arranged for some food shipments for us from his region, which takes some pressure off the locals."

"Half the state wants this to work, the other half just wants us to rig generators and water pumps... and nothing else. And even if we can break that deal, we shouldn't."

"Yeah."

"If this fails, we look like nerds in a really bad movie." He thought for a moment and added, "If it works, though, we're legends."

That was a tingly thought.

"Hey, Pete!" Carter said, hurrying across the launch control room to the launch director's position, where Adams sat, preparing and organizing what documentation he had for the launch—handbooks, checklists, standard procedures, emergency procedures, and the like. There were a lot of checklists. Most of the documentation was supposed to be electronic, but that had been when they had enough people to *make* it electronic. And you had to have all that documentation for the launch. Also for everything leading up to it. It wasn't his favorite task, but it meant they were getting ever closer.

"Hey, Mel," a cheerful Adams said, looking up from the paper-box full of notebooks and stud-bound documents. "What's up? We did it! We have launch in four days, the bird's on the pad, and we're actually ready!"

Well, sort of. The probe was still having parts installed, on the pad, with mass corrections of grams being reported every few hours. Grams mattered for the distance involved.

He shook his head. "Honestly? I never thought we'd manage this..."

"And we still may not," Carter told him solemnly. "You need to talk to the meteorologists right away."

"Oh shit," Adams murmured, sobering and reaching for the console phone.

Much of the infrastructure of the region, such as telephone lines, didn't work, simply because of the lack of people to maintain them. Storms, especially in Florida, tended to take down phone lines and break telephone poles. But the meteorologists were military, and they were at Patrick AFB. Those lines were dedicated and had been carefully buried, and they still worked.

So Adams got an answer on the third ring.

"Patrick Meteorological Division. Anita Jones here."

"Dr. Jones, this is Peter Adams at KSC. I'm the launch director, chief engineer, and mission manager of the Hina Mission."

"Right. We sent a message for you to call us. Thanks for getting back with us so soon."

"What's up?"

"It's not good, I'm afraid, Mr. Adams. Is the bird on the pad yet?"

"It is; the crawler reached the facility yesterday, and we've started the countdown."

"You may want to put the kibosh on the countdown and bring 'er back into the hangar—um, excuse me, the VAB. Hurricane Gertie has strengthened almost to a Cat 5 and the models are showing a westward turn into the central Florida coast."

"Oh shit," Adams murmured, dismayed. "Where does landfall look most likely?"

"It's a little early to say that for certain," Jones replied. "But the model consensus—and the models that seem to be tracking it the best—show landfall pretty much on top of us, give or take fifty miles or so either way. We expect conditions to begin deteriorating in about thirty-six hours from our last update, which was two hours ago. The base commander is declaring a HURCON II."

"Damn, damn, damn," Adams cursed. "When will we violate launch criteria?"

"Based on what I've looked up on your launch criteria, I'd estimate about two and a half, maybe three days max, from now, but I can send you the data to compare to your launch criteria if you like."

"How do you know?"

"Our models give us the wind speed and pressure curves as the system approaches the coast," Jones explained. "It's part of that whole 'forecast cone' structure. Of course, that varies depending on where in the cone you are, but we're showing the center of the cone making a beeline for us. And I can do a decent estimate of when that's gonna exceed your commit criteria, based on knowing what your wind speed launch violations are, and that's been established for years."

"Oh. Okay, then no, you probably know more about that than the folks we have left here," Adams decided.

"Right. So like I said, you're gonna get a violation due to winds in about two and a half or three days. When's launch?"

"*Four* days from now. Right at the end of our window."

"Ooo. That's unfortunate."

"No shit." He flushed in frustration and withheld anger.

"Well, I'd recommend a rollback into the VAB to protect the bird," Jones decided. "You can always roll it back out once the storm goes through."

"Assuming the VAB, as old as it is, and as little maintenance as we've been able to give it the last couple years, can withstand a Cat 5. What's the max sustained wind on this beast?"

"About a hundred fifty-five miles an hour currently, and continuing to strengthen. But the models show it could reach as much as two-hundred ten, two-hundred twenty, miles an hour by the time it makes landfall. Maybe higher."

"WHAT?"

"It's late in the season, the water's warm, and it'll come right over the Gulf Stream, then stall out almost on top of us when the steering currents crap out due to that high pressure ridge in the Gulf of Mexico strengthening and extending north. Never mind that Bermuda high blocking it to the north...and it wants to turn to the right to recurve, but it can't. So the offshore half—and most of the eyewall—will still extend over the Gulf Stream...which, around here, is pretty much just offshore," Jones explained. "This is gonna hammer Florida bad."

"How long will it stay stalled on top of us?"

"We don't anticipate actual landfall for at least a week," Jones sighed. "Brigadier General Mackinaw is flying out all the aircraft he can, loaded with as many personnel as he can, to Tyndall, and battening down everything else."

"Where are you going?"

"We're not," Jones said. "Well, we're moving to higher ground, sure. And higher up in the buildings. But we're essential personnel for this."

"Damn."

"Yeah. Theme park ride, it ain't." They were silent for long moments, then Jones asked, "When does your launch window close?"

"JPL says that we've pushed it about as late as we can push it, and hope to catch the object," Adams said. "'We have those four days. Six barely possibly, but it's iffy. And that's assuming everything goes smoothly and we don't get any serious damage to the VAB or the control center. Never mind the pads."

"Mmph. Looking at my data, here, that doesn't bode well."

He cursed. "This was already a Hail Mary. We cobbled the bird together with short supplies, we were already tight on the window. But it's the only one we had."

"Yeah, I know. Listen, I'll keep on top of this, and feed you more information as soon as I have it, okay? Is there any way you can speed up the countdown?"

Everyone wanted more. He took a breath. "I'll look into it, but I doubt it. Those things are generally as tight as they can get already."

"Okay, well, we'll all have to do the best we can, I guess."

"Yeah. I'm just not sure that's gonna be enough. Listen, thank you," Adams said. "I need to get my people together and see about safing the bird and my people."

"Right. Talk soon."

"Later."

And he hung up.

∽⊙∼

"How long does it take to get the crawler back to the VAB with a load?" Adams queried in the emergency staff meeting he'd called.

"What the hell?! We're four days and counting from launch, Pete!" his flow director and pad ops chief, Greg Crooks, said. "If we roll back, we'll be awfully damn close to the end of the launch window in getting the bird off the ground by the time we can recycle the countdown! We'll never catch the damn asteroid!"

"There may not be anything we *can* do," Adams said with a sigh. "I just heard from Meteorology at Patrick. The model consensus shows Gertie headed right for us."

Curses, mutters, and grumbles went around the room.

"Can it get worse?" Crooks complained. "That's the worst news yet."

"Be careful what you wish for, Greg, because yeah, it can," Adams said, solemn. "It's already a Cat 4, verging on a Cat 5, and it's gonna strengthen—a lot—as it crosses the Gulf Stream."

"How much?" someone asked, fearful.

"They're estimating well above two hundred miles an hour, say two-ten plus, sustained winds in the eyewall," Adams said. "And then stall out once it makes landfall . . . on top of us."

The room fell silent in shocked dismay.

"So there are two things I need to know," Adams continued. "Well, lemme back up and punt. Is there any chance we can shave at least a day, but better, a day and a half, off the countdown checklist?"

"No way in hell," Crooks declared. "We've got it as tight as it'll go now and be sure the bird will fly."

"Shit. Okay, back to those things I need to know, and I think there's actually three. One: how long does it take to do an emergency regress of the crawler? Two: what's the max windspeed the VAB was designed to withstand, and is it in condition to handle the original specs? And three: what's the highest storm surge we've ever had at KSC?"

Eyes grew wide around the room.

"Does anybody know any of that off the tops of your heads?"

Heads shook in the negative.

"Then go find out."

"Pete, there may not be answers to find," Crooks pointed out. "Not now. Not after the outbreak and everything that went with it."

He kept calm, because they needed him to. "Then find what you can. If you can't find VAB specs, find out what the strongest winds were that it's already been hit with. If you can't find the highest storm surge, contact the local National Weather Service office—however you can, to whoever's left there—and see if you can get a table of data. If you can't raise them, Patrick Meteorological might know; ask for Anita Jones. We meet back here in four hours, and I need answers. GO."

Four hours later, they reconvened in the same conference room.

"Okay, guys, what have we got?" Adams asked.

"The standard speed on the crawler is the standard speed on the crawler," Bob Rogers said. "Loaded, it's about a mile an hour. So it'll take us about three and a half hours to get from the pad back to the VAB. We might be able to push it a little and cut that to three hours, but it's risky, on both the bird and the crawler."

"We've got a risky situation," Adams pointed out.

"Still, half an hour? Eh. Probably not worth pushing *that* hard."

"So keep it to the standard speed?" Rogers verified.

"Yeah. We'll just accommodate the time in our planning." Adams looked around. "What about the VAB's ability to withstand the winds?"

"We don't know for sure," Paul Anders said. "Evidently that documentation has been lost in all the ... shit ... of the last couple years. We're still looking, but I dunno if we'll find it in time for this particular situation. That said, I can tell you that the center has ridden out quite a few hurricanes over the years, and we're still standing. Some of the support buildings have suffered damage, but as nearly as I can tell, the VAB has been through winds up to maybe a hundred five, hundred ten miles an hour, and only suffered cosmetic damage. And it's in about as good a shape as it was before the outbreak; we've kept it maintained as well as we could. I've got a team putting the storm shutters over the launch control windows, and those things are pretty sturdy. I think we'll be good."

"So we can move the bird into the VAB and take shelter there ourselves," Adams decided. "And the launch control wing will be safed. That all sounds good. What about storm surge?"

"That's a little more difficult, Pete," Anders said. "We've had a lot of problems over the years with beach erosion in places, and there've been a lotta things tried, none of it really recent due to the outbreak. Some of the railroads and vehicle roads out near the launch pads have flooded over the years. And if we have a really big storm surge, say ten or twelve feet, we could be swimming—the max height above sea level for the entire center is only about ten feet. And it's a stretch for only one storm, but if it sits on top of us long enough and cuts away at the beach, we might lose pad 39A or B, or both. And never mind our current requirements, those are historic sites—the Moon missions launched from there."

"Shit," Adams cursed. "Those are not the answers I was hoping for."

"I know, but it is what it is, Pete."

"Okay," Adams decided. "I guess we move the bird back to the VAB, move all our personnel into one of the higher floors, ride it out, and hope for the best."

Adams got a phone call.

"Adams here."

"Mayor Adams, this is Mayor Binney, Port St. John." The tension in the man's voice was noticeable.

"Yes, what can I do for you?" At least they were talking and not shooting.

Binney's words came out in a rush. "Sir, you know we have a hurricane moving in. You know how urgent the pumps are. We've got to have some support. I'm not threatening, I'm warning. We could lose crops, infrastructure, everything. We're sandbagging and boarding, but we need technical help on the pumps."

Well, didn't that change the dynamic.

"I had actually been sending a couple of experts and a couple of skilled techs right at the moment you got excited a few days ago, Mayor Binney. This could already have been accomplished."

His counterpart sounded a bit less panicky. "Mr. Adams, you may have the benefit of a bunch of geniuses who are calm under fire. I've got mixed people of mixed backgrounds who've survived zombies, some roving gangs, ragged-edge survival and are scared. Either I made an effort by force, or they'd have replaced me, if you get my meaning, or done it themselves."

If the Chief didn't deliver, then the Chief could be sacrificed. Yeah.

Adams said, "I remember a bunch of idiots claiming sunglasses and face masks would reduce the risk of infection. People always want an easy answer."

Binney said, "They do, sir. I promise you and your people no harm if you can get those experts here to help."

"The problem is, once things got hostile, there was a breach of trust. I really hate to be in this position, but I'm going to need ambassadors, shall we say, to good faith."

Jesus, he was about to demand hostages for diplomacy. This wasn't Colonial, it was Medieval.

"Who, though?"

There was only one workable option. "Make it a half dozen children, old enough not to need diapers, younger than thirteen. We'll show them some movies and technical stuff at the museum. They'll be safe."

There was a long pause. "I guess I'll have to arrange that. I'll call back shortly."

"I'll wait for your call."

He hung up. This was just awful.

Four hours later, six children and six technicians passed each other on the causeway, under cover of armed guards. The Port St. John contingent seemed completely cowed by the black SUV with bull bars and a machinegun. It was good to have support. Even if the guy providing it was completely out of his gourd.

The "King" claimed Canaveral as a protectorate, but his communications came down to wanting to see a space launch, and for them to continue afterward. He was in fact a royal Patron.

Adams was making disaster plans to protect the center personnel as best he could, when his phone rang. He grabbed it and absently rattled off, "KSC Launch Control. Adams."

"Pete, this is Anita Jones with Patrick Meteorological Division."

"Oh, hello, Dr. Jones. Do you have any more information for us?"

"Maybe, but I need to know something first. What are your plans?"

"Hm? I...I'm afraid I don't understand the question..."

"What are you doing about the launch?"

"Oh. Well, we've halted the countdown. They're safing the bird now, and prepping for an emergency regress on the crawler, back to the VAB."

"How late can you push the regress?"

"As late as we can. And we already are."

"Good. Hold off on the regress until you hear from me."

"What? But why?"

"Because I've just been made aware of something. While the usual model consensus still shows landfall as a damn powerful Cat 5 on or near the Cape, there's a new model, out of that consortium of universities that's also been reconstructing the radar grid. And it's showing Gertie recurves before making landfall."

"*That* would sure be good. How *much* before, though? Launch scrub criteria are pretty firm, and awfully damn tight..."

"That's why I said wait. We're still refining it in the model runs. But Pete? They've spent most of their time during the outbreak building the model based on historical data. It's *good*."

Adams was silent for a long moment.

"Thanks, Dr. Jones. I'll take all of *that* kinda news I can get. Keep me posted."

"Wilco."

Additional good news arrived in the form of the techs returning from Port St. John, having helped reconfigure some heavy flow pumps to avoid flooding in the lower-lying residential areas nearer the shoreline; some of the locals had spent the same time dredging out the drainage canals that ran through all the neighborhoods, maximizing the ability of the system to shunt flood waters away from populated areas, whether from torrential rain or storm surge. And, the techs reported, the eastern shoulder of U.S. 1—which ran along the coast of the mainland, skirting what was termed Indian River—was being converted into a levee of sorts with what earth-moving equipment was available.

"What about the kids?" Adams wondered. "Did they get back home okay?"

"Without a problem," Carter told him. "We took them around what's still functional of the visitor center and rolled the videos with the transducers. They loved it. Our techs came back, the children went home with their parents, and everybody was satisfied. The kids went back talking about what they'd learned. Their parents asked if we were gonna start holding Space Camp again. They want to send all the kids to Space Camp to get trained on stuff."

Adams raked a hand through his hair.

"Okay, so the kids got home all right," he said. "Good. But *Space Camp? Really?* I got all I can swing a cat at, now. Somebody else is gonna have to set *that* up, dammit."

"Wait, what?" Crooks exclaimed, as he spoke with Adams on the gantry phone system. He and his team were working frantically to prep the SHRUGS launch vehicle, with the Hina probe already loaded, for return to the VAB. It was turning into a hairy process, as a few lines of thunderstorms, spawned by Gertie well outside its wind field, kept blowing across Merritt Island. He was, consequently, having a hard time processing the information Adams was imparting. "The hurricane's gonna turn?"

"It *may* turn," Adams reiterated with emphasis. "So go ahead and finish safing, but don't do anything that would invalidate the portion of the countdown checklist we've already gone through, and don't start the move until the very last second. And you might wanna check with me first, just in case. Consider this a countdown hold until further notice."

"Oh, I see now," Crooks said. "All right, Pete. Pad team will comply. And hope to hell it turns, and we can resume count instead of recycling it."

"Exactly, and good man, Greg. Adams out."

"Crooks out."

"Adams, this is Jones."

"Hey, Dr. Jones. What's the word?"

"The word is—um, wait, you didn't roll all the way back yet, did you?"

"No, the bird's still on the pad, but we're getting close. The winds are awful iffy, and damn, but the lightning in the feeder bands! It's real close to the commit criteria of having to roll back. We had to pull everyone off the gantry for the time being, just to make sure nobody got zapped."

"Good! Because the word is good. Gertie's turning, and there's no going back from that! That Bermuda high shifted and extended southeast like the consortium's model predicted, and Gertie would have to go way out and around it, and by then it'd be up the coast anyhow. It's maybe an hour or two before you'll start to feel the effects of the recurve, and you're not gonna get anything worse in the meantime. In fact, you're coming up on a break in the feeder bands, so even the rain should taper off soon."

"Really? Don't shit me, now."

"No, really. Hold for about another hour, then you'll start seeing sunshine. Once you see sunshine, get your people out to the pad and resume the countdown!"

"Done!"

The pad flow workers looked up as a shaft of sunlight cut through the murk of the clouds. In the northeast, a patch of blue sky could just be seen.

"Huh. That . . . looks good."

"Yeah. Hey, Jim. How's the clock?"

"Eh. We're gettin' tight, Mike. If we resume the count right now, we can maybe, *maybe* launch it just in time to catch up."

Just then, the loudspeakers across the center annunciated. The voice was Adams'.

ATTENTION. ATTENTION. HURRICANE GERTIE HAS BEGUN TO RECURVE. LAUNCH HOLD LIFTS IN FORTY-FIVE MINUTES. REPEAT, WE RESUME THE COUNT IN FORTY-FIVE MINUTES. PLEASE MAN YOUR STATIONS AND PREPARE FOR LAUNCH IN TWENTY-EIGHT HOURS, THIRTY-SEVEN MINUTES.

Cheers could be heard over most of the launch facility. He said, "And tell those probe monkeys there's no more time. If they find more sensors, they'll have to use them on the next mission. It's done."

Unfortunately, their difficulties weren't over.

Cryogenic fuel could create problems that most people never thought about when they fueled their own vehicles. Liquid oxygen, aka LOX, was tanked in the SHRUGS at a pressurized $-340°F$. This tended to cause objects in contact with it, such as pipes, valves, and such, to shrink by an amount determined by the thermal properties of the materials of which they were manufactured. This could, in turn, cause leaks, if adjacent components didn't shrink at the same rate. The historic STS-35 mission teams could attest to that.

So when a LOX spill occurred on the pad, the area had to be evacuated and tanking stopped while the LOX evaporated and all the components came to a thermal equilibrium. That meant an unanticipated launch hold. And that shoved the launch time scant minutes past what JPL considered the drop-dead end of the launch window.

"It's got to be filled, and it's got to be filled on time," Adams pressed on the horn to the gantry phone system from the launch director's console.

"There's a limit on venting versus filling, condensing versus just wasting LOX, Pete," Crooks pointed out, as work continued behind him on the bird. "This is literally as fast as we can possibly do it. Remember when Scotty said he couldn't change the laws of physics?"

"Yeah."

"Yes, well, we already found you a loophole. But goddamn, it's going to be tight."

"Okay...can we overlap processes on the countdown?"

"We already are."

"Can we overlap anything else? Shave off seconds?" They were staring at the ragged edge of the launch window. Anything would help.

"No, that's about the size of it, Pete. I'm sorry. We're doing the best we can."

"I know. I'm sorry, too. We're just that little bit behind from the initial hookup problems, the pad leak, never mind the damn hurricane, and—"

"You're worried we're gonna miss the launch window."

"Yeah. It's already closing hard. This target isn't like the usual shit where we were going to the Station or something, and could just stand down and recycle for the next day or two."

"I'll let the guys know to push everything as tight as they can get it," Crooks offered. "That's about all we can do."

"I hope it'll be enough," Adams said.

"That's it, and there's the final count..." the ground launch sequence engineer murmured from his console in launch control.

No one was sitting; the panoramic window overlooking the launch pads—the storm shutters having been removed some six hours before—showed launch literally in the last fifteen seconds of the window. Now they had to hope JPL's calculations were correct, or slightly favorable.

"Get on the horn and get the word out," Adams barked. "And tell the king to look north."

The control room scrambled to obey.

The disembodied voice sounded over the video broadcast of the night launch. It was also being transmitted on shortwave and AM. Who would see the video was uncertain. However...

The sky lit from horizon to horizon with an orange glare. The rocket rose on a column of liquid golden fire pouring onto the ground, even as a pure white plume of steam shot out to the side, shining in the light of the launch. The ground shook as it had before, and might again.

"...And here we have a pillar of fire lighting up the night sky over the Kennedy Space Center. It should be visible to observers throughout the Florida peninsula and up into Georgia, possibly even the Carolinas, all along the East Coast. The human race has reclaimed our planet from disaster. And more importantly, we are now reclaiming space.

"This is Canaveral Launch Control."

Just Like Home

JODY LYNN NYE

"You get that cable run through the wall to the security lights all right?" Billy Marx asked Orin Feldman.

The lanky youth nodded, wiping his dusty nose on the sleeve of his white plastic hazmat suit. For once, the two teens and their companions weren't wearing them in case of run-ins with endless crowds of infecteds. Those days were over, thank God. Just for the moment, Billy enjoyed the feeling of not having eyes on his back or a plastic shield in his face.

"Yessir," Orin said, gesturing over his shoulder. "Run up the wall, through the ceiling, and down into the distribution circuit. Let 'er rip."

Billy grinned.

He knelt beside the electrical box in the half-finished wall and hooked his end of the cable into the connector. He felt the powerful hum through the insulated fingers of his glove as he fastened the termination down with a nonmetallic screwdriver.

"We're in business!" he said, sticking the tool into a loop on his belt. "Let's go see how it looks."

All around him, the banging and clattering of activity felt so good and positive. For once, they weren't building something purely for defense. No, this was part of a celebration, the best thing that had happened at Foresight Genetics in absolutely months.

After the long, terrifying spell the couple of hundred survivors had spent fighting off victims of the zombie plague and wondering if any trip they took outside the compound of the mountain-top testing facility was going to be their last, the end of the ordeal was in sight. The airborne plague had died out, and the vaccine worked to protect people who hadn't been exposed yet, so the normals around him were safe enough. The hordes of wild infecteds had been culled down to a few, and what betas anyone could find, Billy had heard might prove to be trainable to menial jobs. The aggressive ones might still try to bite but Foresight Genetics was trying to work out some means of taming them a little. It was going to be a long time before civilization recovered back to normal again, and pockets of infecteds still roamed in the ruins of the Tennessee Valley, but those who had taken shelter in the fenced compound at the top of the hill were starting to think what life might be like after the plague.

Ms. Nora Fulton, the little part-Choctaw woman who had lost her husband and young son to an infected, was an important person in both their lives, to most everyone working with Billy and Orin. Once she had found her way up the mountain to Foresight's secured facility all those months ago, she threw herself into the protection of the compound and those who lived inside it as if they were her own family. A dead shot who could use any weapon, she became one of their best hunters, bringing down one after another of the mindless, naked invaders like she was shooting cans off a fence. Her anger was a force of nature. While many of the others had seen the infecteds as "there but for the grace of God go I," Ms. Nora treated them all like rabid dogs. Considering what they did to an unwary person who had been jumped by a pack of them, Billy could see the comparison. Most everybody had lost at least one loved one to the zombies. Only when the scientists in the Hole and Mr. Steve Smith said the betas might be recoverable to a certain extent had Billy started to see them as fellow human beings again. Ms. Nora probably never would, and he didn't blame her a bit.

The person who really got her was Mr. Lou Hammond. A big, balding African-American man who had been a plumber before the virus started around, he had been a solid and calming presence. He started turning up where Ms. Nora went, and always had her back when they had to go out hunting. Even Billy, who admitted he wasn't great at spotting subtleties anywhere, could see that Mr. Lou had become stuck on her. He was pleased but not too surprised when she had told everyone the two of them had gotten engaged.

From the moment that piece of news went around the compound, everyone had a smile on their faces. The plans had really begun to solidify with Ms. Melanie Trimble, the surviving manager of Foresight. Ms. Melanie had a gift for organizing. Up until then, the organization mostly had a grim cast to it. Doling out supplies, counting people in and out of the compound to see who made it back and who didn't, keeping track of the betas they brought in to evaluate, and the spinal cords of infecteds the scientists needed to make the serum. Being able to plan a wedding lifted her spirits.

Like the company name, Ms. Melanie also had a gift for foresight.

"We're all gonna be able to leave here soon," the plump dark-skinned woman had told several key people, including Billy, his mom, and his girlfriend Tee Figueroa, during a very late night secret conference in the cafeteria. "I don't know how you all feel about it, but I'm getting tired of sleeping with five roommates. Three of them snore!"

Billy giggled, and Tee, a petite Latina with long dark hair pulled back in a braid, elbowed him in the ribs. He grunted. His ribs weren't as well covered on his tall, pear-shaped body as they had before the plague started, but he was beginning to fill out again, thanks to more resources becoming available to them from outside.

"We've lived with it because we have to, but now that we can see the end of the plague, we have to think about where we're all going to live from now on. Now, you all know Ms. Nora and Mr. Lou are getting married. They're smart and brave. I can't think of two people who will be more prepared to live outside the compound than they are. So," she began, with a big smile on her broad face, "as a wedding present, I think we oughta fix up a house for them. Just to get the ball rolling."

Orin started up a cheer. Tee reached over and clapped her hands over Orin's mouth in case the noise attracted the attention of anyone else in the dark, echoing concrete halls of the facility. Like it or not, sound carried in there, even footsteps.

"So, you like the idea?" Ms. Melanie asked, surveying the sea of grinning faces. She brandished a clipboard. "Well, then, I've made a sign-up sheet of all the jobs that need doing. And there's lots of them."

The house she had picked out lay downslope about three hundred yards from the facility. The 1940s frame structure had been abandoned longer than the zombie apocalypse had been going on, and wasn't in the greatest of shape, but it had, as Ms. Melanie explained, "possibilities." National Guard Sergeant Angel Velasquez had laughed at her description, calling it a "real fixer-upper." On first sight of the place, Tee had hooted out loud. It was a wreck. Boards leaned away from the siding. One of the two bedrooms was open to the air, the toilet facilities were out back, and the roof sagged like it was tired. She couldn't believe anyone had ever lived in it. Billy just started looking for where the utilities used to come in. If they ever did. The whole place was going to take a mass of work.

They'd been at it for more than two weeks already. Ms. Melanie had been sounding out Ms. Nora about when they wanted to hold the wedding ceremony. She assured the builders they had about one more week to finish. It wasn't much time, considering how much damage had to be repaired in the house and its surrounding yard. Like anywhere the zombies had overrun, the place had stunk of feces, urine, the remains of dead animals and the occasional human being, not to mention rotten food dragged out of the ancient fridge and from the chest freezer in the lean-to beside the dilapidated garage. Most of that got hauled a long way outside and buried, since trash pickup had been stopped everywhere for months.

The volunteers were divided up into teams. Protection was the first group, consisting of the members of the National Guard, serving and retired military, the few security guards who were left, and every hunter in the compound. Anyone who had a decent eye with a weapon took a shift with them.

Demolition and rebuilding came next. Lani Sanders, a chemist at Foresight, had learned carpentry alongside her daddy and her granddaddy. She had declared that the eighty-year-old pine flooring in the house couldn't be saved. The first job had been all hands on deck pulling it up and replacing the termite-eaten joists underneath. A couple of the exterior and almost all the interior walls needed reframing. Once the damaged boards and drywall were out and burning on a pile, they scavenged good wood and panels from all over the Nashville area, along with any decent furniture, appliances, and housewares that could be found in abandoned houses. All of that got put to one side under tarps for the time while the building structure was made sound. Myron Levy, an architect who had escaped Nashville and found his way up the hill to Foresight, laid out a blueprint expanding the little house to have a bonus room and a second bathroom.

"Nobody wants a house with one bathroom anymore," the sharp-faced man said, with a firm shake of his head. His dark hair, going elegantly gray at the temples, danced on his shoulders. "There's zero resale value. You gotta think ahead these days."

Even though he was only eighteen, Billy's specialty in electronics made him the lead on wiring the house, installing ceiling and sconce lights, a satellite dish, as well as motion detectors, proximity alarms, emergency radio links to Foresight and the police station, security doorbells with cameras, and an electric fence surrounding the little two-bedroom house just downslope from the Foresight facility. With so few people left, there was no shortage of pre-plague supplies. Mr. Jud Tomkinson, in charge of Foresight's plant operations, had told him that unless there was an emergency, he could spend all his time working on pulling new wiring and setting up all the fancy bells and whistles. Tee, five years older than Billy, had been a sound engineer in New York and Nashville. She was fixing up sound equipment with speakers in all the rooms.

"You gonna talk about all this on your radio program?" Dieter Vance asked, passing by with a load of PVC pipes under his arm. Billy's hobby as a ham radio operator had brought in news from survivors all over the world, including Antarctica. Desperately hungry for news, everyone had insisted that he broadcast his conversations over the facility PA. They had their spirits lifted by knowing they weren't alone in the world. Billy's ham setup was the only non-government-linked communications system in the compound, as the other equipment was tied to the Hole in Nebraska and a few other secure locations that had come back online. His "program" had made him a minor celebrity around Foresight. He got to announce birthdays, notable moments in history, a running trivia contest, and other memos from the brass twice a day, and was excused from perimeter scouting so he could talk with his fellow ham operators and bring in more news. Billy grinned up at the former recon scout, a small, balding man in his fifties.

"Nossir. Ms. Melanie would take me to pieces if I blew the surprise."

"The hammering and sawing can be heard for miles!" Tee said, puffing a lock of her dark hair out of her eyes. She had a Polk speaker under her arm that Billy knew was worth thousands. It had been scavenged from a club in the music district. "This isn't what I call a surprise."

"Well, Ms. Nora and Mr. Lou have been steered clear of this area on purpose," Dieter said, a wicked twinkle in his eye. "They kind of know, but it's the details that will be the surprise. We want them to like it."

"They'll like it!" Tee said. She shook her head. "This is the nicest thing you could do for them. After everything Nora has been through."

"All of us," Dieter said, his usually animated face solemn. "We all lost someone, but she lost her only child, right in front of her eyes."

The others fell silent for a moment, every one of them remembering his or her dead.

"Infecteds coming this way!" Angel Velasquez barked. "Seven or eight of them!" The National Guardswoman crouched down behind the still-incomplete south fence as the protectors on duty rushed to join her. She waved the barrel of her rifle to the right. "Micky, haul that bale of chicken wire up here! Block that hole!"

Retired Specialist Micky Rollins turned off the welding torch he was using to seal a pipe, but kept the heavy metal mask over his face. Although everyone in the compound had been vaccinated, they were still at risk from injury. The zombies liked to go for the face and try to chew off noses or lips. More than a few of the inhabitants were hoping that a plastic surgeon or two had survived to repair disfigurements. Billy, Dieter, and Tee leaped up to help. Billy made a mental note to send out word over the ham radio to ask about doctors. Soon, he hoped, people would be willing and able to travel again. But not yet.

"Thanks," Micky grunted. The heavyset man guided the big spool into the fence. It didn't close the gap completely. Billy reached into his tool belt for the wire cutters and snapped the cable holding the bale. Together, they unwound it across the open area. From his pocket, Billy produced a handful of zip ties. Hastily, they fastened the metal mesh in place. Micky hauled a tranquilizer gun out from behind his welding apron.

"Good!" he said, calmly. "Y'all just keep on working. Angel and I will take care of this bunch."

Tee stood staring over the chain-link fence into the woods with a forlorn look on her face. She had spent weeks or months holed up alone in a home studio in the suburbs, hiding from zombies and living on what little canned and preserved food she could scrounge. She had nearly been killed a couple of times until a party from Foresight found her. Billy came to put an arm around her slender shoulders.

"It's okay," he said. She turned and buried her face in the breast of his hazmat suit.

Thrashing in the bushes heralded the infecteds bursting out just twenty feet shy of the fence line. Like usual, they were stark naked with torn-up feet, jagged nails, and wild hair. Three men, four women, and so caked with dirt he couldn't tell if they were black, brown, or white, ran straight toward them. Their leader was a tall, wild-eyed man with folds of skin hanging on his gaunt body, meaning he used to be overweight, like Billy had been. Everybody in this world, infected or survivor, had been reduced to subsistence rations. The zombies supplemented theirs with whatever living being they could overpower and eat.

"Arms ready..." Angel said, fixing her rifle through a bend in the chain-link. "And...!"

At that moment, a couple of dirt bikes zipped up the hill with a squall like chainsaws.

"Hold your fire!"

The bikers, in full leathers with visored helmets, circled the infecteds at speed. Weapons coughed, one after another. The zombies screeched and tried to break away. One by one, blue-fledged darts appeared somewhere on each of the scrawny, naked bodies. The leader saw what was happening to his squad, and dived for one of the bikers. He missed, stumbling over his feet. The other biker turned in a hairpin and plugged the leader twice in the back. The male let out a bellow, collapsed to his knees, then fell flat on his face in the dust. All the other infecteds had dropped by then.

"They're out," Billy murmured to Tee. She pushed loose from his embrace. Billy found her a strange combination of vulnerable and tough, and he liked both facets of her. He still wondered what she saw in him.

The bikers pulled off their helmets. Billy recognized Roger Marshall and Elaine Bey, a couple of the hunters.

"Nice shooting!" Angel called to them.

"Thanks!" Elaine said, holstering her tranquilizer rifle in a sheath along the fork of her bike. She was of south Asian descent, with huge dark eyes and magnificent, long brown-black hair that was tightly braided on top of her head. She had been a biathlon competitor somewhere in Florida. "We've been tracking these guys for a few days. We ran them until they were getting tired out so we wouldn't lose any shots taking them down. Glad we got them all."

"We have to drive them like cattle," Roger added. He had silver hair and craggy, reddened skin that made his light blue eyes stand out like LEDs. "If we don't keep on 'em, they scatter."

"My goodness, the house really is taking shape!" Elaine said. "I don't know if Ms. Nora is going to be able to handle living normal again, especially in a place this nice."

"Why wouldn't she?" Tee asked.

Elaine and Roger exchanged bemused glances.

"Well, she's gotten so used to hunting them," Roger said. "She's damned good at it. It's funny, but I think she'll almost miss it when this is all over. Helps her deal, she says. I dunno. Maybe she's getting addicted to the adrenaline. Not me. I wish I could go back to my old accounting office and just have to face the IRS once in a while instead of nekkid people who want to eat me."

Tee laughed. "When all this is over, I don't think I ever want to see anybody naked again!"

Everyone laughed at that.

"Bad luck for you, Billy-boy," Roger said, with a snicker.

"How many more zombies are out there in this area?" Billy asked, ignoring the burning in his cheeks. An idea had popped into his mind.

"Oh, a few groups," Roger said. "Eventually we'll get 'em. Anyone got a truck handy to help us get these guys up to Foresight? We want them evaluated before they wake up. It's easier to cull them that way."

"Sure," Dieter said, rubbing his gloves down the front of his white suit. "I got a minute. Pickup's around the side yard."

"No, wait," Billy said. "Let me. Orin, can you finish connecting the cables?"

"You got it," Orin replied. He shot a nervous glance through the fence at the infecteds, but they were totally out.

Billy collected the keys and drove the battered green Ford around to the south side of the house. With the speed born of long practice, the enforcers loaded the unconscious zombies into the truck bed like so many sacks of fertilizer. Billy climbed into the cab and followed Elaine and Roger up the hill.

"Thanks for your help," Roger said, once they had the infecteds loaded out onto gurneys and strapped down. The big male was already beginning to stir when Ms. Melanie rolled him inside the Foresight plant. "You looked like you had something on your mind, son. Is there a problem of some kind?"

"I dunno," Billy said. He was trying not to squirm with concern. "How likely is it that any more of those zombie gangs are going to come up this way? I mean, in the week or two?"

Roger and Elaine exchanged another glance.

"I don't know," Elaine said. "You're worried that they might come up and spoil Ms. Nora's wedding?"

"Kind of," Billy said.

"Well, we'll let you know if we see any more of them coming close to the end of the week," Roger promised him. "You don't have to worry."

"It's not that," Billy began, then spotted Mr. Lou pulling his little green Prius up the stone drive toward them and clapped his mouth shut. The others noticed Mr. Lou, too.

"Thanks for your help, son," Roger said. "We're gonna get cleaned up and get us something to eat. You all are doing a great job." As Mr. Lou got out of his little car and hoisted a big sack from the back seat over his shoulder, he raised his voice. "Can't wait to hear what kind of stories you're getting from your friends overseas on the next show. When is it, eight o'clock?"

"Oh, yeah!" Billy said, grateful for the distraction. "My Welsh friend Geraint and his friends got airlifted last night to Valley Air Station by the Royal Air Force. I've got stories...."

"Don't spoil it!" Mr. Lou said, coming up with a big smile on his broad, dark face. He clapped Billy on the back with his free hand. "I want to hear the whole thing when I can sit back and enjoy it. Y'all have a good day."

"You, too, Mr. Lou," Billy said, as the big man strode into the facility. "I better go."

"So, Geraint, I've got you on PA," Billy said, leaning into the big microphone, "tell everybody again. How did the Air Force come and get you?"

"Ah, Effy-bach, you'd hardly credit it," came the plummy voice into his can-style headphones. "Effy" was an affectionate abbreviation for Billy's ham call sign, Whiskey Edward Seven Foxtrot Foxtrot Yankee, or WE7FFY. Geraint, all the way over in northwest Great Britain, went by Golf Whiskey Four Echo Hotel

India, or GW4EHI, not as pronounceable. "It was quite the adventure, so it was."

From the pleased looks on Mr. Jud's and Tee's faces, Geraint was coming over just fine on the speakers, rolling R's and over-emphasized diction, and all. The link was clearer than it had ever been, meaning the Welshman had a good signal with boosters to the ordinarily low power frequency. Billy checked his own power readings. Although he had built in capacitance to keep the flow steady, they could still experience a drop in current that would throw his "show" off the air and maybe short out his radio when it came back in. It was a new unit, salvaged from the same sound studio where they had found Tee, but if it got a surge up the line, it could burn the circuitry.

"What happened? It was just last night, wasn't it?"

"Well, then, you know those RAF-eh chappies, they make a big noise doing efferything! So, you see, a monster great hellycopter cooms out of noweah and begins hovering-eh above us out here on Ynys Lawd. Men rrrrappelling down long skinny black ropes. At first, with our rrrraggedy clothes, they thought the five of us, we might be some of the walking-eh dead. But then, they let us get our things and loaded-eh us into the aircraft! A boompy ride-eh, and a welcome one. My, but weren't they glad to see us on the base, and we were grateful too! Ah, the food! The first hot-eh meal was blissful, let me tell you that. I've-eh con-strrructed in my mind the food I would eat when next I was given the chance. I dreamt of the barrrbecue you've described-eh to me, with crrrisped meat on the outside and tangy sauce to dip. I longed for Sunday roast and Christmas-eh puddings, but baked beans on toast and a prrrop-eh brewed cuppa tasted like all my Christmases in my life put together!"

Billy laughed at the humble description. "Beans on toast? That's all?"

"Oh, my boy, it was a feast! And biscuits! Not tasted sweets in a long-eh while, now. I've lost more than four stone. But it's all to the good, it's all to the good. We slept in clean beds, after a genuine hot showah, so we did!"

Billy's audience let out an audible sigh of pleasure. He grinned, and adjusted his gauges on the control board just a little.

"That sounds great, Geraint. I'm really happy you're all okay. Have they started cleaning up the infecteds over there?"

"Ach, yes. We've all had the inoculations now, and there's a muckin' grrreat infirmary like a warehouse on a fenced area of the base, where they take in the walking dead. A few are starting to come out of it now, more every day. You can't call them people, exactly, but we've had our share of village idiots. We can put them to work, hauling stone and carrying out rubbish, perhaps."

"Here, too," Billy said. "We're getting a lot of the betas trained, too, but I don't know how many people we've lost over these months."

Geraint's voice was solemn. "I trrry not to think about that, Effy. We're alive, and we'll make our way back to normal. That's what matters."

Billy cleared his throat. It wouldn't do to let tears clog him up when he had another couple of hours to go talking with his ham friends around the world. "So, what's next for you?" he asked. "I mean, what do you want to do once you can...go home?"

"Well, I know I won't spend all me time in the office-eh! Life's too precious for that. I want to get married again. Mairi and I became very close during all those weeks in the lighthouse. I'm too old and not good enough for her, but she's said she'll have me anyhow. We're planning to travel around once we can, maybe even come over to the States and meet you Eye Are Ell, as the teenagers say. What about you, Effy? You've got your whole life ahead of you? And two pretty girls interested in you at that?"

Tee guffawed, and elbowed Billy in the shoulder. He grimaced. Why was everyone trying to get him settled down so soon?

"There's gonna be a wedding here pretty soon," he said. "It's not me! It's Ms. Nora and Mr. Lou, two of the best hunters in the compound."

"Wish them well for me," Geraint said. "God bless them and let them be happy."

"They can hear you," Billy said. Mr. Jud nodded. "Thanks a lot. I know it's really late over there. Talk to you again tomorrow?"

"I'll be looking forward to it. Bless you, my boy."

Geraint's words stuck with him all the next day while he pulled in wires and ran the pieces of the security system through the walls of the little house. What did come next, once the plague was really over and they were free to live outside the compound?

The question finally burst out of him while he and Tee were helping Dieter put together the kitchen counters across the top of the cabinets taken from a showroom. The new flooring was covered with a heavy plastic tarp to protect it from the light blue paint Myron and the others were slapping on the fresh drywall on the walls and ceiling. The fixtures for the coming track lights were ready, installed by Billy and Orin just that morning.

The section of slate-blue granite between the stove and the sink was hinged at the back. When lifted, it revealed a recess containing control panel with a dedicated line to the compound and a miniature ham outfit Billy was very proud of, override switches for the security lights that now topped all four corners of the fence in the yard and the two gables of the roof, and brackets for Ms. Nora's favorite pistol and two boxes of ammunition. It was a neat little arrangement, but when he closed the top on it, the boom it made had an air of finality about it that broke something loose in him.

"What happens to us when all this is over?" Billy asked.

"What do you mean?" Tee asked.

Billy wiped his nose with the back of his work glove.

"Everything is going to be different. We'll all be spread out across the area. I mean, I don't want to live in one room with my mama forever, but I've met all these good people, made some really intense friendships. I hate the thought of losing touch with all of you. I've hated nearly everything else that has gone on, but I'll be sorry to have that part end."

"How do you think you're gonna get rid of us?" Dieter said, with a rueful grin. "We're old army buddies now, Billy. That's what veterans have. Only we understand what others in the service have been through. And it lasts a lifetime. I can sit down with my guys from the unit, and all one of them will have to say is, 'remember that time in Mogadishu?' And you don't have to say anything else. And, when one of us is having a hard time, we're the only ones who get it. That never goes away."

"Do you ever get over those times?" Tee asked, her dark eyes sympathetic.

"I'll ask *you* that again in five years," Dieter said. "You tell me then. Meantime, Billy, why don't you think about going on like you've begun here? You and Tee have made yourself a radio station right here with nothing but some tin cans and string. Once we can start expanding, you ought to take over one of the big studios down in the city. You've helped us come together and survive just as much as Mr. Jud and Ms. Melanie."

"No, I haven't," Billy protested.

"You bet you have," Myron Levy said, getting down heavily from his ladder with a can of paint in his hand. "My kids and I never talked so much as before we got stuck here, but now we've had something good to discuss, like your stories from the folks overseas. It's keeping us optimistic that civilization didn't end. You oughta think about keeping that up. When the Internet gets up again, you can get an audience all over the world. I'd do your publicity for you."

Billy stopped working, screwdriver in hand, at the thought. It made him go starry-eyed. What if he could turn his cherished hobby into a job?

"What about you, Miss Tee?" Dieter asked. "The government says the plague is over. Pretty soon, everything is gonna be opening up, even if it's smaller than before. Where do you want to be in twelve months?"

Tee laughed. "Well, I'm looking forward to when

people start coming home again. I've been on the radio to Cindy in Nepal for hours and hours. I really like her. *We* figure that once she's back, she and Billy and I are all going to move in together. I've seen some really nice abandoned houses down in town. I've got my eye on a couple that we could clean up and move into."

Billy's mouth dropped open. "Now, wait a minute!" he protested. "I just can't live with two ladies!"

"You're going to turn one of us down?" Tee asked, eyeing him. "After she's spent all those months in Asia pining for you? Boy, maybe you aren't the guy I thought you were. Maybe she and I will move in, and you can go scratch."

The others all hooted as Billy felt his cheeks burn. There was no good way out of that conversation, no matter what he said.

"You're outnumbered, boy," Dieter said, clapping him on the shoulder. "Go with it. We're all making it up as we go along."

"Well, she's better with sound equipment than I am," Billy said, making a playful grimace at Tee. She beamed. "Maybe it'll work out. Ms. Melanie calls it the 'new normal.'"

"That's the spirit!" Dieter said. "I can't wait for it to be over so I can get back to my house. I've been there with a few of the National Guard. It's a mess, but the important stuff is still there, including my granny's cast-iron stove. I just don't know how long it'll be until I can stop rolling out of bed with a gun when I hear the least little noise. What's next is the scary part. If we can live through that and settle in again, I think we're all gonna be okay. You're just going to have to take that jump, but you have to do it with your eyes open to the possibilities. You gotta see where you're going. There will be a period of adaptation. That's normal. Ms. Melanie has picked the right people to start us forward, you know. There aren't two braver people in the compound than Mr. Lou and Ms. Nora."

"Where are they today?" Myron asked, prying open yet another paint can. "I got some colors for the master bedroom, but I don't want to start until she approves it."

"Downhill," Billy said, pointing. "Mr. Lou stopped me on the way out this morning. Something was messing with the water coming up into the compound. Mr. Jud was afraid the infecteds got into the pump house."

"Damn!" Dieter said. "This ain't over yet. I better check." He stepped away and unholstered the shortwave radio on his belt.

"Am I pushing you too hard?" Tee asked, genuine concern on her face. "I know I tease you, but I don't mean anything by it. You're just so sweet and innocent, it's hard to resist."

"No," Billy said, regarding her fondly. "I'm glad you do it. Dieter's right. I've got to move toward the future, but it's hard when I don't know which way to go. All I figured before all this started happening was I'd go to college and study up for a career, and get that going. When we moved up here, I stopped looking ahead."

Tee pushed her hand into his. "We'll figure it out. Who knows when the colleges will start up again, and what can they teach you more than you already know? I can show you how to operate and fix all the technology

I use. Anything we find that's still working in any broadcast facility ought to have a manual somewhere. The zombies wouldn't have been interested in anything that wasn't food. If they haven't wrecked it past repair, we can get it going again and make that broadcast station happen. It'll be scary, but if we're together, it'll be okay. Nora and Lou already know that."

Billy squeezed her hand. He'd never felt protective of anybody the way he did with Tee, but at the same time as vulnerable as a baby. She was so accomplished and smart and brave, and he was just a country kid who knew something about radios. Still, she considered him worthy, an equal, someone she liked . . . no, loved enough to want to start a new life with. That was a big pair of shoes to step into. He gulped a little, wondering what it would be like to have all three of them living together, him, Tee and Cindy. Well, he knew he wasn't going to be in charge, no matter what else.

Dieter came back. He looked relieved.

"It's all right. A rock fell down and squeezed some of the hoses up against the cliff face. Nothing the zombies did. Ms. Nora's going to meet Myron up at the compound and look at the paint chips in a little while."

"We better finish up here," Billy said, gathering up his tools and brushing the clipped ends of wire into a trash bag on the counter. "We've only got a couple of days until the wedding."

"Oh, my God!" Tee said. "I have to figure out something to wear. I'm not going to the only celebration for months in a hazmat suit with dust in my hair. And what do you think they'd appreciate as a wedding gift?"

"Well, this house is from all of us," Dieter said. "We're going to sign a card and frame it in the living room right next to the front door. Right above the switch for the electric fence," he added with a grin.

Tee shook her head. "I'm one of her bridesmaids. I need to come up with something."

"I got an idea for a present," Billy said. "But I don't want to say too much yet."

Since no preachers or religious folk in the area had survived the infected, Ms. Nora and Mr. Lou had decided that the wedding would be just the two of them standing up in front of the community—that was, the people in the Foresight Genetics compound and a few guests who were flying in from The Hole and the nearest military base for the event. The weather cooperated, shining warm and bright. Any storm clouds that threatened had moved away, leaving a blue sky with a few fluffy clouds in it. It wasn't even too hot or humid. Just looking up, Billy thought it could have been any nice day. He went over the sound system again and again until he was satisfied that it and the stack of CDs mounted in the multi-disc player were ready to rip. On strict orders from his mama and Tee, who were going to help the bride get ready in her brand-new master bedroom, no one was to enter the house until after the ceremony, so Tee would set the music running.

Ms. Nora had pretty much put the preparations into the hands of Ms. Melanie. Nobody got individual invitations, but details were posted on every bulletin board, and Billy had broadcast them during his nightly show for the last six evenings. Every scrap of wood, every shred of plastic, every loose nail had been removed from the work site. Once the little house had been finished and inspected by the capable plant manager, she had set them to work decorating the outside for the wedding party.

With plenty of threats and cajoling, Ms. Melanie had gotten the foragers to come up with enough flour, sugar, eggs, vanilla and baking powder to bake a cake big enough for everyone to get a piece. The sparkling confection stood on a table right beside the doorstep under the newly restored wrap-around veranda, in case of rain. Even if the three layers sloped a little to the right under its heavy load of decorative icing, it looked amazingly festive. The scent of sugar and vanilla on the air was so enticing, Billy's stomach growled.

He and the rest of the employees or family members waited in the neatly mowed front yard among a cluster of round tables covered with any kind of tablecloths that the foragers could find, dressed in their best attempt at festive clothing. With months of privation whittling away his pear-shaped body to a tall carrot, he'd scrounged up a pair of black dress pants and a tuxedo shirt from the closet of some long-gone musician in the city. Thank God, the man had gone for clip-on bow ties instead of making Billy have to guess how to tie one. He'd also lifted a handsome Grass Valley switcher from the man's rig in his living room. Although it was unlikely the original owner would ever come looking for his possessions, Billy had left an IOU note, as he always did when taking goods from houses or stores. He preferred to make things right with God than not to take responsibility for his sins. He straightened the tie as Neeta Patel, one of the genetic engineers, pulled up in one of the company vans.

Neeta was grinning as wide as the sky as she jumped down from the driver's seat and pulled open the big side door. The slim woman had on a red silk dress covered with glittering sequins and a pair of black sandals.

"Come on," she said. "You can't hide in here forever."

"I'm not hiding!" Mr. Lou slid out of the first seat and marched up to the white-covered table in the middle of the yard as if he was ready to face the firing squad. A leather-bound Bible lay on the table, surrounded by flowers and candles.

The groom wore a dark gray suit whose strained buttonholes made it look like it had once been too tight but hung around Mr. Lou's shrunken midsection. His hair had gotten pretty long, like everyone else's, but someone had fixed it into a bunch of tiny braids that hung to his shoulders. The combination kind of made him look like a pop star. Mr. Jud Tomkinson, plant manager of Foresight, popped out behind him, wearing a dark blue suit and a pink plastic flower in his buttonhole. He was the best man. Not that he had to keep Mr. Lou from running away or fainting. Mr. Lou looked happier than Billy had ever seen him. This was a new kind of normal, one everyone could really get behind. If only it would last.

"All right," Mr. Lou said, with a grin. "Where is my woman?"

"Real soon now," Billy promised him.

Inside the house, he heard a bunch of giggles erupt. He, Mr. Jud, and Mr. Lou exchanged puzzled glances. Music started to play from the speakers embedded in the posts of the porch.

Suddenly, the door opened, and Tee came out with her hair styled high on her head, wearing a slinky black dress and sandals that laced up her legs. She had a fistful of plastic roses and a look of glee on her face. Carrying the same kind of bouquet, Ms. Melanie emerged in a shiny pink bodycon dress that hugged her comfortable bulk with love. Next, Billy's mother was wide-eyed with delight in a flowered dress that skimmed her feet and a wreath of the artificial flowers on her head. The plant manager and the other bridesmaids filing out of the house could barely contain themselves. Every time one of them glanced at the others, they broke up laughing.

None of the guests could figure out what was so funny until the CD recording of "Here Comes the Bride" started playing, and Ms. Nora stepped out under the portico.

The bride wore camo.

Ms. Nora, a small, very thin woman in her forties, wore a big fluffy wedding dress, with tight-fitting sleeves flared at the wrist and a scoop neck, and a long train that had to be fifteen feet long, all of it cut out of Desert Storm khaki camouflage cloth. She had a veil, too, over her dark, silver-shot hair, made of duck-blind netting. It was totally absurd. It was perfect.

Billy gasped for a moment, then started laughing so hard that tears leaked out of his eyes. Ms. Nora grinned as she passed him. Everybody broke into giggles and guffaws.

Mr. Lou straightened up as the bridesmaids arranged themselves in a semicircle and waited for Ms. Nora to arrive. He beamed at her.

"My God, Nora, you do know how to make an

entrance!" He took her hand and kissed it. All the guests sighed.

"So, you gonna marry me, or what?" she asked, with a challenging look.

"Sure thing," Mr. Lou said. He took a folded paper out of his breast pocket, then paused. "You wanna go first?"

"All right." Ms. Nora didn't speak much at the best of times, so Billy knew it was hard for her to open up in front of all those people, even to the man she loved. She looked up into his face and fixed her eyes on him. "Lou Hammond, you're the best man I know. Sometimes you're the only thing that has made this all bearable. I . . . if there's any time left to us in this world, I want us to spend it together."

She had tears in her eyes, which said more than any of her words. Behind her, Tee's lips were quivering as if she was trying not to cry.

When Ms. Nora fell silent, Mr. Lou nodded. He glanced at the piece of paper, then stuck it back in his pocket. He folded both her hands in his.

"Nora Fulton, you make me smile. Stay with me a while. My whole life sings, it grows wings, I think of things I never did before, when you're with me . . ." To the astonishment of his bride and practically everybody else in the crowd, he went on to rap out his vows. Billy couldn't help himself. He let out a yell of delight, accompanied by all the younger people, even as some of the older ones looked appalled at the eloquent, rhythmic patter. ". . . Be my wife, and I'll love you all my life!"

For answer, Ms. Nora stood up on her tiptoes and kissed him. He wrapped his big arms around her and held her tightly.

"They don't need me to say it," Mr. Jud announced, "but in the eyes of everyone who matters, they're married! Let's hear it for the happy couple!"

Everyone cheered. Ms. Nora's dusky cheeks turned red with pleasure.

Right on cue, the dance music started.

"Everybody on serving duty, get that food out here!" Ms. Melanie commanded. Twenty people streamed into the little house or went to fling open the doors and trunks of the vehicles that had been driven down from the compound. She beckoned to Orin, who was in charge of bringing chairs for them to sit at the white-covered table. Whisking the candles and Bible away, she made room for plates, flatware, and glasses. Billy's mother, smiling with pride, came over to offer them a bottle of champagne.

"Where in God's green Earth did you find that?" Mr. Lou asked.

"My son got it for you. God bless you both."

"Well, thank you," Mr. Lou said, glancing toward Billy. "Thank you."

Billy helped lay out the food on long tables that were set up against the side wall of the house. In future months, a strip of garden would go there, but in the meanwhile, it was convenient to plug in Crockpots. Due to the lack of available game or livestock, most of the dishes were vegetarian, but in the hands of expert cooks who had been making do with practically nothing for months, it all smelled amazing. Billy couldn't wait to dig in. He glanced toward Mr. Lou and Ms. Nora, but they didn't seem interested in getting up to eat. They stared at each other like they couldn't believe they were really married.

Tee came over to grab his arm. Her cheeks were flushed with pink. She looked absolutely gorgeous.

"Come and dance with me!" she said.

"I, uh..." Billy pointed at the buffet.

"Come on!" She pulled him out onto the lawn.

Like him, everyone seemed cautious about celebrating, even such an event like this one. Other couples looked as though they wanted to take advantage of the bouncy music, but until Tee dragged Billy out to dance, no one else did. As soon as she started gyrating and waving her arms, a handful of the youngest scientists and technicians joined in. Mr. Jud and his wife Ms. Sharon whirled onto the grass and started doing something old-fashioned but really graceful. Tee laughed.

Billy studied her. From the frail, terrified creature she had been when a group of scavengers from Foresight rescued her, she had recovered to a vital extrovert. Billy regarded her as if she was a wild animal of some kind. She must have read his mind, because she bared her teeth in a mock growl and brandished her nails like claws.

"Grr!"

"Not a tame lion," Mr. Jud said, as he steered his wife past them.

That was a quote from The Chronicles of Narnia, a set of books Billy had pushed aside as being awfully childish. "What's it mean?" he asked.

"It means you have to take her like she is, son," Mr. Jud said. He winked at Tee. "That's not a bad thing."

Billy decided he was right. He got right into the dancing, and discovered that even if he wasn't very good at it, he was having fun. Tee looked gorgeous, the house was beautiful, and the strong lights that he had installed kept the growing shadows from dimming the celebration.

It got even more festive when some of Mr. Lou's friends produced their own gift for the newlyweds. They had not only found a stash of liquor on one of their runs out to "Wal-Marts" and "Targets," meaning abandoned homes in humble neighborhoods or upscale ones, but they had been using the lab equipment to distill their own country waters.

"Try some!" Chaz Miller said, coming around the dance floor with a tray of glasses. Tee accepted one at once. She sipped the clear liquor and made a face.

"Wow! Fierce!"

Billy started a hand toward one of the glasses, then pulled it back. Chaz grinned. He slapped a glass into his palm.

"You've earned it, Billy. Besides, if you weren't of age before, you sure are now. All of us have aged twenty years. That makes you almost forty. You think you might deserve a drink?"

"Well..." He tried a sip. The hard liquor burned its way down his throat and made him cough. He had drunk his mom's beer on the sly now and again for a few years, but this was exponentially more intense. He gave the glass back, still mostly full. "Let's dance some more, okay?"

"Okay," Tee said, pleased. "Thanks anyhow."

"No problem," Chaz said. "This won't go to waste!"

Finally, Ms. Melanie persuaded Mr. Lou and Ms. Nora to take their first dance together. Soft, slow music came over the loudspeakers, something with horns and strings. As planned, the lighting softened to moonlight. The wedding couple clung to each other and swayed in the middle of the lawn. Half a dozen of the younger guests recorded it with their cell phone cameras.

Suddenly, whooping and the sound of motorcycle engines rose over the music.

Billy stopped to listen. The noise was unmistakable. He raised his arms to get the attention of the rest of the guests.

"Infecteds!" he shouted. "Coming this way!"

The guests abandoned the buffet and the dance floor, and ran for their firearms. Since they had started to try to rehabilitate betas, everyone was armed with sedative guns and nets, with a couple sharpshooters carrying 30-00 heavy-duty rifles in case the infecteds went crazy. Under the instruction of Chaz, who was a Tennessee State Trooper, and National Guard Angel Velasquez, everyone lined up around the perimeter fence. The security lights kicked on to full, and the electric fence crackled to life.

There they were, maybe the last of the infecteds in this area, arms raised against the sudden glare. Billy counted about fifteen of them. Roger and Elaine had done a great job rounding them up. The two motorcycles revved back and forth behind the mob, preventing them from making an escape.

They didn't charge right away. They milled around, almost as if some of the memories of who they had been had analyzed systems. Still naked, still filthy, still scrawny from near starvation, covered with bruises, sores, and gouges, with their feet half worn to bone by stumbling over rocks and roots in the woods, but wily like wild animals. They carried sticks and rocks for weapons, but they were looking for the weak places to get in, to get at the normal—and the food—inside the perimeter fence. They bared broken teeth and snarled, trying to make up their minds whether to charge or not. Billy's gorge rose at the sight of them, but he hunkered down. This was it, a moment that he could remember for history.

The first infected, a male covered in orange clay, charged the fence. As he touched the wire, blue-white electricity arced under his wasted fingers. He screeched and retreated, wild eyes searching the fence line for weaknesses.

Ms. Nora hitched up her skirt and tied it into a knot at her hip.

"Where's my shotgun?" she demanded, heading for the door of her new house.

Billy jumped up to head her off.

"Ms. Nora, don't!"

She rounded on him, ripping off her veil and flinging it to one side.

"What do you mean, don't?" she asked, her eyes on fire. "You think I'm gonna let zombies ruin my weddin'?"

"No, ma'am!" Billy said. He reached underneath the table holding the remains of the cake and came up with a gun. The shining barrel was festooned with handfuls of colored ribbons and a big bow had been tied around the stock. "This is for you. It's a brand-new tranquilizer gun. We all want you to have it. And we've got three boxes of cartridges for you to use. All yours." He held it out. She put her hands on it, and gave him a sour look.

"You ain't gonna let me kill 'em no more," she said.

"It's your wedding day," Billy said, hoping she would relent. "It's a new day. A fresh start. For everyone. These may be the last ones you ever see. Help the ones who can get better. Find a better life, as much as they can have. Find simple jobs to do. Give them a little dignity, even. Help you, too."

Ms. Nora nodded once, then took the gun. She stuck the boxes in one of the pockets in the seams of the wedding gown.

"You're a good kid, Billy," she said. "Thanks."

Billy went to another emplacement. Tee was already there, a trank pistol in her hands. She leaned over and gave him a kiss. He kissed her back, still feeling bold about showing affection like that, and triggered the spotlights.

"You set this up," Tee said, with a conspiratorial grin.

"Maybe," Billy said, then the secret burst out of him. "Yeah, I did. Roger, Elaine, and I discussed it the other day. I wanted to lure the rest of the local infecteds up to the compound for treatment, and this way, it kills two birds with one stone. I figured it would take them pretty much all day to work their way up here, and the motorcyclists to drive 'em toward us at the last minute. I couldn't think what else would make a good present for Ms. Nora. I just had to make sure she didn't take a shotgun to them."

Tee laughed. "You're a lot smarter than you look." Billy was crestfallen. She kissed him again. "You look pretty smart, so that's a compliment."

Billy felt confused, but decided to enjoy the moment instead of thinking about it too hard.

Ms. Nora stalked toward the south fence, her new rifle loaded with the barrel pointing toward heaven.

"I'll spot them for her," Billy said, rising to his feet.

"I'll do it," Tee said. "You're a much better shot than I am."

She stood up and took the handles of the movable high-intensity light, sweeping it back and forth across the open area on their side of the fenced yard. Billy hoped that the power wouldn't cut out from the demand, but everybody except a skeleton crew was down here from Foresight. There shouldn't be too many people using electricity up above except for what was needed to run the coolers and freezers. He crossed his fingers that the transformers would hold out.

Ms. Nora lowered the barrel, and squeezed the trigger. The orange-covered infected dropped. That seemed to arouse the others. They came rushing toward the fence.

"Call your shots," Mr. Jud bellowed. "Don't waste shells!"

Everyone gave Ms. Nora first crack. With her dead-sure aim, there was no such thing as wasting ammunition.

"Yee-hoo!" she howled, hauling back the action on the beribboned gun and dropping in a new shell.

Pop! A big infected male staggered as the trank dart hit him square in his bony chest. He took another couple of steps forward, and collapsed with his arms over the wire strung along the top of the fence. Fortunately, someone had turned off the power so he didn't fry.

In less time than Billy thought possible, the new bride had potted four of the fifteen. The rest of the infecteds collapsed as darts from the rest of the guests took care of the others. Billy just stood and enjoyed the expression of triumph on Ms. Nora's face. She held her new gun up over her head, and Mr. Lou lifted her high into the air.

"Threat's over! Take 'em back to the lab and let's get 'em evaluated," Mr. Jud said, gesturing toward the fence. "And we'll leave the happy couple to themselves."

Billy looked back over his shoulder just in time to see Mr. Lou sweep Ms. Nora up into his arms and carry her over the threshold of their new house, trank gun and all.

"I hate to say it, but that's one of the most romantic things I ever saw," Tee said, shaking her head.

"It's too much to hope we all get to live happily ever after," Billy said, putting his arm around Tee's shoulders and drawing her up the hill toward the compound. "I'll take what we can get a little at a time."

Chase the Sunset

JAMIE IBSON

"Two-Two-Charlie, contact, wait, out!"

Sergeant Catherine "Cat" Cavanaugh dropped the rope and retreated to the relative safety of her G Wagon. The green, militarized Mercedes SUV provided some much-needed speed, in case the infected turned their way. For once, the plan went as expected, and the now un-barricaded door unleashed a small horde of emaciated infected.

"Now *that* is a thing of beauty," Master Corporal Jessie Rowe chuckled. "Are you going to invite the boys to come watch?"

"I—oh." She reached for her radio PTT again. "Two-Two, Two-Two-Charlie. We're on the west bank of Wascana Lake, east of the Arts Center. Bring the C6 and, or, a Timberwolf, soonest, over."

"Two-Two, roger, send a sitrep, over." Warrant Officer Jim Kolar, Two-Platoon's acting platoon commander, didn't often get requests for the medium machinegun *or* their sniper with his .338 Lapua rifle. Heavier ammunition was rare and valuable.

"Two-Two-Charlie. We removed some of the barricades around the Arts Center and released several dozen infected. They are now in contact with local wildlife. May need something heavier than our small arms. Out."

Less than a minute later, Kolar and Specialist Rob George arrived, George hefting the beefy C14 Timberwolf rifle. Jim Kolar was in his forties, with a salt-and-pepper cop mustache and a trim green beret, despite the near-freezing temperatures. Rob was a barrel-chested First Nations man with dual-citizenship. He'd been a Bradley gunner in Georgia and returned to Canada after he mustered out. Then he landed a gig as a network engineer at ASU London, where he'd met Cavanaugh. With the H7D3 plague being what it was, the veteran soldier dusted off his old BDUs and assisted wherever he was needed. In theory, he might have been an Allied Soldier (Veteran, Recalled), but what with the zombie apocalypse and all, no one was looking at the org chart too closely. Cavanaugh greeted them with a wide smile.

"You know that feeling you get, when that gloriously cruel bitch, Mother Nature, does clearance *for* you?"

Kolar cocked an eyebrow puzzled, but George just started laughing. Their sharpshooter pointed to the banks of the shallow, meandering, twisting lake that bisected the southeast quarter of Regina where a bull moose, whose antlers hadn't quite matured yet, was expressing its displeasure to the Arts Centers' recent occupants. *Violently.*

Cavanaugh laughed as it planted its front hooves and double-kicked backward, sending one H7D3 victim flying across the riverbank. He did not rise again.

"Ouch, only a nine-point-two from the Russian judge," Rowe joked. "Lost points on that landing."

Pleased with the result, the moose circled like a bucking bronco, sending infected scattering like bowling pins, and fifteen hundred pounds of angry bull crushed the ones that were still moving. It caught another one on its still-developing antlers, bucked its head, and threw the infected on a high arc. The crack and meaty thump when that infected hit the ground was audible.

"Sergeant Cavanaugh, did you *actually* need the platoon's heavy weapons?" Kolar asked. He was grinning, so he wasn't *mad*...

"Absolutely. If that swamp donkey kaiju motherfucker comes this way, this Tinkertoy is only going to make it angrier," she said, gesturing to her C7. "That's the fourth moose I've seen since we got to Regina, Jim, and then there's the bears, wolves, and worst of all, the Canada geese. I'm thinking we could mostly just open these infected hives up and let nature do its business. We're going to be tight on ammo until we reach Dundurn, so let's get creative and make use of what we can."

"You make a good point," George said. He tapped his Timberwolf's magazine. "I'm down to just three mags. The redcoat's barracks didn't have anything but nine-mil and twelve-gauge, which was a bit of a kick in the nuts."

"Speaking of which," Rowe replied, and pointed. Kolar and George simultaneously winced as the seven-foot-tall beast kicked an infected male in the groin. The male collapsed and curled up in the fetal position, despite the late-winter snow that still covered the ground, and stayed there.

"Is this your clearance plan, then, Cat?" Kolar asked.

"I need to go check on Deadman; they've fired up a neighborhood a few blocks away.

"If it's stupid, but it works, Jim," she replied. "Can I keep Rob? Just in case our megafauna friend wants to get sporty?"

"Sure," Kolar agreed. He shook his head in disbelief as the moose crushed yet another infected into paste. "It's hard to reconcile how enormous they are, isn't it?"

George laughed. "When I was with Third ID in Georgia, folks couldn't accept how big they were. They thought moose were like deer, but a little bigger. When I told them, *slightly shorter than an elephant*, they thought I was crazy. Who's crazy now, *y'all*?"

The moose concluded its rampage, with twenty or thirty dead or dying infected staining the snow red. Its flanks heaved with exertion, but it was otherwise unharmed.

"That it?" Kolar asked.

"Hardly," Cavanaugh smirked. "It's a big arts center. I've got three more doors, and three more ropes. I'll give my swamp donkey kaiju friend here a minute to catch his breath, and then round two. Mother Nature willing, we'll have Regina cleared to high yellow in no time. Then on, to Moose Jaw."

She pondered for a moment. "Anyone know why it's even called that?"

"Two-Two-Charlie, contact! Wait, out."

Cat hauled the wheel over to the left, slammed on the brakes, and yanked her C7 rifle from the bracket. This time, her C7 would suffice. With the armored G Wagon in park, she bailed out and laid her forearm across the hood. Rowe joined her from the back seat, behind her. A near-emaciated woman, with a child in her arms, limped out from the tiny village on the right side of the highway and across the street as fast as her weak, starved legs could carry her. Two infected pursued her out into the open. As they'd found in Regina, and Winterpeg, and every other town, village and hamlet they'd cleared, the winter drove the infected indoors, where food was scarce to nonexistent. The few that had survived the harsh Canadian winter had subsisted on their fellow plague victims, and Cat didn't feel the slightest tinge of guilt when she flipped her selector switch off safe, led the infected a hair, and squeezed the trigger.

The reserve infantry NCO was pretty sure she'd suffered some serious hearing loss over the last many months because the rifle fire didn't bother her anymore, even without earpro. One more reason she was happy to let the lingering winter do the heavy lifting, clearance-wise. The lead infected fell, Rowe fired a split second later, and the second infected dropped, too. The woman ducked, stumbled, and nearly lost her footing when gunfire shattered the quiet morning, but upon seeing the green army vehicle, she changed directions and limped their way.

"Two-Two, this is Two-Two-Charlie, sitrep. Two infected down, two civilians in the clear, moving forward to make contact." She checked the road sign for the small cluster of buildings. "We're just outside Belle Plaine now, over."

"*Two-Two-Charlie, Two-Two-Sunray. We'll be there in five. Over.*"

"Two-Two-Charlie, roger, out."

∽⊖∾

"Warrant Kolar, this is Kaitlyn Tillie, and her . . . adopted daughter, Jocelyn. Kaitlyn, this is my platoon commander, Warrant Officer Jim Kolar."

Kaitlyn sniffed and managed to meet the warrant's eyes for a moment before looking away again. Jim offered his hand to shake and introduce himself, but the woman shied away from it, like a dog that knew it was about to get swatted with newspaper.

"Kaitlyn, I want you to tell Jim what you just told me. Can you do that?"

Jocelyn looked to be eight, maybe nine years old, with fine but unkempt blonde hair and stick-thin limbs. Kaitlyn seemed too young to be the child's mother, early twenties at most, with auburn hair that hung in tight, unkempt ringlets. She might have been pretty, six months earlier, but starvation simply wasn't glamourous. Jocelyn's lip quivered, and she hugged Kaitlyn's leg, hiding behind her protector. Kaitlyn didn't look happy either, but she took a deep breath, looked off towards the city, and spoke.

"There's . . . there's two men in Moose Jaw, who come out this way. I hid here, out of town, where there's almost nobody and almost no zombies. I honestly think the two Miss Cat here shot were the last two. I scoured the houses for what food there was, and we could melt the snow to drink, but there isn't enough to eat. These men, from the city? They'd come out this way, and they'd trade food for . . ." she let out a quiet sob, and hid her face in her hands. Cat patted her on the shoulder, and she leaned in close for support. Kaitlyn gathered her composure with a deep breath.

She dropped her hands again, balled her hands into fists and glared at the distant horizon. "They'd trade me food for sex," she spat, blunt and angry. "I'd hide Jocelyn away in another house when they came through, but they refused to take me away from here, and the weather's been so cold, and there's nowhere to go, but Moose Jaw and they're *from* Moose Jaw, and they'd only give us enough food to last us until they came by the *next* time. I haven't seen them in I don't know how many weeks now, but the food ran out, and..."

She trailed off. Her rage spent, it broke Cat's heart to hear the story again. Kaitlyn had skipped over the hardest part though, the part that made this even worse, the part that made these coercive, manipulative rapists immediately, *definitely* their problem.

"They were wearing CADPAT, Jim, driving G Wagons, and gave her army rations. They're almost certainly ours."

Belle Plaine was one of the smallest villages Cavanaugh had ever seen, and she'd seen a *lot* of small villages. Maybe three dozen houses, a grain elevator for the railway, and a gas station-restaurant-motel called Chubby's, of all things. Cavanaugh found the station's wrench to access their underground fuel tank and had everyone top up while Warrant Kolar briefed Two Platoon's leadership. In addition to that most precious resource, fuel, the gas station had another essential item: *maps*. Jim spread the paper folder out on the counter for all his section commanders to see and found the Lt. Col D.V. Currie Armoury on the map. He studied the surrounding region as they brainstormed.

"Jessie, you were armoured recce, what are we looking at for weapons and equipment?"

"Tap-Vees, G Wagons, and standard green Chevy Silverados, assuming they've got fuel," Rowe replied.

"C6s, 7s, 8s, and 9s. At the reserves level, armoured recce and mechanized infantry are reasonably similar, equipment-wise. It's the battlefield roles that are different."

"And we have to assume they have fuel," Cavanaugh pointed out. "They've been patrolling the area, and raping Miz Tillie for months."

"Could it just be the two of them?" Sergeant Cole Deadman asked. "They've just gone completely off the leash because they're all that's left?"

"I asked Tillie a few more questions," Cavanaugh said. "She found all the guys intimidating and didn't want to say anymore, but there used to be more troops that rolled past. Men, women, older, younger, and she remembered a young female troop named Ellie? She wasn't sure, her co-driver called her Kayden or something like that, but she stopped coming around once the snows arrived, and that's when the assaults began. She hasn't seen anyone other than our two scumbags since. They're almost certainly legit, but whether they're just slipping in a little casual sexual assault into their regular patrols on the down-low, or whether they're all that's left, no idea."

"Understood. Did Miss Tillie and her ward accept a ride back to Regina?"

"Yes," Deadman replied. "Melissa Hanneman is from the Triple Rs; she'll give them a lift back in one of the technicals with Jas Kaur. They've got plenty of room and food at the redcoat barracks."

"Excellent." Kolar stabbed the map with a finger and traced a road north to where it intersected Highway One. "It's a straight shot south along the main drag to the armouries. Cat, you'll take point again, but I want you to take a pair of C9s with you, in case you come under fire. I'll be next in the order of march with Vlasic and the C6. Rowe?"

"Warrant?"

"When your folks moved to the frozen north, you landed here, right?" She nodded and shivered involuntarily. Moving to the central Canadian prairies from South Africa had been a very *cold* adjustment. "Hard as it is to believe, we may need to assault the Dragoon armouries. Would the mall rooftop be a decent place to establish an OP or a firebase?"

Her eyes widened at the request, but she thought for a moment, then traced a route on the map.

"*Och, bliksem* . . . You'd need ladders to get up most places. But there used to be dumpsters on the east side that might still be tall enough for troops to get up. We used to play kickball there, and whenever someone roofed the ball, we'd scramble up and get it back down. Got yelled at by security all the time, but they were mostly just worried we'd fall and break our *domkop* necks. Otherwise . . . there's trees behind the armouries, but they'll just be bare twigs at this point, nothing's got leaves yet. The Carl G would make a *moerse* hole in their back yard from the rooftop if it came down to it, so, yeah. She'd do."

"Perfect." Kolar sketched out the route he wanted Deadman and Kane to take. "One and Two Section will approach from the east, and provide security for Specialist George. He'll scan the windows and initiate if it proves necessary. Go off-road through this park, bypass as much of suburbia as you can, and get to the mall. If the mall doesn't pan out, send one section north and one south. Keep a block back, and radio if you encounter survivors or infected. If things go completely to shit, we'll either withdraw the way we came or thunder-run past while you provide covering fire."

"I see no way this could go horribly wrong," Deadman said, straight-faced. "What's ROEs and equipment?"

"We're trading vehicles," Kolar replied. "I want the big green machine out front, and our bandit technicals skulking up behind, staying out of sight. They've all got big tire bumpers, so use 'em. No gunfire, unless someone's got a gun and they're going to use it."

At Main, Cavanaugh turned south. Burned buildings lined along the west side of the road, the charred wreckage jutted into the sky like the ribs of the roadside corpses, stripped by scavengers and left in ruin. Sections of Regina had looked like this, and Winnipeg before that. The ground had been dirtied and greyed as ash and charred wood mixed with falling snow. Here and there, reddened spots stained the snow where an infected had died, frozen, and was only just starting to thaw out. Vehicles littered the roads, but many of them could just be avoided or driven around.

As they advanced, one particular SUV caught Cavanaugh's attention. A G Wagon, identical to the one she was driving, sat askew across the southbound lanes. The drivers' side door was ajar, and a thick pile of wet, melting snow on the roof dripped to the asphalt. Cavanaugh pulled her armoured car to a halt and dismounted. Harris joined her on her search, while Griffin Lawson and Sunny Singh covered their flanks with their light machineguns.

"Two-Two, Two-Two-Charlie, over."

"Go for Two-Two, over."

"Two-Two-Charlie. Got a G Wagon here, roadside. Dried blood and old brain matter on the interior, and a C7 on the seat." She unloaded and cleared the rifle. A bullet flew from the chamber, and one more round sat on top of the magazine. That was all. "Two rounds left. No sign of the previous occupants, over."

"Two-Two, roger, G Wagon's owner saved the last rounds for themselves, over."

"Two-Two-Charlie, keys are in the ignition, but the battery's dead. We're carrying on. Out."

Cat collected the keys from the ignition, but when she stepped out, her feet almost rolled out from under her. She kicked the snow away until she found the offending items—a pile of spent 5.56mm casings. She brushed more chunks of ice and snow out of the way and, in moments, turned up her first rifle magazine. Snow and ice had melted into the void below the follower, but it would thaw. Harris turned up another one, and then she found a third mag and *more* casings. Someone had done a *lot* of shooting here, and they'd run out of ammo. She put the iced magazines in the trunk—waste not want not—and had everyone mount up.

"We're not gonna come back for it, are we, Sarge?" Lawson asked. Lawson had been a private with the Algonquins and straight out of infantry school when the collapse hit. "Thing's probably haunted."

"One, of course we are. Two, if haunting a thing is possible, we're going to have a harder time finding something that *isn't*."

Farther south, a narrow creek and series of ponds divided the burned neighborhood from the commercial district where the armouries lay. A pack of grey coyotes—the wolflike predators, not armoured vehicles—trotted along the creek, on the hunt. Unlike before, Cavanaugh had no faith in her ability to draw infected and the coyotes together in another "lets-you-and-him-fight" situation. She eased up on the gas pedal, and crept past a Canadian Tire, three abandoned fast food joints, and reached the U-shaped driveway for the barracks. The front lawn of the Currie Armouries had several military vehicles displayed on it, and she wished they were still serviceable. A WWII-era Fox armoured car sat next to a six-wheeled Cougar, an M113 rested next to a white UN-marked track she didn't recognize, they had a Sherman tank, and more.

The barracks themselves were a large rectangular two-story building made of red brick and heavy stone. The remnants of several A-Frame tents with ragged canvas still hung from the aluminum poles all over the grounds in front of the building itself, and the north side of the building appeared to be a fenced-in vehicle park. She saw five-ton trucks, more armored G Wagons, and a handful of the green converted Chevy Silverados.

"Two-Two, Two-Two-Charlie, we're turning in now, over," she sent.

"*Two-Two, roger, catching up now, over,*" Kolar replied. That he'd just dropped Corporal Vlasic off behind the Canadian Tire, to watch them from a second hide with his medium machine gun, went unsaid. It sucked, but they had to assume they were being listened to if anyone in the barracks had a radio. Cavanaugh pulled her armored car to a halt, and Rowe was out the door in a flash, scanning the front of the building with her rifle. Singh and Lawson bailed too, scanning the rooftops and windows.

"Everybody confirm they're still on safe," Cavanaugh warned. "We don't initiate."

Warrant Kolar arrived next with his driver, and two more G Wagons containing the rest of Three Section pulled in behind him.

"How do we gain access, Warrant?" Private Joel Harris asked. He and Lawson had been through battle school together, and even if they kicked ass at clearance, neither one quite seemed to *get* the whole "chain of command" thing.

"Let's try knocking," Kolar replied. "Stack left, Harris, you asked, you can go first."

Harris gulped and pulled his bayonet from its frog. He slammed the butt of it against the door several times. "CANADIAN FORCES! OPEN UP!" he bellowed, then stepped aside so as not to be bowled over by the doors if they swung open. They waited ten seconds, and Harris repeated himself. Another ten seconds passed, and he was about to bash the door a third time when they heard a *clunk*, a *chunk*, and then a *creak* as the door swung open. Cavanaugh and Harris stepped forward, and a slim, dark-haired female wearing a combat T-shirt and CADPAT pants greeted them. She eyed their uniforms for a moment and burst into tears.

"Oh, thank Christ," she gushed and pushed the doors open wider. "Who are you with? Are you here to rescue us? He's, uh, he's in through there," she pointed.

"Who's through there?" Cavanaugh followed the woman inside, flanked by her fireteam. The enormous wooden doors opened into a broad hallway, with offices on both sides, before passing through another broad archway and opening up into what must have been their interior parade square. "Names, soldier."

"Govnar!" the woman squeaked. "Warrant Govnar! I'm Elyssa. Private Elyssa Kaliszewska, Sergeant." She pronounced it *Callie-zoo-ska.* "You aren't—you don't know?"

"Pretend I don't."

"It's easier for you to see for yourself, Sergeant," the young private meekly replied. She looked as browbeaten as Kaitlyn had. A male soldier rounded the corner from the parade square, and four weapons instantly came up.

"Hands! Show me your hands," Cavanaugh ordered, and the surprised soldier did so. His hands shot up, and he froze.

"Is this him?"

"No!" Kaliszewska squeaked. "That's Sergeant Yannick! It's not his fault!"

"What the hell is going on in there, Cavanaugh?" Kolar demanded from the doorway, and entered the hall regardless. The sergeant was older, perhaps Jim's age, had thin, patchy scruff, and wore thick glasses. Harris patted him down, found nothing, and then covered Cavanaugh as she quickly searched young Kaliszewska for weapons. Kolar brought the rest of his team into the hallway and advised the rest of the platoon they'd made contact. Kaliszewska started crying again, and the sergeant was pale with a sheen to his forehead as if he might faint.

"What is it you want to show us?" Cavanaugh asked.

"Govnar's in his office, and . . . and he's got Rylie in there with him."

Kaliszewska led Cavanaugh, Kolar, and the rest of the troops into the central drill hall of the armoury, across the wooden floor, and to a set of offices. Sergeant Yannick, whoever he was, remained utterly mute. As Cavanaugh entered the hall proper, she saw another soldier in a kitchenette off to the side, washing dishes. She was also female, and to Cavanaugh's shock, she wore even less than Kaliszewska, merely a sports bra. She had a shiner, reddened cheeks, and when she looked up to see them, she dropped the plastic dish she was rinsing.

"What's going on, Private? Why isn't *she* dressed either?"

"Govnar, Sergeant—he's through here," Kaliszewska replied without answering Cavanaugh's question. She gestured down a hallway off the drill hall towards an office door marked MAJ. B. C. JAEGER—COMMANDING OFFICER. Cavanaugh pointed a knife-hand at Harris and motioned for him to get behind her. With her rifle at the low ready, she pushed the office door open.

A male in combats sat in the CO's chair behind his desk. He had a grip on a *third* female's ponytail, forcing her to fellate him. She was gagging, audibly.

As the door opened, so did his eyes. "What the fuck!" he shouted, leaping to his feet and dragging the topless woman up with him. Cavanaugh's C7 snapped up, but Govnar held his victim in front of him as a human shield. The other hand, the one not holding his hostage's hair, held a pistol, and he pointed it at the girl's neck.

"Fuck you, 'what the fuck'!" Cavanaugh snapped. "Warrant? We've found our rapist!"

"Hey, take it fuckin' easy," the man said. The change in his demeanor was obvious, but he didn't lower the pistol. "You just surprised me is all. Everyone here knows not to interrupt when I'm enjoying some quality time; no need for the guns."

"*Quality* time?" Cavanaugh repeated.

"You can't blame a guy for wanting a little action, can you?" he countered, but he didn't lower the gun.

"*Quality time!*" Cavanaugh snarled.

"You're makin' me nervous here," Govnar repeated. "It ain't what it looks like! The bitch likes it rough."

"That's not what Kaitlyn Tillie in Belle Plaine said, you piece of filth!"

"*Fuck you*, lady. Just because I want a piece before I share out what little food I've got left doesn't make me a monster. Some people ain't got nothing of value but time. She'd have starved to death months ago if it weren't for me. She should be *thanking* me, that ungrateful bitch."

"That's about enough, Govnar," Kolar spat. "I'm placing you under arrest for sexual assault."

"Fuck you, Judge Dredd, what, you think you're The Law? There *is* no law. The law *died* last fall, along with Canada, and the States and the rest of the fuckin' world."

"Well, gee, I never thought about it that way," Cavanaugh said. The sarcasm was thick. "I suppose you're right."

"What the hell are you talking about, Cat?" Kolar whispered.

"No, seriously." Her eyes hardened, and she spoke even louder. "If there's no government, then there's no law, and if there's no law, then there's no crime anymore. The crime rate just hit zero. Nobody has the authority to arrest anyone for anything."

"See?" Govnar said. "She gets it. No law, no government, I can do whatever the fuck I want."

Kolar gave Cavanaugh a questioning look. *Trust me*, her eyes said back. "And so can I. So, I'm going to kill you."

"*What*?" Kolar and Govnar shouted, at the same time.

"No law, right, asshole? What law is there to protect you from someone like me? Someone who despises rapists with every fiber of her being? You say there's no law in effect? The law is the only thing protecting *you* from *me*!"

"Ho-ho-hold on, hold on a minute. Maybe—"

"No wonder the private said 'rescue'; you've got the women walking around in T-shirts or *topless* when it's minus five outside! Sex or starvation? You're predatory scum!"

"That's enough, Sergeant," Kolar said, but Cavanaugh wasn't finished.

"I should shoot you right now in the kneecaps and turn you over to your 'unit'! See how long it takes for you to bleed out—we've got a trauma medic, *she* could keep you alive a *looong time*, you utter disgrace. The *law* may be dead, but *justice* hasn't gone anywhere!"

Govnar seemed taken aback at first, but then remembered he had both a hostage and a gun of his own. "You aren't doing shit, bitch! You back off and lower your rifle, or the next thing you see is her brains splattered all over your scope. Back off, give me some space, or I kill her now. I know how this shit works. You can't say no to me! You've gotta *negotiate*."

The woman he'd been assaulting suppressed a sob and leaned away from the pistol as he jammed it harder against her jaw. It sucked, but Cavanaugh had to admit she didn't have a shot. The offset between the scope and the rifle was enough that, at this close distance, she couldn't be sure she could take him out with one round and, of course, the scumbag rapist had his finger on the trigger already. Fight was no good; the hostage would die. Flight was worse; this was their problem to solve. Bluster had failed—but she could submit, partially, turn that a bluff, and play for time.

"Okay," Kolar interrupted. This time, *his* eyes said, *trust me*. "That's *enough*, Sergeant. See to the others. I'll handle this."

Cavanaugh cursed, but she knew she might have gone a bit too far. She lowered her rifle and backed up down the hallway.

"That's right, hero, back up. We're going to get mighty comfy in here. Get me some coffee, Judge Dredd, and have one of the girls bring it in. Hurry up."

"That'll take a minute to brew, Govnar. Let's talk about what you want to get out of this," Kolar said, negotiating in earnest this time.

"A tall ship and a star to steer her by."

"I can give you a truck. Full tank of gas. You're all about trades, right? Food for sex? How about a Lincoln Navigator for her life?"

"A *Navigator*? I like the way you roll. Bring it right into the drill hall, and leave all the overhead doors wide open."

"Cover him, Harris," Kolar announced, loudly. "I'll see if I can't rustle up some coffee and a set of keys."

"Covering," Harris replied mechanically, focusing down the scope of his C7. Kolar and Cavanaugh slipped back down the hallway together and ushered Private Kaliszewska away from the line of fire.

"All callsigns Two-Two," Kolar spoke into his radio, once they were far enough away. "Two-Two-Sunray. Things have gone to hell in a hurry, we've got a barricaded soldier with a human shield. Two-Two-Bravo, keep eyes on the black/red corner, over."

"*Bravo, black/red corner, roger, over,*" Sergeant Deadman replied.

"Sunray, out."

"Jess, do you have spare combats?" Cavanaugh asked. "Mine need a good scrub before they're decent again."

"Sure, be right back."

Cavanaugh gestured for the Dragoons to follow her into a side office near the front entrance.

"Elyssa, right?" Cavanaugh began, and Kaliszewska nodded.

"Or Kay-Ten, like my last name. K plus ten more letters..."

"I'm familiar with Polish names, Elyssa." Cavanaugh smiled. She hadn't been living with this nightmare for who-knew how many months, so she put on a brave face. "Introductions. I'm Cat, Sergeant, originally with 4RCR from 31 Brigade, South-West Ontario. Now I'm with this lashup; we're calling it Task Force Sunset." Rowe joined them, carrying a pile of combat shirts. "This is my two-eye-see, Master Corporal Jessie Rowe, six years in Lord Strathcona's Horse."

"And I'm Danielle McLeod," the third woman replied. "Corporal, seven years in. I was a fitness trainer in town before everything went to shit. The girl in there with the warrant is Rylie Hamilton, a new private, like Elyssa here."

"I assume Govnar demanded you remain undressed?" Cavanaugh asked, and both women nodded.

"When we pissed him off, he'd demand articles of clothing as punishment. Don't..." Kay-Ten looked to McLeod, and she nodded. "Don't blame Sergeant Yannick. It wasn't his fault. He won't admit it, but Govnar and Connard abused him, too. He's not a fighter, Sergeant, he's an accountant from Saskatoon who counted bullets at Camp Dundurn."

"Who's Connard?" Rowe asked.

"Another shithead, got bit on patrol two weeks back," McLeod answered. "He and Govnar arrived together, armoured recce liaisons from the Strathcona Horse."

"Oh did they now?" Rowe asked. "I call shenanigans. I've been there six years, never met no Warrant Govnar, never met no Sergeant Connard. And the Strats aren't exactly a great, giant unit where a couple senior assholes could be missed."

Cavanaugh tapped her finger on the SIG Sauer holstered on her leg. "If he's the kind of shit for brains who thinks women are poor, defenseless waifs, maybe..."

"...Maybe we ought to disabuse him of such antiquated thinking," Rowe said. There was fury behind her eyes, and without another word, they turned to find Warrant Kolar.

"Jim, what's your plan here?" Cavanaugh asked. She and Rowe had pulled him aside, and kept her voice low.

"Draw him out, and have George take him down as they go to leave."

"I have a suggestion."

And she told him.

"That's . . . risky," Kolar objected.

"It is," she agreed. "But a helluva lot better than relying on Rob to make a headshot, on a moving target, through door glass, while he may or may not have a gun to a hostage's head. You need to buy us some time to set it up, though."

"I can start by sending him the coffee," Kolar said, thoughtfully. "Drag that out as long as I can manage."

"And here I am, completely out of laxatives and iocane powder," Rowe said with a smirk. "Plus, he demanded 'one of the girls' bring it. We can all guess what he's got on his mind. I'll go. I've a blade in my boot and if he gives me half a chance, I'll cut the fokker's Jakob off and jam it down his throat."

Kolar eyed Cavanaugh. "She's your troop, how do you feel about that?"

"It's her ass, it's her call," Cat stated. "We're low on options and need to draw him out where he's vulnerable so I can take the shot." She gulped hard. "The longer he's in there, the more likely he's going to just start blasting."

Kolar nodded at that. "Agreed. Jess, if you're willing, you'll deliver the coffee. I'll have Deadman bring one of the technicals up."

"Where's my gawddamned coffee, Dredd?" Warrant Govnar demanded. "I'm getting a bit twitchy in here, lacking my caffeine and all!"

"It's almost finished brewing, Govnar," Kolar shouted down the hallway. "Another thirty seconds. How do you take it?"

"Just have the girl bring everything with her. I want

a thermos, a travel mug, milk, and sugar. Make sure the lids are nice and tight, I know what happened on United Ninety-Three, so don't fuck with me on this or she dies."

"You guys have milk?" Jessie whispered to Kaliszewska.

"We had a couple of pallets of American MREs," she whispered back. "They came with juice boxes, but with milk in them instead. They don't go bad for years. I have no idea why."

"That's bizarre."

Kolar confirmed that the tray was prepared, and flashed Rowe a quick thumbs-up. "Okay, Warrant!" he called down the hallway. "We're bringing you the coffee now. Your soldiers out here are afraid, so one of our females is bringing it in, instead. We have Navigators and Yukon Denalis. Which do you want?"

"I like how you assholes roll, chump, but I'll stick with the Navigator. What happened to the hero chick? She was way easier on the eyes than you are, old man."

"We had a disagreement," Kolar replied. "I felt you could be reasoned with; she did not. So she's been relieved." He toggled the PTT on his radio. "Two-Two-Charlie, Two-Two-Sunray. That's a go for the Navigator, over."

"Charlie, roger on the Navigator, over," Private Singh replied.

"So we bring you the Navigator, right here into the building on the parade square, then what?" Kolar asked. "How do we know you're going to let the girl go?"

"I've been thinking about that," Govnar said. "I'm a pretty pragmatic guy. If I let the girl go, your psycho Amazon hero chick kills me out of spite. If I take the girl with me and don't let her go, you assholes chase me down, and the same thing happens. But if I take the girl with me just as far as, say, Highway One, and I let her out there, then we're square. I know for a fact you'll be able to follow my tracks in this snow, no matter where I go. So that's how it's gonna be. I let her out there, and your pet psychopath is less likely to kill my ass dead."

"I can't say I'm real keen on letting you leave with a hostage," Kolar replied.

"I can't say I give a flying fuck," Govnar sneered. "I ain't getting my ass shot off, and you're probably *less* keen on having dead chick brains blown all over this here office, and have it be *your* fault. So that's what I'm doing, or people die. Where the *hell* is that coffee?"

"Coming now," Kolar answered. Jess had been listening to the exchange, took a deep breath, and composed herself. Did she trust the team? Yes, she did. Could things still go horribly awry? Yes, they could. But courage was being afraid and doing your duty anyway. She lifted the plastic cafeteria tray with the thermos, mug, milk boxes, and sugar, and walked down the hallway, into the lion's den. When she entered the room, she kept her eyes low and tried to look frightened.

"And who are *you*, pretty lady?"

"My name's Jessica, Warrant," she muttered.

"*Hello, nurse!* A beautiful redhead with a sexy accent. Where you from? Australia? Kiwiland?"

"Pretoria, Warrant," she said. "That's in South Africa."

"I know where Pretoria is, girl, I just suck with accents. I like you. I think *you're* coming with me instead."

"What?" Jess protested, sounding scared. "That wasn't the deal!"

"I'm changing the deal." The warrant leaned out from behind his human shield and pointed his pistol at her. "Lift your shirt, Red, show me you don't have any weapons tucked into those combats."

Jess raised her eyes and looked him square in the face. She pulled up her combat shirt to expose her midriff and rotated in place. "I'm just a driver, Warrant," she lied. "I just drive the snowplow. We don't have guns enough for everyone."

"Well, you'll do nicely, I think." Govnar smiled with a greasy look on his face and shoved his hostage away. "Get outta here, bitch, Dragan Govnar just traded up." He gestured for Jess to take her place. The traumatized woman stumbled before dashing out of the room to the drill hall. "You know what they say about redheads?"

"Get stuffed, acourse I do, *domkop*. You twats seem to think it's some big secret we never hear. Hardy har har, 'you can sleep with a blonde, or you can sleep with a brunette...'" she trailed off. She couldn't get *too* mouthy, or he might *actually* hurt her.

"But you won't get any sleep with a redhead!" the warrant cackled, and Jessica's loathing for the man plumbed new depths. The hostage disappeared back down the hallway, and Rowe was left alone with the rapist and his gun. He gestured for her to come to him, and she felt *violated* when he wrapped his arm around her waist and slipped his hand up under her shirt. But the muzzle of the pistol pressed against *her* jaw now, and she suppressed a shudder. *It's all according to plan*, she told herself, but that wasn't entirely true. She had a blade in her boot, but couldn't reach it like this.

"Coffee's good and all, chump," her captor called down the hallway. "But I'm still waiting for my ride! Might decide Red here can keep me entertained until it shows up."

"Now hold on, Dragan, I appreciate that you let that young woman go, but taking Jessica complicated things. You fucked us, breaking the deal like that. We've got to get the snowplow out of the way to bring the Navigator in, and she was our driver," he lied. "It'll be just another minute."

"Excuses are like assholes, chump, everyone has one, and they all stink," the warrant replied. "Just git'er done."

Joel Harris eased his up-armored Lincoln SUV through the overhead doors into the drill hall and made an eight-point-turn that left snowy tracks all over the hardwood. Eventually, he got the SUV backed up to the hallway leading to the OIC's office, put it in park, and stepped out. The Navigator had been Joel's pet Mad Max project after the Fall. It had belonged to his parents before they turned, and after they were gone, he went to work in his shop. As the world went to hell, Joel bolted on sheets of armor, or plywood, and affixed chains to the frame. He hung tires off them as enormous, heavy-duty bumpers for high-speed zombie bowling. The sunroof became a turret, and each door had a set of friction-fit rubberized arms to hold an occupant's rifle. The surviving Lake Soups, the Lake Superior Scottish Regiment, had been duly impressed. He'd led their post-apocalyptic patrols as far as North Bay, where they linked up with surviving members of Canada's government, holed up six hundred feet down. Now, they were heading northwest with the rest of their rag-tag platoon, to Edmonton. He'd spent a *lot* of time, energy, and money making the Navigator the perfect war rig. So he *very* much hoped Sergeant Cavanaugh knew what she was doing.

"Doors are open, and the engine's running, Govnar!" Kolar called down the hallway.

"Perfect! Now, all you little do-gooders go for a walk, so Red and I can make our cunning getaway. I'll give you to the count of ten, and if I see a uniform, Red dies first."

"Back!" Kolar called. "Everyone, back!"

He, Harris, Lawson, and the last three Dragoons retreated to the entryway hall.

"We're in the hallway now, Warrant! You're clear to leave!"

"Bring the tray, Red, you're driving as far as the highway," Govnar said.

"Yes, Warrant," Jess replied, keeping her eyes fixed on the floor. Once the cafeteria tray was in her hands, Govnar prodded her with his pistol to get her to advance down the hallway. They shuffled forward, with the warrant using her as a shield to cover his advance. He peered around corners and cleared each doorframe before he committed to entering the drill hall. Her heart pounded in her chest, and she had to remind herself to breathe.

That'd be awkward, she thought. Pass out, and miss the show?

∽⊖∾

"Get ready to take a seat, on my count," the rapist piece of shit ordered. As Jess moved to sit in the driver's seat, Govnar had his eyes glued on the main entrance doorway, and tried to find the edge of the SUV with his right leg. He was getting in the back seat.

Perfect.

"On three, step up into the SUV. Clear?" he asked.

Jessie Rowe nodded. "Clear, Warrant."

"One, two, thr—"

There was a moment, perhaps one-second-long, where Jess was in the clear. Govnar went to step up into the back of the SUV and lowered the pistol to clear the B pillar. As he stepped up, and his butt cheek found the seat, his Browning pointed at the drill hall floor rather than Jessica. During the first half of that second, Govnar began saying the word "three" and ducked to slide onto the rear bench.

The human eye is attracted to movement. It evolved to spot game on the African savanna, back when prehistoric tribes would literally chase their prey until it collapsed from exhaustion. Being able to detect and focus on that movement was a predator's instinct, and it was one of the many characteristics that made humanity among the deadliest persistence predators on the earth.

Some of the deadliest individuals on earth, therefore, are trained snipers. Snipers are very, *very* good at remaining very, very *still*, which makes it unbelievably hard for the human eye to detect them. While Catherine Cavanaugh had not attended the CAF's mysterious sniper school, she was still an infantry soldier and understood the concept. Her dark blanket let her blend into the shadows behind the SUV's dark tint. She only needed to move the tiniest fraction to bring her pistol in line, and then the only thing that moved was her trigger finger. The mid-point of the aforementioned second was when she finished squeezing, and sent a 9mm hollowpoint through Dragan Govnar's temple, from a distance of about four feet.

Time resumed its normal flow as the bark of the pistol shattered the quiet in the drill hall, and the contents of Govnar's head painted the floor for about twelve feet. The Browning Hi-Power in his hand clattered to the floor safely beside him, while blood and brains leaked out a baseball-sized exit wound.

"Tango down," she breathed. Then, she repeated herself more loudly. "Tango down!"

In the front seat, Jess blew out a breath and just gripped the steering wheel for a moment before bouncing out of the cab, as Kolar, Harris, and the others rushed out from the front hall.

"HA! *Jou fokken doos!"* Jess slipped back into her native Afrikaans. *"Bladdy bliksem! Fok jou, boudkapper!"* She punted the body, hard, and felt one of the dead man's ribs crack with the impact, and spat on his leaking corpse. She kicked it again, and then a third time. "And *you!* You sweet beautiful killer you!" Jess dashed to the rear of the Navigator and flung the hatch open. Cavanaugh sat there, mostly covered by the dark blanket, pale and gulping deep breaths. Jessie grabbed her around the midsection and dragged her out in a bear hug.

"Oooohhh, we are So Totally Besties Right Now!" Jess gushed. "If I batted for the other team, I'd have yer babies. Wow. Oh, *God*, wow. I've got the shakes and everything! I don't think I've been this spun up since that...uh...I'm not going to finish that sentence." Jess flushed a bright pink in her cheeks and hugged Cavanaugh even tighter as tears of relief and joy streamed down her cheeks.

"I think I'm gonna be sick," Cavanaugh confessed. She bent over to retch.

"Hey," Kolar said, joining them and kneeling next to her. "Hey. You did amazing back there. Combat breathing. You've done this a hundred times before. In-two-three-four-out-two-three-four..."

Cavanaugh breathed deep and swallowed hard as she struggled to keep her breakfast down. "You have no idea how hard that was," she gasped out.

Kolar studied her, puzzled. "You've killed *hundreds* of zombies since the Fall? Why?"

"And that was the worst. By far. Worse than Thunder Bay, worse than Winnipeg, *way* worse than Regina."

"Why?" Harris asked.

"Because he was still human!" she shouted at the floor. "He wasn't just some naked infected zombie!"

Finally, her legs gave out, and she collapsed to the floor. Jessie Rowe joined her and hugged her close. Cavanaugh's voice became a rasp. "He was a clothed, normal human *monster*, and that made it a hundred times worse. Infected aren't *people* anymore; they're easy. They're predictable. They're just *hungry*, not *evil*. I had to sit back there, watching, waiting, *praying* the perfect moment would appear to shoot him and hope he didn't kill Jessie, or that *I* didn't miss and kill Jessie, or that I didn't fuck up and get Jessie killed...I could barely hear the radio over my heartbeat in my ears."

"And yet, your fears were entirely for her, and not for yourself," Kolar said. "There's cold courage in that. Take all the time you need."

Rob George, Sergeant Deadman, and Master Corporal Kane entered the main hallway with their teams. George took in the leaking mess on the floor and raised his eyebrows. Her shot placement had been precise, making an almost invisible hole in Govnar's ear canal, and a spectacular, messy crater on the other side of his head where the hollowpoint exited. *Impressive*.

"Man, I don't know what the big deal is," Lawson whispered to Singh. "So she blasted one fucking scumbag, so what?"

"So you'll be volunteering to take point on the next life or death crisis, Private?" George snarled. Lawson's head snapped up, *Kolar's* head snapped up, but Rob had no patience for insubordinate noobs and being part of the team without actually holding rank, had its perks. "I'll be damned if I'm going to let you mouth off after one of the finest displays of bravery I've ever seen. Step up or shut up."

The platoon sniper left Lawson speechless, crossed the parade square floor, and took hold of one of the dead man's boots. "With your permission, Sergeant Cavanaugh, I'll dispose of this for you?"

Cavanaugh grimaced, nodded, and Rowe hauled her up to her feet. "Thank you, Rob. Lawson, we'll address this further in private."

Rob dragged the body through the open overhead door and into the icy outdoors. *Let the crows and coyotes have him*, he thought. For that matter, it might lure some infected out of doors, where that frigid bitch, Mother Nature, would further reduce them. He ignored the leaking fluids and grey matter and stripped off the dead man's ID plates.

Lawson was pouting when Rob reentered the barracks. He already had a bucket out and a mop in hand as he swabbed the bloody trail left by Govnar's leaking corpse. Except, the ID plates suggested the dead man wasn't someone named Govnar at all. "Anyone ever heard of a C Bergeron?" Rob asked the others. He handed the metal ID necklace off to Kolar, who studied the plates.

"That sonofabitch," Kolar breathed. "*Chad* Bergeron was a sergeant in the Cambridge Highlanders. He got into all kinds of shit when we deployed with Op Athena. I never met him, but everyone was talking about it. He came home early, disgraced, and accepted a somewhat less than honourable discharge rather than go to jail. They *should* have jailed him. He extorted locals, intimidation, threats . . . He might have killed some folks, but they never pinned it on him. From the stories I heard, he should have been done for murder one."

"I beg your pardon, Warrant?" Yannick interrupted. "Disgraced?"

"No, it's okay, Sergeant, I get it. There's chaos, people coming and going, units getting parted out, people are dying, then some senior NCO shows up claiming to be a liaison from the Regs. Nobody's heard of him coming, but that's SOP for a planetwide SNAFU like this one. He shows up, walks the walk, talks a mean talk, inserts himself into the chain of command, and nobody's the wiser."

"Good!" Cavanaugh interjected. "The stress of my having emptied his cranium is rapidly coming to an end. Time for the pitch, Jim?"

"Sure," Kolar grinned.

Cavanaugh rolled her head side to side, as though limbering up for a race, cracked her knuckles, and smiled to the four survivors. "Ladies, Sergeant, time for us to lay our cards on the table. Task Force Sunset, which I alluded to earlier, is half, more or less, of the in-contact remnants of the Canadian Armed Forces. Task Forces Sunrise and Sunset began at North Bay. There's a NORAD bunker there, where Prime Minister Singer, General Nadarzinski, ten more members of Parliament and assorted aides, boyfriends, girlfriends, husbands, wives, and mistresses, are all waiting out this plague, six hundred feet underground. Sunrise started working its way east, to Petawawa, Ottawa, south to Kingston, then following the Highway One corridor east. *Their* job is to chase the sunrise every day; reconnect with Eastern Ontario, Quebec, and the Maritimes.

"Task Force Sunset's job is to do likewise, but west-bound. Once we're done here, we'll move on to Fifteen Wing and then the ammo bunkers at Dundurn. We have a string of soldiers, militias, survivors, *Canadians*, between here and the Atlantic, and *everyone* needs ammo. Ammo will let the survivors clear infected. Ammo will let the survivors clear bandits, opportunists, and the occasional stolen-valour scumbag who needs aerating. Winter has already done a lot of the heavy clearing for us, but it's still dicey out there. Bagged rations, canned, and dry goods are a finite resource. If our surviving farmers can't get crops planted, then starvation will kill us as assuredly as H7D3, and it takes time and expertise to grow food and rebuild a distribution network. Distributing ammunition first will break trail. Once Dundurn is up and running, we're off to Saskatoon and then the big prize, Edmonton. We know there are survivors—North Bay has satellite comms with the Patricias, the *real* Strats, and the rest of First Brigade. Once we've unfucked their logistics and delivered a couple tons of ammo, it's off to see the Pacific and link up with any surviving units in BC."

Corporal McLeod exchanged a look with Kaliszewska, Hamilton, and the clerk, Sergeant Yannick. "That's a helluva pitch, Cat, but we still don't know what you're selling."

"Sergeant Yannick, you worked at Camp Dundurn, correct?"

"Yes, I ran systems there to track accounting the ammunition and arranged deliveries."

"How'd you like to get back up there? We'll need someone who can run the show, distributing ammunition across six time zones, eventually. TF Sunset is much larger than just Two Platoon, and we have a follow-on security element who can protect you while you get the logistics train rolling. We could get you home to Saskatoon—if you'd like?"

"I'd like that a lot," he admitted.

"And you three badass survivors." Cavanaugh smiled at the other three soldiers. "Have you ever seen the sun setting over the ocean? Would you like to?"

Descent into the Underworld

BRIAN TRENT

"Seems you have unwanted guests," she said, stepping back from the tower viewer and inviting him to look. The Umbrian countryside below was a scene of pastoral tranquility—at least, it appeared that way from the mountaintop. Farmhouses dotted fields of subsistence crops, hemmed in by orderly rows of cypress trees like green spears.

Anna grimaced. "Go on, take a peek. Tourists used to pay three euros to use this, and they never had the view you're about to."

Silvio Cipriano peered through the viewer's telescopic lens. It was aimed on his village's northern border, where fencing terminated at a rocky gulch by the woods.

And someone was there.

Silvio's natural thought was that one of the villagers was collecting timber for fuel. Then he noticed the man's naked condition, the dirt and bloody scratches on his body, the wild hair and scraggly beard. The intruder lurched from the forest, limping rapidly towards the gulch.

263

"It's a zombie," he muttered, using the English word. "One of the shy ones, looks like."

Anna nodded. "And you're about to see him disappear."

He swiveled the view to the watchtower below, a defensive structure he'd insisted the village construct during the previous winter. Sure enough, a lookout was up there—Salvatore, the college kid who'd fled from Rome with his parents—but he was *facing the wrong way*, reclining in his perch with a cigarette in hand, rifle at his feet.

Silvio hissed his displeasure.

"Keep watching," Anna said.

"For what? Our intrepid lookout is not *looking* where he's supposed to. That zombie could wander right into a yard and..." His breath caught. "Holy *shit!*"

From the edge of the lens, a dark flood erupted from the woods. Silvio jerked the viewer back to the gulch to see the largest pack of dogs he'd ever witnessed—some thirty or forty animals strong. They were a gangrel bunch—even before the outbreak, feral dogs had been a problem in Italy, crowding out local fauna, breeding wildly (and interbreeding with wolves), and harassing unwary travelers. The situation had only gotten worse since the Fall. Man's best friend had learned that, in the absence of man, there was strength in numbers.

The zombie whirled in panic, and then the pack was upon him. Jaws snapped, tearing away sheaves of flesh, grasping at every limb. The victim dissolved into dozens of hungry mouths.

If there was any kind of pecking order, Silvio didn't see it. Chalk it up to one more feature of the new reality: any hint of domesticity in canines was long gone. He shuddered but couldn't look away from the carnage; a particularly wolfish-looking dog ripped off the zombie's hand and went scampering off with it. In the village watchtower, young Salvatore had *finally* heard the disturbance, grabbed his rifle, and was staring in slack-jawed amazement through his scope.

Shivering, Silvio stepped back from the viewer. "That's a bad way to die," he said softly. "Even for one of the infected..."

Anna's eyes were bright in the late afternoon glow. "Did I tell you I was a tour director in Pompeii? There were *always* homeless dogs in those ruins, begging for scraps."

"They're not begging anymore."

She heard the anxious tone in his voice. "You should move up here, Silvio. You, your daughter, and your mother. It's not safe down there."

"Nowhere is truly safe." Haunted memories flickered at the edge of his thoughts, and not all of them were from these cruel apocalyptic days. "Do you know what the traders from Venice told me last week? Fishermen are having problems with octopuses! The things have moved into the canals and turned crafty and aggressive. They pull down the nets, they mess with the salt pools." He glanced back to the blood-stained gulch. "It's like with these dogs. Humanity is fighting for its place in nature again."

"There are no octopuses *or* dogs up here."

Silvio's gaze flicked to the wrought-iron gates behind her, where a narrow path led into the mountaintop caves. They had once been a tourist attraction: a twisting, labyrinthine system of tunnels dating back to the Etruscans. Since the Fall, a group of survivors had seen the wisdom in rediscovering their ancestral stomping grounds: Anna's people grew vegetables atop the mountain, but their real achievement was the pigeons: like the bygone Etruscans, they'd taken to raising pigeons for meat. A convenient, sustainable source of protein to replace bygone supply chains.

But as with everything in the post-Fall reality, no group could afford isolation. Trade was how humanity had invented civilization... and it promised to do so again.

As the infected began to wither away with the old year, a Trade Road began forming along the old highways. Italian communities were warily reaching out, eager to barter for essentials. Half-sunken Venice supplied fish, salt, and potassium chlorate (cooked down from seaweed). Boats from the south were bringing lemons and other fresh fruit. A scavenger faction west of Bologna had looted a warehouse of paper products and canned goods. Cheeses and salted pork were trickling in from a repurposed medieval monastery...

Silvio hefted his bag of smoked pigeon meat—an offering from the cave people to prove they were ready to join the effort. "I'll let the traders know your group is open for business," he said.

Anna gave a sidelong look. "You're evading the subject."

"You noticed that, did you?"

"You live in an unprotected village, Silvio."

"Not true. We have a fence."

"And a useless lookout."

"I'll be having a conversation with young Salvatore," he growled. "Believe that."

"One kid with a rifle isn't good security. The caves here are—"

"Dangerous."

She raised an eyebrow. "How?"

"For a little girl," he clarified. And it was true. The mountain's geography made it a natural citadel, but for a child—especially one as relentlessly curious as his Caterina—there were dangers. One misstep and she could fall off a cliffside perch, or go tumbling down a narrow chasm.

"Besides," he added, "I didn't exactly make friends here today."

Anna shook her head. "Is that what you're concerned about? Listen, Giuseppe was a jerk before the world ended. He likes to throw his weight around, figuring no one will stand up to him. You showed him he was wrong." She gave a winning smile. "By the way, where the hell did you learn to fight like that? Giuseppe's a big fellow, but you swatted him down like he was nothing."

Quickly, Silvio said, "He was drunk. It's no measure of fighting skill to topple a drunk."

His new friend looked less than content with that answer, and Silvio cursed himself for being careless. There was wisdom in ending a fight fast—there were no hospitals for fixing a broken hand or repairing a broken jaw.

Yet the truth was that Silvio had been drunk, too—an extra cup of Chianti had put him over the edge. And for a man of his skillset and body count, that was bad business. Giuseppe, the wannabe alpha male of the mountain, had made one too many unflattering comments about Silvio's village and its farmers, and Silvio—already in a dark mood and feeling the wine—responded in kind. Like any bully, Giuseppe had puffed up at the talkback. He'd grabbed Silvio...

...and that had been a mistake.

Anna hunched over the tower viewer again, listlessly taking in the village. "Um...isn't *that* your daughter?"

Silvio brushed her aside and peered through the lens again. Sure enough, he spotted little Caterina. She was not allowed to leave the cottage yard by herself, but there she was, playing in the gulch with her stuffed bunny. Unaware that just around the bend, dozens of feral dogs were feasting on the dead.

A rifle shot cracked from the watchtower. The dogs melted away, dragging what remained of the bloody corpse into the woods.

Silvio sprang back from the viewer. "Goddam it! I *told* her to stay indoors until I returned!"

"The dogs are leaving," Anna pointed out.

"She's breaking the rules!" He hauled the bag of meat over his shoulder and ran full-tilt down the mountain path, terrified that the pack might return and sniff out a second course. Terrified at the thought of losing what was left of his family.

Terrified that wherever he went and whatever he did, violence was always nipping at his heels.

Before the Fall, he had killed forty-three people.

They had been contract-jobs, usually for the Sicilians or Croatians—but they had been *jobs*. Lots of guys who worked the crime syndicates were eager to embrace it as a lifestyle. They strutted through nightclubs coked to the gills, picking fights, starting feuds, attracting attention. Most came from the streets like Silvio, beaten down and impoverished; joining the criminal *nouveau riche* gave them a chance to wear expensive suits, drive sports cars, and fuck surgically perfect trollops.

But Silvio always maintained professionalism. He did his work and went home. He stayed off the radar of law enforcement and rival syndicates. His targets were a means to a paycheck—jobs measured in single-paragraph dossiers and color photos.

He didn't enjoy violence. Didn't enjoy the kill.

Yet I almost killed Giuseppe today, he thought as he ran down the mountain. *It would have been easy: pressing one hand against the man's eyes to draw up his defense . . . and then driving a single blow into his windpipe.*

He'd done it before, and he shuddered, double-timing it to his cottage above the gulch.

"Caterina!" he cried. "Come here!"

The cottage had been his safehouse in the old days, when he needed to lay low after high-profile jobs. It therefore was the most logical destination when the cities began falling . . . first to the infected, then to the unchecked fires. Umbria became a natural place for survivors making a similar exodus.

"Caterina!"

His daughter appeared on the hillcrest, clutching her plush bunny. Her golden hair made her seem a princess from a fairy tale. Her pale dress was dirty from where she'd been playing among the rocks and weeds.

She waved to him excitedly. "Papa! Where did you go?"

"I told you, I had to go to work." Silvio scooped her up, heart pounding.

"Did you see the bird people?"

"I did."

"Did you see the birds? I want to feed the birds!"

Thinking of the pigeon meat in his bag, he decided to change the subject. "What were you doing in the gulch?"

Her smile fell. "Please don't be angry, Papa."

"When I go to work, you are *never* to go beyond our fence!" The dogs' grisly feast replayed in his mind. "Why did you disobey me? Why go into the gulch?"

"I was looking for the treasure."

He blinked. "What treasure?"

"Nana says she heard people digging for buried treasure! Papa, can we look for treasure? Please!"

The cottage's backdoor swung open, and his mother emerged. In the failing light, she seemed a shriveled old woman—a harsh reversion to her days in a crumbling, crime-infested Salerno neighborhood—and it hurt Silvio to see. She'd done her best to raise him, had sacrificed what little she had. In return, he helped raise her out of those slums...

...and yet now, the *world itself* was a crumbling slum. The past was nipping at their heels again.

Silvio put his daughter down. "Wash up for dinner."

"But the treasure..."

"There's no treasure here." He scowled at his mother.

As Caterina scurried inside, the old woman approached, shoulders slouched, anxiously kneading her hands. She glanced to his bag and said, "Things went well?"

"They have food to trade," he said evasively.

"We could use the meat. The fish from Venice don't always arrive fresh..."

"Mama," he interrupted, voice brittle. "What is Caterina talking about?"

The woman looked at her feet. "I didn't tell her there was buried treasure. I said . . . it *sounded* like people were digging. I heard talking. I looked out the window and . . ."

"And?"

The woman's eyes filled with tears. "I didn't see anyone. But . . . but . . . I *heard* the shovels! I heard . . ."

"You were hearing things again, Mama."

He didn't know what the rest of the world was dealing with. Since the Fall, his own life had narrowed from international assignments to the village's day-to-day concerns and the formalization of the Trade Road. The infected had faded; since winter's thaw, they'd rarely been seen at all.

No, the *real* concern was of a skinned knee that could turn septic without antibiotics. Or a broken hand that would cripple a farmer whose life depended on tilling the land.

Or the medicine that kept his mother's mind clear.

The zombies might be gone but so were the pharmacies. Hell, most Italian cities were gone, too—without firefighters, blazes had reduced urban centers to ash; Silvio's flight to the safehouse had been shadowed by a hellish horizon like something out of Dante. Medicine was a fading dream; Silvio knew that by the time Caterina was an adult, the ERs and clinics and online ordering he'd taken for granted would seem like fables too lofty to be believed. The need for medicine—and a dependable supply route—had been the motivation behind his reconnaissance for the Trade Road: helping to connect survivors, tally what they offered, and establish safe stations along the way.

With a heavy heart, Silvio pointed into the gulch.

Mossy boulders lay strewn like giant's teeth. The low hills beyond were a rolling, uninhabited horizon as far as the eye could see—two kilometers if it was a step—and without a single home, shack, or tent. Too rocky to be farmed: bleak and beautiful and bereft of any human soul.

"Look down there, Mama. There are *no* people. When you tell Caterina things like that, she wants to investigate."

"But—"

"You need your pills."

His mother's expression was so lost and frightened that it was a lance through his chest. She was eighty-two, tough as Italian mothers tended to be, but her pills had run out with winter. She was starting to forget things. Twice he'd caught her talking to people who weren't there . . .

"I heard people," she insisted, looking to the gulch. "I think . . . I think they were speaking English! I heard digging! Silvio, why would I imagine something like that?"

"What book have we been reading to Caterina?"

The woman stiffened.

"Mama?"

A tear rolled down her cheek, and her voice broke as she said, *"Treasure Island."*

When the dinner plates were cleared away, Silvio sent Caterina straight to bed without a story. She protested this injustice—their nightly tradition was for him or her Nana to read tales of lofty palaces and deep dungeons, monsters and treasure. This time, he stood vigil as she brushed her teeth. Then he carried her to bed, tucked her in with her bunny, and made sure the ground-level window was closed.

"Papa?"

"Go to sleep," he whispered, blowing out the candle. Withdrawing to the corridor, he saw his mother standing at the end of the hall, looking crestfallen. He hated seeing her like that. "Goodnight, Mama," he said, and she bowed her head and retreated to her own room.

Silvio went outside and sat on the porch steps. He withdrew his hunting knife and a small piece of black pine—as a kid, he'd taken up whittling as a form of meditation, and the habit had persisted through adulthood. Here in Umbria, he'd decided to create a miniature set of fairy tale beings: a king, queen, noble knight, scaly dragon, horses, and a castle; there were no toy stores anymore, no Disney channel, and so when next Christmas arrived, he wanted to surprise his daughter with new playthings. The bunny was getting threadbare.

As he worked, he glanced to the village. It was a portrait of frosted moonlight and rich shadows. A tiny light glinted atop the watchtower; Salvatore had gone to bed, and it was Old Man Matteo's shift in the crow's nest. Silvio had insisted on rotational guard duties for the village's defense, and he had memorized the schedule with the same clinical efficiency that he'd employed when planning his kills. He wished Matteo had been up there earlier, because as a veteran of the Italian Armed Forces, the man was a crack-shot. The dogs needed culling.

He considered, too, what else needed to be done. The fence had to be expanded and reinforced, which meant an organized timber-fetching expedition. When harvest came, new tools and storage bins would be required. And medical supplies...what were they going to do about medical supplies?

His thoughts trailed off as he spotted a lonely figure entering the village from the mountain path. Too far away to glean any details, except for one: it was creeping steadily towards *his* cottage.

Fuck.

Silvio hadn't discounted the possibility that Giuseppe's pride might inspire some attempt at revenge. Honor duels had been part of Italian culture from Salerno right up to the *Cosa Nostra*, and apparently into the apocalypse as well.

He abandoned his whittle-work and ducked into the shadows near his fence gate. His hand tightened on the knife, thinking: *jab the jugular, pull hard across the throat...*

The intruder reached his gate and swung it open. Silvio sprang up—

—and checked his action, recognizing his visitor.

"Anna?"

The former-tour-director-turned-cave-survivalist spun around at the sound of his voice. "Silvio? Hi! I didn't mean to startle you..."

Tucking the knife into his palm, he said quickly, "I wasn't expecting company, sorry. What are you doing here?"

She shrugged. "It's not like I can call ahead, you know? I wanted to apologize again for what happened earlier."

"Not your fault."

"Giuseppe was out of line. He doesn't seem to understand that things have changed. Acting like a belligerent asshole isn't a good survival skill."

Silvio considered her in the moonlight, a chiaroscuro Venus come down from Olympus. She noticed his attention and chanced a smile, but he looked away, ashamed. His wife Maria had been dead less than a year. It was always close in his thoughts. Close enough that it seemed he could still smell her perfume sometimes.

Anna cleared her throat. "Don't judge us too harshly, is what I came down here to ask."

"I won't."

"For what it's worth, Giuseppe isn't a bad guy. He cracked a tooth right to the gum, and it's not like he can go to a dentist. It's getting infected. He's in a lot of pain. This morning I could see he was feverish."

Silvio felt a twinge of guilt. "He needs antibiotics. Believe me, it's the top item on our wish-list."

She blew a stray hair out of her face. "How fragile society turned out to be, huh? I always figured the future would be flying cars and moon-bases, not this... historical reset." She nodded towards the countryside. "But you know... see those straight rows of cypress trees? That's not a coincidence. The Romans planted them, to shade legions on the march. Whenever you see a neat line of trees like that, there's a lost Roman road there. The past is *always* with us."

"No argument here."

The sound of skittering pebbles interrupted the night's solitude. A light breeze set the community garden wavering like a gentle surf.

Anna playfully kicked his shoe. "Want to go for a walk?"

"The world's a bit dangerous for that, don't you think?"

"Something tells me you're capable of protecting us." She grinned. "But okay, we'll play it safe. Show me around your garden. *You* be the tour director."

"This isn't exactly Pompeii, but fine." He shrugged and secretly pocketed his knife. "To our right is a sweet potato crop from the Cipriano Dynasty, planted in the hallowed era of February..."

Together, they strolled along the vegetable garden—high nutrition crops consisting of potatoes, garlic, and onions. The village had partitioned their community garden so that each homestead shared in its development, from maintenance of water lines to tilling new furrows for plantings.

"What did you do before the Fall?" Anna asked.

"Salesman."

"Peddling what?"

"Insurance."

"Oh, the irony." She chuckled, looked at him curiously. "They teach a lot of self-defense in those insurance seminars, do they?"

"Self-defense is a form of insurance, if you think about—"

His words cut off as he heard another rattle of stones, and this time he was able to pinpoint the source: the gulch. It seemed too deliberate to be from the wind.

A person was walking around down there.

Instinctively, Silvio glanced to his daughter's bedroom window.

It was open.

"Goddam it." He sprinted to the window, briefly hoping that Caterina had merely drawn it open for fresh air. Instead, he saw an empty bed. Cursing, he vaulted the backyard fence as a bewildered Anna pursued him.

"Silvio?"

"Caterina!" From atop the ledge, he scanned the gulch. Moonlight glinted off rocks, deepened the shadows.

Anna stood beside him and said, "You think she went outside again?"

"*Someone* is creeping around, and she's not in her bed!" He descended the slope, peeking behind boulders for signs of a mischievous four-year-old. At a particularly flat, crooked boulder, he stopped short, breath catching.

A plush bunny lay in the grass.

Silvio's blood ran cold. Caterina *never* abandoned her bunny; it had become her protective talisman, a surrogate friend in these trying times and, equally, something *she* could protect.

Where the hell could she have gone? He'd only tucked her in twenty, maybe thirty minutes ago. The gulch was deserted as far as he could see, surrounding hills as untroubled as a painting.

Anna came up behind him and saw the bunny. "Is that hers?"

"Yes." He crouched to examine the grass.

"What was she *doing* back here?"

"Looking for buried treasure."

"You put a lot of gold in the ground, do you?"

"Of course not." Silvio ran his fingers along the earth, noting how the grass blades had been trampled, bent backwards against the grain. A short pace away was another flattened patch, and another. It formed an unmistakable trail of footprints into the gulch. He tracked it to the base of a swollen hill...

...where it ended without explanation.

What the hell?

Anna had stayed behind; now, she called to him excitedly. "Silvio! Look at this!"

He turned to see her lying down on her stomach at the base of the flat, crooked boulder. She produced a small flashlight, shining it into a hollow space beneath the rock.

"The tracks go the other way," he protested.

"Look how deep it goes!" She moved the beam back and forth, revealing an oddly rectangular ledge and a dark hollow. An inviting place for a curious four-year-old; Caterina was notorious for crawling into corners of the cottage's root cellar and closets.

He flattened himself beside Anna, pawing around in the recess. "Caterina! Are you hiding in there?"

"It's an ancient well!" Anna cried. "The Etruscans cut wells in this angular style! Looks like someone tried concealing it, to keep people from falling."

Mind racing in terror, Silvio flipped around and inserted himself feet first, bracing his shoes against the sides of the chute. Anna handed him the flashlight and he took it with trembling fingers.

"I'm going down," he stammered, and began a spiderlike descent into the bowels of the earth.

There was no fear he'd known that could compete with the blind, raw panic impelling him on. He fought off images of reaching the bottom of the well to find his daughter's broken, lifeless body. Yet it made horrifying sense. Why else would she have dropped the bunny near the boulder? Why else would she be *nowhere* else in sight? It even explained why he hadn't heard her scream.

He was nearly hyperventilating as he half-clambered, half-slid and, suddenly, he splashed into warm water.

Oh my God!

Silvio used the flashlight to scan the narrow space. The water was shallow.

A human body would float.

Anna landed behind him; he hadn't even known she was following. She took in the secret underground with wide eyes. "Why is this water so warm? It's March! It should be ice cold!"

Silvio let the flashlight beam crawl along the walls, and to his surprise he spotted a jagged, slanting fissure, like a wide lightning bolt. Earthquakes were more common in Italy than people suspected, and this was clearly the result of one or several quakes over the centuries, splitting the clay and opening a deeper passage.

"She could fit through this," he muttered.

Anna touched his arm. "Silvio, does that make sense? Could a child have gotten all the way down here and..."

"And survived the fall? Enough to go spelunking?"

She swallowed hard. "Yeah."

He said nothing. A numbness began to spread through his limbs, but he rebelled against it. Squeezing through the fissure, he stumbled into the next passage and was abruptly neck-deep in water. He dropped the flashlight, and when he plunged his head underwater to retrieve it, his eyes were burning. There was a chemical taste in his mouth.

When he came up for air, he saw that Anna had followed him once again. Her eyes grew wide. "Silvio, are you *seeing* this?"

"This water has chlorine in it," he muttered.

She pointed a dripping hand. "Look!"

And then he saw something that should not exist.

They had wandered into a subterranean lagoon. It filled a cavernous space like the grottos of Capri. The water was preternaturally warm and highly chlorinated, but it was also electric blue in color! By that luminosity, Silvio spotted a pale, sandy beach a hundred meters away, and upon that beach—

Impossible! he thought.

—were dozens of fold-out chairs and striped umbrellas, lined up in a neat row along the shore!

Silvio's mind flipped around as he tried processing the sight. Farther inland from the beach chairs stood a Caribbean-style bar with a thatched roof, festooned in gaudy Christmas lights.

"Am I having a stroke?" Anna asked, jaw agape.

"If so, we're sharing the same hallucination."

"But how is this possible? Do you think—"

He clamped his palm over her mouth. With his other hand, he pointed to the far end of the beach.

The sandy stretch appeared to be deserted, but he'd long ago learned that appearances were deceiving. Shapes moved in the gloom. A cigarette burned a hole in the shadows near a small building marked by lavatory signs.

"Two men," he said grimly.

Anna's forehead creased. "How can this place exist? Who the hell are these people?"

"See the pier? There are pool floats tethered."

"I see them."

"It's dark there. Good cover. And we'll be within earshot of the smoker and whoever he's with. Follow me."

Silvio bobbed along, staying low and tasting chlorine.

As he attained the pier, he caught some of the strangers' conversation. They were speaking English. *American* English. Silvio had never been to America—his assignments were limited to Europe—but he knew enough of their movies and music to recognize the accent. And he had killed American targets; they were easy pickings, always clashing in clothing and mannerism with the countries they visited.

Hiding in the darkness of the pier, Silvio turned to check on Anna's progress.

She was halfway across the lagoon, looking scared but determined, when the gunshot rang out and she collapsed into the water.

The gunshot.

Silvio tasted bitter adrenaline in the back of his throat, and for a moment he was back in his Milanese apartment, sitting at the kitchen table, hands laced around the coffee his wife Maria had just poured for him. The air smelled of her perfume.

He'd just returned from a job across the Swiss border. It had been an ugly hit, and the memory of that ugliness trailed him as he drove straight through the night, anxious and eager to see Maria and their daughter. Not just ugly but risky—a high-profile lawyer for a multibillion-dollar, multinational corporation. Even the *Cosa Nostra* treaded carefully around multinats, who were as corrupt, petty, and vengeful as any "criminal" faction; hell, they were rumored to employ their own wet-work specialists, and at rates that would make the Russian *bratva* seem like two-bit counterfeiters.

Maria pushed the table aside so she could straddle him where he sat. "How was the conference?" she asked.

Silvio raised an eyebrow. "Sorry?"

"Your sales conference."

He forged a tight smile. "PowerPoint presentations and motivational speakers. You really want to hear about that?" His briefcase, resting against a table leg, actually *did* contain pamphlets and Xeroxed corporate flyers; the trick to an effective lie, he'd learned, was to wrap it in layers of corroborating evidence. *Like the suicide note he'd left by the body of the attorney, throat slashed in a Zurich hotel bathtub.*

Maria didn't smile, and he suddenly realized how anxious she looked. "I'm willing to listen to anything right now, *mio caro.* Anything to get my mind off the radio."

"What's on the radio?"

"The virus."

He blinked. "*Virus?* What virus?"

She laughed, but there was no humor in it. "Guess that conference really sealed you away, huh? Some disease in America is making people go crazy."

Silvio didn't know what to say to that. There was a sudden scream—a high keening sound that made him jump—and he instantly looked to the bedroom door where Caterina was still asleep.

But it was only the sound of the tea kettle on the stove. Maria kissed him, hopped off his lap and poured herself some tea. "It's getting really scary," she said. "They're saying it's a bioterrorism attack. A doctor on the radio suggested it might be a weaponized form of rabies, can you believe that?"

Already unsettled, Silvio took out his smartphone and checked the news—he'd driven back from Switzerland with the phone powered down, intent on leaving no digital breadcrumbs to connect him to Zurich. Now he stared in astonishment at news of a mysterious outbreak in New York City. A wave of infections and violence, with spotty rumors of the disease spreading deeper into the country.

Frowning, Silvio paged through the newsfeed. "Maybe we should get out of town for a while. Take Caterina south to the countryside."

Maria turned from the stove, a steaming teacup in her hand. "I was hoping you would say—"

The window cracked behind her. Maria collapsed, the teacup shattering and—

JESUS GOD!

—her head emptying onto the floor.

Silvio threw himself atop her. Part of his mind was performing trigonometry, noticing the height of the bullet-hole in the window and realizing the shot must have come from the nearby grocer's rooftop.

But the rest of his thoughts were focused on trying to stop the bleeding. He tore off his shirt and wrapped it around what was left of Maria's skull. His briefcase was spattered with pink bits of bone and brains.

Caterina's door flung open. "Mama?"

"Back in your room!" Silvio screamed.

His daughter's eyes grew wide as she saw him, blood-drenched and clutching her mother. *"MAMA! MAMA!"*

As his eyes misted over, Caterina seemed to dissolve. He couldn't see her. He could only hear her screaming—as high-pitched as the tea kettle.

And in the following months, as the world fell apart country by country—first from America and through Asia and at last like a wildfire through Europe—he was forever remembering that awful scream. The world died, but a part of him was already dead, and he could close his eyes and feel Maria's warm blood as he'd held her lifeless body...his love...his life...

Anna's head vanished beneath the water. A second gunshot rang out, followed by a woman's cry and the screech of car tires. A scratching guitar riff kicked off a breathless gallop of drum-work.

Silvio found that he couldn't look away from where Anna had disappeared. When her mass of black hair resurfaced, she swam to him and gripped his arm. Eyes pink with chlorine, she whispered, "They're shooting at us!"

"No," he grumbled. "No one's shooting."

"The gunshot—"

"We're hearing an outdoor movie theater, like a drive-in."

Anna considered this. On the beach, the smoker took a final drag of his cigarette, crushed the butt into an ashtray, and disappeared into the lavatory. His partner strayed to the bar to return a bottle of whiskey. Silvio pulled himself along the pier and crept onto the sand, drawing his knife.

Trailing him, Anna whispered, "How can there be a beach and theater underground? This is Umbria, for God's sake!"

"Think about it. And while you're thinking, *stay here.*"

"Where are *you* going?"

"I have to use the bathroom." Mindful of the fellow at the bar, Silvio slipped quietly past the smoking ashtray and entered the lavatory.

A single plug-in light provided the only illumination. A tall fellow stood at the urinal. He wore a red cap, and a sky-blue uniform with a holster-and-sidearm. Silvio waited as the man emptied his bladder; when he turned to use the sink, Silvio struck him with a three-knuckled punch to the diaphragm and dropped him like felled timber.

Then he straddled the man's chest, pressing the knife to his throat.

"The girl," he whispered in English. "What happened to the little girl?"

The man fought for air. He tried focusing on Silvio's face through tears and pain. "How the fuck do you know about that? No one knows!"

"Obviously *you* do." Silvio jabbed the knife deeper, directly against the carotid. At the same time, he soaked up details of the man's uniform. A patch over the breast-pocket read: BOCCACCIO BUNKERS. "Tell me where she is, and I'll leave you tied up here but alive. What happened to her?"

The man licked his lips, and in a husky, smoker's voice, said, "She drowned."

Silvio felt his blood run cold. "Drowned? You mean..."

"The Newells are keeping it quiet, okay? You with the Fontaines? The Chatfields? Listen, the Newells are paying blue-boxes to hush this up. Blue-boxes, man! Porn, liquor, pot...harder stuff if you want! Whoever you're with, it doesn't matter. You keep your mouth shut, we'll give you a cut, okay?"

Silvio didn't have the vaguest idea what the man was saying; the slang strained his limited knowledge of English. "You're lying," he managed.

"I'm not! I helped bury the body!"

"Where did you take her?"

"Topside! We went out to the hills and..." The man squinted at him. "Wait, who the *hell* are you? How the fuck did you get in—"

The knife seemed to move of its own accord. The blade opened the man's throat, and his eyes grew wide as he choked, sputtered, and died; blood spread out along the floor tiles in dark lines.

He wanted to slump back and weep, but footsteps sounded near the door and another man appeared, wearing a similar sky-blue uniform. This second opponent instantly registered the dying body on the floor and the intruder squatting over it. He reached for his holstered sidearm.

Silvio was faster. Snatching the dead man's pistol, he sighted his target and squeezed the trigger. The lavatory wall was sprayed with a ropy sludge of brains. The man tipped backwards and struck the floor hard.

Outside, a movie explosion sounded. An unseen audience clapped and cheered.

He let the pistol clatter from his hands. When Anna appeared in the doorway, he gazed at her with hollow eyes.

She regarded the scene in open-mouthed astonishment. "Jesus Christ," she muttered. "Are you okay? I heard the gunshot and... Silvio? Are you hurt?"

"She's dead."

The two words seemed deadlier than any bullets, and on the heels of this grim pronouncement came the thought: *I deserve this.*

Forty-three murders. For Silvio, it had been the

fastest way out of the Salerno slums. He'd started out as just another low-level killer working for cheap cash, but most low-level killers didn't last long. They were messy, idiotic, and impulsive. They got themselves caught, or pissed off the wrong people and ended up in the obits. Silvio paid attention. Took his first job at thirteen and did it with a knife, wearing latex gloves and with a change of clothes he'd brought in a plastic bag—no loud gunshots or bloody clothes to attract the neighbors. He didn't boast, didn't gamble, didn't bury his nose in cocaine or run with street thugs. He was determined to be professional . . . what they called in the business a "master-class." And it wasn't long before that reputation reached the top ranks of the *Cosa Nostra*.

It was a gruesome career track, but Silvio soothed his conscience by telling himself he didn't enjoy the violence. Didn't kill unnecessarily. Didn't revel in it.

Anna carefully stepped around the bodies. "Silvio, get up."

"My little girl is dead."

"No, she's not."

He blinked at her.

She crouched beside him and touched his face. "Caterina is somewhere in this Stygian pit. And I think I know where to find her."

He pointed to the dead man beneath him. "He told me—"

"I heard," she insisted. "I crept to the doorway when you were talking with him. Had to dive behind a trash-bin when his friend showed up."

"Then you heard what he said!"

"That someone drowned, yes. Someone in the Newell

family, whoever the hell they are. *They weren't talking about your daughter.* I have a sick idea of what's been happening." She regarded the carnage around them. "And I suspect you're exactly the person to resolve it."

"Did you know that most of Pompeii escaped the volcano?"

They were moving stealthily away from the beach, shadowing a lighted cobblestone path and artificial palm trees with polyurethane leaves. Silvio felt like he was on autopilot. Afraid to hope, he fell back on his tactics of adapting to the available terrain.

He didn't know the headcount of this underground bunker, but it was reasonable to assume they'd be able to tell an intruder at a glance. To that end, Silvio had stripped the first corpse of its blood-stained uniform and changed into it, donning the cap and taking the weapon—a SIG Sauer P226 with a fifteen-round magazine—and the clip from the second pistol as backup. Assuming the "public" areas would be under electronic surveillance, he kept to the shadows, head lowered beneath his cap, and shielding Anna with his body as they went.

She nudged him and continued softly, "The volcano was smoking for days. Ancient people weren't stupid. Most fled town. Those who stayed were the wealthiest families, hunkering down with their comforts and riches, waiting for things to pass. Of course, what passed was a pyroclastic eruption..."

"Anna, I don't know what you're—"

"You asked me to think about what this place is." She thumped the badge on his stolen uniform. "*Boccaccio Bunkers* must be a place for rich families in case of an apocalypse. When the virus hit, they packed up and burrowed in."

Ahead of them, the path forked—a three-way signpost indicated the ways to SERENITY BEACH, STARDARK THEATER, and DREAM ESTATES.

"The guards here are ex-military," Silvio muttered. "American. Maybe former SEALs."

"How do you know?"

"A feeling."

She gave a sidelong look. "Are *you* ex-military?"

"Not exactly." He led the way towards DREAM ESTATES. A security gate stood ahead, with an occupied guard station. Yet there was also a wall lined with potted flowers and faux ivy. Silvio hoisted Anna onto its ledge, pulled himself up after her, and dropped quietly to the other side.

"Mother of God," he whispered.

This wing of the bunker resembled a high-priced condo complex, with each unit's façade built directly into the rock wall. A mock dead-end road ran in front, complete with streetlamps and individual mailboxes. Each home sported a minuscule square of Astroturf.

"This was all tunneled out of an existing cave system," Anna said. "The well we discovered? That was probably an Etruscan cistern! Whoever built this place didn't know about it, or they would have filled it in!"

"Which means there's a different point of egress. These people didn't rappel down a chute with my daughter." He looked sharply at her. "You said you had a sick idea of what's been happening..."

"The mailboxes," Anna interrupted. "We're looking for the name 'Newell.'"

As it turned out, their destination was three units

in along the road. The neighboring structures were dark and quiet—apparently, movie night at Stardark Theater was a major social event.

"They won't be at the movie," Anna said softly.

"How the hell do you know?"

"Were you listening to that guard? He told you what was happening before you...um..."

He regarded her, face pitted by darkness. "Before I killed him?"

Anna touched his hand. "You killed him in self-defense, right? It might not hold up in court, but..."

"There are no courts anymore." Silvio walked to the Newell's front door and knocked three times. Music played loudly within—suspiciously loud. The peephole darkened as someone peered through the lens. Silvio kept his face lowered, the BOCCACCIO BUNKERS cap concealing his features.

The door swung open, revealing a well-groomed man with silver hair and an improbable tan.

"Everything okay?" the man barked. "You people swore that everything would be—"

His words dissolved as Silvio's fist caught him in the teeth and shattered them like bone china.

He once killed three Croatian drug-runners operating out of a Nyhavn waterfront in Copenhagen. They'd gotten in the habit of ordering takeout, so one night Silvio intercepted the deliveryman while posing as one of his targets. He poisoned the meal, and delivered it himself. An hour later, he entered the apartment to find two targets dead...but the third leapt out of a closet to tackle him. Despite being poisoned—sweating and shaking violently—the guy had fought like a fucking demon.

Mr. Newell of *Boccaccio Bunkers* put up no such resistance.

The man was sprawled out from one punch, and Silvio leapt over him, plunging deeper into the household. He passed an empty den, glancing at mounted photographs: they variously showed Mr. Newell with a stunning blonde, lots of vacation pics, and a young girl—also blonde—who could be no older than four or five.

Beneath the otherwise deafening music, Silvio heard voices from a corridor. There, a bathroom door was ajar. A little girl cried as a woman scolded her. Silvio burst into the room and the scene pierced his brain in scattered shards.

Mrs. Newell was forcibly washing the hair of a young girl, who had been made to stand before a sink. There was a box of blond hair dye on the counter. The little girl looked up and...

"Caterina," Silvio whispered.

The woman roared in outrage. "What the *hell* are you doing in my house? Who the hell do you think—"

The music covered his next actions. He dragged a semi-conscious Mrs. Newell to the lobby, depositing her alongside her bleeding husband. Then he returned to fetch Caterina, and she wept in his arms.

"Papa!"

"Papa is here," he said, kissing her cheek as he brought her out. He handed her off to Anna and added, "Take her outside. I'll be there in a minute."

Anna hefted the little girl into her arms. "What are *you* going to do?"

He withdrew the knife from his boot. "Personal matter."

"We rescued your daughter! There's no need to—"

"We rescued her," he snapped, "because *these* people took her!"

"This isn't self-defense."

"This is *exactly* self-defense."

"Silvio, we're better than this!"

"*That* platitude was a luxury of the old world," he said thickly, and as he stared at the Newells he felt his vision constricting like a rifle-sight. He recalled the scene from the bathroom. The box of hair dye. The new clothes draped over a hamper. His hands curled around the hilt of his knife. It would be an eight-second job, like butchering chickens.

"Besides," he growled, "if we leave them alive, they'll alert the whole place. As it is, we don't know where we're going. We certainly can't leave the way we arrived."

Anna stared coldly at the couple on the floor. "How do we get out of here?"

It was Mr. Newell, clutching his battered mouth, who mumbled, "The front gate. Turn left at the carousel and go down Market Hollow." He spat a gob of saliva and teeth into his palm.

"Tie them up," Anna told Silvio.

"They abducted my daughter—"

"To replace one who died!"

Silvio felt his venom dissipate as he remembered what the security guard had said: *She drowned... the Newells are keeping it quiet... I helped bury the body... topside!* This must have been what his mother heard from the previous night, when she thought strangers were digging in the hills.

Anna touched his arm and, in a gentle voice, said, "Silvio, let's go home."

"You *can't* take her!" Mrs. Newell wailed, makeup running in greasy rivulets. "You can't do this to us!"

Holding Caterina in her arms, Anna regarded the woman. "I'm sorry for your loss, I really am. Many people have lost loved ones during this."

"I don't care about *them!*" Mrs. Newell screamed, and she pointed a bony finger. "*She's* the right age! No one here has to know! She can *be* Becky!"

Silvio stared coldly. "Her name is Caterina, and she doesn't belong to you." He dragged the Newells to the bathroom, stripped them, and bound their hands and feet with their own clothes. He tried not to think of his knife, or the SIG Sauer in its holster.

As he turned away, Mrs. Newell cried, "We *can't* be the only ones who lost a child! The other families will talk! *They'll talk about us!*"

They were within sight of Market Hollow's garish carousel when klaxons erupted like a scream. Whether they had triggered some surveillance tripwire, or the Newells had hit a hidden panic switch, Silvio didn't know and there wasn't time to care.

Market Hollow was a blasted-out cavern occupied by storefronts with kitschy names—On the Rocks Tavern, Wendy's Hair & Nails, Farmer's Market, and a pharmacy called The Apothecary. Silvio turned in amazement to this latter window, seeing past his reflection to endless rows of medicines, pill bottles, bandages, tissue boxes. Giuseppe's toothache, mama's dementia, the cuts and fevers and injuries that tomorrow was certain to bring... all those needed treatments were *here*.

Six men emerged from the hollow's far end in three-by-three formation, clad in *Boccaccio Bunkers* raiment. Thinking fast, Silvio seized Anna by the neck and shoved her and his daughter to the ground. He waved excitedly to the oncoming men.

"I've got two of them!" he shouted in his best imitation of the guard's husky American accent. "The others went that way! Be careful—they're armed!"

The deception worked...partly. The first set of men darted past, grinning eagerly, looking forward to real action in what must have been a somnolent posting. A fourth man peeled off from his team and followed. The remaining two jogged up to Silvio.

"Take a look!" he insisted, pointing.

The men looked down, and Silvio killed them both with point-blank headshots.

Caterina sobbed. "Papa!"

"Papa's here," he assured her. "We're almost home."

At the end of Market Hollow, a wide stairway was hewn into the rock. On the level below, a heavy-duty, reinforced jeep sat before an immense set of double-doors. White lettering on the wall read: GATE RELEASE. There was also a skinny metal chute climbing into the cavern ceiling with the words OUTSIDE VIEW; Silvio was reminded of war-time trench periscopes.

This is how they come and go secretly, he thought. *The night they buried the dead girl, and hours ago when they abducted Caterina...these fucking Morlocks take a peek to ensure the way is clear. Then they emerge like trapdoor spiders.*

He sprinted to the gate mechanism and pulled the release handle. The doors swiveled inward, spilling dirt and stones. Bright moonlight illuminated the widening gap.

"Silvio!"

Anna waved him over to where she stood before a large whiteboard mounted on the wall. He almost didn't bother with it; he'd seen enough of these people to figure they were best left alone, their life of privileged moles no concern of his now that Caterina was back in his arms. But there was a horrified tone in Anna's voice that made him pay attention, so he hesitated, peering closely at the whiteboard.

"Holy shit," he gasped.

In red marker, someone had sketched a crude map of the village. The position of individual cottages was accurately rendered, and each was designated with a number—several "3"s and "4"s and a "5." They appeared to show the number of inhabitants; Silvio's own cottage sported a "3." The watchtower was drawn with a large red circle around it. And each sector of the community garden contained a list of the crops being grown...

...with the expected dates of harvest.

With Caterina in her arms, Anna touched the board with a trembling hand. "They've been watching us! Watching us *closely!*"

Silvio felt a dangerous fury spread through his veins. *This* was how they knew about Caterina, he realized. *They've been conducting detailed reconnaissance on us. Noting our population, resources, defensive capabilities...*

Perhaps it had begun innocently, as a way of passing the months in quarantine. Idle curiosity, boredom, a kind of game. Yet Silvio gleaned sinister intent in what he was seeing, and he reflected on the shoppes of Market Hollow. *Boccaccio Bunkers* was not a self-sustaining community: when their stockpiles were exhausted, they would starve. Farming, hunting, and bartering with others was the only viable roadmap to future recovery... yet *these* people had opted for total, indulgent isolation.

So what would they do when their coffers were depleted?

"They're planning on raiding us," Silvio hissed. "Once our crops are ready for harvest, they're going to swoop in like locusts and take what they want."

Anna looked stricken. "And they'll kill whoever gets in their—"

A bullet hole perforated the whiteboard two centimeters from her head. She cried out and ducked as Silvio hit the floor and fired at the oncoming rush of Boccaccio security.

"Go!" he cried. "I'll cover you!"

He had to admire the fact that she didn't question this, didn't stare blankly, didn't hesitate. The world had changed and people with it: in the days before the Fall, it seemed the human race had fallen into a semi-coma, coddled by convenience. That dreamy luxury was not to be found in the survivors. Anna acted decisively, dashing with Caterina out into the night. Silvio crawled backwards, emptying his clip and slapping his only spare into place.

Then he was out in the fresh air again.

And he immediately recognized where he was.

It was the gulch behind his cottage. The precise location where he'd been tracking strange footprints that had vanished without explanation, until Anna discovered the Etruscan well.

From the outside, the bunker's doors had been cunningly hidden. The steel had been covered with an outer coat of fake grass, stones, and weeds, efficiently blending it into the hillside. It was here that paying customers had entered when the infection began, arriving by helicopter or private car, gripping their luggage, and hurrying into their sanctuary.

Silvio saw that Anna had scrambled up the slope towards his cottage. He looked to the watchtower and cried out, "Matteo! Over here! We need help!"

Then he climbed the hill, mind racing to consider how his opponents might deploy.

When they did emerge, in the suped-up jeep he'd seen, he was too stunned to immediately react. The vehicle roared into the moonlight like a mythical beast from its lair, hurtling unevenly along the gulch. It banked left and climbed the nearest hill, parking at the summit some three hundred meters away. The far doors fanned open, and three men hopped out, using their armored ride as cover.

One of them shouted, "Hi there! We weren't expecting visitors! Kind of rude not to introduce yourself, you know?"

The jeep shone in the moonlight, the shadows behind it so deep they resembled a chasm.

"You did good!" the man continued, voice cracking in a way suggestive of debilitating pressure, narcotics, or both. "Seriously, well done! I'd love to know how you infiltrated the bunker. More than that, I'd like to know *why*. You break in, murder my people, and shoot up the place. What did we do to you? Are you just a thrill-killing psycho? What's the deal?"

Silvio knew the guy was trying to goad him into giving away his location. The smart move was to stay quiet and wait for their action. Yet he couldn't help himself, and before he knew what he was doing, he called out, "You kidnapped a little girl!"

The man was silent for a moment. "Is *that* what this is about? Jesus Christ! Here I thought I was being clever, slipping in, grabbing the brat, and sneaking back." Another hesitation. "She's your daughter, is that it? Nothing personal, *paisan*. She's the same age as the Newell girl, that's all. Young enough that the family could keep her out of sight, give her a makeover, and no one would suspect there'd been a switch when they see her again."

"You sick fuck!"

A muzzle flashed across the jeep's roof. Bullets thumped against the hilltop, and Silvio ducked, peppered by fresh dirt.

"Hey *paisan*? Listen up! I've killed insurgents in nine countries! I could wipe out your village in a single night! But it doesn't have to be like that! Hand over the girl. The Newells can give her a better life than you can! She'll want for nothing. Believe me, that's a better deal than other survivors are—"

A shot cracked from the watchtower—from Old Man Matteo's IAF rifle. One of the *Boccaccio* security slumped over into the moonlight, dead before he hit the ground.

To Silvio's amazement, his main opponent laughed—a shrill, wild laugh that was partway between a sob and scream. "You stupid piece of shit! Now I'm going to take the bitch by force! I offered you a reasonable trade! *I didn't have to do that!* You think you people have any real power here? I've got a fucking arsenal under your feet!"

Anna whispered, "Silvio? Do you *see* that?"

He swallowed hard. "I certainly do."

"The world is gone!" the man cried, unaware of

the black tide spreading from the forest behind him in eerie, coordinated silence. "My country, your country...it's all fucking gone! People like *me* make the rules now. People like *me* are in charge! People like *me* are the masters of—"

And then the dog pack was upon him. The remnants of *Boccaccio* security shrieked as they were torn apart by dozens of slavering jaws.

Caterina snuggled under her blanket, clutching her stuffed bunny protectively to her chest. Her eyes were bright coins in her bedroom's candlelight. "Papa? Will you read to me?"

Silvio kissed her forehead. "Sorry, my gumdrop. Papa has to go to work. But Nana will read you a story tonight."

A day had passed since his descent into the underworld. Even in an era without social media, the story had gained considerable traction. Both the village and mountaintop cave-dwellers were discussing the strange intruders who had emerged from a secret door in the gulch. A caravan from the Trade Road had arrived that morning, listening eagerly to the tale of a little girl's rescue from flesh-and-blood devils beneath the earth.

Caterina had recovered quickly—perhaps too quickly—from her ordeal. Silvio had assigned a round-the-clock watch detail on the hill since escaping; the only significant occurrence since the midnight shootout had been the bunker doors sealing up once again; by Silvio's reckoning, there were at least two remaining guards of the bunker's security force, as well as unknown quantities of military-grade ordnance, fuel for the jeep...

...and other resources.

One consequence of her abduction, however, was that Caterina was jumpier than before. As a shadow passed behind her bedroom window, she started up in panic. "Papa!"

"It's okay," Silvio assured her. "Some men from the village are out there. And some from the mountain, too. They're all here to keep you safe."

She tilted her head sidelong in a way that reminded him of her mother. "Are they going to look for treasure? They should be careful, Papa. Those people underground were not nice."

Silvio felt his heart harden at his daughter's simple yet accurate assessment. "You're right. They were *not nice*." He kissed her again. "I love you, my gumdrop."

Caterina giggled. "I love you too, Papa."

He blew out the candle and headed outside to join the others.

A full posse had gathered on the ledge behind the cottage, with young Salvatore and Old Man Matteo and even a very repentant Giuseppe from the mountain. There weren't many firearms to go around, though the dead guards had three AK-47s between them, and Anna—she had insisted on being part of the posse—wielded a double-barrel shotgun retrieved from her mountaintop armory.

Silvio walked into their midst, and every head turned towards him. He playfully slapped Giuseppe's shoulder. "How's the tooth?"

The man chuckled. "You could have done me a favor and knocked it out of my mouth."

"Maybe next time." He regarded the group in the faint starlight. "We have a lot of work to do, my friends. A terrifying danger is in the woods. Our fence needs to be expanded. The Trade Road is growing, and it requires formal rest-stops and refueling stations—I want each one marked by a bright green flag, to tell travelers it is safe and under protection. We have much to do, if we want to survive." He hesitated. "No, 'surviving' is not enough. We want to *rebuild*."

The group nodded. Anna held his gaze with steely resolve.

"We have a future to make," Silvio continued. "But first, we must deal with something from the past."

He led the way into the gulch. He checked his firearm and the knife in his boot.

Then he was first to descend into the well.

A Thing or Two

KACEY EZELL

Ryan Hudson straightened up, stretching his back. He leaned on his shovel and swiped his sleeve across his face. It kept the beading sweat from dripping into his eyes, but didn't do a damn thing for the muggy heat that wrapped around him like a sodden blanket. He reached down and pulled his dad's old U.S. Army canteen from its holder strapped to his belt and twisted the cap off. He inhaled deeply, listening to the sound of the leaves rustling overhead in a breeze that somehow never made its way to cool *his* face.

At seventeen, Ryan knew very well that life wasn't fair...but this was just adding insult to injury. He lifted the canteen and drained the last of the tepid, plastic-y water from its depths and lowered it just as the sound of hoofbeats and a low whistle warned him of his brother's approach.

"Well, look at this. Baby Brother, goofing off on the job like always."

Jacob Hudson brought his gelding to a stop and grinned down at his younger brother. Ryan rolled his

303

eyes and flipped the middle finger of his free hand skyward. Jacob laughed in response.

"What are you doing out here?" Ryan asked. "I thought Mom had you sitting with that mare that's trying to foal today."

"Foaled," Jacob said, grinning widely as he reached into his saddlebag and pulled out a forty-ounce black Hydro Flask bottle. "Slick as you please. None of the problems Mom was so worried about, even if it was the mare's first time."

He tossed the bottle down to the ground at Ryan's feet. "Looks like you're empty, bro. Gotta stay hydrated."

"Thanks," Ryan said, meaning it. He put his empty canteen back into its holder and bent to retrieve the bottle. It was cool to the touch. "Oh man," he said as he flipped open the top and took a swig. "I take back everything I ever said about you, Jake. You're a good brother."

"Damn straight I am," Jacob—who would only ever allow Ryan to call him Jake—said. "Anyway, now the mare's foaled, I've come to spell you here. Dad wants you for a run into town."

Ryan lowered the bottle, his eyes going way too hard for a young man of seventeen. "Trouble?" he asked, his voice flat.

Jacob shrugged. "Nothing so bad he thought he should bring us both," he said, his tone taking on a soothing note. "He just said he needed to make a run for some supplies and asked me to send you in."

"Why didn't he just take you?"

"Because he's seen my ugly mug all morning, Ry, and he probably wants you to practice driving." Jacob leaned forward in the saddle and dismounted, then looped his gelding's reins over a nearby branch.

Ryan felt excitement kick through him. "Seriously?"

"That's what he said. He wants to take the Challenger out, now that we got the engine all tweaked to run on Mom's 'shine. I said I'd come finish up here so you could go." Jacob reached out for the shovel.

"Nice!" Ryan said, and handed the implement over. "Thanks! That's really nice of you."

"Yeah, well, Dad's right. I learned to drive before the Fall. It's your turn," Jacob said. "You can make it up to me later." His sly grin promised that Ryan would, indeed, make it up to him, but Ryan didn't care.

"You got it! See you later!" he called out as he turned and half-ran along the path that wound back up the hill toward his family's home. Even running, though, he stepped carefully, making sure that he noted the covert blazes and indicators on the trees that marked the correct trail.

Before long, the upward slope tapered off and the trees opened up to reveal a large clearing. As usual, people moved to and fro between the orderly ring of buildings. Not for the first time, Ryan was struck by how much the community itself resembled the carefully tended beehives that his mother kept behind his family's farmhouse, the largest of the buildings in the compound.

When they'd first arrived here, the farmhouse had been nothing more than a mostly ruined shack lurking in the overgrown clearing. It had been a terrifying time for Ryan and his family. When the initial H3N7 outbreak hit, he'd been a high-school kid like any other, with nothing on his mind but girls and motocross. Then the quarantine order had gone into effect, and his parents had made the decision to break the law and save them all.

They'd packed him and his brother up into The Beast, as his dad's old F-250 was called. They'd grabbed the go-bags and loaded up the back with weapons and all the ammo they could carry. They'd paused long enough to make some coordinating phone calls to members of their Heathen kindred, and then they'd run.

Ryan didn't much like remembering that crazy journey here, but some part of him knew he couldn't just forget. His childhood had ended on that trip, and he'd had to make the kind of choices that haunted one forever.

A little girl from their kindred had become infected. She'd attacked him. He'd killed her. He saved his own life and the lives of the rest of the community... but some nights, he still saw her clear blue eyes and beautiful, softly curling golden hair in his nightmares.

There were other incidents like that one. Other deaths. None bothered him so much as Kelsey's. He kept her name close to his heart like a talisman and hoped and prayed that her ancestors had received her with love.

"Ryan!"

Chuck Hudson's gravelly voice rang out across the clearing, and Ryan shook himself from his woolgathering to see his father striding across the ground. Chuck wasn't a particularly tall man, but he carried himself with the muscular authority of a warrior born and raised. Before the Fall, he'd begun to acquire a layer of softening fat, but there was no trace of that now. From the hard blue eyes behind the tinted sunglasses to the neatly trimmed white beard, to the Thor's Hammer pendant on his chest, to the tips of his steel-toed work boots, Chuck Hudson looked like what he was: a modern day Heathen leader, fighting to keep his family and community alive and thriving, come what may.

"Hi, Dad," Ryan said, straightening his spine as his father approached. "Jake said you wanted me."

"You finish that trench yet?"

"No, sir. Not quite. Jake's going to keep working on it. It's about three-quarters of the way there."

"Good," Chuck said, reaching out to sling his arm around his son's shoulders. "Your mother will be happy to hear it. She's impatient to move forward with improving the defenses on that slope."

Ryan smiled a little. "And we don't want to make Mom unhappy," he said, and it came out with a little more teenaged snark than he'd intended. Chuck reached up and smacked the back of his head lightly.

"Damn straight we don't. I fear no man or God, but only the wrath of my beloved wife. And don't pretend you're any different, boy."

Ryan raised his hands in surrender and shook his hair back out of his eyes. "I'm not! I know. I was just playing around."

"Well, if you're finished playing around, I've got an errand to run. I want you to drive me in to town."

Excitement skittered down Ryan's nerves. "Right now?" he asked.

"You got something better to do?"

"No, sir."

"Then no reason to wait. Go get your rifle, since we're leaving the property."

"Yes, sir!" Without really knowing why he did so, Ryan wrapped his arms around his Dad's torso for a brief, tight hug before letting go and loping off toward the house, where he kept his stash of personal weapons. Not that he'd been totally unarmed, of course. Even on the property, one had a responsibility for one's own safety. It had been a long time since they'd seen infected in any great numbers, but every once in a while a crazy, naked, animalistic wreck that had once been human would come charging through the woods. Thus, his mom's plans and the community policy that everyone leaving the clearing be armed with at least a pistol. Even the kids sent out in pairs to forage carried simple revolvers. It just made sense, even on the safety of the property.

Off the property, all bets were off. Even in friendly territory, Chuck didn't believe in leaving such things to chance. And Ryan fully agreed.

"Mom?" Ryan called as he pushed open the kitchen door of the house. When she didn't answer right away, he stepped inside and headed back to his room. After a few short moments of deliberation, he decided to bring not just his Mini-14, but also a 12-gauge shotgun. Not for the first time, he thanked the Gods and all his ancestors that his parents had raised him and his brother around firearms. The shotgun had been a twelfth birthday present. He'd gotten the Mini-14 for Yule the year before the Fall. Same with the body armor he shrugged over his head and fastened around his waist. He was just loading up his pouches with magazines when his mother leaned in to the doorway.

"Going to town with your dad?" Christine Hudson asked, her voice calm. Ryan turned to her with a smile.

"Yes, ma'am," he said. "Jake says he's going to let me drive."

"You be careful," she said, shaking her dark blonde hair back from her face. "With the engine modifications on the Challenger, it's got a lot of kick. Take it slow and listen to your dad."

"Yes, ma'am," Ryan said again. "I promise."

"Good kid. And if I catch you tracking through my house in muddy boots again, it will be your ass, understand?"

Ryan felt his stomach sink and his face flush as he looked down. Sure enough, a trail of mud prints showed clearly against the restored hardwood of the farmhouse floor.

"Mom, I'm sorry," he said. "I didn't even think—"

"I know," she said, a ghost of a smile playing about her lips. "You're just excited and impatient. I'll take care of it. But you're taking care of my bees for the next two weeks in return."

"Yes, ma'am," he said. "I'm sorry."

"You're forgiven. Now finish arming up and go meet your dad. I'd like you both back before dark."

Ryan nodded, and ducked his head as Christine leaned in to drop a quick kiss on his cheek. Then she turned and walked back down the hallway, leaving the scent of honey and herbs in her wake.

"What happened to you?" Chuck asked when Ryan rejoined him outside on the edge of the clearing. "You look pissed."

"I forgot about my muddy boots and tracked mud inside on Mom's floor," Ryan said, hating the fact that he couldn't seem to keep from mumbling as he spoke. Chuck laughed.

"That was a damned stupid thing to do," Chuck said. "She's gonna make you pay for that."

"Bees for two weeks," Ryan said. "But she didn't say I couldn't come with you."

"Well, let's just get gone before she changes her mind, shall we?" Chuck clapped his son on his shoulder and urged him toward a building half-hidden under the trees near the edge of the clearing.

The barn was the only building besides the farmhouse that predated the Fall. When they'd first arrived, they'd actually taken shelter in the barn, because it had been in far better condition. The property had been in Christine's family for generations, and while the old farmhouse had obviously not been used for several years, it soon became clear that the barn had. Deep in the back, among the piles of rusting farm implements and broken-down furniture, they'd found a treasure shrouded in dusty canvas: a vintage 1970 Dodge Challenger. Ryan remembered that his dad had been awestruck as he breathlessly opened up the hood and found the 440 Magnum engine with the six pack intake. Chuck had run his fingers along the fender with a reverence usually reserved for touching his wife.

They had no way of knowing how long the car had been stored there. It didn't start at first, but Ryan's mom had tinkered with it, and she and one of the other mechanics in the kindred had eventually gotten it to run. More importantly, they'd adapted the engine to run on the product of the other major treasure they'd found in the barn: the still.

"Dad," Ryan said as they opened up the now-clean barn and walked toward the Challenger in its stall. "Did you ever figure out how long this property's been in Mom's family?"

"She doesn't know for sure," Chuck answered. He

grabbed hold of the new cover that shrouded the car and whipped it back. Underneath, the chrome bumper gleamed dully in the midmorning light that streamed in from the door. "Her daddy brought her up here when she was little, and said his great-grandaddy had run liquor down from this mountain during Prohibition. She did say that the still was in operation when she was born. They didn't tear it down and store the parts in here until sometime in the seventies."

"And we put it back together," Ryan finished as he helped pull the cover off and fold it up. "And now we're back running liquor all over the mountains."

"Yep. We got real lucky that your mom comes from a long line of bootleggers. Liquor is the perfect trade commodity in these times. It's fuel, antiseptic, medicine—"

"And a good time," Ryan said with a grin. His dad's teeth flashed in the dimness as he grinned back.

"That too, though I'd rather drink your mother's mead. I'm too old for the still's rotgut."

Ryan snorted and opened the car door. That was a lie. His father enjoyed all kinds of liquor, and could hold his own against any man in the kindred when drinking. Chuck laughed and got in on the driver's side. He turned the key and the motor turned over with its characteristic growl and they pulled forward out of the barn in good spirits.

It wasn't far to the town as the crow flew, but the gravel road they followed off the mountain was long and twisty. Chuck kept up a running stream of commentary as he cut the wheel back and forth, navigating the treacherous switchbacks that carried them down the slope toward the valley below. Before the Fall, the valley had been mostly farmland dotted with homesteads here and there and the occasional suburban bedroom community for those willing to trade a long commute to the city for a quiet, pretty neighborhood.

Now, as Ryan looked out over the vista that stretched below, most of the farmland lay fallow and neglected, and only a tight huddle of buildings at a turn in the nearby river gave any sign of human habitation. Unlike the abandoned farm buildings that had begun to disappear under aggressive kudzu and other plants, the town and the wall that encircled it were solid and in good repair. A thin twist of smoke spiraled upward from a building in the center of town and Ryan imagined that he could catch the distant scent of wood smoke.

As the gravel of their road emptied out onto the cracked blacktop that had once been the state highway, Chuck pulled the Challenger over to the side and cut the engine. Then he looked over at his younger son with a knowing smile.

"Ready?" he asked.

Ryan didn't bother answering with words. He grabbed the handle and threw his door open, barely remembering to safely stow his shotgun before practically leaping out of the passenger side of the car. His dad's chuckles followed him around the car as they swapped places.

"Go ahead and adjust the seat, get settled first," Chuck said as he took hold of Ryan's shotgun and lowered himself down to the passenger seat. His advice wasn't, strictly speaking, necessary, since Ryan was already doing just that.

"I *have* driven before, Dad," Ryan reminded his father.

"Watch your mouth, boy," Chuck growled. "You may have driven the Beast, and you're real good on that motorbike you boys fixed up, but this beauty is something else. There's a reason your mother's people stashed this car away. You'll treat her with respect or she'll bite your ass but good. Trust me."

"Yes, sir," Ryan said, carefully keeping his eyes from rolling.

"Now, you remember how to use the clutch...?"

It took far longer than he would have liked, but as they roared down the old state highway toward town, Ryan flexed his hands on the Challenger's wheel and privately admitted that his dad was right. She really *was* something else. He could feel the powerful torque of her modded-out engine thrumming under his feet and hands. It shivered through his body in an almost sexual way. No wonder men gave their cars women's names and treated them like queens.

Once they got going again, it didn't take but about another half-hour to reach the town's gate.

"Huh," Chuck said as they approached. "Slow down a bit, Ry, this looks weird."

Ryan concentrated on coordinating his feet and hands to downshift as smoothly as possible, then turned his focus outward. His dad's tone held a warning.

"The gates are closed," Chuck said slowly as they rounded the last bend and caught sight of the main entrance to the town. Sure enough, a solid, massive metal barrier easily two stories high stretched from one end of the town wall to the other across the highway's blacktop. "They haven't done that during the daytime since we've been trading with them. Go ahead and stop, but don't cut the engine."

"Yes, sir," Ryan said. He successfully brought the car to a stop and held it, idling, while Chuck opened the door and stood just behind its partial shelter.

"Hello the Town!" Chuck called out, using the voice that Ryan knew had once shouted instructions and details to U.S. Army MEDEVAC crews over the sounds of turning helicopter rotors. "Chuck and Ryan Hudson from up on the Mountain!"

A long pause, then a small window opened high in the massive gate.

"Wait there!" a voice, high and tight with fear, ordered.

Chuck gave an exaggerated shrug. "Okay," he called back. Ryan noticed that his father casually rested his hand on the grip of the rifle slung across his chest. He fought not to shift uncomfortably in his seat.

A loud *thunk* sounded from somewhere behind the wall, and a piercing squeal heralded the opening of a ground-level, pedestrian-sized door in the huge gate. A dark-skinned woman with short steel gray hair in braided cornrows stepped out. Like them, she wore body armor and carried a weapon with the ease of one who had long years of training and familiarity.

"Hey Robin," Chuck called out as she approached. "What's going on?"

"Chuck," Robin said, flashing him a quick smile that didn't reach her eyes. "Sorry about the chilly reception. We've had a little trouble recently. I'm glad you came; we're getting low on our medical stock."

"We're happy to trade," Chuck said, his shoulders easing slightly. "Brought a load down just for you. Want us to pull in?"

"Gate stays locked for the next little while, Chuck, sorry. Gotta do the trade here."

Chuck nodded, then looked over at Ryan and repeated the gesture. Ryan took that to mean that he could relax, so he cut the engine and pulled the keys from the ignition. He stepped out, tossed the keys to his dad, who caught them and unlocked the trunk, opening it with an expansive gesture before handing the keys back to Ryan.

"Twenty-five gallons, 180 proof. Christine's guarantee of purity. Should help with your medical supplies some. You got wounded?"

"A few," Robin said, her dark eyes flicking a warning to Chuck. Ryan understood her nonverbal meaning: a community handled its own problems, until it couldn't . . . then the community typically wasn't long for the world. Harsh, perhaps, but it was the way things were since the Fall. "How much?"

"Got any copper pipe?"

Robin pursed her lips, then nodded. "A couple feet . . . say eight or so."

Chuck turned to look at his son, then turned back to Robin and nodded. "Throw in about four/five yeast starters from within your community and you've got a deal." Chuck said. Ryan inhaled slowly, fighting to keep the incredulity off of his face. Those were *incredibly* generous terms his father was offering.

Robin blinked, and some of the tension cleared from her face, smoothing out her brow and widening her big, dark eyes. She really was a beautiful woman, Ryan suddenly realized, despite the fact that she was his father's age.

"Chuck, I—"

"Copper's hard to get these days," Chuck said, cutting off her low-voiced protest. "And I need it if we're going to keep up with demand. Take the deal or leave it, Robin. I don't have all day to stand out here wrangling in the open with you."

"We'll take it," Robin said, sounding once again like the decisive leader Ryan knew she was. She whistled and waved a hand, and four relatively burly men stepped through the door in the gate. Robin rattled off instructions to the first in line, who nodded and went back inside while the other three slung their weapons and stepped back toward the trunk of the Challenger. The fourth man returned while they were loading up the jugs of 'shine, and he carried an open-top crate with a pile of assorted copper pipe fittings inside. A young kid, maybe twelve, followed him, holding a tray of what looked like plastic cups.

"We had the yeast samples ready," Robin said with a slight smile. "You're always looking for new stock."

"So we are," Chuck said. He glanced in at the copper and nodded, and the man set the crate into the open trunk, where the jugs had just been. Ryan got back into the car and watched in the rear-view mirror as his father shut the trunk, and then stuck out his hand. Robin took it, and the two of them shook in the ancient gesture of a deal sealed and done. It looked like Chuck was about to step back, but Ryan saw Robin pull him close and speak low words into his ear. Chuck's face never wavered, but he gave her a slight nod and spoke as well. Robin smiled a grim little smile and shook her head, then she stepped back and raised a hand in farewell. Chuck touched his fingers to the frame of his sunglasses and walked back to the passenger side of the car.

Without saying anything, Ryan turned the key, listening to the Challenger's engine roar to life. Then he looked over to see his father staring straight ahead.

"Let's go, son," Chuck said, without looking. Ryan waited for a moment, then put the car in gear and pulled away.

They drove in silence for a few miles, with only the engine's purr and the whirring of the tires on the broken blacktop to accompany them. Finally, Ryan couldn't stand it anymore and spoke up.

"So, you want to tell me what that was all about?" he asked, careful to keep his tone mostly respectful.

"What was that all about?" Chuck asked without moving from his half-reclining slump against the passenger-side window. Ryan could hear the fatigue in the words. For some reason he couldn't name, it made Ryan angry to hear his father sounding so tired and beaten down. Chuck Hudson was a warrior's warrior! He didn't get *tired*...

"That!" Ryan said, and some of his rage and incredulity jacked the volume and intensity of his voice up a bit higher than he would have liked. Still, he'd started. Might as well finish. "You practically *gave* that woman our liquor! For what? A box of verdigris-covered junk and some *yeast starters*? That's not a good trade, Dad! Mom's gonna be pissed!"

Chuck finally sat up and glowered at his youngest child through his dark-tinted sunglasses.

"Your mother won't mind one bit," he said, keeping his tone mild, though steel underlaid every word. "Robin is good people, and so are most of the folks in her community. They needed our liquor for their hospital, and they won't take charity. And we *do* need the copper to start that new still, and more yeast cultures are always useful to keep our stock healthy."

"But we should have asked for five times that amount of copper!" Ryan said.

"They didn't have it to give, son," Chuck said lowly. "Like she said, they've had a bit of trouble. That's what she told me when we said goodbye—"

Chuck broke off, and when Ryan glanced over at his dad, he found him staring into the rearview mirror, his eyes squinting slightly behind the dark lenses. Ryan looked back as well, but all he could see was a mostly empty highway, with only a single truck turning off a side road behind them...

Oh. Shit.

"Who do you think that is?" Ryan asked, all of his fire and frustration gone in an instant as he forced his mind to the clear, calm place where he could act.

"We're about to find out," Chuck said. "Be cool for a moment, but slowly accelerate. We don't want to give away all of our advantages."

Ryan did as he was told, gently increasing the pressure of his right foot on the gas pedal. The Challenger responded like a thoroughbred eager for the race to begin. The truck steadily gained ground behind them, getting so close that Ryan could only see the front grille in the rear-view mirror.

"Dad—" he said.

"Easy, son," Chuck said, his voice empty. "This is what I thought. Robin said they'd finally kicked these assholes out of the town. She warned us that they might try to tail us home. But don't worry, we'll lose 'em. Listen very carefully to me, all right? When I tell you, I want you to smoothly and slowly give the car about half of its full gas. Don't floor it, you'll flood the engine and break the back end loose. Just put the pedal down about halfway, until you feel the front end get light and the back end get heavy. Do you understand?"

"Yes, sir," Ryan said, cutting his eyes from the rear-view to the road in front of him, and then to the side mirror when the truck abruptly pulled into the left lane.

"You gotta be real strong and steady on the wheel, Ryan," Chuck said. "Otherwise you'll lose control, okay?"

The truck zoomed forward, bringing the front grill even with their back tires. Ryan glanced down and saw that they were doing about eighty.

"Now Ryan. About half gas!"

Ryan took a deep breath and pushed the pedal down about halfway to the floor. He felt the rumble of the engine increase in pitch, the vibration spreading through the frame and into his body. Almost as if she were an extension of himself, he could *feel* how the Challenger squatted back on her back tires, letting the weight off of her front end. Time seemed to slow as his connection to the machine grew.

Behind them, the truck swerved sharply to the right, coming within inches of their back fender. Despite himself, Ryan flinched, his hands tensing on the wheel just enough. The back end broke loose, lurching to the right. Some instinct from his motocross days kicked in, and while his father yelled for him to hold the damn thing still, Ryan locked the wheel in place and refused to let it move while they rode out the slide.

"Downshift and go! Nice and steady on the gas!" Chuck shouted, and as soon as Ryan felt the wheels bite into the pavement again, he danced his feet on the clutch and the gas, and threw the pistol-grip shifter forward into third gear. He picked the gas back up, and just as his dad had instructed, he steadily increased the gas from fifty percent to sixty...seventy...eighty...

Like a great hunting cat, the Challenger roared as she leapt from her crouch, front tires grabbing the pavement once again as the back tires threw her forward. The RPM needle zoomed from three thousand to eight thousand, hovering near the red line, while the speedometer climbed steadily past eighty, ninety, one hundred...

Chuck let out a whoop of exhilaration and pushed himself up through the open passenger side window. Ryan heard his father's rifle blast twice before Chuck lowered himself down into the seat again, his face flushed red from the wind and the excitement.

"*Damn* fine driving son! Damn fine!" he said, slapping his son on the back as he removed his magazine and replaced it with a full one. "Keep that speed up until we turn off onto the mountain road."

"They'll see our dust trail and be able to follow," Ryan said, as the worrying thought occurred to him. "We're leading them straight home, Dad."

"That's what I'm hoping for, son."

Ryan glanced at his dad. "What?"

Chuck grinned. "Like the old song says, boy. 'I learned a thing or two from Charlie, don't you know?' Just keep driving. We gotta get back in time to warn your mother."

Ryan fought to let his breath out slowly and evenly while his heart rate slowed. He didn't want to let the exhalation rustle the leaves that hung inches from his face. He'd spent enough time in hunting stands to know how to move and breathe without spooking his quarry, though as he sighted down the length of his Mini-14, he realized that this particular target wasn't likely to pay attention. Even if the hammering of Ryan's heart really was as externally loud as it sounded in his ears.

Which was good, because after more than an hour of "go, go, go" it really was hard to be still, no matter how much hunting experience he had.

They'd hauled ass all the way to the turnoff to the mountain and up onto the gravel road that started up the slope. But instead of continuing onto the cliff road they'd taken earlier, Chuck had instructed Ryan to turn off onto a path that was little more than a game trail. Ryan barely had time to wonder about whether they had the undercarriage clearance needed before the track dead ended in a tiny clearing with a deadfall against the rock face at the far end. They'd eased up to the deadfall. Even though he knew it was false, Ryan couldn't see the cavern behind it until he'd come to a stop right in front of the cleverly disguised door. They'd hidden the Challenger behind the door, in the shallow cave beyond, then Chuck had sent Ryan back down another one of the "game trails" that crisscrossed the entirety of his mother's property. Chuck had stayed behind to light a fire in the cavern's natural chimney. The smoke would signal the kindred that intruders were inbound, and would tell them to block the cliff road at its narrowest point, right after it turned back away from the edge and into the forest.

That would force the intruders to take the turn that would lead them gradually down the slope and away from the summit. The kindred, Ryan included, had spent years developing the funneling features that would eventually bog down the most souped-up of vehicles and force attackers to continue on foot if they didn't turn back.

As, it appeared, they hadn't.

Ryan bent his head and sighted along his barrel again as the sound of arguing and cursing drifted up from the forest floor toward him. He watched two men come slowly into view, neither of them moving well. He focused on the ruddy sheen of their faces, they both looked as if the hike had been a struggle so far. Ryan inhaled slowly, waiting to see if any more men followed as the pair trudged up the trail over the small rise a few hundred yards away.

No one did, yet. Better and better.

He held himself motionless for another second, letting them both make their way through the dense undergrowth until they were almost directly below his tree. He raised his head. They had no idea he was there. This wasn't going to be finished with guns.

Fine with him. He reached his right leg back and kicked the lever that rested just below his boot. It stuck, and a cascade of leaves and twigs slithered down the tree branch behind him.

"What was that?" one of the men below asked, stopping suddenly and causing his buddy to bump into him from behind. Ryan gritted his teeth. If he took the rifle shot from here, he'd likely miss due to the awkward angle. Plus, there was no way he was going to get both of them with a single shot. He drew in a deep breath and kicked down on the damned lever with all of his weight. The steel cable that ran down along the tree and under the forest debris squealed as it moved, but it *did* move. Finally.

The bottom of the path fell open beneath the intruders' feet. Ryan heard them scream as they fell. He grabbed his rifle and slid down the branch, hitting solid ground about the same time as he heard the wet *squelch* sound of sharpened steel sliding into flesh.

The screaming took on a howling quality. Ryan shook his head and wiped the sweat off of his brow, then looked up to see his father materialize out of the tree line on the other side of the path.

"Got 'em, son?" Chuck asked, his voice calm and untroubled by the horrific noises coming from the pit yawning between them.

"Yes, sir," Ryan said.

"Good. Let's see what we've got," Chuck said. He pulled his favorite Glock out of his holster and approached the edge. Ryan raised his rifle up and did the same.

Below them, two men sprawled brokenly over the mass of rebar that bristled from the floor of the pit. The taller of the two lay with his neck bent at an awkward angle and a single spike through his lower skull, knocking his jaw completely askew. He wasn't moving.

The other man was.

"Fuck you, you fucking hillbillies!" The man spat, pain creasing his face. He'd managed to fall just about perfectly, Ryan realized. Most of his body slumped between the wall of the pit and the stakes, with only one tall spike spearing through his right upper thigh. "Psycho sons of bitches! When I get out of here—"

"You'll be mindless and naked, and we'll put you

down like we do all the rabid animals," Chuck said, his voice insouciant and bored-sounding.

"Wh-what?"

"Oh, I'm sorry," Chuck said. "That was rude of me. You just got here, after all. You probably haven't had a chance to look around and realize what you've stumbled upon here. This is one of our old infected traps, modified for use by more . . . sentient invaders. Nominally, anyway."

"What you mean, 'sen-shent'?"

Chuck sighed. "Never mind. If you look around, you'll notice the tips of the rebar are stained with blood. Aside from yours and your boyfriend's, that is."

"Hey, I ain't no fa—!"

Chuck held up his hands. "Hey, man, love is love. I'm not going to cast aspersions on your relationship status."

"Apsertions—?"

"Dad," Ryan said, his voice empty.

Chuck let out a sigh. "Yer right kid, I shouldn't play with him. It's not sporting at this point. All right, asshole, here's the deal. That spike that pierced your leg? It was covered in infected blood. Now it may be dormant by now, it may not be. That's the gamble you're taking. So if you can get yourself off the spike and out of this twenty-foot-deep pit before you bleed out, you might be okay. Or you might be a naked fiend running around trying to eat anything in sight. It's in the hands of the fates at this point. Either way, you should have learned your lesson when Robin kicked you out of the town. It's not polite to show up uninvited. Bad things happen that way."

The injured man in the pit gaped up at Chuck, his

mouth dropping open as reality set in...and likely pain too, Ryan realized. Sometimes the body was kind and delayed the response a little. But it always caught up to itself. Always.

"So you're...just going to...leave me?" the man asked, his face growing paler by the moment. Ryan could see a slightly darker puddle spreading on the dirt floor of the pit.

"Yep," Chuck said. "Uninvited guests don't make it down from this mountain. You ready, son?"

"Yes sir," Ryan said, looking unflinchingly at the man he'd just sentenced to a very painful death.

"All right, let's get back before your mother starts to worry."

The man in the pit started to scream, but Chuck turned his back and stepped away, and after a moment, Ryan followed suit. Together, they hiked back up the barely visible path that would lead them to the settlement. The screams followed them for a little ways, but eventually, they faded under the natural sounds of the mountain's forest.

"How long do you think he'll last?" Ryan asked after a while.

"He won't make it through the night," Chuck said, confidently. "If he tries to pull off that stake, he'll tear his femoral and bleed out in seconds. And there are still infected hiding in these woods. They're the scared kind who won't approach a fully armed human, but one helpless, staked to the ground...they'll get to him eventually."

Ryan nodded. They'd all occasionally seen that type of infected during their work duties. It was another one of the reasons everyone went armed.

One of many.

Chuck reached out and clapped his son on the shoulder. Up ahead, the lights of the settlement twinkled through the trees, beckoning them home. "You did good, kid," Chuck said. "It's not an easy thing."

"Maybe not," Ryan said. "But it's necessary, isn't it? We gotta protect our own."

"Damn straight, kid. Damn straight."

Ex Fide Absurdo

CHRISTOPHER L. SMITH & BRENT ROEDER

David Pascoe approached the door with resignation, blowing the sweat from his upper lip. He shifted his plate carrier slightly, allowing some air in between it and his saturated long-sleeved shirt. The summer heat was early this year, as though God thought the Lone Star State needed more time in the Heavenly Oven.

"Less than a minute out here, and I feel like I just stepped out of the shower," he said over his shoulder. "I still don't see why I have to be the one on point, Taylor."

His partner, Alden Taylor, grinned behind his mirrored sunglasses.

"I'm the better shot," he said, "so I'm overwatch."

Pascoe slammed the wooden door with the butt of his shotgun, drowning out his muttered comment. If there were any infected inside, they'd know in seconds. He waited a few moments, listening carefully, then repeated the motion. This time, there were definite sounds of movement—slow, shuffling noises, a low groan, and scratching. Pascoe tightened his grip and flicked the safety off. Taylor nodded, set his feet, and scanned the perimeter. If there was a nest inside, there was a good chance there'd be more nearby. Standard procedure for a nest was to get them bunched up around a choke point, kick the door in, and service the targets. So far, it had been like shooting fish in a barrel, or fishing with dynamite. So far.

More scrabbling and groaning from the other side. Pascoe rapped on the door one more time, took a step back, and tensed.

"Goddammit," came a male voice from the other side. "You trying to bust it down?"

Pascoe relaxed. Zeds didn't answer a knock, and certainly didn't gripe.

"What the hell you want?" A shadow passed over the fisheye as the man inside continued. "If you're looking for trouble, I ain't got nothing to lose, and jail ain't an option."

"Sir, I'm Census Agent Pascoe, and this is my partner Taylor," Pascoe said calmly. "We're from the government, and we're here to help you."

"Ha! Nice try, boy. Ain't no government, and if there was, I'm damn sure I don't need its 'help.'"

"That's why we're here, sir. Can you open the door so we can discuss this face-to-face?"

"How do I know you ain't raiders?"

"Do raiders usually knock?"

"These days, it wouldn't surprise me."

Pascoe sighed. "Do they usually have long conversations after they do?"

"Hmph." After a several second pause, Pascoe heard various chains, latches, and bolts disengaging. The door opened a crack, revealing a bloodshot, rheumy green eye. "You got 'til I need to piss, boy. Get to it."

Pascoe ignored Taylor's soft chuckles behind him.

"You're right, sir. That's why we're here. To establish a legitimate governor of Texas, we need to know how many surviving constituents there may be."

The door opened a bit more, revealing a leathery, clean-shaven face. The man stood slightly taller than Pascoe, wearing clean khakis and a polo shirt.

"Uh-hunh."

"Before we get to the main questions—age, name, etc.—let me ask you the important one. Do you own firearms?"

"Lost 'em all in a tragic boating accident last week."

Pascoe couldn't help but grin. The nearest coast was about fifty miles away in Corpus Christi, and the only visible water was a small pond or tank roughly three hundred feet from the house. He'd seen the sun glancing off it as they'd approached.

"That's unfortunate, sir," he said, jerking a thumb over his shoulder as the door began to close. "However, it's your lucky day. If you look behind me, you'll see a truck parked nearby."

The old man followed Pascoe's thumb with narrowed eyes. Behind him, he knew the old man was studying the late-model white and silver Chevy. Under the camper top, in the bed, were neatly arranged boxes of scavenged weapons and ammo.

"We have quite a few different types, calibers, etc., as well as body armor and ammo. If, as you say, you don't have any weapons, we're authorized to supply you with at least one rifle or shotgun, and a pistol."

"You shitting me?"

"No, sir. You're free to choose what you'd like, except for Moe the two-forty."

"Moe?"

"Moe Dakka. Our nickname."

"I don't get it." The man shrugged. "Anyways, who am I voting for?"

"We're not there just yet. The emergency council is wanting to make sure all Texans who can vote are able to survive long enough to do so."

"Humph." The old man rubbed his chin. "All right, son, I'll tell ya whut—let's just say you don't have to worry about me none, either way."

"Understood, sir. We'll put you down as 'A. Nonomous, declined armament, unconfirmed weaponry.' We'll leave you to your day, thank you."

"You boys seem like nice folk. Be careful out there. It ain't the zeds you need to worry about much, these days."

"Oh?"

"Yup. Rumor has it there's a group running 'round and causing trouble. Seems like once the main danger passed, them fellas got to sowin' some oats. Heard they was out near Bishop, and movin' this way."

"Good to know, sir, much obliged."

"Yup. Take care now."

"What do you think?" Taylor opened the center console, pulling a map from under their stash of grenades. "Should we head towards Bishop and do some reccy?"

"Why do you want to go look for trouble?"

"Don't. Not really. But the council wants to know what's happening, right?"

"Well . . ."

"And," Taylor continued, "seems to me that whoever is out there needs to be counted."

Pascoe shot him a dirty look. Taylor grinned.

"You wouldn't want to be lax in your sworn duty, would you?"

"Oh, sure, play that card again."

"Worked last time, didn't it?"

Pascoe shook his head. "Last time" was really "first time," referring back to when he'd met the now ex-con. Taylor had kept him from going catatonic by doing a fair impression of every drill instructor, ever. It had given Pascoe something to cling to, in the middle of events that should have overwhelmed him.

He knew, unfortunately, that Taylor was right, but dammit, this was supposed to be a cushy, low risk job. Even though the infected "zeds" were less common, due to the harsh winter, severe flooding in spring, and current drought conditions, they were still out there. Pascoe and Taylor had been lucky so far, for various values of "luck," in that they'd only run into a handful of nests. Additionally lucky, since those nests had been small, isolated, and unable to effectively swarm.

He shuddered, thinking of the reports he'd heard on "Devil Dog Radio" about clearing ocean liners. He admired the Marines and what they were doing out there, but he had no desire to follow in their footsteps, thank you very much.

"I see that look in your eyes, bro," Taylor said. "But these are actual living people. All they can do is shoot us, not turn us into slobbering, naked cannibals, right?"

"That's your idea of 'reassuring'?"

Taylor chuckled.

"Fine," Pascoe said, climbing into the truck. "But I'm going to bitch about it the whole time."

∽⊖∾

Pascoe drove carefully along the four-lane road, keeping an eye out for any major obstructions. They'd been lucky so far—the rural highway had been under construction in several places last year, and it appeared that had kept traffic to a minimum. There were very few abandoned cars, unlike the interstates and urban areas. Most of the heavy machinery was along the shoulders, though, leaving the road itself navigable.

"Thinking back," Pascoe said idly, "I should've known this was going to happen."

"What was going to happen?"

"This." He gestured vaguely at the horizon. "Fall of society, cannibal zombie things. The last ten months or so. This."

"Okay, I'll bite," Taylor said, turning. "How come?"

"Paid off my truck. Should've just bought ammo."

Taylor snorted.

"You know what's worse than that?" Taylor asked, as they drove up a small incline. Pascoe risked a quick glance at the other man.

"What?"

"Do you realize we'll never get to see those new Star Wars movies they were going to make?"

"Oh, man, that's just cruel. I bet they'd have been awesome."

"Tell me about it. After the prequels, they only could've gotten better."

"Unless they did something dumb, like making a knock-off Vader, or bringing back the Emperor."

"Ooh, or killing off Han Solo."

"They'd never do that though."

"True. Luke, maybe, but they'd have to make it meaningful, like Obi-Wan."

A flicker of motion caught Pascoe's eye. Off to his left, about three hundred yards away, a group of cars approached the intersection of a smaller road. The dust clouds made it difficult to see exactly what was happening. He slowed, waiting to see which direction the pack would turn.

"Oh, hell yeah. Luke in full Kenobi mode. How cool would that be?" Taylor paused at Pascoe's raised hand. "What's up?"

"Up ahead, could be trouble."

The newcomers turned at the junction, heading away from their position.

Pascoe sat, hands on the wheel of the idling truck, as Taylor scanned the scene with his binoculars. From the top of the slight rise, he had a clear view of the divided highway, and the events playing out.

"This is some Mad Max shit right here," Taylor said, handing over the binocs. "Check it out."

Pascoe took them and focused on the group ahead of them. Four cars, armored with various types of sheet metal and spikes, appeared to be in pursuit of a beat-up U-Haul. The truck was badly dented along one side, and spewing thick blue exhaust.

"Looks like they raided every hardware store in the county," he said. "The worst part is what they did to the new Chargers. That warrants killing on its own."

"Yeah, looks like they've been busy."

Pascoe watched as the group flanked the truck. The driver didn't seem to be panicking, maneuvering purposefully to counteract the others' tactics.

"Must be from Houston," Taylor muttered.

One of the pursuit cars broke left, hopping the median and crossing into what would've been the oncoming lane. Deftly avoiding a few abandoned cars, it accelerated through a clear stretch, pulling ahead of the truck. After a few seconds, the driver angled back across the median, in an attempt to ram their quarry.

The truck driver was prepared, however, accelerating and steering away from the incoming Charger. The move opened up just enough space to where the attacker undershot, fishtailing in behind the truck, and subsequently slamming into one of the other cars.

Both armored cars, locked together, careened onto the shoulder. The cut-off driver's car broke away only seconds before the other slammed into a concrete divider. Pascoe watched as it went airborne, simultaneously flipping and spinning, to land on its roof, belching smoke.

"Whoa! Nicely done, dude!" Taylor slammed his hand down on the dashboard. "If that guy's still alive, he's definitely going to feel it later."

The smoke thickened, flames creeping into view.

"Hunh, well, never mind."

The pack crested the next hill, taking them out of view. Taylor punched him in the arm.

"Well, come on, man, you waiting for an invitation? This is better than Indy."

Pascoe sighed, dropping their truck into gear. He gave the burning Charger a wide berth, just in case it decided to get energetic. As it appeared in his rearview, it experienced a rapid unscheduled disassembly.

He slowed down as they came to the top of the small rise, just in case there was more carnage on the downslope ahead of them. His luck held—the group had made it another mile ahead before stopping their prey. Pascoe brought their pickup to a stop again.

"Okay, let's see what's happening now," Taylor said, as he focused the binocs. Pascoe watched as the ant-sized figures surrounded the truck. "We've got some rough-looking dudes . . . lot of leather and denim . . . moving towards the cab . . ."

Pascoe strained, but gave up at the first sign of a headache.

"Oh, hell." Taylor's whisper barely carried. "They're pulling someone out of the passenger side."

Taylor's hands tightened briefly, his face going blank. He handed the glasses to Pascoe, who took them and sighted the group in.

"New plan," Taylor said, releasing his seat belt. "Drive, slow, until we're halfway there. Let me out, then get up on them. Buy me some time to get set."

"You're kidding, right?"

"No." Taylor's voice left no room for doubt. "It's a priest."

Pascoe watched silently for a few moments. It was difficult to tell, due to the men moving around, but after a few seconds, he saw what Taylor was talking about. The man on the ground had a black long-sleeved shirt with a white collar.

Taylor got out, moved to the back of the pickup, and opened the camper. Pascoe could see him rummaging around briefly, before closing up and coming back with a scoped Barrett.

"Let's go," he said, closing the door. "Nice and smooth, while they're preoccupied."

"You want me to do what, exactly?"

"Do the census thing, tell 'em a story, dress in drag and do the hula, I don't care. Just stall them for a minute."

"This isn't our problem, Taylor..."

"Yeah, it is, OFFICER Pascoe," Taylor hissed, glaring. "We're doing this."

Pascoe nodded, realizing nothing he said would convince the man otherwise. He put the pickup in gear and made his way forward, keeping the speedometer just under thirty.

"Here," Taylor said, after a minute. "Edge closer to the culvert there. Don't stop, just slow down."

Taylor waited until they were at a crawl, then opened the door and rolled out in one smooth motion. As Pascoe accelerated again, the door swung closed. His next few moments were spent trying to figure out what he was going to say, as well as watching the men ahead of him react.

As he hit what he figured was the two-hundred-yard mark, the sound of his engine caught the men's attention. Three of the six visible had turned to watch his approach—the two with rifles keeping them slung at a low ready position—while the others crowded around their victims, using rifle butts and kicks to keep them subdued. At one hundred feet, he stopped the truck, put it in park, and got out.

Plastering what he hoped was his most innocent—and most importantly, harmless—"hey guys, I'm just doing my job" smile on his face, he got out of the truck and started forward. The other members of the gang had now turned to see what was going on, watching him with a mix of wariness and curiosity. Pascoe stopped after ten steps, grinning and waving like an idiot.

The armor on the Chargers made it impossible to see into them from his angle, but their doors appeared to be welded shut. If there was anyone inside, they were a low priority threat. Two of the raiders kept a foot each on the beaten and bleeding occupants of the U-Haul.

Pascoe took a deep breath.

Showtime.

"Good day, gentlemen," he said, still smiling. He held up his clipboard, hoping that its fabled powers of persuasion and access held true, even outside of a military installation. "My name is Pascoe, and I won't take up too much of your time. I can see you're busy."

"Whatcha think you doin' here, man?" The speaker, one of the first to notice his approach, was the only man not carrying a rifle. Instead, he carried two holstered pistols, slung low like an old west gunfighter. The tattoos visible along his neck and cheeks identified him as someone who had done time.

"I've been instructed by the Emergency Council of the State of Texas to perform a census in this area. What we're trying to do is make sure that all eligible voters are accounted for, and have the ability to defend themselves during the current crisis."

Several of the others traded glances, chuckling.

Come on, Taylor, Pascoe thought.

"Like I said," he continued aloud, "I just need to get some basic info, and I'll leave you to your business. Shouldn't take but a moment."

"You got some stones, *pendejo,*" the leader said, "I'll give you that."

Pascoe kept his grin in place and looked over the other man's shoulder. He used the clipboard to point at the two standing over the priests.

"I'll start with you two, so you can get back to what

you were doing," he said, then indicated the others in turn. "Then you, you, and you."

"Ain't no one telling you shit." The leader scowled, taking a step forward. "You got five seconds before I gut you and leave you bleedin'."

"No need for hostility, my good man," Pascoe said. With his arms out, he spread the fingers on his left hand. He folded in his thumb. "I'm simply trying to—"

"Time's running out." Another step forward. Pascoe stepped back as he curled two fingers.

"Three." The two men flanking the leader adjusted their rifles.

"I'll just put y'all down as 'capable and armed'..." Pascoe retreated as he talked, now showing only his pinky.

"Two."

"I'm from the government, and I'm here to help you." He made a full fist. Nothing happened.

"One."

Pascoe brought his right arm across his chest, kept it parallel to his left, and swayed his hips. After a second, he reversed the pose.

"Aloha, oe...aloha oe..." He sang, still dancing backwards. The raider's faces all showed confusion, and the leader paused a few feet away.

"What the fu—"

One of the men over the priests dropped, his chest exploding into crimson. A moment later, his buddy next to him fell as well, his body armor disintegrating. Two more of the raiders dropped just as the crack of the shots caught up.

Pascoe drew his pistol, putting three rounds center of mass on the leader before turning his attention to the man at his two o'clock. He fired just as the other man's rifle barked, his first two shots on target, but his third going wide as his breath exploded from his lungs.

He and both of the bandits hit the ground simultaneously, neither of the other men moving. He winced at the pain in his chest, but fought through it to pull at his armor and inspect his torso. His relieved sigh ended with a gasp. The close-range shot hadn't penetrated, just hurt like a son of a bitch.

At the bandit leader's groan, Pascoe ignored his own discomfort and made his way to the other man. He too was wearing a vest, but it seemed one of Pascoe's shots had gone through. Pascoe relieved the man of his weapons, just to be safe.

"Hurts, don't it?" He punctuated each word by stepping on the man's chest, allowing himself some satisfaction as the other paled. "Figure those priests didn't like it much either."

"Now," he continued, "What are we doing out here, besides harassing men of the cloth?"

"Fu— AH!" Pascoe applied pressure before the word finished.

"Let's try that again."

"Alacrán is coming," the bandit gasped, "He'll know where we are."

Pascoe grunted, putting all of his weight on one foot. The man screamed, then passed out. Macabrely satisfied, Pascoe moved over to the priests.

The younger man was clearly dead, his wide, unblinking eyes still showing shock and surprise. The older priest lay still, but his chest rose and fell weakly. At the sound of Pascoe's footsteps, he managed to turn his head.

"It's okay, Father," Pascoe said, soothingly. "I'm not here to hurt you. Wait one second."

One of the fallen bandits had a camelback. Pascoe removed it, struggling slightly with the man's dead weight, and brought the spout close to the priest's lips.

"Take it slow, sir." He waited as the man took a few careful sips, then said, "Can you tell me what happened?"

"The Cathedral. *Ave Crux, spes unica.*" The priest coughed, bloody foam splattering the ground around him. Pascoe couldn't tell if it was from his busted lips, or internal bleeding.

The sound of a gunshot behind him grabbed his attention. He turned to see Taylor walking towards him, pistol at his side.

"You left an enemy behind you alive," he said, breathing hard. "Not a good strategy these days."

"You okay? Seem to be a bit winded."

"Yeah, been a while since I humped a bitch like this," Taylor said, stroking the Barrett. "But you're worth it, baby, you know I love you." He stopped and nodded at the priests. "What's the situation?"

"Not sure, was just getting to that." Pascoe turned back to the priest to see him motioning for him to come closer. He put his ear next to the older man's lips.

"Moving relics..." he gasped. He held out a leather-bound Bible, wrapped in a rosary.

Pascoe waited until the next coughing fit subsided, then tried to give him some more water. The priest shook him off with more violence than he'd expected, knocking the camelback out of his hand.

"You must hear the Call of God," the priest said,

pressing the Bible to Pascoe's chest. As Pascoe took it, the priest let go, signing the cross as he did.

"*In Hoc Signe Vinces,*" he gasped, slumping back. "Corpus Christi Cathedral, the Ghost protects."

Pascoe closed the man's eyes gently as a final breath rattled through his chest.

"What did he say?"

"Something about relics, the Call of God, and something Latin. Also that a ghost is protecting the Corpus Christi Cathedral," Pascoe said. "That mean anything to you?"

"Hm. Maybe he meant Holy Ghost?" Taylor rubbed a hand over his head. "I guess he meant the Holy Spirit was protecting the cathedral."

He moved over to the back of the truck. Pascoe followed him, stuffing the Bible in a cargo pocket.

He moved over to the back of the U-Haul.

"Let's see what they were so desperate to take there."

The rear was secured, but not locked. Taylor disengaged the latch and heaved, rolling the door up. Inside, the space was dominated by a huge brass bell, with other, smaller items haphazardly arranged around it.

"Whoa, looks like someone cleaned house."

"The Father there said 'moving relics.'"

"Hell of a haul, that bell must weigh hundreds of pounds. All of this other stuff is pretty high end too. Look here." Taylor hefted a box full of silver and gold chalices. "Must be thousands here, in precious metals alone."

"Someone went to a lot of trouble," Pascoe said, nodding. "We should get it off the road. Map says there's a small town up ahead. We could find somewhere to stash it."

"Yeah . . ." Taylor said, eyes distant. He shook it off, rolled down the door and re-secured it. "We need to take them with us, give them a proper send off. Help me get them in the back of the pickup, there's room."

It took a few minutes, but after rearranging the crates of guns and ammo, they were able to gently place the two dead men in the bed of the truck. For good measure, they stripped the raiders of anything useful, as well. When they finished, Taylor closed the tailgate and camper cover, then walked toward the priest's van.

"I'll take this one, you get ours. Find a service station we can park in."

One of the raider's radios crackled to life. Pascoe couldn't follow the rapid fire Spanish. Taylor apparently could, though, and stopped moving. After a few seconds of silence, the voice came back. This time, Pascoe recognized a word.

"Alacrán," Pascoe said, as Taylor's face grew dark. "That's what the leader told me when I questioned him."

"What exactly did he say?"

"'Alacrán is coming.' That mean something?"

"Maybe," Taylor grunted, "probably nothing. Let's get moving."

Pascoe shrugged, and climbed into the Silverado. Something in the side mirror caught his eye—a quick flash, but when he turned to look, there was nothing. It was possible the camper's back window had caught the sun just right, playing tricks on his still-wound nerves. His time in the sandbox had taught him to never ignore his instincts, though, and they were screaming that something wasn't right. He'd take the rear slot and keep his eyes open.

The moving van coughed as Taylor tried to start it, finally grumbling to life on the third try, belching thick black exhaust. With a wheeze and some screeching, it rolled forward. Pascoe gave it some room, then followed.

It took an hour to arrive, locate, and sweep a suitable location, an old service station near the small town's main street.

It was only a matter of minutes, and some heavy exertion, to get the roll-up door open and the van inside. He pulled their Silverado around behind the building while the fumes from the van's exhaust cleared, and checked the perimeter. The station—and several other businesses near it—had been closed long before the current situation started, Pascoe realized. It had been stripped of anything remotely useful—everything remaining was either built into the structure, or bolted down.

That didn't mean precautions were unwarranted, however. He hadn't seen any signs of pursuit, but that didn't mean it wasn't there. The raider's radio squawked a constant stream of agitated Spanish from Alacrán and his men during the drive, doing nothing to alleviate his paranoia. Pascoe took one last careful look around before straining to pull the doors back down again, the stubborn pulley mechanism sending out a shower of red flakes with every turn.

"That's one way to see if the town's clear," Taylor said, sliding out of the driver's seat. "Every zed in the county could've heard us coming. Any movement out there?"

"Not that I could see, but we'll keep an ear out just in case."

"All right, what've we got here?" Taylor looked around

the shop and nodded. "Nice. Homey. Could see us making a nice life for ourselves here."

"Oh ha ha. Now really, we need a plan here."

"Been thinking about that," Taylor said, rubbing his chin. "Way I see it, we owe it to the priests to finish the job."

"Owe it to them? Taylor, we stumbled across these guys in the middle of nowhere. If we hadn't been near, we'd never know about this. Why is it now our responsibility?"

"God works in mysterious ways, bud."

"So does your thought process."

Taylor ignored him.

"This old girl ain't going anywhere fast, if at all," he said, kicking the van's tires. "Repairs are out of the question. I could feel the tranny skipping as we drove. Burning oil, too. Piston rings are likely shot, and it was knocking like a coked-up Jehovah's Witness. Could throw a rod any moment."

"Okay, so we leave it here, see if anyone that cares is still alive, and come back later."

"No." Taylor shook his head. "I don't think this is a 'do it when it's convenient' kind of thing. We're being tested."

"I swear if you say 'We're on a mission from God' I'll shoot you myself." Pascoe paused, shaking his head at Taylor's grin. "You were totally going to say that, weren't you?"

"Maybe. We'll argue about this later. For now, let's find some place to bury the priests."

"There's a patch of grass around the side that should work," Pascoe said. "I'm serious, Taylor, this isn't our problem."

Taylor started towards their truck. "One thing at a time. There's an entrenching tool in the back. Why don't you see if there's anything else to dig with?"

Pascoe finished hammering the crude crosses into the ground, and stepped back.

Taylor kept staring at the cross at the head of the older priest's grave, his hands folded in prayer.

"Hey," Pascoe said gently as he pulled the Bible from his cargo pocket. "You want me to read something, or do you want to say a few words?"

"We can't leave it."

"Leave what?"

"You heard the priest. We need to hear the Call of God," Taylor said, turning to face his partner.

"Why is this so important, Taylor? You can't tell me that these trinkets are worth the trouble."

"Yeah, they are. Not monetarily. Well, not just monetarily. Sure, there's some gold and silver here, but it's more than that."

"What they represent is more important than just the money? I get it."

"Yeah. But no. These items were donated, or the money was donated by parishioners to buy them. Their value isn't just the money, it's the spirit in which they were given. The people in that congregation wanted to be proud of their church. To show God that they would give what they could to make their place of worship beautiful."

He jerked a thumb towards the garage.

"A copper chalice isn't fancy, or expensive, but it'll last for generations. It'll tie great-grandchildren to their ancestors. We can help keep these items in a community that will respect that connection, not just use them for money or trade them for terrestrial power."

"You don't think that the Church saw them as a financial investment? A rainy day fund, if you will?"

"Sure, but the difference is the congregation would benefit from it, not some rando who only sees the melt value. Take the bell. It's a couple hundred pounds of bronze. Not exactly a wealth of metal, even these days. But, it has a history. Deaths, births, marriages—history. Church bells have called the faithful, and more importantly, called *to* them. Let them know that God was there, even in their darkest hour. They gave people hope, when there was nothing else that could."

Pascoe studied his friend carefully.

"It's deeper than that, isn't it?"

Taylor opened his mouth, paused, then snapped it shut. Pascoe knew he was right.

"Should've stopped running my damn mouth," Taylor muttered, shaking his head. Pascoe maintained eye contact for several tense seconds until Taylor said, "Guess it's time we had that talk."

He seemed to consider his words carefully, before starting again.

"You know why I got popped last year? It wasn't because I was sloppy. Hell, I smuggled more dope from Matamoros to San Antonio than you could imagine, and the border boys been none the wiser. So why this time?"

Pascoe thought for a moment. "Someone tipped them off."

"Bingo." Taylor tapped his nose. "Any guesses as to who?"

"Shit, that list could be a mile long and two wide. A girlfriend's angry husband, jilted ex—"

"Nope," Taylor said, smiling. "I'll give you a hint—he's tall, muscular, very handsome, shaved head..."

"No way. You?"

"Had to make it look convincing."

"Okay, hang on now. You gave yourself up? For what?"

"Needed to get closer to some folks on the inside, follow the threads, cultivate some assets. Not to mention, time on the inside for a small potatoes bust would help my cred."

Pascoe sat back, contemplating his friend. Taylor was roughly mid-thirties, and from what he'd seen, highly trained. During his tours overseas, Pascoe had made friends with some special forces guys. They'd come and go without notice, seemingly able to disappear into the local population with little effort. Taylor carried himself similarly.

"You were undercover. DEA?"

"Secret Service. Counterterrorism. These guys weren't just buying new cars and guns. A lot of that money was getting funneled back to the middle east. I'd been working my way up through the ranks, but hit a small snag. It was time to go in deeper."

"Okay, so you were a Fed. How does it all tie to this, though?"

"I'm getting there." Taylor's shoulders slumped as his eyes grew distant. "You were in the service, Pascoe. You know what it's like when you doubt the mission, and what you tell yourself to keep going."

Pascoe nodded. "The Greater Good."

"Yeah. That's what I told myself. 'I'm changing things for the better. Saving more than I'm hurting.' Whatever the rationalization was for that day."

"Like you said, you were looking at the big picture."

"That big picture gets harder to justify when you see some kid swallowing balloons of smack, and you're keeping your head down so you can build a case. One of those balloons busts open in his gut, well, that's just a small price to pay for that fish on the other end.

"It scratches at your soul, man," Taylor said quietly. "Every time, that darkness gets a little more hold on you. But you can't tell anyone, relieve yourself of that burden. That's how you get pulled off duty, retired early, or killed. Only person you can talk to is God, and hope he's listening.

"I'd hear the bells," he continued, waving a hand towards the truck, "and they gave me hope. They brought some light back into the dark parts. This was a sign. God listened. He heard me beg for a chance to make up for all that shit. I got a long way to go to balance the books. This is one of the steps."

"One of them?"

"Heh. You think this is it? Hell no, man, this path started when I met you. I realized it when that girl came at me in the trailer. You think Leyva would've stuck by me? Sumbitch was trying to sell me out. Damn well wouldn't have stopped that rabid prom queen until she'd finished with me."

"Who knows, he might've."

"Maybe, but I guarantee you he wouldn't have felt bad about it. Not enough to have nightmares." Taylor stopped as Pascoe shot him a look. "I hear you at night, bud. It's not every night, but I know when it hits you."

Pascoe looked down at his feet.

"God put a good man in my path. He showed me the journey wasn't going to be easy, but I'd have help.

He felt I was worth saving, and I'll damn sure do my best to earn it."

"And you think this is it?"

"Yeah, I do," Taylor said softly. "We can deliver some hope. Some light in the dark, for others out there."

"Fine. Fine!" Pascoe said, throwing up his arms. "You do know that means we have to move all of the stuff into the truck, right?"

"No one said he had to make it easy."

"I think we have a problem," Taylor said, carrying a load from the back of the van.

"What, another one?" Pascoe didn't look up from consolidating crates of weapons. With how much room the bell would need, he was concerned they wouldn't be able to carry everything.

"I thought I saw a zombie in the distance."

"How's that a problem?"

"I think they're wearing clothes," Taylor answered.

"And you don't think it's a regular survivor, do you?"

"After our run-in with the others, no."

"Well, we're not ready to go here unless you want to abandon some of this stuff."

"I'll go scout it out," Taylor said, as he started pulling gear. "If there's a threat I'll deal with it, or slow them down if we need more time."

"Of course we need more time," Pascoe snarled. "We still have to move that stupid bell."

"Don't insult the bell, it's our mission."

"Our mission is heavy and I don't want to have to move it alone."

"Come to me, all you who labor and are heavy laden, and I will give you rest," quoted Taylor.

"Spare me the sermon and help me out."

"I'm going to head out the back and try to sneak up on them," Taylor said, grabbing a submachine gun out of a crate. He disappeared around the front of the van.

Pascoe felt his temples throb as he stared at the bell and muttered, "Well, fuck—"

With everything out, there was now room in the bed of the truck. What hadn't occurred to either him or Taylor was that the tailgate was about six inches higher than the floor of the van's cargo area.

"Damn it." Pascoe scanned the repair bays, hoping to find something useful.

There were lifts, but with no power, they were out of the question. Any floor jacks had disappeared long ago. Pulling out a flashlight, he started rooting around through the detritus in the corners, desperate to find something. A flash of reflected light caught his eye.

He moved the various greasy rags, papers, and discarded bottles of motor oil. Underneath, he found a worn, but seemingly sound, wheeled mechanic's sled. It looked just tall enough to get the bell level. The next problem would be moving the bell inside the camper. There was just enough room for it to fit height-wise, but he didn't think he'd have enough raw power to shove it forward by himself.

Motor oil on the other hand... Things were always easier with lube. Each bottle he found had a little left in it, less than an ounce in most cases. Fortunately, there were plenty. In short time, he had scrounged up most of a quart.

"It might just do the trick, if I'm careful..." he muttered to himself.

Pascoe climbed into the van, and after several

minutes of creative cursing, managed to get the bell firmly on the sled. A few more minutes of effort got everything lined up with the tailgate. With a satisfied grunt, Pascoe climbed into the truck to prepare the bed.

And watched in horror as the bell rolled away from him, slamming into the cab of the moving van.

"Oh, come on," Pascoe snapped. He noticed that the back of the van floor was a bit warped, probably from the battering it had taken during the chase. The ammo crates would be too bulky to wrestle into place while trying to hold the bell. He needed something to wedge under the wheels.

After getting the bell back into position, he cleared his pistol, jammed it behind a rear caster, then carefully let go. Everything stayed put. With a sigh of relief, he once again climbed into the truck to spread the oil.

With a groan, one of the front casters gave out. The sled leaned forward, bringing the edge of the bell just below the tailgate.

It took everything he had to not scream. Instead, he sat down heavily, sinking his head into his hands. Something poked him in the ass.

"Of course. Can't just have a moment, can I?" he said quietly, digging around in his pocket.

The cross of the rosary-wrapped Bible had turned the wrong way. Pulling the book out, he cocked his hand back to heave it at the source of his frustration, then stopped.

After a few seconds eyeballing both the gap and the book, he stood up.

"O Lord, you are my rock," Pascoe said, looking up towards the sky. "With your help I can advance. I hope you understand."

Finishing the prayer, Pascoe stuffed the top of

the Bible under the caster, bringing the sled back to level. After a brief pause to make sure the bell wasn't going anywhere, he opened the motor oil.

"All right, let's get greasy."

Pascoe wiped his hands on an oily rag, and admired his work. Once the bell was in place, everything else was easy.

"It's a miracle," he said, chuckling.

With a crackle, the bandit's radio in the cab came to life, spewing Spanish. While he'd worked, he'd occasionally heard idle conversation, but nothing that had sounded urgent. This time, the voice on the other end was agitated, the words punctuated with what he recognized as profanity.

As if in response, he heard several gunshots in the distance.

"Oh Christ." After slamming the tailgate and camper closed, he moved towards the cab.

Pascoe's head snapped around at the sound of his name, followed by something unintelligible. In the distance, Taylor was running straight at him, arms pumping in effort. Pascoe hopped into the driver's seat, and started the truck. He pulled out, heading towards Taylor.

Taylor wasted no time, climbing into the passenger seat before the vehicle had stopped.

"Floor it, we need to get out of here," he gasped.

"What's going on?"

"They tracked us, it's a trap."

"Shit." The truck's engine roared as Pascoe stood on the pedal. Just as they got up to speed, a tricked-out car came around the corner in the distance. Pascoe slammed on the brakes. "Dammit, they're ahead of us."

"Flip around!" Taylor leaned out of the window, firing rapidly at the other vehicle.

"Working on it!" With the extra weight, the Chevy handled like a pregnant hippopotamus. By the time Pascoe finished the three-point turn, the other car had closed the gap. Taylor's suppressive fire kept them at bay as they approached the service station. "Who are these guys?"

"They're . . ." Taylor's explanation was cut off by Pascoe hitting the brakes again. "What now?"

"Cover me!" Pascoe put the truck in park and bailed out, sprinting towards the moving van. He'd left the Bible wedged under the mechanic's sled. In seconds, he'd retrieved it and made it back to the truck.

"Almost forgot it," Pascoe explained, dropping the truck into gear. Several more cars had appeared behind them.

"You're trying to get us killed over a Bible?"

"Well, you're trying to get us killed over a bell!" Pascoe tossed the Bible on the center console. Taylor ignored him, hanging out the window to fire at their pursuers.

"I've got an idea," he said, coming back in. Grabbing the Bible, he opened the console, and removed some grenades before shoving the Bible inside. After slamming it shut, he leaned out and tossed the frags. Five seconds later, they heard the explosions.

Pascoe risked a quick glance to see the lead car in flames. The others swerved to avoid it, as well as the telephone poles crashing down across the street.

"Damn, I'm good," Taylor said. "That'll buy us a little time. Make use of it."

"'We'll go take down some names.' 'It'll be easy. What could possibly go wrong?'" Pascoe muttered. "Now we're being pursued by bandits."

"They're not just bandits," Taylor said. "They're cartel. My cartel."

"Oh this gets even better. And the Alacrán guy?"

"He was in too. Started sniffing around, digging into my cover. I thought I'd taken care of him when I set myself up. Made sure only he and Don Cortez knew where I was crossing."

"That's Machiavellian. I'm impressed."

"Yeah," Taylor said. "Apparently not permanent. I imagine the world going haywire at the time gave him some opportunities. Too bad."

"Think maybe you should have mentioned him before this?"

"Probably." Taylor checked his rearview. Satisfied, he continued, "If we get out of this, Pascoe, I promise I'll make it up to you."

"If."

"Keep the faith, my friend. We're on a mission from God."

Pascoe glared silently at the road in front of them.

Pascoe stopped the truck in front of the steps of Corpus Christi Cathedral.

"Check the door! I have overwatch," Taylor said as he hopped out of the truck. He grabbed Moe and a box of ammo from the back seat, then climbed onto the truck's roof. Pascoe slid out of the driver's side.

After running up the front steps and peering through the padlocked door's barred windows, Pascoe yelled, "It's abandoned!"

"It can't be! The priest said to come here!" Taylor responded.

"I don't see signs of anyone, and this place is

sealed up." Pascoe rattled the heavy chain. "Look at the boards over the window—whoever did this took the time to screw them in flush to each other."

"The priest told us to come here." Taylor's voice carried a hint of desperation. "*He* was coming here. Why, if there weren't people?"

"Did he know, or just hope?"

"You're the one who talked to him," Taylor responded. Pascoe shook his head, and ran towards a building on the other side of the complex.

Behind him, the two-forty chattered as Taylor engaged...something. Shortly after, he heard the squeal of tires and what sounded like a severe crash. Hoping that his partner could keep things under control, he continued towards what he assumed was the rectory.

The building, also boarded up, made it clear that no one was inside, and hadn't been for a while. Snarling in frustration, he ran back towards Taylor. As he rounded the corner, he slowed to take in the scene.

A hundred yards out, one armored Charger sat smoking, another abandoned—both surrounded by multiple bodies.

"They're catching up! We need a plan," Pascoe said, running back to the open driver's door. "We're almost on empty, and we don't have anywhere to go."

"This has to be it! The priest said that God was protecting this cathedral!" Taylor lobbed a grenade. "Frag out!"

"He didn't say God. He said the Ghost." Pascoe opened their map.

"Same thing."

"No," Pascoe said. "He didn't say the Holy Spirit, or the Holy Ghost. He just said 'the Ghost.'"

"Is this really time to argue about the Trinity?"

"Not Holy Ghost, Blue Ghost! The USS *Lexington*!" Pascoe pointed to the map. "She's anchored just across the bridge. What if the Blue Ghost is protecting them because they forted up inside it?"

"Hell, let's give it a shot." Taylor said, firing. "Not like we could make it anywhere else."

Shoving the map into the back seat, Pascoe looked down at the open center console. "Where's the Bible?"

"What?" Taylor asked. "I think we have more important things to worry about."

"We can't leave without it. I almost made that mistake once," Pascoe said as he started to search the cab of the truck. "What did you do with it? It was with the grenades!"

"I don't know," Taylor snapped. "I just tossed it out of the way."

Grabbing their last grenade, Pascoe pulled the pin and hurled it at their pursuers.

"They'll have more, it's not important!" Taylor jumped down as Pascoe ran around to the passenger side.

"It was to the priest," Pascoe said, searching the ground. "Got it!"

"Can we get out of here now?"

Tossing the Bible onto the dash, Pascoe slid to the driver's seat and slammed the truck into gear. As they sped down the street, Taylor yanked open the glove compartment, threw the Bible inside, then slammed it closed.

"Check the map," Pascoe said. "I need to know where to go."

"Aim for the big ship."

"Have you ever been there?"

"Well, no," Taylor admitted.

"So. Check. The. Map."

"All right, all right," Taylor said, wrestling with the half folded, half crumpled paper. "Freeway is ahead, get on it."

Pascoe nodded, dodging a few cars here and there that had been abandoned in the streets. Most of the cities had been under strict curfew before everything fell apart, and as a result, travel had been minimal. After everything went to hell, there weren't enough survivors to cause a fender bender, much less a traffic jam.

"Our Lady of Blessed Acceleration, don't fail us now" Taylor said, crossing himself.

"Shit!" Pascoe hit the brakes. Taylor snapped his head up and at the sight of the cars blocking the road ahead of them.

"This don't look like no expressway to me!"

"I think we can get through, there's space between them," Pascoe explained. "This isn't a traffic jam, it's deliberate."

"I hope you're right," Taylor said. It sounded like a prayer.

"We'll know in a second." Pascoe started forward, aiming for the first break in the formation. Whoever had set it up had given just enough room between the rows to make a tight turn, and had staggered the breaks. Agonizing seconds crawled by as he made his way through the ranks.

As they crested a slight rise, he could see that the obstruction only extended another hundred yards.

Pascoe sighed with relief as they cleared the last vehicle. The truck shuddered as he accelerated towards the bridge. He risked a look behind them. The bandits had made it to the blockade, and were filing through it. Taylor kept a running commentary.

"Six bogeys, first one's through.

"Next one. They're forming up.

"Here they come."

"That's our exit." Pascoe pointed ahead of them. Fortunately, this ramp was clear. He took it at speed, not slowing until they approached ground level.

"There's a crossover just ahead," Taylor said, studying the map. "Take it and head back the other way."

Pascoe cranked the wheel, skidding over the grass median and onto the road next to it in a tight U-turn.

"That works too," Taylor said, dropping the map on the dash. "*Now* aim for the big ship."

"I see it," Pascoe answered. The truck fishtailed as he accelerated through a turn.

"I hope you're right about the church," Taylor said, checking behind them. "We're still ahead, but our friends are catching up."

Pascoe grunted in response. They were close, but still needed to navigate through the small retail community near the ship.

"Tattoo shops, beachwear, jet ski rentals," Taylor said, as they sped by. "This place has everything."

As they rounded what Pascoe hoped was the last corner, he swore. Ahead, several cars, an anchor, and an airplane blocked the entrance to the pier.

"Damn, that's blasphemy," Taylor muttered. "Practical, but blasphemy."

"Shit!" Pascoe yelled, pulling up in front of the barricade. He pounded on the steering wheel with a fist, then climbed out of the truck. He stood there, studying the blockage. After a moment, his shoulders slumped.

"And I don't see anyone moving around," Taylor said, at his shoulder. "You'd think that they would react to people rocking up on them. They must have been overrun."

Head down, Pascoe walked back to the cab and grabbed the map. There had to be somewhere—anywhere—they could go.

"We need," he started, but was cut off by a shriek of tires. Across the small parking lot, half a dozen modified cars and trucks came to a screeching halt. Armed men piled out of the vehicles and took up firing positions.

Pascoe grabbed a rifle from the back seat, slapped in a magazine, and hunkered near the truck's tail lights. Taylor had armed himself and moved behind the engine block. When no one started shooting, Pascoe carefully looked at the bandits.

A man approached the front set of cars, carrying a megaphone. Unlike the others, he was in a neatly pressed suit—jacket worn open over body armor.

"You are both very brave, and very stupid to steal from me," he said, amplified voice carrying easily over the distance.

"*We* stole," Pascoe scoffed.

"These things belong to the Church, not some two-bit *mojada*, Alacrán!" Taylor yelled. "We won't give them up. We're on a mission from God!"

Alacrán looked startled, then squinted, studying them. After several seconds, he spoke again.

"Is that you, Taylor?" After no response, he continued, "I guess I shouldn't be surprised *un pinche traidor chuppa verga* like you survived."

Pascoe watched as Taylor grinned, winked, and shouted something in Spanish.

"Open fire!" Alacrán yelled. The truck rocked as bullets tore into it.

"Jesus Christ, Taylor, what did you say?"

"I told him his Abuela's tamales were dry and tasteless."

"Dear God, man."

Pascoe waited for a break in the incoming fire before retaliating with unaimed shots of his own. With any luck, it would at least get the cartel thugs to take cover. Suddenly, a voice boomed from behind him.

"THIS IS A PLACE OF SANCTUARY. CEASE HOSTILITIES OR WE WILL FORCE THEM TO CEASE."

The cartel force replied with another volley.

"YOU AT THE TRUCK, STAY DOWN."

Pascoe crouched, head covered, as Hell rained down in front of them.

Ears ringing, surprised to be alive, Pascoe surveyed the area. Alacrán's men had fled in any vehicle still operational, leaving their dead behind.

Pascoe walked around their truck, surveying the damage. The side panels and camper resembled metallic Swiss cheese, and several different fluids leaked from under the engine block.

"Damn," he said, patting the fender. "You served well, faithful servant."

In response, the Silverado sank on its shocks with a wheezing sigh.

Movement on the pier caught his eye. Two men in black shirts approached warily from the *Lexington*. As they got closer, Pascoe could make out the starched white collars. He carefully slung his rifle.

"May God be with you, gentlemen," the older priest said, striding forward. "Sorry for leaving you out there, but we wanted to get an idea of who we might be dealing with. We saw you on the bridge and knew there was trouble, but couldn't tell who was the cause."

"Well, we appreciate the help," Taylor said. "Would you happen to be from the cathedral?"

"Why yes, I am," the priest said smiling. "I am Monsignor Gallardo, Vicar General of the Diocese of Corpus Christi. And, for now, the diocesan administrator."

"Does that mean you're in charge?" Pascoe asked.

"Yes, my son." The priest's smile grew. "That means I am in charge."

"Well, have we got a surprise for you," Taylor said, grinning.

Monsignor Gallardo cocked an eyebrow, and followed him to the back of their truck.

With a flourish, Taylor opened the camper shell. It promptly fell off its hinges, smashing to bits on the ground. Without missing a beat, he yanked on the tailgate's handle. The whole panel came away from the frame, landing next to his feet.

"Ta dah!"

"Oh, my." Monsignor Gallardo's eyebrows shot up.

"I see you came across Fathers Jimenez and Nguyen," he continued, frowning. "They didn't make it back last year. We assumed the worst. How are they?"

"I'm sorry, Monsignor," Taylor said. "They didn't make it."

"The younger of the two..." Pascoe began.

"Father Jimenez."

"Father Jimenez," Pascoe corrected, "had passed by the time we got to him. But Father Nguyen told us to come here. He was very adamant."

The monsignor crossed himself and quietly said a prayer. Pascoe shot a glance at his partner.

"They were very dedicated men," the monsignor said, after a moment. "Both to God and what they felt was their duty."

"Well I'd say they accomplished it," Taylor said. "They were able to get these relics into safe hands."

"Yes, yes. Of course you have our thanks for returning everything," Monsignor Gallardo said, frowning. "But the confusion comes from why 'everything?' While the crosses and gilded chalices are nice, they aren't necessary. The bell, though, that is quite the surprise."

"Church bells bring hope, Monsignor. They were there for me when I needed guidance, a way through my own personal darkness."

"This bell in particular?"

"Well, no, but some like it."

"Ah, I see now," Monsignor said. "But, my son, those were different times. Now, the bell's silence brings that hope, for its song brings the infected."

"Then why go through the trouble of bringing them all this way? Why did Father Nguyen take the chance and go after them in the first place?"

"Only God knows, my son. As the end approached, we had our parishes group together to store these things. Why they took the truck with everything in it? My only guess is that it was due to expediency. As to what they were going after, well, that I can explain. Our church was blessed with a gift of pieces of the One True Cross seventy-seven years ago. While chalices and bells are nice, they are things that can be replaced. That relic is not—it's a reminder of what Jesus did for us so many years ago. It's unfortunate that Father Nguyen didn't find it."

"The pieces of the cross, Monsignor," Pascoe said, "Um...what would they have been stored in?"

"Well, before all of this madness began, they were displayed proudly and prominently at the altar. To preserve them, they were encased in glass, along with other indulgences. The glass itself was embedded in a silver disk, mounted inside a golden cross." He grunted as he lifted an item from the back seat of the truck. "This one, actually. But as you can see, the relic is missing. Father Nguyen must have hidden the Cross in another location, which he carried to the grave."

"There's one more item, Monsignor," Pascoe said, feeling his cheeks flush. "It, um, wasn't exactly handled with care, though."

He walked to the passenger side, and opened the glove compartment. After a few seconds, he pulled out the greasy, scuffed-up, rosary-wrapped bible. He handed it to Monsignor Gallardo.

The monsignor took it, brows furrowing. Then his face broke into a grin.

"Oh, Father Nguyen, you sneaky genius." Looking at Pascoe, he said, "You never thought to examine this?"

"Not really, Monsignor. I didn't think there was anything special about it. I thought it was Father Nguyen's Bible, and I brought it along because it seemed important to him."

Monsignor Gallardo unwrapped the rosary, opened the Bible, and flipped quickly past the first third.

Chuckling, he said, "Important, indeed."

With a smile, he tipped it so Pascoe could see. Nestled inside was a small glass vial. Within it, three slivers of dark, petrified wood.

"My friends, you have truly done God's work. Thank you for bringing this treasure home."

The Best Part of Waking Up

MIKE MASSA

Billy Joe Destrehan liked to believe that he knew it all, but deep down he knew there were only two things that he could reliably do well. Make coffee and blow shit up.

Given the right equipment and supplies he could either always pull the perfect espresso shot or improvise the ideal explosive charge, from moving several tons of dirt to popping a door lock without disturbing the framed art on the adjacent wall. It was a question of attention to detail and the application of core principles. At the moment, however, Billy Joe was in spectator mode. He watched his brand new boss, a gaunt and visibly frustrated U.S. Navy senior chief, reread some handwritten notes lying on the laboratory table. Billy Joe suspected he knew what the problem was. Experience in handling eccentric managers kept his teeth together.

It required effort, because there were clues to the senior chief's frustration scattered around the white-painted, ad-hoc lab that served as the Naval Station Guantanamo Bay Special Projects workshop. For starters, temperature-labeled beakers full of previous experiments were visible, and they suggested to Billy Joe the old guy was wasting his time. But Senior Chief Machinist's Mate Lando (my daddy really liked the movies, see?) Washington had been crystal clear. When the armed trusty escorting a group of parolees had dropped Billy Joe off with his new minder not even half an hour earlier, Washington made it plain that the comfy job in Special Projects depended on staying quiet unless and until called upon. During introductions, the Senior, as he preferred to be called, shared his readiness "to blow your terrorist ass away for damn near any reason, up to and including putting artificial sweetener in my coffee." Post-Fall, Billy Joe had accumulated considerable experience with crazy bosses and he recognized absolute sincerity when he heard it. Besides, Washington wore a Beretta 92F on his hip and all Billy Joe had was a note pad.

Billy Joe cleaved to his decision to leave his new boss strictly alone. However, a half hour of zero conversation and successive flopped experiments turned the experience of silently watching the bustling man in dark blue coveralls from mildly annoying to tiresome. Billy Joe nerved himself to speak.

"So, tell me about yourself, Fresh Meat," Washington suddenly ordered, not bothering to look up. Billy Joe almost started in surprise. "How did you end up in Commodore Wolf's lockup?"

"It wasn't Wolf's camp," Billy Joe replied without thinking, but then considered the question. He wasn't anxious to unpack that particular can of worms so he decided to share just the barest outline, as well as conceal his incipient resentment over this latest nickname. "I worked for the losing side in a little war in Tennessee.

I got shot and missed the last big fight. Afterwards, they captured me in bed and once I was well enough, Mr. Smith, ah—Commodore Wolf's brother—gave us the option of working or not eating. I like eating."

"And that's it?" Washington asked, and his unsmiling brown eyes punctuated the question before the man returned to his instruments. "Just the wrong place and the wrong time, eh? The paperwork they gave me yesterday says that your little group was particularly nasty. Right crazy fuckers. Slaves and shit? Way I heard it, Smith's brother only left off killing you out of hand since he didn't actually catch you doing anything."

"The guy that was in charge needed my skills," Billy Joe replied, recognizing that Washington already knew plenty. "I did what I had to do in order to stay alive. That meant being useful for engineering and chemical work."

Washington made little "keep it going" gestures.

I wonder what else is in my file?

"I mostly did explosives."

"The Gleaners' bomb man, that's right," Washington stated, eyes still on his work.

Billy Joe decided that wasn't a question. There was a pause, and Billy Joe watched the buzz-cutted Navy man fiddle around. Surrounded by Pyrex flasks, rows of test tubes and neatly racked laboratory tools, Senior Chief Washington checked the reading on the digital thermometer clipped to a graduated cylinder. Inside, a clear liquid danced, boiling merrily. Then he adjusted one of the empty beaker lined up just so on bench.

"A hundred and thirty-one 'cee' this time," the senior added, nodding in a satisfied manner as he confirmed the temperature. Then he addressed Billy Joe again, his voice hardening. "And?"

"Yeah, the Gleaners' bomb man," Billy Joe agreed reluctantly. "But I also did some engineering—electrical, chemical, and so forth. Look, I wasn't crazy about working for the Gleaners, but they offered a worse deal than Smith. Any failure to cooperate cost big. They turned you into a slave. Or worse."

The less time he spent thinking about the Gleaners, the whole Watts Bar episode, and most especially about that devil Tom Smith, the happier Billy Joe was. Joining the Gleaners hadn't exactly been his first choice, but he'd found a niche there. Unfortunately for the Gleaners, they'd underestimated the opposition. Some well-organized and, more importantly, better-led survivors from New York City, of all places, had kicked their teeth in. The story among the Gleaner survivors was that Smith the Younger had fed Harlan Greene, the leader of the losers and Billy Joe's previous boss, into the intake of a hydroelectric dam. Not that Billy Joe missed that psycho Greene, but then Smith had detained anyone who'd been swept up with the Gleaners. The bank people got around to interrogating him and by a narrow margin, deferred outright execution, and instead set Billy Joe to forced labor, pending reevaluation. That meant clean-up work, mostly disposing of thousands of rotting zombie corpses while under armed guard. Lab work in Guantanamo Bay, Cuba, looked like a tall, cool drink of water in comparison.

"Well, Fresh Meat, plenty of bad things have happened to lots and lots of good people," Washington said. "Commodore Smith is the new Secretary of War under Vice President—sorry, make that President Staba. And she's decided the Secretary of War's existing policy of 'what happened in the compartment stays in the compartment' applies to detainees."

"Sorry, Senior, I don't know what that means," Billy Joe replied, a little confused. He glanced around the converted hospital lab and shrugged to illustrate his confusion. "I've been on labor details since I left the hospital tent, and they didn't tell us a lot. Then the guards loaded us in a bus, put us on the airplane and now I'm here."

"I'll give you the long explanation later," Washington said flatly. "For now it means you get to prove you're fit to rejoin the human race. And I'm the one marking your report card, got it?"

"Yessir!" That didn't sound great, but it beat burying rotting corpses.

"Don't call me Sir, sonny," Washington growled. "I work for a living, and now you do too. Pass me that can."

Billy Joe let his eyes track along Senior Chief Washington's surprisingly skinny arm pointing towards a shelf labeled "Nuclear Chemistry." A silver aluminum container, different from the one Washington had been using, shone in the fluorescent lighting. All identifying marks were covered in heavy, olive drab tape. Billy Joe lifted it down, noting in passing that the lid was also taped. Someone had used a black marker to label it "Contaminated Ferric Oxide."

The internal foil cover parted with a nice hiss to reveal rusty-brown granules, which the grizzled submariner sniffed appreciatively. Billy Joe continued to observe as Washington ignored the open jar he'd used before, instead applying the white plastic sampler to scoop up a single measure of new material before meticulously scraping the excess back into the container. He emptied the scoop into one of the clean, empty beakers. After repeating the process, Washington resealed the can and passed it back to Billy Joe, who put it back where he'd found it.

These final steps confirmed what Billy Joe had suspected was the point of the apparatus and procedure he'd seen so far. He couldn't fault Washington's technique but he knew it wouldn't make a difference to the outcome. In response to a grunt and gesture, Billy Joe passed an insulated glove to Washington. The senior put it on his left hand before carefully removing the thermometer from the cylinder. The bubbling liquid steamed as he poured it into the waiting beaker and the granules quickly dissolved, leaving a swirling dark brown, almost black liquid. The apparent chemist removed his glove, and set it aside so he could use both hands to turn the beaker this way and that, studying the color. Finally, Senior Chief Washington leaned over to sniff the result, and grimaced.

"God, I even hate the Italian instant."

"I still can't get over how clean everything is," Billy Joe said, looking over as another parolee slid onto the old-style cafeteria bench. Jerome Knight had been another Gleaner, really not more than a foot soldier. The faded prison tattoos that peeked from his collar and wrist cuffs offered hints of even earlier history. "I'll give the Marine neat freaks who tidied this base up that much. Smells a lot better than the last place, too."

Before being relocated to Cuba, away from the now resolved conflict where many had died on both sides, the Gleaner detainees had been quartered in tents, not far from the mass burial pits filled with the results of the climactic battle of Watts Bar Dam. Early burials of the thousands of dead zombies had been hasty and shallow, and the smell of decomposition still lingered over the area. The wet, muddy Tennessee winter had exacerbated the already poor conditions. Billy Joe had nightmares about it. By contrast, this place was literally a tropical paradise. The Marines had even lined up decorative rocks in front of the red-tiled stucco buildings and painted them.

"Fucking Marines," muttered Knight. "I'm glad most of them are gone, busting their asses to clear Washington, New York and all the other zombie shit-holes. Maybe now I can take a shot at one of the hot mamas walking around with all babies..."

There were a lot of babies around. The video the Navy had made the ex-Gleaners watch, documenting the first days of the Smith Family provided the answer. Billy Joe had to admit the visuals were soberingly effective, showing the brilliant night-time satellite view of the Earth rapidly dimming as one illuminated city after another was blotted from existence by the plague. The entire world went dark, except for a tiny, flickering point of light in the Caribbean, the evening lights of Wolf Squadron. As the survivors rescued everyone they could find, the light slowly grew, and the tally of the saved climbed into the thousands, the clip ended with a subtitle: "Welcome to Wolf Squadron. The hell with the darkness. Light a Candle."

The now-dated video was used to orient new arrivals, talking up the urgency of rescuing all they could. Many of them were civilian women who'd all gotten pregnant more or less simultaneously, since they'd all been trapped at sea about the same time, at which point there presumably hadn't been a lot else to do. Thousands had been successfully recovered, and with the passage of time, there were a lot of moms at Gitmo. Most of them seemed to be young, pretty and single. Billy Joe and the other probationers frequently saw them, a vision from the world they'd lost, smiling and pushing full tandem strollers around the housing on base, sharing babysitting duties so that others could work. They were utterly, unmistakably out-of-bounds to the likes of the probationers.

"Watch your mouth, Knight!" Billy Joe said urgently. "You know the women are off-limits!"

"Yeah, whatever," his seatmate groused, his acne-scarred face screwed up in distaste as he stared at the unappetizing fish and rice curry, a staple at the Guantanamo dining facility. "I'm sick of the same food every day. We ate better when Greene was in charge, and we didn't have to pay in stupid chits, neither!"

He loudly slammed his change down next to his metal tray. The chits were just color denominated poker chips with serial numbers melted into the plastic. They'd replaced the old cardboard counters that had been used by the government militia after the Chattanooga battle. Billy Joe fingered the "change" in the pants pocket of his lightweight khaki boilersuit; those suits served all the probationers as a uniform, distinct from the green camouflage utilities of the Marines, the incomprehensible blue digicam of the regular sailors, or the dark blue coveralls of the sub guys.

"Put a sock in it!" hissed another parolee, looking over his shoulder furtively as he joined the table. Even Smitty, no genius by any measure, knew it wouldn't pay to be overheard speaking like that. Even though Billy

Joe knew the Navy file listed this probationer as Edward Smith, he'd answered exclusively to Smitty for as long as Billy Joe had known him. And who would argue with him? Where Knight tended to get lost in his uniform, every motion Smitty made threatened the seams of his overalls. When the burly parolee tapped the bright white probationer's patch on his chest, his biceps strained his suit's fabric as through he was smuggling cantaloupes in his shirtsleeves. "See this? We're all being judged, every second. Greene and the Gleaners are dead. I'm not spending the rest of my life on some shit detail because you're tired of the menu. Until we get made, we all make nice. Then we cut this piece of shit off our clothes."

"Sorry, Smitty!" Knight not-quite whined. "It's just—"

"I said shut it," Smitty bit off. For a moment, he seemed to radiate hostility and barely controlled rage, but a patently false smile quickly slid over his previously bared teeth. Billy Joe knew that the tall, slick-headed man had been selected as a Gleaner soldier for his intimidating strength, and his cunning had drawn his old boss's approval. "Pick up your money and smile like you're having a great time. Make like B.J. here. Nice and quiet, being useful. Getting in good with the man, right B.J.?"

"The name's Billy Joe."

"Sure, sure," Smitty said silkily, smoothing over Billy Joe's objection. "So what does your boss have you doing now? It's got to be better than the scavenging they got me doing."

"We spent a couple weeks trying to rebuild the main generators so the Navy could re-task the sub we're using to power the base," Billy Joe said, willing to go along with a show of amity. Smitty was right about the importance of not only working hard, but convincing the new management of the human race that the former Gleaners were treading the straight-and-narrow once and for all. "While we're waiting on new parts, he has me working on some remote detonators. The plan is to demolish some of the damaged buildings in town."

The Navy base lay at the mouth of a large salt-water bay in southeastern Cuba. Farther inland, across the fenced and chained harbor causeway that divided the base from Cuba proper, lay the actual city of Guantanamo. Fortunately, the number of zombies had radically fallen, thanks to some hush-hush experiments coordinated from the old Camp Delta where the Taliban and Al Qaeda prisoners had met their end during the early days of the plague.

Security was tight on that part of the base and the parolees had been invited to not speculate. However, whatever they were doing there meant the orderly, centrally managed process of looting the former Cuban city could proceed much more easily than had been the case months previously.

"Why not just use the military stuff instead of building new electronics?" Sylvie James asked. "Don't they have a base full of gear?"

The wiry, hard-eyed ex-Gleaner had taken advantage of the previous group's focus on competence over sex. Billy Joe had seen her drop a drunk Gleaner foot soldier with a knee kick, and then cool him with an economical strike to the temple. Sylvie been one of the few women who'd stuck with soldiering, striving to become an officer in the Gleaner militia, taking after her old boss, Eva O'Shaughnessy.

Speaking of which, Billy Joe thought, *I hope that scary bitch is rotting in hell.*

"The plan is to save the good stuff for emergencies,"

he replied, shrugging. "What I'm making isn't much more powerful than really big fireworks set off by remote control. There's plenty of old cell phone parts and other electronics. What I really could use is some genuine coffee. Actual beans, roasted and ground. My boss is crazy for the stuff, and I mean that literally. Developed some kind of obsession with it while he was trapped on his sub, probably. He's been experimenting with everything he can find and he's pretty influential with the Navy. Could help us get in good with management, if you see what I mean. Have any of you seen anything like that come in?"

"Nah," Sylvie replied. "I've been working on sweep team inventory and the only coffee I've seen is freeze-dried and not much of that. Everyone wants coffee so it goes directly into restricted storage."

"There's some irony for you," Billy Joe said, shaking his head. "This place was practically the birthplace of coffee in the Western Hemisphere. Used to export tens of thousands of tons of the stuff from plantations not even thirty miles away. Might as well be on the dark side of the moon until we clear out that way."

"Look at you, college-boy!" Smitty exclaimed softly, smiling widely enough to be seen though not overhead. Billy Joe's incomplete university education had been a source of amusement to the Gleaner rank and file, just as his proximity to the old boss had been a source of jealousy. "You're practically a coffee genius now. Thing is, except for the hospital and managing people like us, the military is moving most of their stuff outta here to Florida. Coffee is a so-what compared to that."

"Coffee was the second largest commodity in the entire world, right behind oil," Billy Joe replied in a tight, controlled tone, omitting the words "you idiot." "It was worth tens of billions of dollars before the Fall. Sooner or later we're going to have an economy again, and it's going to have to be based on something. Paper dollars aren't worth shit. We can't use chits forever. The economy has to be based on something and we're right here where coffee started, practically. Wouldn't hurt to get an early start on that, right? If everyone wants coffee and we have the solution, we'd be made for sure. We could lose these stupid probation uniforms. We could be somebody."

"Hmm, that's not a bad idea, B.J.," Smitty said, rubbing his chin. It looked like he was actually giving it some thought and a shrewd expression slid across his face. Billy Joe watched Smitty glance around the other tables where other ex-Gleaners sat in their little cliques. "We'll keep our eyes open. Sylvie, you'll check to see if any of those Cuban survivors know anything about it, but on the down-low?"

"No problem, Smitty," she answered.

"And keep your mouth shut, Jerry, right?" Smitty ordered. "Make nice, big smiles, right? You don't tell any of the others till I say, right?"

"Right, Smitty."

"Yeah, coffee's not a bad idea at all, B.J.," Smitty added, leaning over to steal a stale Twinkie from Billy Joe's tray. "I like it."

"My name's Billy Joe."

"Crack-Crack-Crack-CRACK!"
The plumes of dirty brown smoke that jetted from around the circumference of the concrete apartment block contrasted against the clean blue sky. Each

report was delayed by a millisecond from the one preceding. Fully thirty explosions sounded, causing the smoke-blackened shell to shiver and then collapse inwards. Billy Joe reflexively shielded his eyes from the billowing smoke and dust that rushed outwards. Meanwhile, the excitable locals who'd been rescued and now served as a basic labor force, alongside a dozen or more probationers, yelled enthusiastically.

After several minutes, the cloud began to dissipate, whisked away by the persistent breeze and a lonely-looking zombie dazedly stumbled into view. Moments later a single shot from one of the security Marines dropped it almost a hundred meters from the nearest potential meal. Nothing else moved.

"Check fire, check fire!" an angry voice sounded to Billy Joe's side, likely one of the Marine sergeants who oversaw the details of an operation like this. "Confirm targets as hostile before engaging!"

"Stupid git," Senior Chief Washington said, squinting through the remaining dust to gauge how thoroughly the building had been demolished.

"Senior?" Billy Joe knew the military wasn't crazy about the new orders to refrain from shooting zombies out of hand.

"Only supposed to shoot the aggressive zombies, the alphas," Washington relied, sparing Billy Joe a glance. "Fresh Meat, weren't you listening at the brief? The new intel is that the other kind of zombie, the ones that run away and hide, are different. We're supposed to try to save them."

"Saving zombies seems pretty crazy to me, Senior."

"Well, the secretary of war and the commanding general here at Gitmo aren't asking, they're telling," the older man said to Billy Joe, wiping dust from the rectangular tablet computer he held. "The shy ones, the betas, those are people. The studies in Florida show that most of them can be taught to do simple tasks, which is more than I can say about you. On the other hand, while I didn't hire you for your opinion, this controller you whipped up worked pretty damn well. Nice job."

As Billy Joe watched, Washington carefully tapped two buttons that had been blinking. Previously, "Master Arm" and "Detonate" had been limned in yellow and red. A few taps later both were grayed out and the overlay read "Safe."

"Thanks, Senior." Billy Joe meant it. His efforts to adapt dissimilar parts and write some software had resulted in the converted controller that Washington now held, as well as a backup. That didn't count the scratch-built radio link or the fully assembled four dozen charges he'd estimated, well, over-estimated, that would be needed. Moreover, the work had required a high degree of precision. As far as he could tell, every single charge he'd placed had gone high order, leaving not a single squib behind to delay efforts to clear the wreckage. It was a new sensation to be appreciated. He hadn't been asked to hurt anyone, well, except zombies, and even those casualties were incidental. His contribution was actually helping to make things better. Billy Joe was surprised at how good it felt. Even better, good results tended to put Senior Chief Washington in a receptive mood...

"Senior, I had a little help," Billy said, deciding to take a risk. He waved at the short, dark-skinned man who'd remained inconspicuous by standing well back. "This is Julio Cabrillo. He's a part-time cell phone salesman we rescued a week ago. Julio was a big help when I had to rewrite some code and update the firmware on the charge sequencers. Julio, this is Senior Chief Washington."

"Senor, *mucho gusto*," Cabrillo said, looking apprehensive.

"Fresh Meat, you let a Cuban handle explosives in my lab?" Washington growled. "Are you aching to go back to burying zombies? I can probably find some that aren't dead yet and let you wrestle them all by your lonesome."

"Negative, Senior!" Billy Joe replied decisively. He'd learned that unlike the Gleaners, Washington could be counted upon to react even more negatively if he cowered or tried to kiss ass. "I really needed the help with programming, and I never let him touch the controlled items, either the electrical caps or the C-4. Everything's accounted for. Besides, I think he's got some information that's going to really interest you."

"And that is?"

There was a pregnant pause and Cabrillo seemed to wilt under the Navy noncom's steely gaze.

"Go on Julio, tell him!" Billy Joe said impatiently, tugging Cabrillo even closer.

"*Jefe, me familia trabajan*—my family work at Hacienda y Cafetal Gelaberto," the slightly built Cuban said, doffing his wide brimmed hat. "I live there, my family work the crop for five *generaciones*, even before Castro."

Cabrillo punctuated the last comment by spitting in the dust.

"What's he talking about, Fresh Meat?" Washington

asked, cutting his eyes towards Billy Joe. "You have precious few seconds left before you need to start getting used to the smell of dead bodies."

"The Gelaberto Coffee plantation, Senior," Billy Joe said, simply. "It was part museum and part working coffee plantation. Three hundred acres of mature Arabica and Robusta plants. Wash troughs, a big stone drying apron and what sounds like the better part of three tons of bagged coffee beans, in the green and ready to be roasted and ground."

"Are you fucking shitting me, Destrehan?" Washington asked, apparently shocked enough to use Billy Joe's last name. "Coffee? Real coffee?"

"Aye-firmative, Senior," he answered happily. "And the best part is that it isn't even an hour's drive away!"

"You burned them," Washington stated accusingly. "Be careful, I said. It's a delicate job, I said. But you had to hurry. Hell, I can taste the scorched bits!"

"Senior, two months ago you didn't have any coffee at all." Billy Joe couldn't hold back any longer, but he kept his tone light. His old barista job hadn't involved roasting, but Julio had seen it done and this was the best batch so far. "Then, all you had was instant and you didn't like that. You were changing the water temperature and trying to make it taste better, even the fancy Italian stuff you overpaid for. Thing is, the taste of instant coffee is locked-in the moment it's packaged after roasting, brewing and drying. This is fresh-roasted coffee, and we only toasted it to the first crack. It has a perfectly mild flavor."

Washington sniffed the coffee again and grudgingly took a sip before putting the mug down.

"You wrote the procedure, outlined the principle of the thing and we paid perfect attention to detail," Billy Joe added for good measure, sounding a bit defensive, even to his own ears.

"Two months ago I was still on the WESTPAC cruise from hell," the senior replied, giving Billy Joe a bit of side eye as he pushed the coffee aside to cool. Billy Joe watched him don a blue baseball cap whose gold embroidery spelled out "USS *Columbus* – SSN 762," which the senior had already informed him was the best damn nuke in the entire fleet. "And you were still in that prison camp run by Commodore Wolf's brother. Instead of enjoying air conditioning and fresh roasted coffee, you were burying corpses. So, if my bitching about coffee bothers you, say the word."

"Sorry, Senior," Billy Joe said, swallowing. "Just trying to help."

"Ah, hell, it's all right," Washington said, waving away the disagreement. "You were right about the instant, you were mostly right about using Julio to get the detonators done on time and finding out about the Cafetal. Getting fresh coffee, burnt or not, is actually genius."

"Thank you, Senior," Billy answered quietly. Getting a compliment was a new experience. Sharing the credit was also a new thing, but it felt good too. "We really should thank Julio. He provided the info and did a lot of the work."

"And where is Mr. Cabrillo?" Washington asked, theatrically looking around the mostly empty lab.

"He's visiting his sister in the betas' compound," Billy Joe answered quickly. "The doctors say she's going to be fine after some decent nutrition."

"Damn lucky, finding her like that. What were the odds that a zombie would be smart enough to hide in a coffee warehouse and then get found by a member of her own family?"

"They were both from the Cafetal, but all he knew was she'd been infected and then fled in order to keep from getting anyone else sick. Or worse."

"Still, damned lucky." Washington eyed his steaming coffee longingly. "With a little more luck, she'll be one of the good ones and can have some kind of life again. Julio told me he thinks she even recognizes him."

Both men sat and thought about that for a bit. For some reason the plantation had been almost empty of corpses and the presence of aggressive infected had been almost nil. The Gitmo Marines had been able to recover or rescue half a dozen betas during the coffee operation. Most had fought to get away, but all were being treated for their health problems and attended by a psychologist who'd been rescued from a boat months earlier. Billy had thought that the plan to try to train them to do basic chores was optimistic. Then he'd met Katerina Cabrillo, Julio's sister. She'd calmed considerably after seeing her brother, who visited her for hours every day. She was even wearing clothes now, which was a good thing because as soon as she'd left decontamination, her original beauty had caught everyone's eye. At least, those of the men. Billy Joe had felt vaguely ashamed for even noticing. Even more so for the fantasy of claiming rescuer's rights that briefly occurred to him. Recalling that impulse refreshed the shame of even thinking such a thing. That was probably why he didn't watch his mouth in the next breath. The shame led to anger, and predictably, the anger disconnected Billy Joe's brain from his idiot mouth.

"Seems like a lot of effort to try to save them," Billy Joe said, breaking the silence. "Especially when there are so many humans that need rescuing."

"Boy," Washington bit out and then visibly controlled himself. "Boy, just when I start liking you, you go and say some damned foolish thing. Remember what I told you a couple weeks ago about things that happened in the compartment staying in the compartment?"

"Yes, Senior," Billy Joe answered as briefly as he could. It didn't take an empath to note Washington was suddenly and genuinely furious.

"You said before you didn't understand what it meant, so I'm going to spell it out for you, simple-like," the Navy noncom said, his hard brown eyes pinning Billy Joe's gaze. "What it means is that everyone, Gleaners included, gets the benefit of what amounts to a general amnesty for anything that anyone did to survive prior to rejoining the human race. People were trapped inside rooms, compartments really, on cruise ships and warships and every little kind of dinky yacht and fishing boat. We could hear them, thousands of them, you know, on the passive sonar systems on the sub."

Billy Joe watched the senior chief's eyes slide off to one side, staring through the wall opposite his bench.

"We'd creep really close, and the fancy sonar we have means you could hear a mouse fart in a hurricane at ten thousand yards. Sonar so good you could hear the moans and growls of zombies inside a ship, right through the hull. Sometimes, you'd hear the sobbing of an uninfected person talking to themselves, waiting to die. Starvation usually, sometimes thirst or just despair. You could hear uninfected humans preying on each other, desperate. They did things, terrible things to stay alive. All we could do was listen. Subs are based on the coast, and some of us had families that might have made it out. Those people we could hear, the zombies we could hear, they could have been our families for all we knew. Maybe the ones killing. Maybe the ones dying."

Billy Joe kept still and didn't say a word as Senior Chief Washington's angry voice slowly dropped to a whisper.

"But we just listened. We couldn't help anyone, not till we made contact with Commodore Wolf—Secretary Smith," Washington continued, sitting up slightly at the memory of those days. "And he and his family were saving people, starting with little boats and working all the way up to the freaking *Voyage Under the Stars*, a thousand-foot-long ocean liner. Hell, Smith's daughter personally cleared a sailboat belonging to the wife of the chief of the boat from the missile boat *Florida*, and wasn't that a fucking shot in the arm? It was the Rebellion blowing up the Death Star, it was the charge of the Light fucking Brigade, and Wolf Squadron kept rescuing people and bringing back hope. And when Wolf got us the vaccine, we could finally get off the subs. But we needed, still need, people. Lots more than we have."

Washington slowly reached for his coffee cup, but didn't raise it. He kept talking and his eyes, shadowed by the overhead lights, remained fixed on the far wall.

"So, even if you did terrible things in order to survive inside your compartment, including killing zombies—who are humans by the way and don't you fucking forget it—well, you get a pass." Billy Joe listened carefully as Washington continued. "The President, get that sonny, the President of the United States, has decided that even possible criminals get a chance to rejoin society. So except in extreme cases like your old boss, you get a fresh start, dated to the day you rejoined the human race, see?"

"Yes, Senior."

"Well, we aren't in the compartment anymore." Washington was still whispering, but he blinked and slowly turned his head to look at Billy Joe. The senior chief's deep-set brown eyes were lined, haunted... and fierce. His dark face could have been carved from old mahogany. "Everyone's responsible for all their actions. Everyone gets to contribute if they can. Even a zombie. Even a Gleaner piece of trash who might be an electronics expert. Even a broke-dick nuke sailor without a boat."

Washington visibly shook himself and stared into his cup, suddenly silent.

"Well, I'm glad for Julio, Senior," Billy Joe said carefully, trying to defuse the tense atmosphere by returning to the earlier conversation. "His family was from the Cafetal, and he knew she was infected and ran away. But I think he was as surprised as anyone else that she was still alive. With a little more luck, she'll be one of good ones and can have some kind of life again."

"Maybe," Washington replied in a more normal tone of voice, sipping his coffee to see if it was the right temperature. "Goddammit, now it's cold. Isn't that always how it is? Coffee's either too hot or too cold."

Let's not dwell on my slip of the tongue. It's bad enough that I thought about Julio's sister naked. Now I'm suggesting she's not human. What the fuck is wrong with me?

Billy Joe took a deep breath and held it before slowly exhaling through his nose.

Time to change the subject.

"I made a little something that will help with that, Senior," Billy Joe slid a slightly oversized insulated metal mug across the slick surface of the lab table. It stopped right in front of the senior chief. "The scroungers have been bringing in a *lot* of used cell phones and I've been trying to think what else we could make. The lithium-ion batteries have enough juice to run a hefty resistor coil for a couple hours and it's preset to 140 degrees Fahrenheit, which is just about sipping temperature. I adapted a traveling mug, so it already had the lid and insulation. If you want it hotter, I can tweak it, but I think this is the sweet spot."

Washington raised his eyebrows.

"Keeps your fresh-roasted, just-brewed, authentic Cuba cafecito hot for hours, Senior," Billy Joe said, trying to relax after the intimidating monologue the senior had just delivered. The prototype had been easy, but the work to miniaturize it and make the cup look decent had been hard and he was proud to finally show off the result.

"Keeps my coffee hot for real, Destrehan?" Washington asked, surprised. He opened the lid to see if it was filled, and then turned the cup over, examining the construction and weighing it in his hand. "Heavy. Nice, but heavy."

"It's the battery pack, needs to be big enough to power the resistors to keep the coffee warm," Billy Joe answered, feeling the start of a shit-eating grin from spreading across his face. "This one's only a prototype. With the right parts we could make some more, maybe give some to the big brass. Then sell the rest."

"What's this?" Washington asked, pointing at a small aperture. "Charging port?"

"Yep," Billy Joe said, nodding happily. "Plug into a wall, into a car, into a computer and it recharges in about an hour. I call it a *Chispa*."

"What's that mean?"

"It's the Spanish word for spark or ember," Billy Joe answered. "Julio again."

"Not bad, Destrehan," Washington said, starting to carefully pour his coffee into the heated mug. "No bad at all. But for now, these belong to the base. You're not to 'sell' them, copy?"

"Copy, Senior."

"I got you the fucking spic, and you were supposed to use him to get the fucking coffee!" Knight growled at Billy Joe from close range, necessarily so since he had Billy Joe's shirt front bunched in one grimy fist. "So how are we going to turn that into money now?"

"Back the fuck off, Knight!" Billy Joe yelled back, sweeping the other man's hands away and making him stumble. "I'm not in charge and I can't control everything. The Marines who did the clearance recovered the coffee and now it's under lock and key."

"But it's your boss who has the key, right B.J.?" Smitty observed from his slouch in an ocher-colored easy chair. He had his feet up on a battered coffee table which was covered in old magazines. They'd borrowed some furniture from here and there and turned one of the many empty rooms in the old base hospital into a lounge. They even had a couch long enough to nap on. "Which means you have access to the key too."

"No, I don't," Billy Joe replied, keeping an eye on Knight, who was standing just outside arm's distance, his fists balled at his sides. Behind Knight, Sylvie watched them both, her smirk clearly visible over the other man's shoulder. She seemed relaxed, one hip perched on an examination table while she used a looted nail file to smooth her manicure. "I wear the same probationer uniform you do, and I'm watched, just like you are."

"So what do we do about getting a better gig, like the one you got?" Smitty asked, his tone artificially reasonable. "I went out of my way to get you the Cuban you needed in order to make the coffee thing happen. Now you're sitting pretty, working indoors while we're still sweating outside, and under the Marines' guns, to boot."

"We all have the same chance to start over," Billy Joe replied, stepping a little farther away from Knight, whose tattoos seemed darker against still-flushed skin. Billy Joe moved to a chair opposite Smitty. "There aren't enough people to do all the things that need doing. You could go into electronics, or power systems, or even try out for soldiering. I invented a coffee cup that stays hot—"

"So you think I should keep busting my ass?" Smitty cut him off, eyes slitted. "You brag about your lame Radio Shack project? That's your answer? You thought you were all that when you were Greene's pet bomber. Did you tell the new boss everything you did? Does the Navy know how you helped him do all that nasty shit? I bet not."

"I did what I had to!"

"All the men said that," Sylvie contributed from the back row. "Boo-hoo, I have to blow up that house full of kids, or Greene will kill me! Oh no, I have to participate in that gang rape, or they won't respect me! But now you want to start over. Pretty convenient."

"All of us did shit we didn't want to," Billy Joe answered, his voice climbing an octave. "And I sure as shit never raped anyone."

"Oh?" Sylvie remarked, cuttingly. "All the women in the recreation hall were volunteers, were they?"

"I don't know!" Billy Joe said, stung by the implications. He found his own weapon and raised his voice to deliver it. "Did you ask them when you visited? Were all your refugee girlfriends actually into other women or were they just tired of starving?"

"Enough," Smitty ordered flatly, his hand forestalling Sylvie's charge as she rose angrily from her spot. Smitty confirmed that the door was fully closed and that no one was looking in the little round observation window installed on all the hospital room entrances. "B.J., you have a smart, wiggly brain, I'll give you that. I don't know what your plan is, but I expect you to figure out how we all get ahead on this scheme. Keep your mind on the job—and the job is helping all of us get off the working details and into a nice, cushy jobs where we can get made. Got it?"

"Yeah, I got it," Billy Joe replied. "But . . ."

"I noticed that you've gotten pretty buddy-buddy with that spic we got for you," Knight interrupted. "Him and his pretty retard sister. I know what you're after. If you can't get me a better job, maybe you can set me up, eh? I don't mind seconds."

"Fuck. You," Billy Joe said distinctly, turning his

head to stare at Knight. He fell his pulse begin to pound, but remained icy calm. "Fuck you twice."

"You better wake up, dumb-ass!" Knight replied, closing the distance, his armed cocked back. "You better remember where you come from!"

"Shut it, both of you." Smitty raised his voice just a bit, cutting across Sylvie's sudden high pitched giggle. "Sit your ass down, Jerry."

Knight grudgingly moved away again, sitting on a rusty folding chair.

"Sure, a little tail would be nice," Smitty went on, as soon as he seemed confident that calm had returned. "But no man ever died from not getting any, right Sylvie?"

"I wouldn't know about that," she replied tartly. "I'm not a man. But I am getting tired of this probationer status bullshit."

"You and me both," groused Knight, his eyes now as feral as any zombie Billy Joe had seen.

"I'll have a look around, Smitty," he said evenly, keeping his eyes just unfocused enough to take in the whole room. "I'll think about it."

"Uh-huh," answered Smitty. "Why don't you go do that. Now would be good."

Billy Joe turned and walked out of the room. As the door swung shut, he couldn't stop himself from one quick glance over his shoulder. The quiet smile on Smitty's face told him that the ex-Gleaner noticed.

"Wake up!" an insistent voice rang in Billy Joe's ear. "Wake up, Destrehan. Now!"

"Wazzama?" Billy Joe managed. A bright yellow light flicked on, blinding him. "Wuhssa?"

"You awake?" Washington's voice penetrated Billy Joe's fog. "All the way? Bad news, Cabrillo's dead. One of the betas beat him to death and assaulted his sister."

"What!" Billy Joe was suddenly and awfully awake. "That's impossible!"

"The dead guy and the traumatized girl seem to disagree," Washington said, standing fully upright. The lines on his face were grim. "The react team heard the screams and tazed the beta. Big male. He must have gotten aggressive; maybe thought he was in a dominance fight. Maybe got scared. Security came to me because Cabrillo was one of ours."

"Betas run, Senior." As he spoke, Billy Joe had already swung his legs out of bed and was pulling on his boilersuit. "It's what they do. They never fight if they can run. Where's Katerina?"

"The corpsmen took her to Urgent Care," Washington replied, stepping back as Billy Joe stomped his feet into his boots.

"I'll meet you there, Senior," Billy said, brusquely passing the man and heading out the door. He had a feeling that if he wanted to be sure, he had to talk to Smitty right then, not wait for morning.

"Wait, where are you going?"

Billy Joe heard him, but didn't pause. He ran, not to Urgent Care, or the betas' detention wing. A uniformed Gleaner parolee wouldn't be allowed into either location, even one that worked for Senior Chief Washington. Instead, Billy Joe ran to the lounge that Smitty and the rest had created. A terrible feeling of responsibility began to fall, but he fought it off.

You don't know that Smitty or Knight did it. You don't know. Could be coincidence.

It was only a few minutes' run, but his heart sank as he saw the electric light leaking from under the door. There wasn't any practical reason for the other ex-Gleaners to be up at this hour. Billy Joe blew through the swinging door, taking in the scene.

Three faces, variously surprised, angry and scared, gaped in mid-argument. The bright examination lights overhead laid bare their collective guilt.

"Close the door, you fool!" Smitty said, his voice taut with control. "And you two, shut up!"

"What's going on?" Billy Joe asked, but he knew. He knew the moment he was Knight in an unfamiliar gray coverall. The sense of blame finished cloaking him with guilt, an icy touch that kissed the back of his neck, making his skin ripple. His stomach roiled and when he swallowed, the bitter taste of bile burned on the back of his tongue. "Knight, you sonavabitch, what did you do?"

"I didn't do anything!" Knight answered, his face somehow empty and scared at the same time. A swollen lower lip distorted his sneer. "I just wanted to see, that's all, just look! She'd been naked for months; she didn't even care!"

"Such an asshole," Sylvie said. "Now all of us are going to hang, hang, hang, all because you wanted to see some tits."

"Both of you shut up, I said." Smitty stood from where he'd been sitting next to Knight. He faced Billy Joe. "Does anyone know where you are?"

"No, I just heard Julio is dead, killed by a beta...?"

"Good!" Smitty said, breathing a sigh of relief. "Real good. That's exactly the plan."

"What fucking plan?" Billy Joe shouted, causing Smitty to rise and close the distance in an eye blink.

"Keep your goddamn voice down or I'll fix it so you can't talk above a whisper, college-boy," Smitty said, breathing heavily as he loomed over Billy Joe. "You understand?"

"I just want to know what happened to Julio," Billy Joe replied, taking a step back, raising his hands placatingly. "What happened to Katrina?"

Smitty looked at him and then strode two steps back to Knight.

"Tell him."

"They're not really human, you know," Knight offered from his chair. He raised his head, which moved his collar enough to reveal deep parallel scratches gouging the amateur tattoo on his neck. "It shouldn't even count."

SLAP.

Knight spilled onto the floor, stunned.

"I said to tell him, not make excuses," Smitty ordered, keeping his hand raised for another strike. "Now get your ass in that chair and repeat what you told us."

Billy watched the erstwhile ex-Gleaner clamber back into his seat, holding one hand to the palm print that reddened his cheek. The miserable man outlined a simple tale. After his shift he'd taken a few drinks. He saw Julio and his sister walking outside and he followed them back to the rooms reserved for the betas. After waiting for the man to leave, he approached the woman with some candy he'd filched. She'd not objected when he'd begun to remove her clothes, but the brother had returned. The fight was short. The erstwhile cell-phone repairman had been no match for an angry and scared ex-con. Knight had struck Cabrillo's throat, fracturing his windpipe and suffocating him. Panicked, Knight had opened the doors to the other betas' rooms and fled.

"I didn't mean to kill him," he pleaded, finishing his account. "And I never meant to rape her, I swear. I just wanted to look."

During the account, Billy Joe experienced an odd shift in his perception. It was as though his vision narrowed gradually, focusing ever more closely on Knight until he was looking through a narrow straw, only able to see Knight's face and the dirty hands he was nervously twisting in his lap.

"You pig," Billy Joe heard himself say, almost conversationally. "You piece of shit. I hope they do hang you. I'll pull on your fucking legs when—"

Billy Joe didn't finish. Instead, a sharp pain bloomed in his jaw and he too was knocked to the floor. He blearily shook his head and when his eyes focused, he was staring at the khaki pant legs of Smitty's boilersuit. Partially stunned, he scrabbled backwards until his back met the wall, and Smitty addressed him.

"Why am I the only one doing the thinking, B.J.?" the burly man said, squatting in front of Billy Joe. He continued in a low, menacing tone. "That's supposed to be your job. No one wanted to hurt anyone, but accidents happen. Damn shame about the Cuban, but nothing we can do now. No point in fighting about it or confessing. Won't bring him back. It would be a black mark against all of us, including you. Nod if you understand."

Billy Joe stretched his jaw and nodded. He could taste a little blood in his mouth.

"What happened is that you didn't see anything

and you didn't hear anything," Smith explained, his voice gravelly with the promise of violence. "If anyone asks, Knight's trying to be righteous, same as you. He's never said a thing about women or betas. All of us are just trying to be better citizens, grateful for a second chance. Nod if you understand."

Billy Joe ducked his head a second time. He'd always been a technical guy, leaving the hands-on stuff to Gleaner rank-and-file. But even dazed, the anger he'd felt towards Knight still roiled his stomach.

I'll say whatever they want and leave. Then I'll report these assholes.

"And if you think that you can run away, report what you think you know, and walk away afterwards..." Smitty stood as Knight and Sylvie flanked him. All three looked down at their fellow probationer, disdain plain in their eyes. "...remember this: even if the military thinks we're all the same, the days of the Wild West are over. Every crisis has a cycle, and it's come around again. Now they need things like proof and reasonable doubt. Maybe you don't care 'bout that. Did you fall for that 'light a candle against the darkness' bullshit video? I hope not. Even if you tried to talk, it would be three of us and one of you. It should be all of us against everyone else, including the system. The courts and 'justice' are back. There's the suckers who believe that crap and there's those that understand and work outside the system. That's us. As long as you remember that, you get to benefit with us, same as us. Nod. If. You. Understand."

Billy Joe nodded, even as Smitty kept talking. *But I'll still tell, you shitheel.*

"All right then. You and I had a fight over a card

game, Jerry. Sylvie walked in and broke it up, which is how you got those scratches, B.J., and talked to you the next morning about calming down, maybe playing cards less often. Simple story, no need to be fancy. Now, everyone go to bed. Tomorrow's a new day and everyone, including B.J., is going to be a team player."

"There's nothing I can do right now, son," Senior Chief Washington said, holding his hands palm outwards. Billy Joe thought the gesture was pretty close to the gesture for surrender. "You gave a deposition on what you heard. I corroborated with what I knew and what I think. I also fought like hell to talk about your contribution."

"They're walking?" Billy Joe said disbelievingly. "I wrecked my reputation, destroyed every relationship I have with any probationer and then waited for two weeks just for this? Julio is dead and his sister is curled up in a cell, alternating between catatonic fear and being batshit crazy whenever she sees a man! And the person responsible walks?"

"He doesn't get to walk," Washington rebutted. "Knight's going to be watched every day. All three of them, for that matter."

"So am I," Billy Joe replied dejectedly. He plucked at the mustard-colored fabric of the boilersuit. "So is every person that wears one of these. Some of them are really trying. I was really trying."

"I know you are," Washington replied doggedly. Billy Joe watched his mentor's face. Washington had a slightly hangdog look and the reason wasn't long in coming. "But I've got more bad news. You can't doss down here anymore. The investigation turned up that the probationers were sleeping all over the place and the base C.O. is cracking down. You have to go back to the dorm."

"What?" Billy Joe almost yelled. "I can't go there; they all hate me! I didn't do anything wrong—I did everything right!"

"I know," the Senior Chief said regretfully, and turned his office chair to one side, looking out the window. A couple of larger Wolf Squadron yachts were entering the bay, likely to refuel from the fuel coaster that one of the submarines had towed in. The sparkling blue water was at odds with the dark emotions in this compartment. "And I'm sorry. It's exactly what I said when the executive officer told me that the investigation had closed. But there was no physical evidence. The advocate general took statements from everyone and in the end it came down to a classic 'he said, they said' case. Since I didn't witness anything, my opinions were taken as just that. I tried to explain that you were anything but a regular probationer, but in the end that's all they could see. And all the probationers are going to be watched more closely for a while. But not forever."

Both men sat for a while, alone with their thoughts. Billy Joe continued to rethink his decisions at every step, much as he'd done daily since he'd tried to turn Knight in.

Which step could I have taken to keep Julio alive? What if Smitty is right? The cycle repeats and we're stuck in it.

"But not forever," Billy Joe murmured. "I'm an idiot."

"What's that?" Washington asked, tapping his fingers on his desk. "Who's an idiot?"

"I'm the idiot," Billy Joe replied, more loudly this time. "Smitty was right. It all went exactly as he said it would. The old system is back. It's easy to manipulate. Either you manipulate it or it manipulates you and you end up on the bottom."

"That's pretty dark, Destrehan."

"I'm sorry, Senior," Billy Joe said, apologizing politely. He had work to do and he couldn't do it here. He decided to imitate the military people he saw all over the place and be formally polite. "You're right, of course. I better get my stuff out of the lab and over to the dorm until this blows over. Permission to get started, Senior?"

"Sure thing, kid," Washington answered, looking a little puzzled at the sudden shift in Billy Joe's tone. "See you later."

Billy Joe's hands were full, so he used his elbow to swing the annex door open.

"Look who came crawling back!" Knight smugly crowed as the door squeaked shut. Feet up and arms crossed behind his head, the man gave off an air of irritating self-assurance. "I guess you want to celebrate with the winners."

Sylvie looked up from a small mirror, her dark eyes flashing with anger and contempt, before returning to admire the earrings she was holding up to the side of her head. That brief glimpse told Billy Joe where things stood between him and the most reasonable of his group. He moved to the table to set down his box.

"Come to your senses, boyo?" Smitty's voice boomed from behind the couch, and a moment later the man sat up, twisting around to face the door. "The little inquiry went just the way I expected. We're not trusted, but we're not in jail either. I just love the phrase 'reasonable doubt,' don't you?"

"I was scared, Smitty," Billy Joe said. It was true, because he was scared and he remained scared. The fear threatened a stutter badly enough that he had to think about enunciating each word. It was a tense coiled spring, poised to unleash something awful. Billy Joe knew that all the ex-Gleaner probationers were going to be labeled as untrustworthy, possible rapists and murderers. He knew that these three would make sure that none of the other probationers ever trusted him. Worse, he wondered if Washington could afford to still work with him, might even disown him. "I don't have your experience."

"You tried to drop the dime on Jerry, here," Smitty replied, swinging his legs to the ground and standing up. "That means you tried to rat all of us out."

"No!" Billy Joe answered, desperate. "I liked Cabrillo. We worked together. I understand it was an accident, but I was scared we'd get found out. I didn't want to lose what I had. Everything's been dark for so long and Cabrillo was the first friend I'd made..."

"Fucking whiner," Sylvie said, pushing a backing onto the little glittering silver skull and crossbones earring. "And now what, you want to beg forgiveness?"

"Fuck that," Knight offered. "What was that you said before? Yeah, fuck you twice."

"We could still try the coffee thing," Billy Joe said, practically begging. "Look, I made you all your own *Chispas* so you could try them out." He set out three insulated mugs, each uniquely colored and labeled with their names. Then he withdrew a thermos of hot coffee and filled each one.

"That actually smells nice, B.J.," Smitty said, strolling over to the table. He looked over the mugs. He picked up the orange one and tried a sip. "Tastes good, too."

"The coffee never gets cold, see?" Billy Joe explained eagerly. "There's a charging port so you can run it on your desk, or recharge it if you take it somewhere. Coffee is the first consumer good that we might be able to produce. Remember how coffee chains were big business? Everyone wants coffee."

"Gimme that, asshole." Knight roughly shouldered Billy Joe aside. He selected the sickly green mug and poured his own coffee. Knight plucked a stainless steel flask from his boilersuit pocket and waved it. "Sylvie, you in? I've got a little flavoring."

"Sure," Sylvie said, uncoiling from her perch. "But I don't drink with stool pigeons."

"That's your cue, college-boy," Smitty said, with exaggerated kindness. "We'll think about this. But you shouldn't expect us to trust you right away. You're going to have to show us that you understand how the world works. Idealism is out. Practicality is in."

"Sure, sure thing, Smitty," Billy Joe said, collecting the box but leaving the coffee makings where they sat. "I appreciate it. Really, I . . ."

"Yeah, bye-bye asshole," Knight said, splashing liquor into his mug. "Don't let the door hit you on the ass on the way out. And check on the retard chick for me, eh?"

"What were you doing with those assholes, Destrehan?" Washington stopped him just a few steps from the door. "I went looking for you but you weren't at the dorm or the lab. Why did you run off to see these pricks?"

"They did it, Senior," Billy Joe said, sliding a tablet PC out of the cardboard box and dropping the empty container to the stained linoleum corridor floor. "I can't prove it, but that prick Knight murdered Julio and let the remaining infected out of their rooms. The others covered it up. Smitty bragged about how the so-called law was impotent and he was right! You know it and I know it. And the system still failed. There won't be justice for Julio or his sister."

"What the fuck are you doing?" Washington's eyes widened as he recognized the tablet screen of the duplicate explosives controller light up. Before the older man could move, Billy Joe tapped the "Master Arm" button. The "Detonate" control began to blink a bright blood red. "Where did you get the backup controller? Give that over."

"I'm sorry, I can't do that, Senior," Billy Joe answered sadly, taking a half-step back, keeping outside the senior chief's lunging distance. "Those people are a cancer left over from the old world. We can't begin again with that kind of sickness waiting to create the next problem. The evil just persists. It's up to us to work around the system, catch the stuff that gets by."

"What did you do, boy?" his mentored demanded. "Where are the charges?"

"There's too many bad people out there, Senior," Billy Joe answered defiantly, hovering one finger over the pulsing "Detonate" button. "I can't beat them hand-to-hand. I wasn't able to persuade them. But I can use the tools I do have. The coffee mugs have a battery to warm the coffee, but each of the ones in that room is also sitting on a microcap, forty grams of C-4 and the same in notched wire. Right now the cancer is drinking coffee, planning how it's gonna move on from this little victory, and be part of the future. I can't allow it."

"You don't want to do this, son," Washington said, softening his tone. "There's no going back from this. It's the principle of the thing."

Billy Joe took a deep, shuddering breath. He looked back towards the room. The three ex-Gleaners were holding their mugs together, making a toast.

What if he's right? Am I screwing this up again?

"You're right, there's too many bad men out there, Destrehan," Washington said gently, extending his hand again. "But at the core of it, we need good people to hold the line. Don't do it. You're a good man."

Billy Joe couldn't meet Washington's eyes. He kept looking at the window. Knight was taking a big swallow from his new mug. Billy Joe could see a happy glint in the Gleaner's eye.

"If I'm a good man, Senior, then why do I want so much to do bad things?"

He mashed the button.

About the Editors & Authors

John Ringo brings fighting to life. He is the creator of the Posleen Wars series, which has become a *New York Times* best-selling series with over one million copies in print. The series contains *A Hymn Before Battle, Gust Front, When the Devil Dances, Hell's Faire,* and *Eye of the Storm*. In addition, Ringo has penned the Council War series. Adding another dimension to his skills, Ringo created nationally best-selling techno-thriller novels about Mike Harmon (*Ghost, Kildar, Choosers of the Slain, Unto the Breach, A Deeper Blue*, and, with Ryan Sear, *Tiger by the Tail*).

His techno-thriller *The Last Centurion* was also a national bestseller. A more playful twist on the future is found in novels of the Looking-Glass series: *Into the Looking Glass, Vorpal Blade, Manxome Foe,* and *Claws That Catch,* the last three in collaboration with Travis S. Taylor. His audience was further enhanced with four collaborations with fellow *New York Times* best-selling author David Weber: *March Upcountry, March to the Sea, March to the Stars* and *We Few*.

There are an additional seven collaborations from the Posleen series: *The Hero,* written with Michael Z.

Williamson, *Watch on the Rhine*, *Yellow Eyes*, and *The Tuloriad*, all written with Tom Kratman, and the *New York Times* bestseller *Cally's War* and its sequels *Sister Time* and *Honor of the Clan*, all with Julie Cochrane. His science-based zombie apocalypse Black Tide Rising series includes *Under a Graveyard Sky*, *To Sail a Darkling Sea*, *Islands of Rage and Hope*, and *Strands of Sorrow*. A veteran of the 82nd Airborne, Ringo brings first-hand knowledge of military operations to his fiction.

Gary Poole has worked in the entertainment and publishing industry for his entire adult life. He's worked directly with John Ringo and several other authors on over a dozen novels and anthologies. He is also a film and television screenwriter, the managing editor of a successful alternative newsweekly in Tennessee, hosts a popular morning radio show, and has voiced well over three thousand radio and television commercials.

Kevin J. Anderson has published more than 170 books, 57 of which have been national or international bestsellers. He has written numerous novels in the Star Wars, X-Files, and Dune universes, as well as unique steampunk fantasy novels *Clockwork Angels* and *Clockwork Lives*, written with legendary rock drummer Neil Peart, based on the concept album by the band Rush. His original works include the Saga of Seven Suns series, the Terra Incognita fantasy trilogy, and his humorous horror series featuring Dan Shamble, Zombie P.I. He has edited numerous anthologies, written comics and games, and the lyrics to two rock CDs. Anderson and his wife Rebecca Moesta are the publishers of WordFire Press. His most recent novels are *Vengewar*, *The Duke of Caladan*, and *Stake*.

Rebecca Moesta (pronounced MESS-tuh) is the bestselling author of forty books, both solo and in collaboration with her husband, Kevin J. Anderson. Her solo work includes *A Christmas to Remember* (based on the Hallmark TV movie by the same name), Buffy the Vampire Slayer and Junior Jedi Knights novels, short stories, articles, ghost writing, and editing anthologies. With Kevin, she wrote the Crystal Doors trilogy, the Young Jedi Knights series, movie and game novelizations, lyrics for rock CDs, graphic novels, pop-up books, and writing books, such as *Writing as a Team Sport*.

Brendan DuBois is the author of the Lewis Cole mysteries and numerous short stories, which have earned him a Shamus Award and three Edgar Award nominations. Around one hundred of his stories have been published in anthologies and magazines. He is best known for his alternate history novel *Resurrection Day*, which won the Sidewise Award for Alternate History. In 2010, the readers of *Deadly Pleasures and Mystery News* awarded him the Barry Award, for Best Mystery Short Story of the Year, for his story "The High House Writer," which was published in the July/August 2009 issue of *Alfred Hitchcock's Mystery Magazine*. DuBois is a former newspaper reporter and a lifelong resident of New Hampshire, where he lives with his wife and pets.

A 2019 Dragon Award finalist, **Jason Cordova** is a kaiju enthusiast. A former high school basketball coach, he has authored over 15 novels and been in dozens of anthologies. He currently lives in Virginia. You can find him at www.jasoncordova.com.

Lydia Sherrer writes the ongoing best-selling urban fantasy series, Love, Lies, and Hocus Pocus—The Lily Singer Adventures, a magical epic full of snark, tea, and a talking cat. In addition to her urban fantasy series, Lydia Sherrer has written the epic fantasy *When the Gods Laughed,* which was included in the *USA Today* Best-selling box set "Wrath and Ruin." Her latest project is a gaming adventure sci-fi collaboration with John Ringo involving monster hunting in augmented reality, with an expected release in 2022. Lydia Sherrer lives in Louisville, Kentucky, with her spouse, adorable spawn, and feline overlords. She subsists on tea and chocolate and hates sleep because it keeps her from writing.

Michael Z. Williamson is retired military, having served twenty-five years in the U.S. Army and the U.S. Air Force. He was deployed for Operation Iraqi Freedom and Operation Desert Fox. Williamson is a state-ranked competitive shooter in combat rifle and combat pistol. He has consulted on military matters, weapons, and disaster preparedness for Discovery Channel and Outdoor Channel productions and is Editor-at-Large for Survivalblog, with 300K weekly readers. In addition to these activities, Williamson tests and reviews firearms and gear for manufacturers. Williamson's books set in his Freehold Universe include *Freehold*, *Better to Beg Forgiveness*, and *Do Unto Others*. His novel *The Hero* with John Ringo has reached modern classic status. Williamson was born in England, raised in Liverpool and Toronto, Canada, and now resides in Indianapolis with his wife and children.

A veteran of more than twenty years in the civilian space program, as well as various military space defense programs, **Stephanie Osborn** worked on numerous space shuttle flights and the International Space Station, and counts the training of astronauts on her résumé. Her space experience also includes Spacelab and ISS operations, variable star astrophysics, Martian aeolian geophysics, radiation physics, and nuclear, biological, and chemical weapons effects. She has authored, coauthored, or contributed to some 50 books, including the celebrated science-fiction mystery, *Burnout: The Mystery of Space Shuttle STS-281*.

Jody Lynn Nye lists her main career activity as "spoiling cats." When not engaged upon this worthy occupation, she writes fantasy and science fiction books and short stories. Since 1987 she has published over 50 books and more than 170 short stories. She specializes in science fiction and fantasy stories that blend action and humor. She's also one of the most successful collaborators in the business, with about a third of her novels either collaborations or sequels to others' works. She collaborated with Robert Asprin on the MythAdventures series, collaborated with Anne McCaffrey on both the Dragonriders of Pern series and the Doona series, and coauthored the *Visual Guide To Xanth* with Piers Anthony. Over the last twenty or so years, Jody Lynn Nye has taught numerous writing workshops and participated at science-fiction conventions on hundreds of panels covering the subjects of writing and being published.

Jamie Ibson is from the frozen wastelands of Canuckistan, where bear, northern tundra kaiju, and cobra chickens battle for domination in the wilds between hockey rinks and Tim Hortonses. He is a former infantryman, and retired from law enforcement in early 2021. He has been publishing short stories since 2018 and his first novels came out in 2020. His website can be found at ibsonwrites.ca. He is married to the lovely Michelle, and they have cats.

Brian Trent's speculative fiction appears regularly in *Analog, Fantasy & Science Fiction, The Year's Best Military and Adventure SF* (winning the 2019 Reader's Poll Award for his story "Crash-Site"), *Terraform, Daily Science Fiction, Galaxy's Edge, Nature,* and numerous year's best anthologies. The author of the science fiction thriller *Ten Thousand Thunders*, his work has also appeared in a number of Baen Books anthologies including *Cosmic Corsairs* and *Weird World War III*. Trent lives in New England. Visit his website at www.briantrent.com.

Kacey Ezell is a USAF helicopter pilot who writes sci-fi/fantasy/alt history. She co-wrote *Gunpowder & Embers* (Last Judgment's Fire Book 1) with John Ringo and Christopher L. Smith, was a Dragon Award finalist in 2018 and 2019, and her stories have twice been featured in Baen's *Year's Best Mil/Adventure SF* compilation. In 2018, her story won the Baen Reader's Choice Award. She has several books published by Baen, Chris Kennedy Publishing, and Blackstone Publishing. Find out more at www.kaceyezell.net.

A native Texan by birth (if not geography), **Christopher L. Smith** moved "home" as soon as he could. Attending Texas A&M, he learned quickly that there was more to college than beer and football games. He relocated to San Antonio, attending SAC and UTSA, graduating in late 2000 with a BA in Lit. While there, he also met a wonderful lady who somehow found him to be funny, charming, and worth marrying. (She has since changed her mind on the funny and charming.) Christopher began writing fiction in 2012. His short stories can be found in multiple anthologies, including John Ringo and Gary Poole's *Black Tide Rising*, Mike Williamson's *Forged In Blood*, Larry Correia and Kacey Ezell's *Noir Fatale*, and Tom Kratman's *Terra Nova*. Christopher has cowritten two novels: *Kraken Mare* with Jason Cordova, and *Gunpowder & Embers*

with Kacey Ezell and John Ringo. His cats allow his family and their dogs to reside with them outside of San Antonio.

Brent Roeder is a neuroscience Ph.D. candidate (though hopefully by now a full Ph.D.) researching how to restore damaged memory function. A life-long geek, he enjoys world-building and writing sci-fi and fantasy to relax from work. Very occasionally he even remembers to finish a story.

Mike Massa is a longtime contributor to the Black Tide universe. He's co-written two novels with John Ringo including national bestsellers *Valley of Shadows* (2018) and *River of Night* (2019), as well as five short stories. He also writes fantasy, Mil-SF and nonfiction. Currently, Mike works for an award-winning research university, integrating machine learning and artificial intelligence technologies into practical applications for logistics, predictive maintenance, and cyber-defense. Or, you know, Skynet. Whichever comes first.

EXPERIENCE THE WORLDS OF THE LEGENDARY
JERRY POURNELLE
NEW YORK TIMES BEST-SELLING CREATOR OF *FALKENBERG'S LEGION*

"Possibly the greatest science fiction novel I have ever read."
—Robert A. Heinlein on *The Mote in God's Eye*
by Larry Niven and Jerry Pournelle

"Jerry Pournelle is one of science fiction's greatest storytellers."
—Poul Anderson

"Jerry Pournelle's trademark is first-rate action against well-realized backgrounds of hard science and hardball politics."
—David Drake

"Rousing. . . . The best of the genre."   —*The New York Times*

THE BEST OF JERRY POURNELLE (ed. by John F. Carr)
PB: 978-1-9821-2500-4 • $8.99 US / $11.99 CAN

THE LEGACY OF HEOROT SERIES

The two hundred colonists on board the *Geographic* have spent a century in cold sleep to arrive here: Avalon, a lush, verdant planet lightyears from Earth. They hope to establish a permanent colony, and Avalon seems the perfect place. And so they set about planting and building.

But their very presence has upset the ecology of Avalon. Soon an implacable predator stalks them, picking them off one by one. In order to defeat this alien enemy, they must reevaluate everything they think they know about Avalon, and uncover the planet's dark secrets.

LEGACY OF HEOROT (with Larry Niven & Steven Barnes)
TPB: 978-1-9821-2437-3 • $16.00 US / $22.00 CAN
PB: 978-1-9821-2544-8 • $8.99 US / $11.99 CAN

WELCOME BACK

Officer Turner held up the clipboard, took a pen out of his shirt pocket and said, "Okay, let's step up, and don't rush. There's plenty of time, and there's plenty of room at Rockland. One at a time, give us your name, and if you're a parent or a legal guardian, give us the name of minors that will be accompanying you."

His words seemed to hang in the cool Atlantic air. No one moved.

Fred struggled to keep the expression on his face calm and bland.

"Really?" Turner asked. "Come along, now. Who'll be first?"

Fred didn't dare move, to look behind, to break the mood.

Lieutenant Porter said, "What's going on here? What's wrong with you? Don't you want to leave, be safe? There'll be good food, no shortages, electricity. You'll be safe."

Now Fred looked behind at his townspeople, his friends, all of whom who had done so much to stay alive and together this past year.

He turned back to the two well-dressed and well-fed men.

Fred said, "You said yesterday, 'welcome back.' Am I right?"

The two men exchanged glances. "Yes," the Navy lieutenant said. "Was that a problem?"

Fred said, "'Fraid so. Most of us took that as an insult, Lieutenant, 'cause we never left America. We were right here."

—from "Liberation Day"
by Brendan DuBois

BAEN BOOKS by JOHN RINGO

BLACK TIDE RISING: *Under a Graveyard Sky* • *To Sail a Darkling Sea* • *Islands of Rage and Hope* • *Strands of Sorrow* • *Black Tide Rising* (edited with Gary Poole) • *The Valley of Shadows* (with Mike Massa) • *Voices of the Fall* (edited with Gary Poole) • *River of Night* (with Mike Massa) • *We Shall Rise* (edited with Gary Poole)

TRANSDIMENSIONAL HUNTER SERIES (with Lydia Sherrer): *Into the Real*

TROY RISING: *Live Free or Die* • *Citadel* • *The Hot Gate*

LEGACY OF THE ALDENATA: *A Hymn Before Battle* • *Gust Front* • *When the Devil Dances* • *Hell's Faire* • *The Hero* (with Michael Z. Williamson) • *Cally's War* (with Julie Cochrane) • *Watch on the Rhine* (with Tom Kratman) • *Sister Time* (with Julie Cochrane) • *Yellow Eyes* (with Tom Kratman) • *Honor of the Clan* (with Julie Cochrane) • *Eye of the Storm*

COUNCIL WARS: *There Will Be Dragons* • *Emerald Sea* • *Against the Tide* • *East of the Sun, West of the Moon*

INTO THE LOOKING GLASS: *Into the Looking Glass* • *Vorpal Blade* (with Travis S. Taylor) • *Manxome Foe* (with Travis S. Taylor) • *Claws that Catch* (with Travis S. Taylor)

EMPIRE OF MAN (with David Weber): *March Upcountry* • *March to the Sea* • *March to the Stars* and *We Few* (collected in *Throne of Stars*)

SPECIAL CIRCUMSTANCES: *Princess of Wands* • *Queen of Wands*

PALADIN OF SHADOWS: *Ghost* • *Kildar* • *Choosers of the Slain* • *Unto the Breach* • *A Deeper Blue* • *Tiger by the Tail* (with Ryan Sear)

STANDALONE TITLES: *The Last Centurion* • *Citizens* (edited with Brian M. Thomsen)

To purchase any of these titles in e-book form, please go to www.baen.com.